May Day

Book One of American Sulla

A novel by

Thom Stark

Copyright Notice

Dedication

This book is dedicated to my beloved wife Judy, without whose unwavering belief and support it could not have come to pass.

About the cover

The cover of this book is a painting by Dave Michael Rogers done as a work for hire based on two photographs: Skyline of New York with One WTC by Cathy Baird, from Wikimedia Commons (which is licensed under the terms of Creative Commons Attribution 2.0 Generic), and an unattributed photo of the August 24, 1968 French Canopus thermonuclear test at Fangataufa atoll (also in the public domain). Both photographs have been manipulated by the artist to produce the composite image used as this book's cover, and the title, subtitle, and author credit have been added by Thom Stark. The resulting image is copyright © 2015 by Thom Stark, with all rights reserved thereunto.

About the back cover

The back cover of this book consists of portions of two uncredited Department of Defense photographs, both of which are, by definition, in the public domain. Both photographs have been manipulated by the author. The resulting image is copyright © 2013 by Thom Stark, with all rights reserved thereunto.

Acknowledgements

The author wishes gratefully to acknowledge the persons, organizations, and institutions upon whose contributions he has so heavily depended to make the content of this work as accurate and readable as possible. The reader should keep in mind, however, that any errors or mischaracterizations of fact it may contain are entirely and exclusively the responsibility of the author, and not those named below.

The friends, family members, and strangers who sponsored the author's failed Kickstarter and successful Indiegogo fundraising campaigns are all exemplary human beings. Without their help, the author might have found himself homeless well before this book could be finished. A complete list of those who contributed to one, the other, or both efforts can be found at the end of this volume.

For the description of the May Day nuclear explosion, the author is indebted to Carey Sublette's Nuclear Weapons Frequently Asked Questions, Section 5.0: Effects of Nuclear Explosions at nuclearweaponarchive.org/Nwfaq/Nfaq5.html. The author made extensive use of Google Maps, Street View, and Google Earth to establish geographical locations, exterior descriptions, and latitude and longitude, where those are specified, and of Google proper to find documents, maps, images, and other resources that added greatly to the background and detail of this book. For information regarding the floor plan and general architectural details of the White House, www.whitehousemuseum.org was invaluable. For details of the layout of the White House Situation Room, the author relied heavily upon NBC's May 2, 2012 Rock Center special "Inside the Situation Room". For research regarding military ranks and ratings, insignia, uniforms, unit designations, and weaponry, Wikipedia articles were the author's almost-invariable starting point. For physical details of the National Military Command Center's Emergency Conference Room, www.fas.org/nuke/guide/usa/c3i/nmcc.htm images were the author's primary reference. The author's principle sources for House and Senate procedures, and the layout of seats at their daises were those bodies' respective web sites, www.house.gov and www.senate.gov. Countless other Internet-based resources provided other data and details that are key to the credibility (or lack thereof) of the narrative.

Susan Thornton, author of the short novel *From Time to Time*, did yeoman work proofreading the earliest draft of this book, persuading the author to spell-check the ms, and generally cheerleading. David Strom, editor and author of hundreds of technology-related articles, two books, and the weekly *Web Informant* column (www.strominator.com), was kind enough to act as a beta reader for the book. He pointed out an embarrassing geographical blunder the author hastily – if sheepishly – corrected, and provided welcome encouragement. Finally, Hilary Lauren, author of *Killing Karl*, generously volunteered to edit the ms. She was instrumental in persuading the author to rethink his determination to reproduce regional dialects at the expense of readability, and also offered a host of other general and specific recommendations whose adoption has, in the author's opinion, significantly improved the narrative. Any violations of his or her preferred stylebook guidelines (*e.g.* – the use of punctuation within and surrounding quotation marks) that the critical reader may encounter are the results of artistic choices by the author, and exist in the text despite Ms. Lauren's editorial advice, rather than because of it. Hilary rocks.

Prologue

May 1, 2020, 11:38 am EDT

West Street, New York, NY

The box van – stolen in New Jersey two weeks earlier, and since heavily modified – turned left at the traffic light off West Street onto Albany, then left again onto Washington. It descended into the gaping maw of the World Trade Center's delivery entrance. No one noticed its springs sagging despite the super-duty suspension upgrade it had received. The radiation detectors above the ramp that led down into the WTC delivery level registered no unusual neutron flux from its malignant cargo.

The driver's paperwork appeared genuine. His vehicle's New York license plates (purloined in the Bronx, just two hours earlier) raised no suspicion, so the guards in the gatehouse at the bottom of the ramp allowed him to pass through to the complex's underground traffic circle. He followed the signs around the perimeter of the WTC Plaza, until he turned off at the loading dock for 1 World Trade Center. At the direction of the building's cargo master, he backed up his vehicle to the waist-high secondary dock. Carefully setting the parking brake, he turned the engine off, and the four-way flashers on.

The driver – whose laminated photo badge identified him as Arlington Joseph Smith, but whose real name was Tariq Abdullah Aziz – climbed out of the van, and carefully locked the driver's door. He walked around to the rear of the vehicle, and unlocked the double doors. With visible effort, he tugged them open.

Nestled on a flatbed dolly inside the oddly thick, dull-gray walls of the cargo compartment was what appeared to be a heavy-duty Canon copier/printer. Aziz extended a short, reinforced ramp between the rear of the van's cargo compartment and the lip of the loading dock. Muscles bulging with the effort, he pushed the dolly and its deadly cargo out of the van, onto the dock's surface. His face was already shiny with sweat.

Locking the van's cargo doors, Aziz pushed the copier-laden cart across the loading dock toward the freight elevators. A bored security guard asked for his paperwork. He gave it a cursory examination.

"Sixty-third floor," he said. He pointed to an elevator at the far end of the bank. "Take number four."

Aziz nodded, reclaiming his paperwork from the guard.

"T'anks," he replied.

Carefully controlling his breathing, Aziz pushed his burden down the hallway to the fourth elevator, the cart's tires softly thumping over the joints in the tile floor. Straining, Aziz positioned the cart directly in front of the elevator's doors, then pressed the button to summon the cage.

The doors parted to reveal the padded walls of the elevator compartment. Summoning all his strength, Aziz shoved his cargo over the slight gap between the elevator cage and the doorframe. Quickly, he followed the cart into the elevator. Before it could crash into the back wall of the cage, he pulled mightily on its handle to counter the copier's momentum. He wanted to make sure he left sufficient space between the back wall of the elevator cage and the front of the cart to allow him to push, rather than have to pull, his burden out at his destination.

Once the doors closed, leaving him alone in the elevator for its swift ascent of the first 40 floors, Aziz allowed himself the luxury of filling, and refilling his burning lungs with one deep, racking breath after another. Pulling off his baseball cap to wipe his streaming, shaved head on his sleeve left the khaki material wet with his sweat. Soon, though, the express portion of his ride came to an end. He replaced his ball cap and, with a major effort, forced himself to breathe normally.

To his relief, no one else entered the elevator before it reached the 63rd floor. When the doors opened there, Aziz braced his back against the wall of the cage and, exerting his maximum strength, forced the copier-laden cart over the gap and into the hallway of Global Financial Corporation's Private Banking department. Leaving his burden sitting in front of the freight elevator, Aziz strode down the hallway to the auxiliary reception desk which guarded the entrance to the actual suite of business offices.

"Gotta delivery here," Aziz told the fashionably-dressed Asian receptionist.

She appeared to be in her mid-twenties. The nameplate on her desk identified her as Alicia Takahashi.

"Whom is it for?" inquired the receptionist, looking up to meet his eyes.

Her tone was professional, neither hostile nor friendly, her voice an accent-free contralto.

Aziz pretended to peruse his clipboard, then shrugged.

"Name uh the guy is Carson ..." He squinted at the paperwork in his hand, "... or mebbe Carlson?"

Aziz looked up at Alicia Takahashi, and grinned ruefully.

"Never can read that dispatcher's chicken scratches," he confided, "Guy shoulda been a doctor."

"Let me see, please," Takahashi requested, reaching out for the clipboard.

She examined the slightly sweat-dampened, multi-part form.

"That will be Randy Carlson, one of our office assistants," she said.

Takahashi handed the paperwork back to Aziz.

"I'll page him for you," she told him. "Please have a seat over there."

She gestured to a utilitarian grouping of chairs and a couch around a coffee table next to her desk.

Aziz walked over to the seating area, but did not sit. Instead he stood, facing the wall, and pretended to examine a large abstract painting that hung there, over the couch. The shapes and colors meant nothing to him. Instead, his mind was focused on keeping his breathing slow and regular, and on his rising excitement at the fast-approaching end of his mission.

"Mr. Carlson will be right with you," Takahashi told him, re-cradling the multi-line phone on her desk.

She returned her attention to the textbook on business administration she had been studying when Aziz first approached.

"T'anks," said Aziz

He turned back to his apparent inspection of the jumble of shapes and colors before him.

- *It's happening.* - he thought, taking care to conceal his exaltation at the prospect. - *All that training, all that preparation. And now, at last, it's finally happening.* -

One of the enameled, metal doors on the other side of the reception desk opened. The young, dark-featured man Aziz knew as Ali bin Hamzah emerged, dressed in a white polo shirt and tan chinos.

"Mr. Carlson is here," Takahashi announced.

"Thanks, Alicia," Hamzah said.

He crossed to where Aziz, who had stepped into the center of the corridor, stood waiting, clipboard in hand.

"I'm Randy Carlson," said Hamzah, putting out his right hand, "You have a delivery for me?"

"Yes, sir," responded Aziz, handing him the clipboard. "You ordered a Canon Imagemaster Advance, Model 2020?"

"Yes I did," said Hamzah.

He nodded at the gleaming machine sitting on its cart in front of freight elevator number four.

"That it?" he enquired.

"Yes, sir," Aziz replied.

"Great," said Hamzah. "Let me give you a hand with it."

"T'anks."

The two men strode down the hall to the copier. Together they pushed it back up the corridor to the double metal doorway.

Aziz felt a tremor of excitement run through him, as Hamzah punched in his access code on the keypad beside the doors. With a soft click, they unlocked. Hamzah opened both doors, and set their stops, then helped Aziz push the laden cart across the threshold, into the exclusive precincts of Global Financial.

Re-closing the doors, Hamzah pointed left, down the carpeted hallway.

"The copier room is this way," he said.

Aziz took Hamzah's continued pretense as a sign that unbelievers might be listening. He nodded, grateful for the months of acting classes that allowed them both to pretend so convincingly to be strangers.

"Yes, sir," he responded.

Aziz and Hamzah pushed the cart down the hall. Its tires left deep grooves in the carpet behind them. Along the way, they passed several glass-walled offices, whose occupants appeared to be absorbed in the data on the monitors that cluttered their desktops. At last, they reached a doorway on their right, which opened into a large room. Illuminated by overhead fluorescent panels, it was crowded with office machines of various kinds. Across the room was a ten-foot-wide gap along the wall, to which Hamzah gestured.

"It goes there," he instructed.

"Yes, sir," replied Aziz.

Together, the two men maneuvered the heavy cart across the room. Grunting with effort, they pushed the copier into position. Hamzah picked up its electrical cord, and plugged it into an outlet on the wall.

Hamzah glanced over his shoulder to be certain there was no one else within earshot.

In a voice pitched just above a whisper, he said, "Brother, you should have the honor."

"Insha'Allah, my brother," replied Aziz.

He reached for the copier's keypad, noting with pride as he did, that his hand did not tremble. Methodically, he keyed in the digits 01052020.

"Allahu akbar," he cried.

Then he pressed Enter.

May 1, 2020, 11:56 am EDT

1 World Trade Center, New York, NY

The explosive shaped charges surrounding an approximately 11-pound sphere of plutonium at the heart of the Canon Imagemaster instantly crushed it against the beryllium reflector at its center. The storm of neutrons from the resulting critical mass shattered atomic nuclei in the compacted ball of Pu-239, disgorging an exponentially-increasing cascade of free neutrons. The energy released by the fissioning atoms caused the resulting plasma to expand, until the distance between its individual nuclei grew too great to sustain their chain reaction. At that point, slightly over half a microsecond after the explosion began, the plasma ball reached its maximum temperature of nearly 100,000,000 degrees Centigrade – 10,000 times hotter than the surface of the Sun.

Most of that energy radiated away as gamma and X rays, forming an isothermal sphere. The sphere began rapidly cooling, as it expanded. By the time it had grown to 13 meters in diameter, its temperature had declined to a mere 300,000 degrees Centigrade. Its expansion had also slowed, to the point that it began transferring some of its kinetic energy to the material surrounding it: consuming metal, glass, plastic, wood, textiles, and people in the process. They all became part of the highly ionized plasma. The growing fireball now emitted a flash of light in the visible and near-ultraviolet spectra that was 10,000 times as bright as the noonday Sun – and continued to expand.

When it reached the desk of Alicia Takahashi, the isothermal sphere was still hot enough to instantly convert her, the book she was reading, and the desk itself into plasma – into ions, stripped of their outer electron shells, rather than atoms – and incorporate all three into itself. Its expansion continued.

Traveling at the speed of light, the electromagnetic pulse generated by the explosion reached to the horizon in something under a half a millisecond. It caused the circuitry of every silicon-based, electronic device within a dozen miles that was not protected by a Faraday cage to melt, and fuse into inert junk. Cell phones, electronic ignition systems, computers, television sets, pacemakers, and a myriad of other technological staples of city life, all went instantly, permanently dead. Every battery within miles died, as well.

The high-temperature superconductor bus line that connected the massive substation beneath the tower at 7 World Trade Center to the heart of the Financial District efficiently transferred the gargantuan electrical surge to Wall Street, a half-second before the blast front arrived. The rampaging EMP methodically slew New York City's electrical grid. It induced massive current flows, destroying transformers, meters, and switches so swiftly, they were ruined beyond repair before the circuit breakers designed to protect them could be tripped. The massive imbalance in the Northeastern Power Grid caused by the abrupt disappearance of New York City's load crashed the system within minutes, as section after section automatically shut down to protect itself from hundreds of megawatts of electricity run wild.

When the shock wave reached a diameter of 220 meters – about 15 milliseconds after the nuclear detonation began – its rate of expansion slowed to a mere four kilometers per second. It began to separate from the surface of the isothermal plasma sphere that generated it. That separation triggered a second flash of light, which appeared to observers much brighter than the first, because its radiative surface was so large, even though its surface temperature now was a mere fraction of what it had been.

By the time the fireball grew to its maximum 600 meters in diameter – about three-quarters of a second after the chain reaction began – its temperature had fallen to the point that it had almost stopped emitting light. By then, it had completely vaporized most of the Freedom Tower, as well as portions of several adjacent buildings. The expanding shock wave pulverized what remained of 1 World Trade Center, along with square blocks of the nearest skyscrapers. The atmosphere rushing in to fill the vacuum created as the fireball began to collapse blew hundreds of thousands of tons of highly radioactive dust into which the buildings and their contents had been transformed up and into the sky, to form a gigantic mushroom cloud.

The heat of the explosion now fell off rapidly. At a distance of a kilometer from the hypocenter, it was finally incapable of causing fourth- and fifth-degree burns, and its ionizing radiation was no longer invariably fatal.

Fully a third of those exposed to its effects could at least theoretically be expected to survive the experience – assuming they did not first succumb to shock, dehydration, infection, or physical injury.

Meanwhile, the shock wave continued to expand in all directions, diminishing steadily in strength as it spread. By the time it reached two kilometers in diameter, its impact alone was no longer capable of killing a human being outright. However, the storm of debris it drove before it and carried behind was still lethal. The blast front remained powerful enough to shatter every window it struck for more than a mile in every direction – and to spray the insides of the buildings they had adorned with shards of deadly, glittering shrapnel – as well as to puncture the eardrums of every person within a mile of the hypocenter.

When the blast front reached its limit of expansion, close to two kilometers from Ground Zero, the pressure wave reversed direction. The atmosphere immediately flooded in to fill the vacuum the collapsing shockwave created. The in-rushing air swiftly fanned the flames the fireball had ignited into a towering firestorm.

Lower Manhattan began to burn.

May 1, 2020, 9:00 am PDT (12:00 pm EDT)

The Commonwealth Club, San Francisco

William Orwell Steele, President of the United States, stood at the podium looking out over the crowded hall.

- Power suits and power ties. Captains of industry. Masters of the Universe. Movers and shakers all. God help the mark. - he thought.

Tall and lean, with a thick shock of mostly-brown hair, Steele had deep blue eyes, a long, straight nose, a firm mouth, and a strong chin with a faint cleft. During his campaign, media commentators had routinely described him as "movie-star handsome." He knew that to be only a slight exaggeration. More than three years in office had lined his forehead, and grayed his temples, but he still radiated strength and command.

He took a sip from the glass of water on the top of the podium, and began to speak.

"Members and directors of the Commonwealth Club, honored guests, and members of the Fourth Estate, I thank you for inviting me here to speak to you this morning," he said. "At the invitation of the Club's Board of Directors, I take as my subject the topic of multi-lateralism in the evolving world economy."

- A topic on which I used to think I was well-qualified to speak. It's amazing how much humility three-and-a-quarter years in the White House shoves down your throat. -

The President allowed himself a disarming smile.

"Please contain your excitement," he requested.

Laughter filled the room at this sally.

"America's status as the single remaining superpower has been in decline for nearly two decades now," he continued. "With our disastrous adventure in Iraq, and the descent of that country into what it is now clear was inevitable civil war upon our departure, the notion that we should naturally become the world's policeman in the 21st century has become little more than a sad joke. At the same time, with the confluence of near-universal outsourcing of our domestic industrial production to developing countries, and the persistent global economic recession – which has shrunk our middle class to near-extinction, and pushed far too many of our working-class citizens into impoverishment from which they have little prospect of escape – our rank as the mightiest economic engine in the world has suffered badly, as well. Now, we are economically beset on all sides, and facing a teetering mountain of national debt that has only grown higher and steeper, thanks in large part to our chronically-deadlocked Congress. We have finally reached the point where we have no choice but to admit to ourselves that our long, and dearly-held national belief in America's inherent exceptionalism is, in fact, merely a collective delusion."

Steele paused to gauge the effect of his opening salvo. He noted reactions ranging from stony politeness to outright hostility from most of those in the first few rows of the audience. Here and there among them was a scatter of nodding heads and thoughtful expressions – but they were in the distinct minority.

"To the contrary," the President told them, "the truth is we are every bit as as vulnerable as the next country - vulnerable not only to bad decision-making by our politicians, but also to foolish choices by our corporate leaders, to irresponsibility on the part of our regulators, and to partisan myopia on the part of our highest courts. It is now painfully clear that we must fundamentally change the way we think of ourselves and others; must elementally alter the way we treat the citizens of our own and other countries; and, most crucially, must transform the way we lead this nation, both in the public and the private sectors. As a society, we can no longer afford the luxury of parochial arrogance, heedless cupidity, and smug isolationism. It is time – indeed, it is well past time – we admitted that we need the rest of the world as much as it needs us. No longer can we deny that our economy has become so inextricably entwined with those of the rest of the developed, and developing world that, from hence forth, we all stand or fall together."

- The wingnuts will be all over me like a coat of paint for that. Fuck 'em. It's the truth, and these people need to hear the truth, if anyone does. -

"Falling," he observed, "seems like a bad choice to me."

There was an encouraging murmur of agreement from his audience.

"So," Steele posited, "the question then becomes: 'What specific steps must we take to implement these changes?' What is our optimum path forward?"

He paused to sip from the cut-crystal glass atop the podium.

As he set the glass back down on the podium, Special Agent Roger Waters, head of his Secret Service detail strode up to him, and whispered urgently in his ear. For a moment, the President's face was a study in shock and horror – but only for a moment. Then he straightened, unconsciously squared his shoulders, and turned back to the microphone.

"Ladies and gentlemen," he said, "I regret to say we'll have to leave it at that, for now. I thank you for your attention, but I'm afraid I have urgent business to attend to."

Without another word, William Orwell Steele turned and walked away, as his Secret Service phalanx fell in around him.

May 1, 2020, 12:05 pm EDT

North Cove Marina, New York City

Clarabelle Wong shuffled towards the Hudson River, her arms outstretched before her, like a zombie in a cheap horror movie.

Melted flesh hung in tatters from her arms. Her hair and ears were blackened crusts. She remained clothed, only because what remained of her red track suit was fused to the skin of her sides and shoulders. Her back, her buttocks, and the backs of her legs were more than naked – they were burned to the bone. So was the back of her skull.

After nearly two weeks in New York City, Clarabelle had almost completed the list of must-see attractions on her vacation itinerary.

When the bomb went off, she was standing on the Esplanade at the Southwestern end of North Cove Marina. Facing away from Manhattan, she was focused on taking a cell phone photo of Ellis Island, a kilometer distant across the Hudson River. The tower of the World Financial Center had partially shielded her from the blast, so she had escaped being more-or-less instantly vaporized. Instead, the pressure wave slammed her hard against the seawall; the heat flash had burned the flesh from her bones; and the gamma and X-ray radiation had stormed through the genetic material of her body's cells like the Visigoths through Rome.

As yet, she felt no pain. Shock spared her that, at least. But she was terribly, terribly thirsty, and she felt feverish, and sick to her stomach. Water was what she wanted, more than anything else – cool, refreshing water.

Overhead, the mushroom cloud over lower Manhattan blotted out the Sun.

May 1, 2020, 9:21 am PDT (12:21 EDT)

The Presidential Limousine, Highway 101, San Francisco, CA

"Let me get this straight," asked William Orwell Steele, "The explosion was how large?"

"We estimate – that is, the DoD estimates – it was in the 20 kiloton range, sir," responded Ronald Wheaton, his Deputy Security Advisor.

"Goddamnit," the President scowled, "I don't know what that means. Translate it into terms a non-expert can grasp."

"Well, sir," Wheaton replied, "it was about the same size as the bomb we dropped on Nagasaki."

"Okay, that helps," Steele responded. "Go on."

"However, this one did a lot more damage, sir," Wheaton added.

"Why?" the President challenged.

"Well, sir," Wheaton said, "for one thing, it was contained within the Freedom Tower. Just for a few milliseconds, of course, but that was long enough to ensure that most of the blast's force was horizontal..."

"And?" Steele prompted, impatiently.

"And that meant that it destroyed most of Lower Manhattan, sir," Wheaton told him.

"*Most* of Lower Manhattan? My god."

The President's face was gray with shock.

Wheaton nodded.

"Unfortunately, sir," he said, "that's not even the worst news."

"It's not?" Steele demanded. "Then what is?"

Wheaton shook his tousled, ever-so-slightly-graying curls.

"Sir," he replied, "I'm afraid the worst news is that, because it vaporized most of the World Trade Center, the explosion has generated a whole lot more radioactive fallout than the Nagasaki bomb did. And, again unfortunately, the wind is blowing that fallout straight up the coast toward Boston."

"Jesus H. Christ," said Steele. "Is there anything we can do about that?"

"Other than to alert the people in the path of the fallout cloud to evacuate, if they can? No sir. I'm afraid not," Wheaton replied.

"Jesus H. Christ," the President of the United States repeated. "Jesus H. *fucking* Christ."

May 1, 2020, 12:38 pm EDT

50 Hudson St., Jersey City NJ

Aragorn Northcutt Hardcastle, Senior Vice President of National Treasuries Trading for North America, awoke in darkness, silence, and pain.

The last thing he remembered was the incredibly brilliant flash of light, that had jolted him out of his focus on the bank of monitors that ringed his desk – and distracted him from noticing they had all gone blank simultaneously. He recalled standing, to stare through the glass of his office on the 35th floor of the Goldman Sachs Building at the giant, roiling fireball blossoming across the Hudson River; straining to comprehend the horrible, repellently beautiful spectacle unfolding before him.

- *My god!* - He remembered thinking. - *It's an atomic bomb! A fucking atomic bomb!* -

Then ... *something* had happened. Thinking about it now, he still couldn't wrap his mind around just what it had been. He knew only that he was blind, and deaf, and in horrible, excruciating pain. He tried to move his right arm, which was draped across his face. The wave of agony that instantly crashed over him at the effort caused him to black out once again.

When he awoke, some unknown time later, he smelled smoke.

May 1, 2020, 9:47 am PDT (12:47 pm EDT)

Air Force One, somewhere over Nevada

William Steele sat behind the desk in the tiny communications studio aboard Air Force One, waiting for the red light atop the unblinking eye of the television camera to glow. His mind was awhirl with the data with which he had been bombarded since his conversation with Ronald Wheaton, his Deputy National Security Advisor, in the limo on the way to San Francisco International Airport.

Beside the camera, crouched the floor director – Bob something-or-other – counting down the final few seconds to what would be perhaps the most important speech of his presidency. The temperature in the little room was stifling from the intensely-bright television lights, despite the continuous soft whir of air conditioning.

The floor director, holding up all five fingers of his right hand, announced, "Five." His thumb folded across his palm. "Four." His index finger bent to cover his thumb. "Three." Folding his middle finger down against his thumb and forefinger, Bob mouthed, "Two." His ring finger joined the others. His little finger came down to make a fist. He raised his index finger and brought it sharply forward to point directly at the President, as the red light mounted on the camera lit up.

For a long moment, the President sat silent, looking not into, but beyond the camera, as if gathering his energy. His demeanor was calm, his expression grim, his gaze intense.

"My fellow Americans," he began, "it is with great sorrow and great anger that I come before you today. I am sorry to report that, at noon today, thus far unidentified forces of terror detonated a nuclear weapon in the heart of New York City. It destroyed much of the island of Manhattan, and created a cloud of nuclear fallout that is expected to reach Boston within the next 36 hours.

"I am therefore declaring a state of national emergency," Steele continued, "and invoking martial law, beginning immediately. I have ordered all civilian air traffic grounded, and our national borders sealed. This means only active duty military, and State Department personnel on official business will be permitted to leave the United States, and only American citizens bearing valid passports will be permitted to enter.

"I have requested that Congress meet immediately to ratify these declarations. I am now on my way back to Washington to meet with my Cabinet, the Joint Chiefs of Staff, my advisors on national security, and the leaders of both parties in Congress, so that we can begin the important work of rescuing and caring for the survivors of this cowardly attack."

The President's grim expression softened to one of concern.

"If you are in the path of the fallout cloud, you will receive instructions from local authorities on when and how to evacuate. In the meantime, I urge you to remain indoors. If you are currently at work, please stay there. If you are at home, do not leave, particularly if you live, work, or go to school anywhere in the New York City metro area. It is dangerous for you to be outside – nuclear radiation is invisible, but, if you are exposed to it, it can make you very sick, or even kill you." Steele's hands came up in supplication. "I urge you to wait for your local authorities to tell you when to evacuate, and to give you instructions on how to do so safely.

"I have directed the National Guard to mobilize along the expected path of the fallout cloud, and around the New York metro area. I have also ordered the call up of our nation's military reserve forces. I will be dispatching units of the Army and Marines to these areas, as well. Please cooperate with them. If they ask you to leave your home, your school, or your place of employment, please do not argue with them. Take comfort in knowing that these are your fellow Americans, and that they have your safety and well-being as their highest goal."

The President paused for a moment. His expression once again became flinty.

"Know this, too," he said. "In time, we *will* identify those responsible for this outrage, and we *will* bring them to justice. That is not our first priority. At the moment, our prime responsibility is to the thousands – and perhaps even millions – of injured and homeless victims of this cowardly assault, and to those of you who are in danger from the approaching fallout cloud. But believe me when I say that identifying, seeking out, and returning a full measure of retribution upon those who have dared to wreak this outrage on our country, and our fellow citizens *is* a priority to which we shall turn our full attention at the earliest possible moment." Unconsciously, Steele clenched his fist. "Let those who are responsible for this crime understand that they will pay for it, in full – and soon."

The President again paused. The anger faded from his features.

"I will speak to you again," he promised, "after I return to our Capitol, and have had the opportunity to more fully assess the damage this attack has caused, and make more detailed plans to cope with its aftermath. In the meantime, my fellow Americans, we must not give in to fear and panic. That would surely mean victory for those who perpetrated this crime. Instead, let us have courage and confidence that our nation *will* survive this time of trial, and that we *will* soon emerge from it; still strong, determined, and proud. Let us demonstrate to the world that America is, as it has always been, the greatest country on Earth – and that we, its people, are, as we have always been, our nation's greatest strength.

"I thank you for your attention, and your cooperation," Steele concluded. "May God bless America."

For a lingering moment, the red light atop the camera continued to glow, as the President sat, gazing intently into the camera's lens, jaw set, deep blue eyes resolute. For that moment, to his unseen audience, William Orwell Steele seemed to embody the very American virtue his final words had celebrated. For that moment, President William Steele *was* America.

Then the red light winked out. A moment later, Steele slumped tiredly in his chair.

- *So much for the end of American exceptionalism.* -

May 1, 2020, 1:01 pm EDT

1st St., Hackensack, NJ

Nakeesha Gramble pedaled her Big Wheel up First Street. Her short legs pumped furiously. The tricycle's plastic wheels rumbled rewardingly on the concrete sidewalk.

Nakeesha loved her Big Wheel. Her Momma's boyfriend Donell had given it to her for her fifth birthday, just two months earlier. Nakeesha loved Donell, too. He was always nice to her. He brought her presents all the time: clothes, Barbies, her precious Big Wheel. He smelled nice, and he looked *fine*, and her Momma really liked him. But Donell had stopped coming around, all of a sudden, a couple of weeks after her birthday. Momma said the Po-Po got him.

Nakeesha hated the Po-Po, because they made Donell stop coming around.

Nakeesha hated Momma's new boyfriend, Marq, too. He did things to her, when Momma took one of her naps – things Nakeesha didn't like. Momma took a lot of naps, now that Donell had stopped coming around, so Nakeesha had taken to riding her Big Wheel around the neighborhood, every time Momma's head started to nod. She'd call, "'Bye, Momma!" and race out the door, before Marq came out of the bathroom.

As she pedaled past the parking lot of the Center for Food Action, sudden darkness descended over Nakeesha. Then big, fat raindrops began to fall on her. The raindrops were black. They made ugly blotches where they landed on her sky blue jumper.

Ordinarily, Nakeesha paid little attention to the weather. Sunshine was nicer than rain, of course, but even being rained on was better than letting Marq do things to her. But there was something about this rain that frightened Nakeesha. It seemed wrong for it to be black. It smelled funny to her, and the raindrops were so big that, when one of them landed on her hand, it hurt a little. Then one hit her in the eye. It burned something awful.

Growing more afraid, Nakeesha turned her Big Wheel around in the very next driveway. Legs pumping furiously, she fled toward home and the comfort of Momma's presence. Somehow even Marq seemed less scary than the black rain.

Around Nakeesha, the sprinkle of oversized black raindrops abruptly turned into a roaring downpour.

May 1, 2020, 11:30 am MDT (1:30 pm EDT)

Air Force One, somewhere over Colorado

"Ladies and gentlemen, may I have your attention, please?"

Yvonne Clevinger, the President's Press Secretary, paused for a moment to allow the members of the press pool to settle down. There was a low rustle of notepads and pens being readied, then quiet descended on Air Force One's press cabin.

Clevinger glanced briefly down at her notes, then back up at the assembled journalists, attentive in their airline-style seats.

"The President has asked me to apologize to you all for the delay in briefing you," she told them. "He wanted us to have as much information as possible available for you at this first briefing, which is why it has taken this long."

Softly, she cleared her throat.

"As you know from the President's speech," she went on, "at approximately noon today, there was a nuclear explosion in New York City. Satellite imagery indicates that the blast originated at the site of the World Trade Center, and that, most likely, the actual Ground Zero was the Freedom Tower, at 1 World Trade Center."

A buzz of interest filled the room. This was the first members of the press had heard this particular detail, and it shook them all.

"The World Trade Center has been destroyed, as has much of Lower Manhattan," Clevinger continued. "Brooklyn and Jersey City have sustained blast damage, and infrared satellite imagery leads us to believe that much of Manhattan is currently on fire."

Gasps and murmurs swept the room.

"Due to the electro-magnetic pulse from the explosion," the Press Secretary resumed, "all radio, TV, cell phone, and Internet communications with the city have been disrupted. We currently have no contact with anyone on Manhattan Island, at all. Because of severe radiation danger, we have not yet been able to send any members of the

National Guard, the Army, or the Marines into New York proper, although units of all three branches of the armed services are now being marshaled near the perimeter of the blast zone. We expect reconnaissance missions by air and ground to begin within the next few hours." She looked up from her notes. "There is no reliable data on casualties yet, and we expect that accurate figures will take weeks to compile – if not longer."

Unable to contain themselves, journalists began hurling questions at Clevinger. She held up a hand to forestall them.

"Please hold your questions until I'm done telling you what we know," she requested.

"But, what about ...?" Reed Bullock, the Fox News reporter demanded.

"Please." Clevinger stared him down, her hazel eyes unyielding. "Otherwise we'll never get through this."

She lifted the sheaf of papers on her podium, then let them fall back to its surface.

"As the President announced," she continued, "a cloud of extremely radioactive fallout from the bombing is traveling up the Atlantic coast. With winds currently from the south-southwest at approximately 15 miles per hour, we expect the cloud to reach the Boston area sometime within the next 24 hours."

"How radioactive is it?" came a voice from the back of the room.

Clevinger recognized it as that of Preston Hollingsworth, the White House reporter for MSNBC.

"We can't be sure what the level of radioactivity will be once the fallout cloud actually reaches Boston," she replied, "but we believe it's virtually certain to be lethal to anyone caught outside without protection."

A collective gasp of horror filled the room. The implications of Clevinger's statement were clear enough. This would be a nuclear nightmare far worse than Chernobyl or Fukushima, and it was happening on American soil. Clevinger could almost smell her audience's fear.

"Because this cloud is dropping a stream of highly-radioactive dust particles as it travels," she explained, fighting to keep her voice from trembling, "even once it moves out over the ocean, it will leave behind an extended zone of contamination that will render large areas of the Northeastern seaboard uninhabitable for months, or possibly even years to come."

"Oh, God," someone said. Sheila Cubbins, the NPR reporter, began to cry.

"Obviously, evacuating those in the path of the fallout cloud is our highest priority," Clevinger said. "For that, we're counting on you folks to help us get the word out."

"What about the people in areas the cloud has already passed over?" demanded Bullock.

The Press Secretary blinked solemnly.

"It may already be too late for them," she said. Her voice broke.

"Most of them will probably die," she told them.

May 1, 2020, 2:10 pm MDT

MTA Subway Line 7, New York City

Eydis Finnursdottir welcomed the clamor of voices that was becoming audible in the darkness ahead.

She had been a passenger on the 7 line when the power failed, and the subway train on which she was riding ground to a halt. That was somewhere beneath Sixth Avenue, halfway between the Grand Central and Times Square stations. The blackness aboard the stalled train was absolute – even the emergency lights had failed to come on. Around her, the initial calm of the other passengers – phlegmatic New Yorkers, for the most part, accustomed to the occasional breakdowns of the MTA's flagship technology – eventually began to give way to the same creeping panic that groped her heart with clammy fingers.

"Dis is takin' a long time," came one nasal, female voice with a strong Brooklyn accent.

"No shit," agreed a deep, male voice, in tones of purest Bronx.

"Where are da Goddamn lights?" questioned another Bronxian.

"And why doesn't my cell phone work?" a woman demanded, her voice rising in fear.

"Hey, mine don't work neither!" cried a man, his baritone voice cracking.

"What da fuck is goin' on here!" someone shouted.

After that, all semblance of conversation had disappeared. Fear ran rampant through the stranded crowd of passengers, until, finally, a commanding voice cut through the panic with a roar.

"Shut up!" it demanded. "All of yez, just *shut up!*"

What had been well on its way to becoming a mob almost gratefully accepted the admonition of this Brooklynese apparition. Quiet descended.

"Alright," their new leader said. "This ain't no normal-type power failure, like. There oughtta be emergency lights out there, and in here, but there ain't none."

There was a general murmur of agreement with this observation. Obvious as it might have been, no one else had realized there were supposed to be battery-powered emergency lights at regular intervals along the subway track.

"All our cellies is out, too," the Brooklynite observed. "That ain't normal, neither. That means we prob'ly ain't gonna get rescued any time soon."

A renewed hubbub broke out at this prediction.

"Shut *up*, I said!" he barked.

The panic again receded.

"Now, the way I see it," he told them, "we can sit here and wait til the MTA pulls its thumb outta its ass – an' who knows when *that's* gonna happen – or we can get our shit together, and rescue our own selves."

"How?" asked the woman from Brooklyn.

"Easy-peasy," the leader replied. "First of all, I gotta open the emergency exit. That's right here ..."

There was a sliding noise.

"... an now it's open," he continued. "Now, all you people gotta come here, so's we can all hold hands, like."

Tentatively, Eydis rose from her seat. Blindly groping, she made her way toward the voice in the blackness. With her hand outstretched before her, she blundered into the back of someone in a wool coat.

"Please excuse me," Eydis apologized.

"Not to worry," said the woman from Brooklyn.

They had fumbled for each other's hands, clasping them together, before continuing their creeping progress toward the voice of authority at the end of the car. Both women were grateful to be actually doing something – anything – rather than simply waiting helplessly in the dark.

Slowly, the passengers assembled, urged on by their anonymous leader. Eventually, they stretched in a line, hand-in-hand, down the aisle from the subway car's emergency exit.

"Okay," said the Brooklynite. "I'm gonna climb down here, like. Then all of you gotta climb down onto the tracks after me. Don't worry, I'll help you. Then we're all gonna join hands, and walk back to Times Square Station. Okay?"

They had done so, stumbling along in a single file, holding hands to keep themselves together.

Their leader had cautioned them to, "Stay clear of the third rail. If the power comes back on, you could fry like a egg."

It was slow going, despite the dim light from their otherwise-useless cell phone screens.

The Brooklynite who led them – whose name, Eydis learned, was Robert "call me Bob" Bildinsky – frequently barked his shins on unexpected obstacles. Each such encounter was marked by fluent cursing. Once he had actually fallen, and Eydis had learned a whole new set of English vulgarisms as a consequence. But, as time crept by in the penumbral gloom, they made steady progress towards Times Square Station. Now, at last, they were within earshot of their destination.

Eydis was grateful beyond measure.

The track had been dry when they started off, but water had begun to rise around their ankles some time after their journey had begun. Now it was almost up to their knees, and wading through it was difficult, and frightening. Soon, though, in fact, any minute now, Eydis expected there would be light, and their ordeal would come to an end.

- What a tale I will have to tell, once I am back in Reykjavik! -

Then they arrived at Times Square Station. Hands reached down to lift them up, onto the platform. Eydis felt she might faint with relief.

It was crowded. Very, very crowded. In fact, it was jam-packed with bodies. The heat and the stench of terrified humans on the unventilated platform was overwhelming. Eydis struggled to understand why the crowd didn't simply take the stairs up to the street, and simply leave this stinking, dark, broiling-hot place.

Then someone who had seen the explosion told her about the bomb. And the gray, snow-like drifts of fallout covering the streets of Manhattan. And the black rain.

Suddenly, Eydis was more afraid than ever.

May 1, 2020, 1:34 pm CDT (2:34 pm EDT)

Air Force One, somewhere over Nebraska

"It's simply not going to be possible to evacuate everyone, Mr. President," said Stephen Dawkins, the President's Science Advisor, speaking by radio from Washington, DC.

His voice, emanating from a speakerphone on the conference room table, was blurred by crackling static, and a persistent high hiss.

"Unless the wind shifts to the East in the next 12 hours or so – and NOAA says that's unlikely, with tropical storm Beth moving up the coast – the Fallout Zone will stretch as far as 50 to 75 miles inland, by the time the cloud reaches Boston," he continued. "New England freeways and secondary roads are already jammed with traffic. It's total gridlock in the Boston area, now. God only knows what's going to happen by tomorrow morning."

"What about an airlift? Can't we rescue at least some people that way?" asked the President.

"We're looking into that, Mr. President," Dawkins replied. "The problem is, Boston Logan is already one of the busiest airports in the country. Hanscom Field, Worchester Regional, Beverly Municipal, and Norwood Memorial aren't much better – and most of those runways are too short to accommodate jumbo jets."

"What about military airfields? Can't we use those?" Steele suggested.

"All closed years ago, sir," Dawkins responded, "except for those on the Massachusetts Military Reservation – and that's nearly 50 miles from Boston. I'm sorry."

"Fuck," said the President.

There was silence in the conference room for several uncomfortable seconds.

Then, "What about evacuation by sea?" he asked.

Over the speakerphone, the baritone voice of Admiral Harlan Adams, Chief of Staff of the Navy, replied, "Unfortunately, Mr. President, we've already ordered all naval vessels in the Fallout Zone to weight anchor and head Southeast at flank speed."

"What … Why? And why was I not consulted?" Steele demanded, his jaw tightening.

"I apologize, Mr. President," Adams replied. "The Chiefs unanimously agreed it was necessary to act immediately, if we're to save any of our fleet assets in the area from serious contamination. As it is, some of the slower boats – oil tenders and the like – are liable to get pretty heavily dusted, regardless. They just don't have the legs to avoid the fallout."

"I see," said Steele. Again there was silence in the room.

"Here's the thing, sir," Dawkins ventured, at last, "If people stay in their homes, they'll probably receive a lot less radiation than they will if they're caught in their cars when the cloud arrives."

"How so?" the President inquired, his curiosity aroused.

"The air gap between the roof and the ceiling of most buildings will considerably reduce the amount of primary radiation they'll experience," Dawkins explained. "We can thank the inverse square law for that. In a car, they'll be a lot closer to the primary emissions source – the fallout, that is – and they'll get a lot of secondary emissions from primary collisions with the metal in their car roofs."

"In other words …" Steele prompted.

"In other words, sir," Dawkins told him, "they'll fry a lot faster in their cars – and an awful lot of them will be in their cars by the time the cloud arrives."

"That's unacceptable," the President protested.

"It gets worse, sir," Dawkins said, grimly. "Even staying in their homes, they'll receive a lethal dose within days. It'll just happen faster if they're in their cars. Unfortunately, once the fallout cloud arrives, the whole environment will likely be too contaminated to permit us to rescue most of them – and, even if they survive until help arrives, the radiation they'll be exposed to during the rescue attempt will probably kill them."

"And there's nothing we can do about that?" Steele asked.

"No, sir, there's not. I'm sorry, sir," Dawkins told him.

There was silence in the room.

May 1, 2020, 3:15 pm EDT

Interstate 90 westbound, Watertown, MA

Sean Halloran Sr. swore mechanically at the traffic sitting motionless all around him. His heart wasn't really in it, though. He had already exhausted his store of stock and original profanity, vulgarity, and general malediction twice over, along with his reserves of vehemence. Now he was coasting on linguistic momentum alone.

"What the fuck is the holdup?" he demanded for the dozenth time, despite knowing very well what was causing the gridlock.

Every driver around him had evidently turned on his or her radio when the power failed, just as Sean had done. Like him, they all had heard the same, unbelievable news. Like him, they had listened with mounting panic to the President's speech. And, like him, they had all made the same decision: to run, as fast as possible, away from the approaching fallout cloud.

"Honey, calm down," his wife Fiona replied – for the dozenth time. "It's just a traffic jam. It'll clear up soon."

"Ya think so?" Sean responded. "Ya think so? 'Cause I don't think so. No, I don't think it's gonna clear up any fuckin' time soon, Fiona. An' ya know why I don't think it's gonna clear up any fuckin' time soon? Do ya have any fuckin' idea why I don't think it's gonna clear up any goddamn time soon?"

Fiona cringed.

"Because of the bomb?" she offered, timidly.

"You're goddamn right, 'Because of the bomb!'" Sean roared, pounding his fist on the steering wheel of his idling 2016 Chevrolet Sierra crew cab pickup truck. "Because of the fuckin' *bomb*, Fiona! Because of the fuckin' *bomb*!"

Fiona began to cry. Sean Jr., who was strapped into his car seat in the back of the Sierra, began to cry, too.

May 1, 2020, 3:30 pm EDT

Air Force One, somewhere over Ohio

"To be honest, Mr. President, at this point, we have no clue who's responsible."

Arleigh Solomon's rumbling basso sounded clearly from the speakerphone. The Secretary of Internal Security – the recently reorganized, and renamed Department of Homeland Security – was famous for his unapologetic bluntness.

"Half-a-dozen different groups, from someone calling themselves 'Al Qaeda in America' to the Afghani Taliban, have claimed responsibility for the bombing on Jihadi websites. It's unlikely any of them is the true culprit. My guess is that whoever is actually behind this is going to keep as low a profile as possible for the foreseeable future. They'll remember what happened to bin Laden and his crew, and stay on the down low. The NSA agrees with me on that, by the way."

"And the CIA?" asked the President.

"Not as much," admitted Solomon. "But, quite frankly, sir, those guys still couldn't find their collective ass with both hands and a roadmap."

Steele sighed.

Since his administration assumed office, a series of highly-public *faux pas* on the CIA's part had highlighted serious shortcomings in the Agency's core competence – and helped make the reorganization of the cumbersome dinosaur into which the DHS had evolved politically unavoidable. The bungled assassination of the head of Pakistan's Directorate of Inter-Service Intelligence just six months ago had been the final straw. The United States' relations with the Islamic nuclear state – never close or comfortable – had teetered on the brink of total rupture ever since.

"What about state actors?" the President asked.

"Very possible, sir," Solomon replied. "In fact, if I had to bet, that's where I'd put my money."

"Pakistan?" Steele suggested.

"Seems like the obvious suspect, doesn't it, Mr. President? On the other hand, it'd be just like the *Pasdaran* to pull something like this, and let us blame it on the obvious suspect. Those Iranian bastards are subtle." Solomon snorted. "Hell, come to that, I wouldn't put it past the Israelis, either – except that, if it was them, I'd've expected them to plant clues pointing to Iran, instead."

"If I understand you correctly, Arleigh," Steele observed, "clues are in somewhat short supply at the moment."

"Yes sir, that's a fact," Solomon agreed. "At the moment, we can't even access the scene of the crime, so to speak – and I doubt we'll find much to go on, once we do. I'm afraid nuclear weapons are pretty effective at erasing fingerprints."

Steele sighed. "Keep digging, Arleigh. Find out who did this. I don't care what it takes – *find* those assholes."

"Yes sir," Solomon promised. "We'll find them."

May 1, 2020, 4:00 pm EDT

New Jersey Turnpike, Elizabethport, New Jersey

Colonel Arif Fahrood Khan wiped his vomit-flecked lips on his sleeve, tossed his dirty-blond hair out of his ice-blue eyes, and staggered back through the bushes to his stolen bicycle. He had left it parked on its kickstand, on the shoulder of the otherwise-vacant northbound Long Island Expressway. Wearily, he remounted the Schwinn, and continued his now-increasingly-laborious journey south towards Washington D. C. and the sanctuary of the Pakistani embassy.

- Allah has passed judgment on me. I will die the death of a fool, instead of that of a martyr. Ah well. Allahu akbar. -

He knew he deserved his fate, not because of the deaths of so many infidels – that was a reason for pride, not regret – but for having failed to consider the consequences of the Sword of Allah's EMP on the vehicle he had chosen for his escape from the bomb's deadly effects. He had failed to take into account that all modern automobiles depended on electronic ignition and other computer-controlled systems. As a result, the bomb had rendered his Subaru immobile, along with all the other cars in the Bronx he might have stolen in its place. Trapped by his own foolish oversight, Khan had been reduced to stealing this ridiculous bicycle in his effort to escape the Sword's deadly power.

At least he had the sense to torch the garage in which Tariq Aziz's box van had been modified with lead shielding, and a super-duty suspension. He had taken pains to make it look like an accident, just in case any arson investigation might ever be conducted.

- Not that that's bloody likely. The infidels will have their filthy hands full enough, just coping with the dead. -

The thought comforted him, as a coughing fit shook him, forcing him to stop until the spasm passed.

There was death in his lungs. That he knew. The painter's mask he had worn during the initial stage of his journey had not been effective enough to protect him from inhaling particles of the gentle, gray snow of fallout that had drifted down all around him, as he pedaled through the deserted streets of the Bronx. Nor had the baseball cap and raincoat he'd worn at first – long since abandoned, as he reached the verge of heat prostration – kept the deadly stuff from accumulating on his head and shoulders.

Khan – Colonel Arif Fahrood Khan of the Inter-Service Agency to his supervisors and his teammates, Timothy Hilliard according to the passport tucked into his shirt pocket – despaired now of ever reaching Washington. It was clear he had already absorbed a more-than-lethal dose of radioactivity; clear that he would soon be incapacitated; clear that he would never again see his beloved Peshawar. Never again would he hear the blessed words of his beloved imam, and never again hold his beloved wife Roshina.

- Ah, Roshina – truly the light of my life. May Allah forgive me for loving you more than Him."

Khan spat on the roadside. His spittle was threaded with blood.

- Not a good sign. I wonder if I will last long enough to find a car to steal? Perhaps then I can make it to our Embassy before I die? Insha'Allah – it will be as Allah wills. -

Sighing, he stood on the Schwinn's pedals, and resumed his slow journey South.

May 1, 2020, 4:30 pm EDT

Air Force One, entering Washington, DC Special Flight Rules Area

"Let me get this straight, General," the President said, "you're telling me there won't be boots on the ground in Boston any earlier than midnight – and you would prefer holding off on sending in the first wave of troops until the day *after* tomorrow?"

"Yes, sir," responded General Winston S. Chung's voice from the speakerphone, "that's the course of action the Chiefs of Staff unanimously recommend."

"Damnit, General, *why?*" demanded William Orwell Steele.

"Mr. President," Chung replied, "forgive me for being blunt, but 'boots on the ground' aren't useful, if the troops wearing those boots aren't prepared to do anything other than stand around in them. It's true we could physically get at least a token force to the Boston area inside of the next couple of hours – but it would not be equipped to accomplish anything useful. Most of the troops we will be committing to this mission are currently stationed at Ft. Bragg. To get them to the Boston area, along with all the ancillary support, command-and-control, logistics, and other infrastructure they'll need to actually accomplish the assignment you've tasked them with, requires a good deal of planning and organization.

"Your own science advisor's forecast indicates that, by tomorrow night, the greater Boston area is going to be a radioactive killing zone. If you insist on ordering me to commit our troops, without giving us sufficient time and resources to prepare for their deployment, they will arrive there, to be optimistic, perhaps 18 hours ahead of the fallout cloud. They will have with them no anti-radiation suits, no radiac units, no radiation-shielded command-and-control or logistics facilities, and no vehicles equipped to allow them move around in the area without being exposed to lethal doses of radiation. Sir, I cannot more strongly advocate against so pointlessly putting our people in harm's way, to no useful purpose – and I assure you that the other Chiefs are in full agreement with that position."

There was a long moment of silence.

Finally Steele said, "Thank you for your honesty, General. I appreciate it."

He paused to gather his thoughts.

"All right, I'll tell you what I'd like you to do ..." the President announced.

"Sir?" Chung asked.

"Get your ducks lined up to start moving troops – and all their associated impedimenta – into the region the moment we develop a reliable picture of where the borders of the Fallout Zone are likely to be," he instructed. "I want their deployment to commence no later than 0600 Monday morning. In the meantime, get with the Energy Department, and start working on a plan to evacuate as much of the civilian population as possible from the Zone, without exposing your personnel to unnecessary risk in the process."

"Yes sir," Chung replied. "Right away. And ... thank you, sir."

May 1, 2020, 5:03 pm EDT

Northern State Prison, Newark, NJ

Donell Jackson was worried. Arun "Big Sugar" Washington had sent word he wanted to speak to Jackson – and a summons from Big Sugar was more than enough to worry any sane con. Washington was a powerful *don*, even by comparison with other gang bosses in Northern State Prison. The thought that he might inadvertently have done something to earn his ire made Jackson's heart race with fear.

Donell had once stumbled into Big Sugar in the prison dining hall. Some joker had hooked his foot, as he was making his way through the checkerboard of crowded tables. Jackson discovered the arm on which he had caught himself was as hard as oak, and bigger around than his own thigh. Sweating with terror, he had profusely apologized to Washington, explaining that he'd been tripped.

"I am aware of that," Big Sugar replied, before turning back to his meal in dismissal.

The next morning, the body of the inmate who was responsible for tripping Donell was discovered in his cell, drowned in his own toilet. The dead man's cellmate swore he had seen and heard nothing. A 30-day stretch in Administrative Sequestration had done nothing to change his story.

Donell had lived in fear of the huge, soft-spoken gang boss ever since.

Now he was being ushered into the boss's own cell. Jackson's nerves were twanging with vigilance and anticipation.

Washington nearly overflowed an easy chair that might as well have been a throne.

"Hello, Donell," he said, motioning Jackson towards the cell's single bunk. "Please have a seat."

Donell sat.

"Would you care for some pruno?" Big Sugar asked.

"Uhh … sure," Jackson replied, then hastily added, "I mean, 'Yes, thank you, Big Sugar.'"

Washington regarded him levelly. "I see that you're afraid of me," he observed. He motioned for one of his underlings to pour Jackson a cup of the prison-made wine.

Donell, accepting the proffered beverage, found himself tongue-tied. He tried to speak, but failed, and settled for nodding vigorously, instead.

"I know you are an intelligent man," Big Sugar continued. "If nothing else, your fear demonstrates that. It's clear to me that you're also an educated man. You've been very skillful at concealing both of those things from your fellow inmates, which I take to mean you're also a wise man. I find that combination of traits interesting."

Jackson gulped, and managed to croak, "What … what makes you think I'm educated, Big Sugar?"

Washington smiled, revealing a mouthful of elaborate gold inlays.

"Today, in the yard, I overheard you say, 'That's a nuclear bomb!'" he responded. "Were you as under-educated as the typical penitentiary resident, you would most likely have said, 'That's an A-bomb!' or perhaps, 'That's a nook-u-lar bomb!' That you correctly used, and pronounced the word 'nuclear' reveals your education to me."

Donell well remembered the moment the Eastern sky had lit up, brighter than the noonday sun, casting harsh horizontal shadows of him and his fellow inmates against the Admin building. He had turned, startled, towards the fading brilliance, watching in awe as the erupting cloud of smoke and dust over Lower Manhattan formed into the iconic mushroom cloud of a nuclear explosion. For nearly a full minute, he stood in the exercise yard, watching the cloud grow and expand, before the remnants of the shock wave reached Newark, still powerful enough to feel like a slap against his body. He had been unaware Washington was listening – unaware even that he and his crew were nearby – and equally unaware of his own surprised comment on the spectacle they had all witnessed.

"Uh … excuse me for saying so," Jackson replied, "but you sound as if you're pretty well-educated yourself, Big Sugar."

"Please, Donell," Big Sugar responded, "call me 'Suge'. And, yes, I, too, have benefited from a higher level of education than the majority of our peers."

"That's ... interesting," Jackson said.

He took a sip of pruno to give himself a moment to think before continuing.

"So ... Suge ... may I ask why I'm here?" he inquired.

Washington smiled broadly.

"Indeed you may, Donell," he replied, "I have called you here to invite you to join my organization."

Jackson was instantly wary, although he was also flattered by Big Sugar's invitation.

Joining Washington's mob would bring with it an instant upgrade in Donell's status among the prison's population. On the other hand, it would also likely make him a target, not only of inmates jealous of his new eminence, but of Northern State's Correctional Officers, who closely monitored the prison for gang activity. His status as a newly-minted mobster would raise his profile with the bulls. That could easily result in his being reassigned from the general population – where he was free to walk the yard six hours a day, and was allowed to work in the laundry five days a week – to the Security Threat Group Management Unit.

Jackson had already done one 30 day trick in Administrative Sequestration for fighting, beginning on day one of his term at Newark. Some hog had chin-checked him, and he'd had no choice but to clock the sucker back. That was fine with him. The way Jackson figured it, it was better to do 30 in AdSeq than to be turned out as a punk, and spend the rest of his bid getting ass-raped every night.

But 30 days was more than enough. The very last thing Donell wanted was to be sent to GMU – Northern State Prison's maximum-security gang unit. There were some seriously bad dudes in there, and spending 23 hours a day in lockdown wasn't what he'd call easy time. There was also the issue that membership in Big Sugar's crew would undoubtedly carry with it obligations he might find less than welcome – and, once accepted into its ranks, leaving them might well prove impossible.

"Again, if you don't mind my asking, Suge, why?" Jackson replied, playing for time. "I mean, why me – and why now?"

Big Sugar nodded, still smiling.

"I do not at all mind," he responded. "Asking questions, rather than blindly agreeing, demonstrates an admirable and intelligent, caution, on your part. Donell, I have invited you to join us primarily because I am constantly in search of talent. As you might imagine, I have my pick of brawn – a resource in which Northern State is especially rich – but intelligence and education are a different, and much rarer, quality. My organization can always use a bright, educated man. The prospect of conversation with an intellectual peer is a minor personal inducement, as well, but it is the good of the organization that is my paramount consideration. As to why I have chosen to extend the invitation at this particular moment, the fact is that I anticipate a major disturbance in the near future, and I wanted to recruit you before it begins."

Donell was shocked. "You're expecting a riot?"

Washington nodded gravely, his expression inscrutable.

"Yes, Donell," he confirmed. "I am expecting precisely that."

May 1, 2020, 6:30 pm EDT

The House Chamber, Capitol Building, Washington, DC

"Mr. Speaker, Members of this House, Senators, and distinguished guests, thank you for inviting me here to speak to you tonight," the President said. "I have come to urge you to pass – without delay, and without amendment – a bill, sponsored here by Representatives Karman and Hardin, and in identical form in the Senate by Senators Roland and Kurzweil, that will ratify my declaration this morning of a nationwide state of emergency and martial law, effective immediately, and for the duration of the current emergency.

"As you know, at noon today, this great nation suffered an act of nuclear terrorism against its largest, and most populous city. Tens or hundreds of thousands – perhaps even millions – of our fellow Americans were killed in the blast. Hundreds of thousands or millions more were injured or rendered homeless. Even now, an unknown number of our nation's citizens remain trapped in the rubble, exposed to radioactivity they can neither see, nor taste, nor smell, but which is nonetheless silently killing them.

"As I speak, the cloud of radioactive fallout from that attack is making its way up the coast toward New England. By this time tomorrow, that cloud will be passing over Boston, with potentially horrific consequences. It will leave behind it a trail of invisible poison which my Science Advisor, Professor Steven Dawkins, and Dr. Ramamurthi Singh, my Secretary of Energy, tell me will persist and remain deadly for as long as years to come."

Steele paused to survey the chamber, crowded with the powerful, before continuing.

"The challenges we face in the coming days – and, yes, months, and even years – will be epic in scope and difficulty. Meeting them will demand of us both great effort, and the expenditure of vast amounts of our national treasure. But they are challenges we cannot, must not, and will not decline – for millions of our fellow citizens' lives hang in the balance.

"Nor are these trials the only challenge that confronts us. At the moment, we have no way of knowing whether or when our enemies will strike next. It is conceivable that this bombing is merely the beginning of an extended campaign of nuclear terrorism by the so-far faceless forces of evil. So we have no choice: we must be vigilant, we must be resolute, and we cannot afford to compromise, for we cannot afford a repeat of today's events. We must be free to employ all necessary methods to discover who is responsible for this unparalleled atrocity; to find them, and to bring them to justice – for we must, and we *will* bring them to justice.

"Tonight I ask, for the good of the country we all love, that you join together to swiftly authorize this measure. I beg you: give us the power we need to marshal all our resources to cope with this national emergency. Allow us to deploy American military forces on our own soil, so that they may help rescue, and provide succor to the survivors of the blast and the fallout cloud, prevent civil disorder, and keep the peace domestically. Do not hesitate, and do not delay. Your countrymen are counting on you. You must not let them down.

"I thank you, in advance, for your patriotism. And may God bless America."

The standing ovation lasted for nearly 20 minutes.

May 1, 2020, 7:00 pm MDT (9:00 pm EDT)

Patriot Radio Studio 1, Athol, ID

The red "on air" light lit, as Merlin Friend's earphones filled with the sound of distant trumpets. The tread of pounding hoofs passed from right ear to left, and off into the distance.

Friend leaned forward, his lips close to the Neumann BCM 705 microphone that dangled from the boom in front of him, and confided in his distinctive baritone, "Good evening, Patriots. This is your friend Merlin, coming to you, for what may be the last time ever, live from Patriot Radio Studio 1, in Coeur d'Alene. Tonight, the traitors and dupes in our Congress are, even as I speak, handing that socialist spawn of Satan, William Orwell Steele, the sword he will use to sacrifice our blessed Lady Liberty upon the alter of the New World Order, and deliver our helpless nation into the clutching hands of the Bilderbergers, the Trilateralists, the Masons, and the other embodiments of the worldwide Illuminati conspiracy!

"These are dark days, indeed, my friends. Just seven hours ago, our self-appointed Tyrant directed the CIA to set off a nuclear weapon inside the Freedom Tower – a false-flag operation that was specifically designed to give him an excuse to seize absolute power, by declaring a nation-wide state of martial law! Even now, our elected representatives in that den of cowards, thieves, and traitors we call Congress are voting to ratify his declaration! Imagine that: an avowed socialist, the handmaiden of the New World Order, will, in just hours, become the first-ever, officially-sanctioned American dictator! Mark my words, Patriots, our beloved country will never emerge from its subjugation to this evil Tyrant, unless *you* act *now* to stop him!"

Friend had backed away from the microphone, so as not to overload the delicate ribbon of the Neumann's acoustic transducer, as he allowed his voice to rise to a shout. Now he paused for dramatic effect, admiring his own sense of theater.

"My friends," he continued, leaning forward again, "*you* are America's final hope – its last remaining Patriots. It is *you*, and *you alone*, who must rise up against the Tyrant, before the minions of that evil despot can wrest away your ability to resist him. This is why *you* have so long, so fiercely defended your sacred Second Amendment right to bear arms – so that *you* can oppose this evil incarnate, and thwart the Tyrant's malevolent determination to enslave our helpless nation!"

Friend leaned back from the microphone, and raised his voice.

"The black helicopters are on their way – *right now*!" he cried. "The FEMA death camps are ready and waiting – *right now*! The gun-grabbers are at your door – *right now*! And only *you* can stop them! *Only you*! *You* cannot count on your neighbors to stop them; *you* cannot count on the police; *you* cannot count on the Constitution. Only *you* can stop them. Only you."

Friend's lips were almost touching the microphone now.

"*You* are America's last, best hope, my friends," he murmured. "*You* are Lady Liberty's last line of defense. Thomas Jefferson himself told us, 'The tree of Liberty must be refreshed from time to time by the blood of patriots and tyrants.' *This* is that time. William Orwell Steele is that Tyrant. And *you*, my friends, are those patriots. Do not be afraid. Do not allow yourselves to hesitate. Our country needs you. It lies helpless, desperately in need of your courage, your determination, and your patriotism. Only *you* can save our country. Only you."

Friend paused for effect. The silence stretched, nearly to the breaking point, before he spoke again, this time in a businesslike tone and at a normal volume.

"We'll be right back," he said, "after this word from our friends at Goldmine."

May 1, 2020, 7:53 pm EDT

Northern State Prison, Newark, NJ

The riot began just as "Big Sugar" Washington predicted it would.

The correctional officers were attempting to herd the prisoners of Housing Unit A out into the prison yard, towards the dining hall. A convict named Alvin "Cowboy" Clemson was at the head of the file of the cons walking the yellow line down the long corridor to the outside. When the door swung open, Clemson nearly leaped backwards in fright.

Big Sugar's gang had spent all afternoon industriously juicing the grapevine with word that the fine sifting of gray ash and dust that had covered the yard was radioactive poison. Like everyone else who'd heard the rumor, Clemson was deathly afraid of coming into contact with it.

He shook his head so violently that Donell Jackson could hear his ears rattle.

"Uh-uh, boss!" Clemson objected. "Ah ain't a-goin' out there, no how!"

A beefy, harassed-looking guard named Timothy Timmons – the inmates called him "Tim-Tim" – belly-checked Clemson into the wall.

"You looking for a write-up, Cowboy?" Timmons demanded.

Clemson defiantly gave him the eye. "You put yo pen to the wind, Tim-Tim," he invited, in a strong West Texas accent. "Ah still ain't a-goin' out in that pizen. No how, no way."

Enraged, Timmons grabbed Cowboy by the shirt front – an act forbidden by prison system rules. The beefy CO hauled him off his feet, into a nose-to-nose confrontation.

"You giving me attitude, chump?" Timmons growled. "'Cause I'll red-tag your ass right now. You hear me?"

"Fuck you, Tim-Tim," Clemson said. His voice was level and calm. "Y'all kin write my ass up all you want, but Ah still ain't a-goin' out theah. Furilla, son."

"Bet me," Timmons snarled.

Then he physically threw Clemson out the door, into the yard. Cowboy sprawled on his back in the poison dust.

Pandemonium erupted.

What had been a docile, if resentful, line of convicts instantly turned into a raging mob. Each man was grimly determined not to be forced out into what Big Sugar Washington's rumor mill had convinced them was certain, agonizing death. Every inmate was now convinced the guards were intent on doing exactly that. The men in French blue tried their best to use their nightsticks, and pepper sprays, and physical presences to cow the rioters into submission – but there were far too few of them, and their weapons were much too puny to cope with the angry, highly-motivated throng of prisoners fighting for what they were convinced was their very survival.

Within seconds, the mob overwhelmed their guards, and stripped them of their arms. The prisoners formed savage circles around each officer; kicking them and beating them with their own batons.

Then Big Sugar's gangsters swung into action. With calculated brutality, they blindsided those who had taken the COs' truncheons, confiscating those weapons for themselves. Washington's minions mercilessly wielded them against unprotected heads, throwing back those who had been assaulting the now-helpless men in uniform.

Washington himself disdained the use of armament. He relied instead, on his enormous physical strength, and his sheer size and mass to bend the shouting, struggling convicts to his will. When one unfortunate was foolish enough to take a swing at him, Big Sugar calmly broke first his arm, then his neck. He casually tossed the still-twitching corpse into a knot of wild-eyed prisoners, flattening them against the wall.

In no more than two minutes, half-a-dozen bruised, but still very much alive Corrections Officers were huddled behind a cordon of Washington's men. The seething mob was forced to stand off in helpless fury, howling their murderous rage. Donell Jackson, who had, to his surprise, somehow acquired a billy club during the melee, stood with Big Sugar's gang, confronting the mob of bloodthirsty convicts.

Jackson found himself deeply impressed, not only with Washington's physical prowess, but with his generalship. Big Sugar had accurately predicted both the timing of the riot, and that the bulls' attempt to force the inmates to enter the contaminated prison yard would precipitate it. He had properly briefed, and deployed his men so as to take maximum advantage of the situation. They had swiftly gained complete control of both the COs and the mob, all while sustaining neither casualties to their own forces, nor to the officers who were now their hostages.

- If the motherfucker was white, he'd be Batman. -

Washington moved quickly to leverage his control of the guards. He began by advancing into the no-man's-land between his gang and the furious mob. Once there, he imperiously raised one hand to focus attention on himself. The crowd, stung by curiosity, quieted momentarily. Big Sugar took advantage of the opportunity to raise his head, and stare directly into the video camera which was mounted in a wire cage in a corner of the corridor.

"I know that you are watching," he announced to the unseen officers in the control booth, "and I know that you can hear me. I want you to unlock all the doors in the tier. If you do not comply with my demand, I will turn Officer Timmons over to these gentlemen, to do with as they will."

That statement was met with a feral howl from the mob, so brimming with menace that it caused the hair on the nape of Jackson's neck to stand up.

"I will give you 30 seconds to comply," Big Sugar told the unseen COs.

Slowly, the seconds ticked by. The crowd was silent, expectantly counting to itself. When, by Jackson's reckoning, nearly a minute had elapsed, Washington spoke over his shoulder, without turning away from the mob.

"David," he requested, "would you be so good as to bring Officer Timmons to me?"

David "Little Boy" Shabazz, Big Sugar's chief enforcer – a man nearly as physically imposing as Washington himself – immediately turned to pluck Tim-Tim from the floor. Little Boy hustled Timmons forward, to stand shakily beside Washington.

Timothy Timmons was in sad shape. His blue uniform shirt was torn, and stained with blood that had flowed from his badly-broken nose down the front of his blouse. Both his eyes were blacked. Lumps were rising all over his face. One earlobe had been raggedly bitten off. Tears leaked from the corners of his swollen eyes. He trembled like a kicked puppy.

The mob bayed its blood lust. It surged toward the trio of men.

Big Sugar merely lowered his gaze from the video camera to the scrambling crowd. He thrust out his arm, palm up, like a traffic cop.

"Halt," he commanded.

The mob obeyed.

Washington again lifted his eyes to confront the unblinking gaze of the surveillance camera.

"I shall count to ten," he said, in the sudden silence. "One."

At "Seven" the mob began to mutter in excitement.

At "Nine" Officer Timmons fainted, his 200-pound frame sagging in Little Boy's iron grip.

Before Big Sugar could form the word "Ten", there was a loud clack, as the remotely-operated door locks disengaged.

The crowd of cons moaned its disappointment, but Big Sugar Washington merely smiled an ineffable, Buddha-like smile, knowing he had won.

Within an hour, every Corrections Officer in the building surrendered to Big Sugar's men. They were safely locked in a cell, guarded by Washington's underlings. Donell alone accompanied the capo to the control room, where he spent much of the next hour negotiating by telephone with Nathaniel Lundegran, the Warden of North State Prison.

"Come now, Nathaniel," Big Sugar was saying, "we are both men of integrity. Let us focus on solutions that benefit us both."

Lundegran's voice cracked with umbrage at Washington's unwanted familiarity.

"'Men of integrity?' *You*?" he scoffed. "You're nothing but a common thug, Washington!"

"To the contrary," Big Sugar replied, his tone unruffled, "I am a most uncommon thug, Nathaniel. At the moment, I am an uncommon thug, who literally holds the lives of several dozen of your officers in the palm of my hand. It therefore behooves you to treat me as if I were, indeed, the man of integrity I claim to be, does it not?"

"You'll pay for this, Washington," Lundegran growled, "I swear it."

"In the next world, perhaps," Washington agreed cheerfully. "In the here-and-now, however, I expect you will thank me, in the end."

"What?" Lundegran exploded. "Why, you scumbag, when I get through with you, you'll be lucky to get life without parole! In solitary!"

"Come now, Nathaniel," Big Sugar replied. "Consider that, had I not intervened, six of your men would now be deceased in ways that would have mitigated in favor of closed-casket funerals. You have me alone to thank that they are, if somewhat the worse for wear, still very much alive. I assure you that I intend them to remain in that condition, regardless of the outcome of our little colloquoy. I ask you, are these not the actions of a man of integrity?"

"Get to the point, Washington," Lundegran rasped. "What the fuck do you want?"

The mob boss smiled at Jackson.

To the Warden, he responded, "Ah, the sweet sound of reason, at long last."

"Fuck you, Washington," said Lundegran, tiredly. "Just give me your demands."

"I have none," Big Sugar replied.

"Fine," the Warden snarled, "I'm hanging up now."

"I do, however, have some suggestions I believe you may find have merit," Washington continued, unperturbed.

There was a moment of silence, which elicited another grin from Big Sugar.

"I'm listening," Lundegran admitted, eventually.

"Let me begin by pointing out that which is now common knowledge," Washington replied, "At approximately noon today, New York City was destroyed in a nuclear explosion."

"So what?" Lundegran snorted.

"Just this," Big Sugar told him, "that explosion produced copious quantities of nuclear fallout. Northern State's exercise yard – in fact, the entire exterior of this facility – is now liberally covered in that deadly substance. When your officers attempted to compel the convicts whom I now control to march through that poison, they rather naturally objected. That speaks poorly of your own understanding of the hazard we all face – and I speak not just of me and my men, but of you and yours, as well. If I am not mistaken, it is a danger with which we will have to cope without assistance from outside forces for the foreseeable future."

"Like I said," Lundegran interrupted, "cut to the chase, Washington. What the fuck do you want? Other than to bore my ass to death, I mean."

"What I most assuredly do not want," Big Sugar said, "is to be forced to choose between radiation poisoning and starvation. That is an issue which should concern you, as well, Nathaniel. Tell me, how many of your second-shift officers reported for duty today?"

"Go fuck yourself," the Warden replied. "That's classified."

"I thought as much," Washington responded calmly. "So you are short-handed. I suspect that condition, too, will continue for some time to come. Understand, Nathaniel, we are an island in a radioactive sea. If we do not all work together to survive, we shall all soon drown in that sea."

"What. The fuck. Do you *want*?" Lundegran demanded. His question was punctuated by thumps, as if the Warden were pounding his fist on his desk.

"Here is what I propose ..." Big Sugar told him.

May 1, 2020, 9:30 pm EDT

The Oval Office, Washington, DC

"Mr. President," announced Ardin Wildehoof, William Steele's private secretary, "the Congressional delegation has arrived."

"Thank you, Ardin," said William Orwell Steele. "I'll see them now."

He snugged up his black-and-red-striped tie, and smoothed back his slightly graying shock of brown hair.

"Yes, sir," replied Wildehoof.

Seconds later, Marlon Roosevelt, Steele's personal aide, opened the door through which Wildehoof had departed, and held it to admit the Congressional party.

Vice President Diana Hunter, in her capacity as President of the Senate, led the delegation. Hunter was elegant, as always, in a Donna Karan suit, her frosted, auburn hair impeccably pinned up in her trademark French twist. Immediately behind her stumped Alvin Spreckels, the Republican Speaker of the House. Spreckels was a hulking bald man in a Navy blue Armani suit, his jowls spilling over the four-in-hand knot in his crimson-and-silver rep tie. Following them came the Senate Majority and Minority leaders, Vittorio Donofrio and Hale Davies: Donofrio a squat fireplug in a custom-made Italian suit, and yellow, watered-silk power tie; Davies a florid blimp in an off-the-rack navy suit, and vest, sporting a red polyester tie.

Bringing up the rear were Kendall MacMillan, and Darcy Peligroso, the House Majority and Minority leaders. MacMillan, who was gaunt, yet sported a discrete paunch, wore a double-breasted midnight-blue suit with cuffed pants, and a blood-red power tie. Peligroso resembled a dump truck wearing a Navy pinafore over a parti-colored blouse. Her bulldog face was unflatteringly framed by a gray, pageboy haircut. Harry Walters, the official White House photographer, followed a respectful three paces behind them.

Steele stood to greet the dignitaries.

He walked around the Resolute desk, to the pentagonal rug which bore the Great Seal of the United States, on which stood the nation's top legislators. The President held out his hand to his Vice President, who had been his principal opponent for the nomination, four years earlier. Steele leaned forward to put his cheek next to hers, as if delivering an air-kiss.

"How's Ben?" he murmured.

The Vice President moved as if to offer her other cheek to him.

"Not good, I'm afraid," she whispered. "But thanks for asking."

Hunter gracefully backed away. She regarded him for a long second, her expression unreadable. He was startled by the fatigue lines around her tawny eyes.

Steele knew her husband had been diagnosed with advanced pancreatic cancer in February, and that his prognosis was poor. For many years, Benjamin Hunter had been a power player in Washington politics. The Vice President had depended on him for advice and support as heavily as Steele had once depended on his beloved wife Julia. He and Diana Hunter had been distant, since their rough-and-tumble rivalry during the last Presidential campaign, but he felt great sympathy for her now.

Aloud, in a firm, steady voice, Hunter said, "Congratulations, Mr. President. The Senate has ratified your declarations of national emergency and martial law for the duration by a vote of 99 to zero, with one abstention."

"Thank you, Madam Vice President," replied Steele. "Do I take it the abstention was by the senior Senator from Vermont?"

"It was, indeed, Mr. President," Hunter confirmed.

"Ever the conscience of the Senate," observed Steele. "Well, good on Vincent."

The President turned to Spreckels, and offered him his hand.

"Mr. Speaker," he said.

"Mr. President," Spreckels responded. "It is my pleasure to announce that the House has also ratified both of your declaration – although I regret to announce that there were six votes opposed."

"Really," Steele said, making it a statement, rather than a question.

"Yes, sir," Spreckels replied.

Steele turned to MacMillan, eyebrows raised. The Pennsylvanian shook his head, jowls wobbling, magnificent, pure-white toupee undisturbed.

"Mr. President, I am ashamed to say that all six of those voting 'Nay' were, indeed, members of our caucus," he confessed. "I assure you, however, that I did my best on your behalf. If I had had another 24 hours, I believe the vote would have been unanimous."

Steele smiled, and offered MacMillan his hand. "I'm certain you did all you could, Ken. The resolutions passed, and that's the important thing."

He put out his hand to Donofrio.

"Thank you, Vittorio," he said

"My pleasure, Mr. President," responded the Senate Majority Leader.

"And I thank you for your support, and for that of your party," the President said, turning to the senior Senator from Mississippi, and offering his hand.

"You are very welcome, Mr. President," replied Davies. "In such circumstances, we must all put aside partisan differences for the good of the nation."

"Absolutely," said Steele, looking Davies directly in the eye.

After a long moment, he turned to shake hands with Peligroso.

"Thank you, Darcy," he said.

"No need to thank me, Mr. President," Peligroso responded. "Duty demanded it."

It was no secret that there was little love lost between the President and the House Minority Leader. Steele thought of Peligroso as an insufferable boor, while Peligroso considered the President a meddling upstart. Their mutual dislike was always cordial, but the coolness between them was evident even to casual observers.

"Mr. President," interrupted Harry Walters, "If I could impose on you for a moment …?"

"Of course, Harry," replied Steele. "Ladies, gentlemen, if you don't mind, Harry would like to take a few photos to document this historic occasion …"

May 1, 2020, 10:00 pm EDT

Wooten Rd., Sandston, VA

Richard Wayne Lee – R. Wayne, as he preferred to be known – sat at his kitchen table.

His pistols were laid out in an arc above the Big Shot gun cleaning kit from Cabela's on his left, and an ashtray, a butane lighter, and a pack of Marlboros positioned to his right. He had just finished scrubbing out the bore of his Smith & Wesson .44 Magnum Stealth Hunter with a brass brush. Now he was screwing the pad holder onto the end of the cleaning rod, preparing to clean out the filings and excess gun oil. It was a Friday night ritual he treasured – cleaning his guns while listening to Merlin Friend's radio show, live from Patriot Studio 1.

"We're back," Friend's voice confided, "live from Patriot Studio 1 in Coeur d'Alene."

Lee silently parroted the line.

It was a ritual, like cleaning his gun collection, and it comforted him at least as much as reading his Bible. Much as he loved the Lord God, and his only Son, fervently as he believed in them both, his guns were like the children he'd never had. And Merlin Friend was ... was his friend. A better friend than any of his old Post Office co-workers had ever been, that was sure. A friend who confided in him, who *agreed* with him about so many of the things that troubled him about the people who ran their country, and the world.

Merlin – he liked to call the pundit by his first name – was a friend who taught him things, too. Merlin drew connections other people didn't seem to see: connections between that socialist traitor William Orwell Steele and the damn Bilderburgers, for instance; connections between the traitors at the Federal Reserve and the infernal international Jewish banking conspiracy, for another. And Merlin gave him advice. Valuable advice, like investing in gold Krugerrands through his sponsor, Goldmine. With the economy the way it was – in the crapper and circling the drain – it only made sense to put his retirement money in gold, where it would be safe when the monetary system collapsed.

Not that he'd be likely to live to see that, of course. Damn cancer would get him, soon enough.

"Grade 4 small cell carcinoma of the lung, Stage IV," the damn doctors called it.

He coughed; a rusty, hacking noise, and spit black stuff into the wastebasket beside his chair. For a moment, he felt light-headed. But that was just the damn drugs, of course. He'd never even been much of a drinking man, and now he was taking narcotics day and night, like a common street junkie. It just wasn't fair – not to a man who'd spent 30 years working for a living, carrying that damn bag in every damn kind of weather, through rain, and snow, and sleet, and, yes, dark of night, too. And now, just two years into his retirement, the damn doctors had handed him a death sentence – and made a damn drug addict out of him, to boot.

It just wasn't fair.

"It wasn't enough for him to try to raise our taxes," Merlin sneered, "It wasn't enough to make us taxpayers carry all the welfare cheats: the professional 'single mothers', the shirkers on Medicaid and SSI. It wasn't enough to make our proud nation the laughingstock of the world. No, Patriots, that wasn't nearly enough treason for William Orwell Steele! Determined to completely enslave us to the socialism to which he owes his true loyalty, earlier today our so-called President – although I assure you he is not *my* President, because *I* didn't vote for him – ordered the CIA to set off a nuclear weapon in New York City! And, less than an hour ago, the traitorous swine in our invertebrate Congress handed him the sword he demanded they give him to stab Lady Liberty in the heart, cut off her head, and mount it on a pole on the White House lawn!"

Friend's voice was thick with contempt.

"Mark my words, Patriots," he predicted, "there will be no Presidential election this coming November – just wait and see. In fact, there will never be a Presidential election in this country again ... unless *you* act to stop this evil man, and his evil plot."

- Damn right. - Lee nodded his agreement.

He set the Stealth Hunter back in its accustomed place on the far right of the array of weapons on his kitchen table. Picking up the Sig Sauer P220 Carry .45 automatic next to it, he set it down in front of him. Then he began unscrewing the patch holder from the cleaning rod.

"Only *you*, Patriots. Only *you* can stop this madness."

"Damn right, Merlin" Lee said aloud, as he reached for the .44/.45 brass brush. "*Damn* right."

May 1, 2020, 10:30 pm EDT

The Cabinet Room, Washington, DC

"I think we have to assume the worst, Mr. President," said Secretary of the Treasury Anderson Connaught IV. "The NYSE is finished. Even though its data should, in theory, be current, up to within a second or so of the event, it will be months before it can resume operations. As you know, Wall Street was so close to Ground Zero that it had to have been completely destroyed in the explosion. So we have to assume the entire brain trust is gone, along with the physical infrastructure that supported it. The German Bourse, the InterContinental Exchanges, the London Stock Exchange, The Nissei, all will take staggering losses. And the insurance sector will undoubtedly be bankrupted by – well, the physical asset losses in New York City alone will easily total several trillion dollars, not to mention its liabilities in the Fallout Zone. Likewise, the health care industry will probably collapse from the financial strain. The effect on the Federal Government in Social Security, disability, and unemployment claims will be devastating, as well – and we can't forget the costs of rescuing, transporting, housing, and feeding all those refugees."

"So we're in for a major economic recession, then," William Orwell Steele replied.

Connaught shook his head.

"Mr. President," he demurred, "I'm afraid that would be a best-case scenario. Given the state of the Chinese and European economies, and our own pre-existing issues with balance of payments and persistent stagflation, I'd say we're in for a severe – and probably prolonged – global depression."

"How long do you think we have before it starts?" Steele asked, visibly shaken.

"Until Monday, I would think," replied the Treasury Secretary.

"Monday?" Steele demanded, incredulous.

"I'm afraid so, sir," said Connaught. "In fact, the Asian markets – the Hang Sen and the Nikkei, primarily – are a day ahead of us, so we'll get some indication of just how bad things will be on Sunday. But I suspect we won't know the real extent of the damage until Monday, when the European markets will have their first opportunity to react."

"And just how bad do you think it will be, Andy?" the President asked.

"I'd expect that world markets will drop by a minimum of 50 percent in value, Mr. President," replied the Treasury Secretary, "although 70 to 80 percent is more likely."

"You expect stocks to lose 80 percent of their value on Monday?" Steele asked.

"Yes, sir, I do," responded Connaught. "Perhaps more."

"Damnit," the President remarked.

The Cabinet members sat silent around the long table.

"All right," Steele said, at last. "Is there anything we can do about it? Anything to reduce the severity of this ... global depression?"

Connaught shrugged.

"Nationalizing the insurance industry might help," he suggested. "But it'd cost us big time in inflation."

"Quantify 'big time' for me," Steele requested.

"Mr. President," Connaught replied, "the Chinese are in no position to absorb the amount of new paper we'd have to issue. The Saudis will help – they're not going to have a lot of choice about it – but we're still talking about creating something on the order of 20 to 50 *trillion* dollars in new public debt, in order to purchase the insurance industry's liabilities for this disaster. The *only* way we can do that is to print money. And, keep in mind, sir, that we're going to be on the hook for the costs of everything from dealing with the refugee crisis to decontamination of the fallout zone, in addition to the price of propping up the insurance industry."

He sighed.

"That's a *lot* of paper, Mr. President," Connaught observed. "A lot. At a guess – and, at this point, it's only a guess – I'd say we'd be looking at a 100 percent annual inflation for the foreseeable future, at a minimum."

"At a minimum." Steele made it a statement, not a question.

"Yes, sir," Connaught said. "Worst case? I couldn't give you an upper limit, with any degree of confidence. If we add 50 trillion dollars to the existing debt crisis, we could easily be looking at Weimar Republic numbers."

"So, we're completely screwed," said Steele, "economically speaking."

"Yes, sir," said Connaught, "I'm afraid so. If we decline to bail out the insurance sector, it will collapse. That much is certain. The only thing that's uncertain is whether that would be worse for the country – economically speaking – than nationalizing the industry. At this point, I can't predict which option would be the least unpalatable. I can, however, say with a high degree of confidence that the banking sector is going to suffer every bit as badly as insurance will."

"How so?" inquired the President.

"Because the banks have a lot of money invested in stocks and bonds – and a lot of money tied up in the insurance sector, as well, sir," Connaught explained.

"So, the economic crash you're expecting ... ?" Steele left the question hanging.

"Will wipe them out," replied Connaught. "Completely."

Once again, there was silence in the Cabinet Room.

May 1, 2020, 10:30 pm EDT,

Easau Piltch's living room, North Monroe Street, Arlington, VA

"We're back," said the voice of Merlin Friend, "and on this segment of Patriot Radio 1, we'll be talking live with Representative Easau Piltch, of our very own 1st Congressional District. Congressman Piltch was one of the handful of patriots who voted against making the Tyrant William Orwell Steele the military dictator of these United States. Welcome, Congressman!"

There was an immediate, earsplitting shriek of feedback from the home entertainment system in Easau Piltch's living room.

"You have to turn your radio down, Congressman," Friend told him.

"Well, why didn't you say so?" Piltch asked him.

He leaned over to turn the volume control on his receiver/amplifier down one notch. Then he sank into an overstuffed recliner, directly in front of one of the entertainment system's speakers.

"Thank you, Congressman," Friend said.

There was another instantaneous blast of feedback, this one so loud that it made Piltch's eyes water.

"Please turn your radio *all the way down*, Congressman," Friend said, in a voice that carefully concealed his mounting impatience with the Honorable dolt from the 1st Congressional District. "You can turn it back up after we're done talking, all right? For now it'll just be you and me on the telephone, talking like normal people."

"Sorry about that, Merlin," Piltch apologized. "I'm not used to being on the radio like this."

"Congressman Piltch," Friend said, speaking for the benefit of his audience, "you are one of the six patriots in the House of Representatives who had the courage to look William Orwell Steele straight in the eye, and tell him, '*No! No*, I will not hand you the sword you seek to stab Lady Liberty through the heart! *No*, I will not vote to make you Dictator of these United States! *No*, I will not hail you as William the First, King of the United States of America! *No*, Mr. President, this I will not do!'"

Piltch felt his heart swell with pride. By God, it was nice to hear praise like this, especially from Merlin Friend! Why, the way his fellow congressmen had behaved, you'd think his "no" vote had been somehow tantamount to treason, instead of the pure act of true patriotism and courage that Merlin Friend just told everyone it had been. True to his name, Merlin really was a friend – a friend with a radio show that almost everyone in his district listened to. That made this the perfect opportunity to seal his upcoming re-election bid!

"That's why the voters of the 1st Idaho Congressional District elected me, Mr. Friend," Piltch explained. "To represent their best interests in Washington, DC – and to defend their liberty to my dying breath."

"Let me just say that we, the voters of the 1st Congressional District, appreciate your courage, and your patriotism," said Friend. "And, please, call me Merlin."

"I'd be honored to, Merlin," Piltch told him.

"Congressman Piltch," Merlin asked, "Given the nefarious actions of William Orwell Steele – ordering the destruction of New York City by nuclear fire, seizing unlimited power to rule by decree, fitting the shackles of socialism to the helpless citizens of these United States – isn't it time our listeners exercised their Second Amendment right to take matters into their own hands? Has the time finally come for armed resistance?"

Piltch gulped at the man's audacity. His eyes darted about the living room of his oversized Tudor revival rental house.

He wanted to scream.

- *Are you insane, Merlin? We just ratified Steele's declaration of martial law, and you're advocating an armed rebellion? Good God, man, have you no common sense at all?* -

Instead, he said, "Er, no, Merlin, I think that would be ... premature."

"But, they're coming for our guns, Congressman," Friend maintained. "Surely you're not advising your fellow Sons of Fallen Patriots to sit idly by, and permit themselves to be stripped of their inalienable right to bear arms?"

"Of course not, Merlin," Piltch assured him. "But, there's such a thing as due process. As you know, I myself am a member of the Sons of Fallen Patriots, as well as a lifetime member of the NRA. I assure you I am as committed to preserving the Second Amendment as I am to worshipping our Lord Jesus Christ as my personal Savior. But we are a nation of laws, Merlin. We must give those laws a chance to work, before we declare that all is lost, and call our brothers to the barricades."

"But, with Congress backing his declaration of martial law, hasn't the Tyrant placed himself beyond the reach of the law?" Friend insisted.

"Not at all," Piltch assured him. "In fact, on Monday, I will introduce on the floor of the House of Representatives, a bill of impeachment of President Steele."

"Really?" Friend queried.

He sounded impressed. He really *was* impressed, despite himself. Piltch evidently had more on the ball than Friend had credited him with. Even if the bill was quashed – and Friend fully expected it would be – the fact that it had been introduced at all would raise the visibility of the Sons in the public's eyes. And, when the President's allies in Congress tried to make it go away, he'd have a field day decrying their perfidy ... yes, there was definitely hay to be made there!

"Congratulations, Congressman!" Friend said. "By this time, Monday, you will have earned the thanks of a grateful nation, twice over. You heard it here, first, Patriots! On Monday, Congressman Esau Piltch will introduce a bill to impeach the Tyrant! Call your own Congressman *right now*, and urge him to vote for Congressman Piltch's bill! It's up to *you*, Patriots! Only you can bring this monster down! Only *you*!"

He let the silence stretch two more, delicious seconds, before he continued, "We'll be right back, after this word from our friends at Goldmine. Stay with us for more with Congressman Esau Piltch after the break."

May 1, 2020, 11:30 pm EDT

The Cabinet Room, Washington, DC

" ... and FEMA will focus on providing housing, food, medical care, and support services to the refugees," the President summarized.

Dr. Marcus Aurelius Clement, his personal physician, leaned forward from his seat behind William Orwell Steele, to whisper briefly in his ear.

"Ladies and gentlemen," the President announced, "Dr. Clement has advised me that I've been awake since 0330, Washington time, and I urgently need to get some rest. I agree. So, is there any other issue that simply can't wait until tomorrow?" His gaze swept the table.

"All right, then," he concluded, when no one spoke up. "This meeting is adjourned until – let's say 0900 tomorrow morning."

Steele stood, turned to Andover Philips – his Chief of Staff, his former campaign manager, and one of his oldest friends.

"Join me in the Residence, Andy," he invited.

"Of course, sir," Philips replied.

The President caught his physician by the sleeve.

"You, too, Marcus," he insisted. "I hate to drink alone."

"It will be my pleasure, Mr. President," Clement assured him.

Steele gathered up the papers sitting on the conference table in front of him. He made his way around the chairs that fringed it, and exited to the corridor outside the Cabinet Room. At the end of the passageway, he passed through the cloakroom, and out the door to the West Colonnade, which was held open for him by a Marine in full dress uniform. The President strode past the darkened Press Corps offices.

He didn't bother to check whether he was being followed.

After all, he was the President of the United States of America. Of *course* he was being followed. He would be followed all day, every day, for the rest of his life. After almost three-and-a-half years in office, he was, if not exactly comfortable with that state of affairs, at least thoroughly resigned to it. True privacy was a luxury Presidents could not afford – and even ex-Presidents had to be protected from maniacs and extremists. He had long since accepted the fact that he and his Secret Service detail would very likely grow old and gray together.

Steele entered the Palm Room, through a door held open by another Marine. Trailing his entourage, he passed into the Center Hall of the Residence's ground floor. At the elevator lobby, Harold Burley, the operator, still wearing his tuxedo, despite the hour, held the door for him.

Andy Philips, Marcus Clement, and Roger Waters, the head of his Secret Service detail, all entered the cage with the President. Their ascent to the second floor was brief. The little group crossed the Center Hall, where Waters left them to make a final security inspection for the night.

Special Agent Nicolas Mason, Chief of the President's third-shift Secret Service detail, opened the double doors to the Presidential living room for them. The three men were greeted by Steele's six-year-old Great Dane, Duke. The excited animal demanded a thorough petting by each of the three men, which all seemed happy to supply.

Eventually, Steele told him, "That's enough, Buddy," and the dog retreated into the President's private quarters.

As they entered the large room, still furnished largely as it had been during the previous Administration, Steele asked, "Andy, would you do the honors?"

"Certainly, sir," responded Philips. "Scotch for you?"

"As usual," Steele confirmed.

"Laphroig okay?" Philips asked.

"Absolutely," Steele assented.

"Doctor?" the Chief of Staff inquired.

"Oh, red wine, I guess," said the President's physician, absently. "I'm not picky."

"Anderson Valley Cabernet or Napa Valley Merlot?" Philips asked.

"Merlot is fine," Clement told him.

Philips handed out their drinks: a double Scotch, neat, for Steele, a glass of Merlot, along with the split bottle from which it came, for Clement, and a shot of Makers Mark black label on the rocks for himself.

They took seats around the coffee table. Philips and Clement each chose wingback arm chairs. The President sprawled across a matching loveseat, facing them, with Duke sitting on the carpet beside him. The Great Dane rested his big, square head on his master's knee, his eyes fixed adoringly on Steele.

"Well, this a fine kettle of crap, ain't it?" the President observed, sipping his single malt.

"Outstanding, sir," opined Philips, his expression sour.

"The question, as I see it," Steele said, idly scratching Duke's massive head, "is not so much, 'What can we do to help?' as it is 'What can we do to keep things from dissolving into absolute chaos?'"

"Surely it's not that bad, Mr. President," objected Clement, frowning.

"Oh, it most assuredly is that bad, Marcus," the President replied.

He gestured to his Chief of Staff.

"Tell him, Andy," he directed.

Concerned, Clement turned to Philips.

Philips gazed into his drink for a long moment, his expression grim.

"It's like this, Doctor," he said, at length. "The only good news is that this will undoubtedly guarantee the President's re-election. He won't even have to campaign ... much. Which is good, because he's going to be up past his ass in alligators for the foreseeable future."

"If that's the only good news, what's the bad news – apart from the obvious, I mean?" Clement responded.

Philips looked across at Steele, who shrugged.

"Well, let's start with the economy," Philips said. "It's going to crash – hard. And it won't just be us. We're going to take the whole world down with us. Then there's the international relations problem."

"Which is what?" Clement inquired.

"Dr. Clement, how is it you can live in this hothouse Beltway atmosphere, and not have any feel for politics whatsoever?" Philips asked.

"Clean living, regular exercise – and I don't own a TV," the physician replied.

"I'll have to try that some century," Philips mused, pulling a face. "Basically, the problem is that, as President Steele was saying as recently as this morning, the economies of the major powers have become so hopelessly interdependent that our downfall is going to pull Asia, the Euro sector, and the Russians all down with us. India, South America, and the Middle East will follow us down the drain, as well. And Africa – well, Africa was a basket case before this morning's events ... and I sure don't see this making things any better for them."

"So, is that it?" Clement queried.

Philips shook his head.

"Oh, no," he replied. "You see, sooner or later, we're going to find out who did this to us."

Clement frowned in puzzlement. "But, that'll be a good thing, won't it?"

Steele and Philips exchanged a glance.

"No, Marcus," said the President, "It won't."

"How so?" Clement asked, adding, "Mr. President," as an afterthought.

Philips answered.

"Because the odds are that one – or more – of our valued allies in the war on terror is behind this attack," he explained. "And we're going to have to punish that ally, or those allies, in a spectacularly unpleasant and public fashion."

"You don't mean … I mean, you're not thinking about …" Clement stammered.

"Going nuclear? Indeed we are. In fact, I don't see any way around it," Steele told him.

"Jesus Christ!" Clement replied. "That's … terrible."

"Indeed it is," Steele agreed. "It's terrible, it's inevitable, and it's unbelievably dangerous in a world where every two-bit dictator on the planet currently has, or is trying his level best to get his hands on, nuclear weapons of his own."

"But … for God's sake, why then?" the physician demanded. "Why risk it?"

"The Pee-pul," said Philips mockingly. "The fucking, pinheaded pee-pul."

Clement turned almost pleadingly to Steele.

Steele nodded.

"I'm afraid Andy's right, Marcus," he agreed. "Either we nuke the perpetrators into the pre-Cambrian, or the loyal and wise people of the United States of America will have our heads on pikes – and force the folks they replace us with to nuke 'em, instead. The people will want revenge, and nobody and nothing is going to talk them out of it."

"And that means …?" Clement asked, his voice trembling.

"War." Steele and Philips spoke as one.

May 2, 2020, 12:03 am EDT

Cathedral Heights, Washington, DC

Colonel Arif Farood Khan knew he was swiftly nearing the end of his strength.

The well of the passenger seat beside him reeked of his vomit. He had repeatedly befouled his trousers. Were it not for his determination to reach the sanctuary of the Embassy of Pakistan, he would long since have given up. Like a dying dog, he would have sought out some hiding place in which to curl up and wait for the end. But duty and fanatical resolve drove him on beyond the ragged end of his stamina.

"Turn right on Connecticut Avenue in 100 feet," directed the clinical female voice of the GPS unit built into the dashboard of the stolen Toyota minivan.

Khan wiped at the crusts in the corner of his eyes with the back of his hand. When he glanced down, he saw streaks of blood there.

"Turn right now on Connecticut Avenue," the GPS unit instructed.

He made the turn, feeling feverish. His mind felt strangely detached from his failing body, as if he was observing himself from some great height. In the back of the minivan, the carcass of its owner shifted with the centripetal force. Is lolling head thumped softly against the rear hatch.

Khan sighed.

The infidel woman's body was a burden of which he had been unable to rid himself.

In his anxiety to flee the scene of the carjacking, he had simply lifted her lifeless legs into the cargo compartment, leaving her cart full of groceries standing in the parking lot. Making his escape, he discovered the shoulders of the New Jersey turnpike lacked sufficient cover to allow him to simply pull over, and roll her carcass out of the minivan. By then, he no longer possessed the necessary strength to carry her corpse any distance from the vehicle. So it and his damnable bicycle had both accompanied him all the way to Washington, as unwanted cargo.

"Turn left onto Van Ness Street Northwest in 100 feet," the GPS advised.

Khan put on his blinker. A surge of nausea hit him, and he retched in strangling agony. He could taste the bile – and the blood – on the back of his tongue, but his stomach was utterly empty. Nothing came out of his mouth except his gasping, foul breath. His mouth was so very dry.

"Turn left now onto Van Ness Street Northwest," the GPS demanded.

Khan had to hold onto the steering wheel with both hands to keep from falling over as he made the turn.

- *Just a little longer. Insha'Allah, just a little longer.* -

His vision was fading rapidly now.

He realized he was gradually going blind shortly after he had entered Maryland. Now he knew that, even if he lived that long, he still would not see the dawn. It did not matter. He had done his duty.

He had struck a greater blow against the infidel than anyone before him – greater than Salah ad-Din, greater than Osama bin Laden, greater than any *Jihadi* before him. Surely, on *Yawm al-Qiyamah*, he would enter through the *Jihadi* gate *Bab ul-Gihad*, into *Firdaws*, the most exalted realm of *Jannah*, there to dwell in the company of the prophets – including the Prophet himself, might blessings and peace be upon him – along with the most pious of believers, and his fellow martyrs to Islam.

- *And my beloved Roshina, restored to virginity again, to be with me forever.* -

"Turn right onto International Court Northwest in 100 feet," the GPS directed.

Khan shook his head to clear the clinging cobwebs from his brain. It made him dizzy. He was taken again by a fit of retching.

"Turn right now onto International Court Northwest," the GPS instructed.

Khan complied. Right turns were easier than left turns – the driver's door supported him. It kept him from falling over.

- Just a little longer. Allah give me the strength to last just a little longer. -

"Turn left to stay on International Court Northwest in 100 feet," the GPS informed him, as he passed a row of parking spaces on his right.

His sight was steadily darkening now. All but a narrow tunnel of vision was swirling blackness. His mouth hung open, and his breath whistled ominously in his lungs.

"Turn left now to stay on International Court Northwest," the GPS ordered.

Khan turned left. The Embassy of Brunei passed unseen on his right. The semicircular driveway of the Nigerian Embassy came and went on his left. Then he was at the end of the cul-de-sac, pulling into the driveway to the Embassy of Pakistan. His desperately-husbanded strength entirely gone, Khan tried and failed to shift his foot from the gas to the brake. Coasting now, the stolen Toyota crashed into the Embassy's wrought-iron gate.

"You have arrived at your destination," the GPS announced.

May 2, 2020, 12:30 am EDT

The President's Bedroom, Washington, DC

William Orwell Steele stared at the barely-seen canopy over his bed, waiting for sleep.

It was at times like this that he most acutely missed Julia – his beloved wife, *confidante*, partner, and muse – dead now nearly four years. He missed her gentle breathing, the smell of her, the taste of her lips and her sex, her warmth, and the familiar topography of her lean, athletic, responsive body. The assassin's bullet that had struck her down that September afternoon in Cleveland had taken from him the most important person in his life. The immense, instantaneous wave of public sympathy that followed her murder made it obvious that he would win the Presidency – but the taste of his inevitable victory had been ashes in his mouth.

The media had gone into a feeding frenzy at Julia's death.

Around-the-clock coverage of her funeral was only the beginning of its obsession with the "Death of an American Princess", as MSNBC had labeled it. There had been endless, extended obituaries, testimonials, remembrances, anecdotes, each framed by images of his frozen-faced grief, as he waited by her grave for the funeral cortege. Their weeping daughter Artemis, Julia's grief-stricken parents, the massive crowd outside the cemetery gates, all had been fodder for the insatiable 24-hour news cycle.

None of that had mattered to Steele. He had lost his other half, and the emptiness of that loss had become his entire universe. Everything and everyone else was merely an intrusion on his private grief. He had gone through the motions of formal mourning like a zombie, lost in his pain. He remembered almost none of it.

Andy Philips – then his campaign manager – practically dragged him back out on the campaign trail. Philips insisted that it would be good for him to immerse himself in the non-stop parade of photo ops, debates, and interviews. Slowly, he had begun to recover. But his pain and loss never really went away. They had merely been buried under the relentless tide of his obligations as his party's standard bearer.

He had been elected President in a landslide greater than Reagan's 1984 victory. His days immediately were filled with details and responsibilities much graver and more momentous than any he had experienced during the campaign.

His days were full, and the distraction was welcome. It was at night, at moments like this, that he felt the loss of his soul mate most keenly. Alone in the bed that Julia had never had the opportunity to share with him, he mourned her afresh.

He had refused Dr. Clement's offer of an Ambien to help him sleep. Now he began to regret that decision. He was profoundly exhausted, both mentally and physically, and tomorrow promised to be every bit as demanding as today had been. Still, sleep eluded him. Despite the staggering burden of his responsibilities, and the myriad critical issues that clamored for his attention, it was her memory that dominated his thoughts.

- Oh, Jules! How am I going to get through this without you? -

May 2, 2020, 01:30 am EDT

50 Hudson St., Jersey City NJ

Aragorn Northcutt Hardcastle lay awake in the ruin of his office on the 35th floor of the Goldman Sachs Building.

He was freezing, but the agony of his shattered body was so great, he barely noticed the cold. Outside, stars were visible through the gaping hole that had been the wall-to-wall, ceiling-to-floor glass window that looked out across the Hudson to Lower Manhattan. He could not see them. Hardcastle had always treasured that view. Now he saw nothing but darkness.

Hardcastle was sure he would die soon. He longed for it. Anything – *anything* – would be better than this unending torture. His twisted, broken body was an unendurable burden to him, his thirst, an unbearable torment. His blindness was a mortal blow.

He had prided himself on his tennis game. Even should he somehow survive, somehow be rescued, and nursed back to health, he knew he would never again serve a corner court shot with the Pure Drive racket his opponents so often admired. Never again would he thrill to the whistle of the air through its strings, never again magnanimously offer "Good game" to another easily-crushed opponent.

Nor, he knew, would he ever enjoy the talented mouth and equally talented pussy of that gorgeous – and profoundly ambitious – little Vanessa from Arbitrage on the 34th floor. God, how that bitch could suck! But she would never want anything to do with a blind man. That was over, just as his career was over. Over and done with. Gone with the wind.

Hell, his wife would probably divorce him, too. He'd made all the money he was going to make; which undoubtedly meant she'd take him for all she could. A goodly chunk it would be, too. She'd want their estate in the Hamptons, and she'd probably get it. And the summer place on Martha's Vineyard, and the winter home in the Keys, as well. Not that it would matter to him.

After all, what good is a fortune to a blind man? If he couldn't *see* the beautiful things he possessed, he might as well not have them. He owned two Jackson Pollacks – *two* of them! They might as well be blank canvases, for all the enjoyment he'd get out of them.

Awash in self-pity, Aragorn Northcutt Hardcastle lay awake in the ruin of his office, and suffered. And longed for death.

May 2, 2020, 02:30 am EDT

Clay St., Hackensack, NJ

Nakeesha Gramble could not sleep. She was dizzy and nauseated. It felt as though there were ants crawling all over her.

The oily, black rain that had made such ugly splotches on her pretty blue jumper had soaked her corn-rowed hair. But, when she got home, the power was out, and she was scared to take a bath in the dark. So, she settled for rubbing her hair dry with a towel. Then she went to see if her Mama would give her the reassurance she needed.

Her Mama was still napping. Nakeesha could not wake her, even though she shook her and shook her. The only good thing about it was that Marq was napping, too, so she didn't have to let him do bad things to her. Feeling very alone, she'd gone to her room to play with her Barbies, until it started to get dark outside.

Her Mama and Marq woke up at about the time the streetlights normally came on. The power was still out, so her Mama found some candles, and lit them, which cheered Nakeesha up, for a while. The stove didn't work, so her Mama made peanut butter and jelly sandwiches for dinner.

But Nakeesha wasn't hungry. In fact, Nakeesha was starting to feel sick at her stomach. She was so sick, she'd gone into the bathroom – now a darker and scarier place than ever – and thrown up. Afterward, she'd felt a little better for a while, but then she'd been sick again. That time, there wasn't anything left in her stomach for her to throw up. But she'd tried, gagging and retching and managing to bring up only a little vile-tasting liquid. The effort left her weak, and her ribs were sore, and she really, really wanted her Mama to tell her it would be all right, and hold her head for her. But by then her Mama was taking another nap.

Marq made her do the thing with her mouth that she hated so much. That made her feel even sicker. Nakeesha started to cry, but Marq made her finish, anyway. Then he had stuck himself with the needle he kept in Mama's bedroom, and went to lie down with her Mama. Nakeesha started feeling cold. After another bout of dry heaves, she had gone to her bedroom. She crawled under the covers, curled up into a small, tight, Nakeesha-shaped ball, and cried herself to sleep.

But now she was awake in the deathly stillness. Invisible ants crawled all over her. Very, very soon, she knew, she would again have to go to the scary, dark bathroom to throw up.

May 2, 2020, 03:30 am EDT

40°24'26.74" N, 73°35'19.95" W, Atlantic Ocean

Commander Anson McDonald, Captain of the Virginia-class nuclear submarine USS Alligator, stood on the tiny bridge of his boat. He scanned the sky with a pair of Avangard night vision goggles, desperately wishing for another cup of coffee.

Lieutenant Morris Abrams had wakened McDonald less than an hour earlier. The third watch Officer of the Deck had handed him his first mug of joe, along with an "eyes only" VLF radiogram. The 'gram directed him to surface the boat, report its position via satcom radio, and await rendezvous with a UH-1Y copter. Additional orders would be hand-delivered, post-rendezvous.

With its clip-on 6x magnifier, the AN/PVS8 was heavy and awkward. Its Kevlar head strap assembly gave McDonald a headache every time he used it, so he'd been taking frequent breaks from scanning the skies.

The voice of Lieutenant Abrams issued from the annunciator bolted to the bridge's handrail.

"Radar contact, Skipper," Abrams told him. "Bearing 270."

McDonald grunted in annoyance. Despite the superb optical and radar capabilities of the mast array at his back, and the advanced displays available on the command deck, he had irrationally that expected he would spot the approaching Super Huey first.

- Must be getting senile. -

"Roger that," he responded, "All stop. Chief of the Boat to the aft deck."

"All stop, aye," Abrams replied. "COB to the aft deck, aye."

McDonald allowed himself the luxury of scanning the sky to the west, looking for the approaching Super Huey. A minute later, he spotted it, just as it cleared the horizon.

- Hell, the radar mast has 45 feet on me. No wonder it saw the damned thing first. I am getting senile. -

Aloud he muttered, "You kids get off my damned lawn!"

He pushed the annunciator button with his thumb, and said, "I'm on my way down."

"Captain is vacating the bridge, aye," the OOD acknowledged.

McDonald clambered down the ladder until his head was level with the deck, then unhooked the massive hatch, and pulled it closed behind him. He paused to spin the wheel that extended the lugs to secure the hatch, then continued down to the deck below the sail. He made his way through the narrow passageway to the lockout trunk – the advanced airlock system that allowed Virginia-class subs to deploy and retrieve SEAL frogmen, while the boat itself remained fully submerged. He passed through the watertight door, and stepped into the trunk itself. Careful to seal the door behind him, McDonald ascended the ladder to the aft deck of the 'Gator.

Chief Petty Officer Arthur Mueller, Alligator's Chief of the Boat, stood on the now-wallowing submarine's aft deck, awaiting the Super Huey's arrival. He snapped off a crisp salute, as McDonald emerged from the lockout trunk. The Captain nodded, and returned Mueller's salute.

"As you were, Chief," he said.

The COB responded by relaxing only marginally.

"What's the scuttlebutt?" McDonald inquired.

Mueller shrugged.

"'Need to know', Skipper," he replied laconically. "Some of the men are wondering why we're surfaced, but they know better than to ask too many questions."

"What's your take, Chief?" McDonald asked.

"I don't know, Skipper," Mueller responded. "It must be something important, is all I can say. I guess that's pretty obvious. Sir."

"I suppose we'll find out Real Soon Now," McDonald said.

"Aye, sir," Mueller agreed.

The fast-approaching Super Huey was now visible to the naked eye.

"Wave her in, Chief," McDonald told Mueller.

"Aye, sir," Muller acknowledged.

Using red, lighted, signal wands, he directed the chopper to the aft deck. It set down moments later, slewed sideways, so that its cargo doors were facing fore and aft on the sub's narrow deck. They slid back, and men in Marine MARPAT camouflage began piling out. One of them – a tall, black man in his late twenties with a shaved head and lieutenant's silver bars on his collar – approached McDonald. The junior officer came to attention, and saluted the Alligator's Captain.

"Lieutenant Roger Young reporting, sir," he told McDonald.

McDonald returned his salute.

"At ease, Lieutenant," he replied. "Welcome aboard the Alligator. I understand you have orders for me?"

"Yes, sir," responded Young, handing a large, sealed, red envelope to McDonald.

McDonald tore open the envelope. His eyebrows rose, as, turning to take advantage of the portable floodlights Mueller had rigged, he began reading the Operational Order. It was from Admiral Harlan Adams, Chief of Staff of the Navy. With the thumb of his free hand, the Alligator's skipper unconsciously stroked the pencil-thin mustache that adorned his upper lip.

In the military-standard, five-paragraph format, the OPORD directed him to transport Alpha Team, Force Reconnaissance Company, 2nd Marine Division, to 40°42"47.27N, 74°01'31.64W – the New York Vessel Traffic Area. Alpha Team was to deploy, via Combat Rubber Reconnaissance Craft, to conduct a recon and radiation survey mission in the Lower Manhattan blast zone. Alligator was to retrieve Alpha's members, upon completion of that mission. McDonald was specifically ordered to take "all necessary steps" to ensure that his boat was not contaminated in the process. Those steps were to include jettisoning all of Alpha Team's clothing, equipment, and supplies. Once Alligator had retrieved Alpha Team, he was to contact COMSUBLANT via satcom radio, for further instructions.

McDonald thoughtfully folded the OPORD in quarters, and stuffed it into one of the leg pockets in his working uniform. Then he turned to Lt. Young.

"Well," he said, "I have my orders. I assume you have yours?"

"Yes, sir," Young replied, patting one of his own breast pockets.

"Then we'd best be about them," McDonald observed. "The Chief will show you where to stow your gear."

He waved offhandedly in the direction of the equipment storage compartments in the towering sail structure.

"Are you permitted to fraternize with my crew?" he asked.

"No, sir," Young responded.

"Then, once you get your gear squared away," McDonald told him, "the Chief will see you to the lockout trunk. He'll get your team chow and beverages. I think you'll find we have one of the best cooks in the service."

"Thank you, sir," Young replied, "but, if it's all the same to you, my people will probably just want to sack out until shortly before we deploy. It's been kind of a long night."

McDonald nodded. "By all means, Lieutenant. Whatever – as we swabbies say – floats your boat."

A brief grin flashed across Young's face. "Aye, sir," he said.

May 2, 2020, 04:30 am EDT

Port Authority Bus Terminal, New York, NY

Eydis Finnursdottir lay curled into a tight ball on the cold tile floor of the Times Square Port Authority Bus Terminal, surrounded by a sea of other, similarly-uncomfortable humans. Head pillowed on her day pack, she tried desperately to will herself to sleep.

It had taken hours to worm their way through the packed multitude on the subway platform, as unseen water steadily rose over her shoe tops. Gratefully, she had followed her new friend from Brooklyn up the motionless escalator, through the echoing halls of the subway station, to the Port Authority building. They had gingerly felt their way, hand-in-hand, through the utter darkness, until they reached the relative sanctuary of the gigantic terminal building. Long after she was sure she must burst from the pressure in her bladder, they had at last found a rest room. It, too, was crowded. In the profound darkness, Eydis had become separated from her companion.

Only then did it occur to her that she had never thought to ask her new friend's name. Despairing, she nevertheless found a sink in which to rinse her sticky face, and quench her burning thirst. Then, alone, she had groped her way back out of the restroom, and into the vastness of the main terminal floor.

It was ... less dark ... than the subway had been. The sun had long since set, but some slight glimmer of light allowed her to make out, not the features, but at least the shapes of those around her.

She was dreadfully hungry. Her last meal had been breakfast, some 18 hours earlier, by her reckoning – but, as she discovered, the restaurants in the terminal had sold out of their food stocks hours ago. The kiosks and carts likewise had been stripped of their edible wares by the ravenous horde of refugees. There was not so much as a candy bar or a bag of chips to be had at any price.

Eydis's empty, complaining belly added to her misery, as she lay huddled on the tile floor, part of the carpet of bodies that covered every available inch of space. Every so often, as those around her also strove to find a less-uncomfortable position, she would be jostled into full wakefulness – struck by a random limb, or poked by an unseen knee or elbow. Still, it was hard for her to be resentful, when she thought back to the nightmare of the subway platform. Bad as her present circumstance was, she knew well how much worse it could have been, had her nameless, lost friend from Brooklyn not rescued her from that packed crush of humanity, down in the airless heat, fetid stench, Stygian darkness, and rising water of the platform.

But she was still hungry, and the floor was cold and uncomfortable. And sleep would not come, no matter how she longed for it.

May 2, 2020, 05:30 am EDT

Wooten Rd., Sandston, VA

Richard Wayne Lee lay – or half-sat, rather – in his bed. His upper torso was propped on a pile of pillows that allowed him to breathe, despite the spreading cancer in his lungs. He was wide awake, with the words of Merlin Friend echoing over and over again in his mind.

- Only you. -

It was almost as if Merlin Friend's was the voice of Jehovah, speaking directly to him – and he, R. Wayne Lee, was a latter-day Job, put to the ultimate test of faith.

- Only you. -

How, though? How could one retired postal carrier with terminal cancer strike the blow that would free his beloved country from the yoke of the socialist Tyrant? And why should it be *him*? Wouldn't some other, younger, more able-bodied man be better suited to the task?

- Only you. -

Then inspiration struck R. Wayne Lee.

Lately, he had begun to think about disposing of his possessions. He had no wife, and no children to whom he could will them. His sister was dead, his younger brother a hateful stranger.

- A damned Democrat! He probably even voted for that socialist Tyrant, Steele."

He'd been planning to sell his precious Cessna 140, since he could no longer pass a flight physical. The only question had been where the money from that, his house, and his gun collection would go after his death. Now, suddenly, he was grateful he had put off the sale – because now he finally understood how he could use the Cessna as part of that blow for freedom that Merlin Friend had told him he must strike.

- Only you. -

Yes, indeed.

- *Only me.* -

May 2, 2020, 06:30 am EDT

Central Park, Schenectady, NY

Sean Halloran Sr. rubbed his bleary eyes. He reached for the pack of Marlboros on the dashboard of his Chevy Sierra. It was already light enough for him to see there were only three cigarettes left in the pack.

"Goddamnit," he said, in a tired near-whisper.

He guiltily looked over at his wife, huddled against the passenger-side door frame. Her coat was tucked around her shoulders, as a blanket to ward off the night's chill. His muttered curse hadn't wakened her. Fiona was still gently snoring. Halloran switched his gaze to the rear-view mirror. He was further reassured to see his son slumped forward in his car seat, each breath blowing bubbles of drool that slid down his chubby cheeks, as he slept.

- Fuck it, then. I'm havin' one. Three should be enough to get me through til breakfast. -

Sean Sr. was frustrated, angry, and exhausted – but his strongest emotion was one of fear. That his family had been reduced to sleeping in his truck, because none of the motels at which they had inquired along Interstate 90 had had vacancies was a source of shame and frustration. But the thought that their home and his livelihood were both now lost, 100 miles or more to the east, and the prospect of replacing either one seemed dim, and downright terrifying. There simply wasn't much stretch left in their credit cards, and their checking account balance was miniscule, at best.

The previous night had been a long and sleepless one for Halloran. It had not so much been his physical discomfort, as his emotional turmoil that had kept him awake. Fear had played the largest role in his insomnia – fear for his family, fear for his country, fear for the future.

- We're fucked. Completely fucked. -

And now he was almost out of cigarettes.

May 2, 2020, 07:30 am EDT,

North Cove Marina, Lower Manhattan, NY

Lieutenant Roger Young, Commanding Officer of Alpha Team, Force Reconnaissance Company, 2nd Marine Division, watched awestruck, as the F470 Zodiac Rubber Combat Reconnaissance Craft in which he rode steered its careful path through the debris that covered the surface of the North Cove Marina.

A half-hour earlier, as he had surveyed the destruction that was Lower Manhattan from the deck of the U.S.S. Alligator, none of what he had seen looked real to him. Instead, the vista possessed the visual aspect of a big-budget disaster movie, with state-of-the art computer graphics. From the half-kilometer distance of the 'Gator's deck, each particular had seemed too pixel-perfect to be authentic – exquisitely detailed and elegantly rendered. Every nuance seemed too-carefully thought out; each element painstakingly placed for maximum effect; the details of devastation just so. From the ominously-smoldering circular mountain of rubble surrounding what had been the Freedom Tower, to the grayish-black coating of dust covering every surface. From the towering column of smoke rising from the still-burning wreckage, to the black V's of circling birds, and the light haze softening the harsh disaster-scape's edges, it had all seemed somehow illusory, somehow dreamlike.

There was nothing the slightest bit dreamlike about what he observed around him now. Corporal Pruitt, handling the tiller, carefully steered the Zodiac through the densely-littered waters of the almost totally demolished North Cove Marina. Privates Kelly and Gonzales, in the bow, used the oars he had not expected they'd need to fend off the floating tangle of broken masts, dead fish, life preservers, splintered sections of boat hulls and decking, and bloating bodies that covered the surface of the Marina's brackish waters, threatening to foul their little boat's propeller.

Lt. Young had never been in combat – his commission was still too new, his country at precarious peace with the rest of the world since his enlistment. Training simulations had not sufficiently prepared him for the reality of his first encounter with mass civilian casualties. Nor had his imagination readied him for the spectacle of mobs of ravenous gulls battening on the bodies of fish and humans alike.

Kelly pushed aside the corpse of a middle-aged, Asian woman, fused to the remains of a red track suit. He stretched to grab hold of a cleat on the remnant of one of the stubby docks that had, until yesterday, held the Marina's fleet of small, rental sloops.

Now those craft were sunk or demolished. The initial blast, and the reverse-pressure wave that followed, had smashed them, and their proud and extravagant larger cousins into each other, and into the Marina's docks, breakwater, and sea wall. All but two of those structures, and most of the wooden wharf from which they had projected were gone, now just components of the flotsam through which Alpha Squad's F470 had just picked its way.

Gonzales handed Kelly a line. Kelly secured the Zodiac to what remained of the wharf. At the rear of the craft, Pruitt angled the tiller to push the rubber boat's stern against the dock, as well. Private Weisbogel snubbed another line around a second cleat, mooring the F470 to the partially-intact structure.

"All secure, sir," reported Sergeant Cukela, Young's second-in-command, his voice distorted by the vocal port on the M50 General Purpose mask he wore.

Young mentally shook himself from his horror-stricken reverie.

"Let's get topside," he ordered.

For the next few minutes, Alpha Squad busied itself with the task of transferring its personnel and equipment to the remnants of the partially-ruined dock, and the badly-damaged wharf to which it was attached.

Their task was hampered by the Mission Oriented Protective Posture Level 4 clothing they wore. The cumbersome masks hampered their vision, the protective hoods limited their heads' range of motion, the heavy rubber gloves impaired their ability to grasp and manipulate their equipment, and the over garment and rubber boots interfered with their movement. Despite the relative cool of the early May morning, even modest activity in their MOPP 4 suits was sweaty and dehydrating work.

- Thank God for small favors. At least we didn't have to wear body armor, too. -

Using a folding, Portal boarding ladder's swivel hooks to anchor it to the top of the seawall, Alpha Squad clambered onto World Financial Center Plaza. When he set foot on the Plaza, it took Young, who was second-to-last of the six to climb up onto the concrete surface, a moment to comprehend what he was seeing.

The Freedom Tower, which should have been plainly visible from the Plaza, was entirely gone. Both the World Financial Center and Three World Financial Center skyscrapers had collapsed in the blast. Their wreckage had fountained down upon the Plaza, in piles so deep they had spilled over the seawall on both sides of Alpha Team's entry point. The Securities and Exchange Commission building, which had sat between them, was completely buried under their ruins. Only a modest declivity between the twin mounds of debris marked its grave.

On the portion of the seawall that was not buried under debris, there were human-shaped shadows, but no corpses were visible. Young saw no intact structures in any direction, although the smoldering mountains of rubble from disintegrated buildings effectively blocked his view of anything beyond the blast's epicenter. A foot-thick layer of grayish-black dust covered everything in sight. The air was thick with what would have been choking gray smoke, were it not for the protection of the team's M50s.

Private Weisbogel, whose job it was to monitor the IM-174A/PD radiac, spoke up, breaking Young's reverie.

"Lieutenant, sir," he reported, "begging your pardon, but it's fucking *hot* here!"

"How hot?" Young asked.

"Off the scale, sir," Weisbogel replied.

"That's bad," Young observed.

"Yes, sir," Weisbogel agreed. "The scale tops out at 500 centi-Gray per hour, so ..."

"I get it, Private," Young responded.

He turned to his squad.

"Okay, listen up, team," he told them, "we're taking serious rads just standing here. Kelly, Gonzales, you get samples of this dust. Don't touch 'em with your hands, even through your gloves. Use the sampling spoons – and throw the spoons away once you have your samples. Sgt. Cukela, take photographs. Private Weisbogel, you walk to the end of the marina and back, if you can. Take and record readings every ten feet. We rendezvous back here in five minutes."

"And then, sir?" Gonzales inquired anxiously.

"And then we bug the hell out of here," he replied.

Lt. Young started forward.

He was determined to climb the steep pile of rubble to the top of what he had decided to call SEC Pass. Young wanted to see for himself – assuming that turned out to be possible, within the five minute time limit he had just laid down – just what Ground Zero of the Freedom Tower bombing looked like. He did so despite knowing he would be exposing himself to significantly higher radiation levels than the dangerous dose he was already absorbing on the Plaza.

- It's all in a day's work. And I have a report to make. -

May 2, 2020, 08:30 am EDT

NYISO Primary Control Center, Rensselaer, NY

Walter Watson ran the fingers of his left hand through his thinning red hair. His hand came away wet with sweat, which he absently wiped off on his khaki Dockers. He glanced up one final time at the wall of giant monitors that displayed the status and recent history of the hibernating New York state power grid.

Watson began to speak into the red telephone handset pressed against his right ear.

As the Chief Operator of the New York Independent System Operator's day shift, he had been on duty at noon the previous day, when Consolidated Edison's New York City power distribution systems abruptly disappeared from NYISO's Energy Management System dashboard.

Every one of ConEd's FACTS devices had stopped reporting within milliseconds. The resulting electrical power imbalances brought down not only NYISO's own distribution network, but every connected system in the Northeastern Grid. Like toppling dominoes, the region's power plants – including every nuclear generator in the northeastern United States and Eastern Canada – had been forced into emergency shutdown. Every protection Intelligent Electronic Device attached to the system had tripped its relays. Every static and dynamic Volt-Amphere Reactive compensator across nearly a quarter of North America's largest cities had gone offline within less than a minute. Homes, factories, and businesses from Quebec to Virginia all went dark.

Field crews from the each of the power producers, system operators, and distributors who together made up the Northeastern Grid worked frantically around the clock to repair the damage that was done when rogue currents induced by ConEd's sudden disappearance rampaged through the network. Every kind of apparatus, from the largest substations to local poletop transformers, had to be checked. Many needed to be reset, repaired, or replaced. That job was far from complete, even now. Within the Fallout Zone stretching northeast from New York City, there were tens of thousands of Phasor Data Concentrators and other data collection devices that could now only be accessed remotely, because the radiation danger made it impossible for even the hardiest field crews to safely check them in person.

But, bless their hard-hatted hearts, the field operations boys had worked their collective asses off. In Watson's opinion, the result was little short of a miracle. Yesterday afternoon, he would have bet his left testicle it would be at least a week before the system could be restored. In point of fact, it would be far more than a week before power returned to the Fallout Zone, or the upwind boroughs of New York City. Even so, what had been accomplished thus far amazed him.

"All right," Watson said, "NYISO is good to go. Nine Mile Point, let's start with you. Please bring Unit 1 online."

On the wall of giant display screens, power level indicators began to rise, as the nuclear reactor complex on the shore of Lake Ontario began feeding steam to its generators. Data point lists on the Predictive Grid Control System GUI, which heretofore had been just solid columns of zeroes, began to fill with numbers.

A spontaneous cheer erupted from the Operations floor, as the Eastern Grid began, slowly and cautiously, to rise from the grave.

May 2, 2020, 9:30 am EDT

Northern State Prison, Newark, NJ

He hadn't gotten a wink of sleep, but Donell Jackson wasn't complaining. Far from it. He had spent the night as Big Sugar Washington's envoy. Shuttling from cell block to cell block, he had explained Washington's deal with Warden Lundegran to one gang boss after another. It hadn't been easy. He'd had to deal with a lot of skepticism – and he was frequently grateful for the company of David "Little Boy" Shabazz, whom Big Sugar had assigned as Jackson's bodyguard.

Washington had persuaded Warden Lundegran to allow gangs of convicts – including at least one representative from each tier – to use fire hoses to sluice the gritty fallout dust off the yard. Correctional Officers were to coordinate their efforts via walkie-talkies. That would clear the way for the prisoners to march to the dining hall in relative safety, and go a long way towards cooling off the seething resentment the attempt to force them to walk through the fallout had created. Big Sugar also got Lundegran to agree not to lock down the general population, so long as there was no additional rioting. That had taken hours of negotiation, but the capo's remorseless logic had finally prevailed.

Then the real work – getting Northern State's many gang bosses to agree to be bound by the agreement Washington had patiently worked out with the Warden – had begun. Big Sugar himself dealt only with the most powerful mob bosses in Northern State. Jackson carried Washington's message to second-tier gang leaders. Nonetheless, they were still formidable men in their own right, and dangerous if crossed.

Over and over, Donell hammered across the same points. Northern State was surrounded by a sea of radioactive poison. Attempting to escape was tantamount to suicide. The badly-outnumbered and exhausted Corrections Officers had to be protected from reprisals by inmates, because, sooner or later, the government was going to show up in force. And they would all suffer, if the Feds found they had allowed the guards to be mistreated.

Having delivered the bad news, he then stressed the positive parts of Big Sugar's deal. Lundegran had agreed not to lock down the general population, so long as there was no more rioting. Because the prison's guards were so badly over-stretched and under-staffed, the mob bosses themselves would be responsible for policing the pop. They would therefore enjoy greatly increased power, with the Warden's actual blessing.

The experience had often been frustrating, but overall, it had been enormously rewarding, as well. Watching the wary gangsters slowly, grudgingly come to accept the situation that Washington had instantly, and intuitively grasped gave Jackson a feeling of accomplishment unlike any other he had experienced. He thought he now understood why teachers spent their lives educating children. It exhilarated him to witness comprehension dawning in the eyes of the gang leaders whom he had spent so many hours persuading to support Big Sugar's treaty.

Now, that difficult task was accomplished. Washington and Jackson had gotten all the necessary parties to sign off on his deal with the Warden.

"You've done well, Donell," the mob leader told him.

Jackson basked in Washington's praise. What he'd accomplished last night gave him a feeling of accomplishment. Having Big Sugar publicly acknowledge his achievement in front of his entire gang felt like winning a medal.

Washington swept the cell with his gaze.

"I think Donell has earned his place in our organization," he said.

There was a general murmur of agreement.

Big Sugar turned back to Donell.

"Well then," he announced, "that leaves only your initiation ceremony to make it official."

Donell Jackson's heart sank. This – and the unlikelihood of ever being allowed to leave – was the hardest part of joining a mob. He had hoped that Washington would spare him the ordeal. It certainly was nothing to look forward to.

Big Sugar Washington smiled at him.

"Don't worry, Donell," he said, "your new brothers will be gentle. Won't you, boys?"

The gang exploded into raucous, mocking laughter.

Then the beating began.

May 2, 2020, 10:30 am EDT

The Cabinet Room, Washington, DC

"What about the refugee situation?" asked William Orwell Steele.

Jefferson Raymond, Director of the Federal Emergency Management Agency – now once again a stand-alone agency, after the Department of Internal Security reorganization – responded to the President's question.

"As we see it, Mr. President," he replied, "the optimum choice for a primary intake facility and relocation camp is the decommissioned Seneca Army Depot. The Depot is on the Finger Lakes, about halfway between Syracuse and Rochester, New York. It has the advantage of several hundred currently-unused, existing structures, mostly former munitions bunkers. They could easily be repurposed as temporary shelters. It's only ten miles or so off Interstate 90, which, as you know, has become the main evacuation route for Boston refugees. As an alternative, we're considering Fort Monmouth, NJ. It's less developed than Seneca, and is also rather inconveniently far away from the New England coast. However, we think it makes better sense to hold Fort Monmouth in reserve, to house evacuees from New York City, when and as we're able to rescue them."

The President nodded.

"That makes a good deal of sense," he told the FEMA Director.

"Mr. President," Raymond continued, "we're projecting that 80 percent of the Fallout Zone evacuees will choose not to take advantage of government-provided shelter – and I should note we have a high level of confidence in that number. Even so, that leaves potentially tens of millions of newly-homeless citizens for whom we will have to provide at least temporary living quarters. Obviously, the Seneca camp alone will be incapable of accommodating all the refugees we anticipate. Although it will require repairs, the former Sampson Air Force Base runway, which is immediately adjacent to Seneca, could be returned to service fairly quickly. It is long enough for even C-5A's to land and take off, which means we can use Seneca as a point of departure to disperse fairly large numbers of refugees to other relocation camps around the country."

Diana Hunter spoke up. "Excuse me, Mr. President, but may I suggest that, as a matter of policy, we not refer to these facilities as 'relocation camps'? Instead, I think we should call them 'temporary housing facilities'."

Raymond frowned, but Steele held up a hand to stop his objection.

"Could you explain your thinking on this issue, Madam Vice President?" he asked.

"Certainly, Mr. President," she said. "Speaking bluntly, conspiracy-theorist bloggers and pundits are already actively promoting the idea that this administration intends to abuse its martial law powers to create a permanent dictatorship. FEMA 'relocation camps' are as much a part of their standard vocabulary as black helicopters. I strongly suggest we take care to choose our own terminology so as not to play into their hands. 'Temporary housing facilities' doesn't fit their dictatorship meme, whereas 'relocation camp' does."

"Good point, Diana. 'Temporary housing facilities' it is."

The President turned back to Raymond.

"Jeff," Steele inquired, "how long will it take to get Seneca up and running as a 'temporary housing facility' for Fallout Zone refugees?"

"We can begin accepting applications later today, Mr. President," the FEMA Director replied. "I believe we can have Seneca fully operational as what the Vice President has termed a 'temporary housing facility' by ..."

He turned to conduct a whispered conference with his assistants, who were seated behind him, then continued, "... late Sunday or early Monday. As you might imagine, making that happen will, for the most part, be a matter of logistics."

"The sooner the better," Steele told him. "Draft the local National Guard, if you need to, but get it done."

Raymond rose to his feet, "If I might be excused, then, Mr. President?"

"By all means, Mr. Director," Steele agreed.

He turned to the Chairman of the Joint Chiefs of Staff.

"General Chung," he asked, "what resources do we have available to begin evacuating New York City?"

Chung said, "Let me defer that answer to Admiral Adams, Mr. President."

"Admiral Adams?" Steele inquired.

The Navy Chief of Staff replied in a raspy voice, "Well, sir, luckily our newest supercarrier, the John F. Kennedy, is conducting shakedown exercises off Newport News. If we offload her aircraft, she can handle a couple of thousand refugees at a time. The problem, of course, is radioactive contamination. If we use her to transport civilians from the Fallout Zone – and especially from Manhattan – we risk exposing her crew to potentially unacceptable levels of contamination. Meanwhile, the ship herself will essentially be out of service, until such time as she can be thoroughly decontaminated."

"Mr. President?" Steven Dawkins, the President's Science Advisor spoke up.

"Dr. Dawkins?" Steele replied.

"Sir," Dawkins replied, "in my opinion, Tropical Storm Beth – which is bearing down on New York, as we speak – could be a significant factor in the Manhattan rescue effort. In fact, it may be something of a mixed blessing."

"How so, Steve?" The President asked.

"Well, sir, Dawkins told him, "admittedly, high winds will pose challenges, both in sheltering the refugees on JFK's exposed flight deck, and in transporting those refugees safely. On the other hand, Beth is expected to drop a significant amount of rain on New York – six inches or more, if NOAA's most recent forecast is accurate. That should help the effort in two ways: first, by washing much of the fallout off New York's streets, and into its storm sewer system; second, by virtually eliminating airborne radioactive dust particles. While that inevitably will create an environmental nightmare in the Hudson River, Long Island Sound, and Raritan Bay estuaries in the long term, in the short term, it should help minimize the refugees' exposure to radiation. That could greatly reduce the problem of decontaminating both them and the JFK."

"That's good to hear, Doctor," Steele responded.

Dawkins nodded. "In fact, Mr. President," he continued, "decontaminating most of the refugees – at least the ones we're likely to see in the first few trips – may be as trivial as requiring them to discard their shoes before boarding the JFK."

"Dr. Dawkins," Steele smiled, "you have just made my day."

The President turned back to the Navy Chief of Staff.

"Admiral," he asked, "how long will it take to offload the JFK's planes? And what effect would leaving them aboard have on her passenger capacity?"

"Sir, she can easily fly any and all of her aircraft to NAS Oceana or Patuxent on her way to New York," Adams explained. "As for leaving them aboard, although that certainly is an option, it would cut her passenger capacity approximately in half. She can safely carry ... let's say 1,200 civilians on her flight deck. With her hangar deck available, she could accommodate roughly twice that number."

"What about the other ships in her strike group?" Steele asked.

"The other vessels in JFK's battle group consist of a cruiser and two guided missile frigates, Mr. President," Adams replied. "None of them has a lot of deck space, and there's not a lot of room to spare below decks, either. And, if I may speak frankly, sir, decontaminating them would be a bitch."

"Very well, let's leave them out of our calculations for the moment," Steele said. "What other resources can the Navy bring to the party?"

"Well," Adams began, "nominally there are more than a dozen COMLANT Sealift vessels home ported at Norfolk."

"I sense a 'however'," Steele predicted.

"Yes, sir," Adams agreed. "'However,' the majority of them are currently deployed to the Persian Gulf and/or the Indian Ocean. Therefore, they're effectively unavailable to participate in the New York rescue effort – at least, in the near term. If I recall correctly, there are currently two cargo carriers in port, but they are both undergoing refit, and neither of them is currently seaworthy."

"So you're saying there are no other ships available, besides JFK?" Steele demanded, incredulously.

"By no means, Mr. President," Adams replied. "What I'm saying is that there are no other Sealift vessels – which is to say, ships belonging to the U.S. Navy – available. However, what's available in relative abundance are U.S.-flagged civilian craft. In fact, unless they've already run for it, there are very likely a fair number of such ships currently docked in and around New York City. And, if push comes to shove, under martial law, you have the authority to commandeer foreign-flagged ships, as you deem necessary. Sir."

"Well, damn," Steele said. "I suppose I do, at that."

He looked down the table at Kenneth Watanabe, the White House Counsel.

"I do, don't I, Ken?" he asked.

"Yes, Mr. President," Watanabe replied, nodding. "The Admiral is correct."

"All right, get me a list of those ships ..." Steele commanded, looking around the table for a recipient of the order.

"My job, I think," Secretary of Commerce Marcy Collins volunteered, getting up from her seat. "Mr. President," she added.

"And mine, Mr. President," said Ricardo Guitierrez, Secretary of the Navy. "I suspect our database of Merchant Marine vessels will prove useful to Secretary Collins," he explained.

"By all means," Steele replied.

He stretched in his seat, and glanced at the wall clock.

"Ladies and gentlemen," he said, "it's now nearly 10:00. I for one feel a pressing need to unload about a gallon of coffee."

Laughter greeted the President's confession.

"Unless there is business you think is more urgent than that," Steele told them, "I suggest we take a short break and reconvene here at 10:10."

With welcome smiles on most of the participants' faces, the Cabinet meeting began to dissolve.

"Mr. President?" said Diana Hunter, rising to her feet as Steele passed her seat, "Might I have a word in private?"

"Can it wait, Diana?" Steele responded. "I really do have to pee."

"Yes, sir. It's regarding a ... private matter, you might say."

Steele frowned.

"My schedule for the day is overly full, as you might imagine," he said. "Would it be acceptable to have that 'word' tonight, at the Residence? Say, nine-ish?"

"Mr. President," Hunter replied, "Walter Reed's visiting hours extend to 11:00 for oncology patients – but Ben is likely to be unconscious by eight or so. So, yes, thank you, nine-ish should work."

Steele looked grave.

"It's that bad?" he asked.

"Mr. President, my husband is dying," the Vice-President replied.

"I am so sorry, Diana," the President said. "Is there anything I can do?"

"No, sir," the Vice President demurred. "But thank you for asking. May I give Ben your regards?"

"By all means, please do," Steele told her.

Benjamin Hunter had been his wife's campaign manager in the race for their party's nomination. His was the hand behind some of the most vitriolic and damaging attacks of what had been a particularly brutal primary season. But that had been four years ago. From Steele's perspective, Hunter's impending death earned him a large measure of forgiveness for his political sins.

"Would you care to join me for dinner?" the President asked.

"That would be lovely," the Vice President responded.

May 2, 2020, 12:02 am EDT

Port Authority Bus Terminal, New York, NY

Eydis Finnursdottir sat sobbing. She hugged her knees to her chest, curled into a tight ball of misery.

Eydis was exhausted and starving. Her hair and skin felt greasy, and she was overwhelmed with despair and loneliness. She had eaten nothing in more than a day. During her long night on the cold, hard floor of the terminal, she had managed only snatches of sleep. Because of her exertions and the terror of her experience on the subway platform yesterday, she was sure she smelled bad, and looked worse. Everyone who knew and cared about her was more than 2500 miles away. She was a stranger, alone in an alien city in an alien land, trapped in a building full to bursting with foreigners, surrounded by drifts of radioactive death.

"Are you all right, Miss?" asked a warm, concerned, male voice.

Eydis looked up to find the voice belonged to a 20-something man.

He was dressed in hipster black from his untied Converse All-stars to his stylish scarf. He had curly black hair, a short, straight nose, a neat v-shaped soul patch under his lower lip, and a small, pointed chin. A subtle ring of eyeliner surrounded the deepest, darkest eyes she had ever suddenly, unexpectedly, longed to throw herself into, and drown.

"I …" she faltered. "It's nothing. I am just tired."

She managed a wan smile. Her heart fluttered in her chest like a bird, trapped and trying to escape.

"Is there anything I can do to help?" the gorgeous stranger asked, crouching to bring his eyes level with hers.

- Yes, yes, please yes! Rescue me from this horrible nightmare, take me away to your castle in the clouds, bathe me in soothing oils, feed me ambrosia, and make love to me until we die of ecstasy! -

"You're very kind," she husked, instead, "but I am all right, really."

"You have a lovely accent," the man observed. "Is it Scandinavian?"

"Icelandic," she confessed. "I am from Reykjavik."

His dazzling smile stormed her heart.

"I'm sorry," he confessed, "I'm afraid I don't know much about Iceland ... but I love Björk, if that's any help."

Eydis laughed. "Well, now I am jealous of Björk," she told him.

"Don't be," he instructed. "It's strictly a physical thing with her ... I just like to dance."

His smile was blinding.

"May I sit with you?" he asked.

- *Forever!* -

"Yes," Eydis said, her emerald eyes shining, "Please do."

He plopped down beside her. Half-turning to face her, he stuck out his hand.

"I'm Greg Shergold," he said.

"I am Eydis Finnursdottir," she said, shaking his hand awkwardly.

"Eydis? A beautiful name, for a beautiful woman," he told her.

Eydis felt her insides melt completely away. She was left breathless, and filled to bursting with joy.

May 2, 2020, 1:22 pm EDT

The West Wing Press Briefing Room, Washington, DC

"And, finally," White House Press Secretary Yvonne Clevinger told the assembled Press Corps, "the President has declared tomorrow a National Day of Mourning for the victims of the May Day bombing. The official commemoration will begin with a noon service at the National Cathedral, at which the House and Senate chaplains will co-officiate. The President and Vice President will attend the service, of course, and we expect that most of Congress will also be there. Tomorrow afternoon, there will be a memorial concert at the Kennedy Center. The President and a number of other dignitaries will speak, followed by event-appropriate musical selections from a variety of artists. As of right now, the National Choir of Men and Boys, and the Washington Metropolitan Youth Orchestra are the only confirmed acts. Unfortunately, due to the current ban on civilian air traffic, many other excellent performers will be physically unable to appear, but I'm sure there will still be quite a few additions to the list before the end of the day."

Clevinger looked up from the podium.

"That concludes the scripted part of today's briefing," she stated.

The Press Secretary smiled, a wan, but genuine smile.

"I'll take a few questions," she announced, "but I ask you to please be brief – in other words, no two-parters."

Hands, including many clutching pens, notepads, and smartphones, shot up all over the room. Clevinger decided to pick a potentially hostile questioner first.

"Mr. Bullock?" she called.

Reed Bullock of Fox News began, "Regarding the FEMA relocation camps …"

Clevinger looked pained.

"Please, Mr. Bullock," she corrected, "they're 'temporary housing facilities', not 'relocation camps'."

Bullock waved her objection away, as if it were a pesky insect.

"Po-*tay*-to, po-*tah*-to," he said dismissively. "The question is, where are you going to stash all those people, and, once they're in the camps, how long will it be before you let them out?"

"Mr. Bullock," Clevinger said firmly, "anyone who takes advantage of FEMA's offer to provide temporary housing will be free to vacate that housing any time he or she chooses to do so. These facilities will be open to inspection by the press. And no one – I repeat 'no one' – will be forced to accept these accommodations against their will. They're being provided as an option, not a mandate."

Bullock started to speak. Clevinger interrupted him.

"Uh!" she warned, holding up an admonitory finger. "As for locations other than the Seneca Army Depot, those will mostly also be decommissioned military bases – at least, to begin with. The President has chosen them primarily because of logistical concerns: they all have airstrips capable of landing jumbo jets adjacent to them, and most have vacant structures that can readily be converted to temporary housing. Also, because the Federal government owns them, the paperwork and expense involved in requisitioning them for FEMA's use will be minimal. Our displaced citizens demand, and deserve immediate action to assist them in their time of need, and the President is determined to provide that assistance in as timely – and cost-effective – a manner as possible. Next question?"

She ignored Bullock's attempt to follow up, and instead pointed to the MSNBC correspondent. "Mr. Hollingsworth?"

"Does the Administration have any idea yet who was behind the attack?" asked Preston Hollingsworth.

"Not that I'm aware of," the Press Secretary replied. "Please keep in mind that, as he announced yesterday, the President's immediate focus is on the victims of the attack, rather than on its perpetrators. Yesterday, President Steele promised he will see to it that those responsible for the nuclear bombing of Manhattan will be found, and made to pay the price for their crime. I can assure you that he means every word of that promise."

"I ask," Hollingsworth responded, "because there are rumors going around that a revived Al Qaeda network is responsible."

"And, from what I understand," Clevinger shot back, "there are also rumors that Martians were responsible. If there's any substance to either of those rumors – or to any of the dozens, or hundreds of others making the blogosphere rounds – I can only tell you that I have not personally been so informed. Mr. St. John?"

Martin St. John of Reuters, asked, "When, exactly, do you expect the USS Kennedy to reach Manhattan? And will the media be permitted to cover her mission?"

"Weather permitting," Clevinger told him, "the JFK should reach Manhattan sometime before midnight tonight. Obviously, tropical storm Beth will have an influence on her actual schedule."

There was a general nodding of heads at that *caveat*.

"As for press coverage," she continued, "it would be up to her captain whether or not to allow it – but I suspect that physically getting your reporters onto the JFK without violating the civilian no-fly rule currently in effect will be your real obstacle."

"Then the Administration does not intend to make an exception to those rules for the media?" Bullock demanded.

"Not as far as I know," the Press Secretary replied. With an internal sigh of resignation, she said, "Mr. Bonsalle?"

Bernard Bonsalle, was the correspondent from the Libertyfire blog – and the current representative of the rotating pool of reporters from independent blogs.

He stood, and declared self-importantly, "As I'm certain you are aware, there has been significant pushback against President Steele's declaration of martial law. There's been talk that he'll cancel the upcoming Presidential election, and that democracy may, in fact, never be restored to the American people. Are you prepared to confirm Steele's intention to cancel the election, and make himself dictator-for-life of the United States?"

Clevinger's hazel eyes flashed with anger, as a murmur of disapproval at Bonsalle's act of *lèse majesté* spread across the Briefing Room.

"First of all," she replied, biting off each word as if it were Bonsalle's head, "there is no greater champion of democracy alive today than *President* Steele. I can assure you he issued yesterday's declaration of martial law only with the greatest reluctance. No one looks forward more eagerly than the President does to its end. I also think it's important to point out that, last night, Congress voted overwhelmingly to approve his declaration – in fact, the vote in favor was nearly unanimous. Just as importantly, I'd like to note that your characterization of the amount of pushback against the President's declaration of martial law as 'significant' is misleading, at best.

"In point of fact, only a small number of extreme-right-wing bloggers, and podcasters have voiced any real objection – your employer being one of them."

She held up a hand to forestall Bonsalle's objection.

"Right now," she continued, "the President is completely focused on the tasks of rescue and recovery from this national disaster. The Presidential campaign is at the very bottom of his current list of priorities. I'm absolutely certain he has no plans to cancel the upcoming election. I'm equally sure he hopes that martial law will be a mere historical footnote, long before November 3rd comes along. Finally – and this is my own personal opinion – the notion that President Steele has any desire to become 'dictator-for-life' of the United States is utterly ludicrous. As far as I'm concerned, only a raving lunatic would seriously suggest such a thing."

Clevinger made a visible effort to calm herself.

"Ms. Colson?" she invited.

Susan Colson of ABC asked, "Will the President himself be holding a press conference any time soon?"

"I don't know," Clevinger replied, "but I imagine so. I'll ask him about it the next time I see him."

She gathered up the papers on the podium before her, and swept the room with a glance.

"That's all for now," the Press Secretary concluded. "Thank you for your time and attention."

May 2, 2020, 2:28 pm EDT

The White House Situation Room, Washington, DC

William Orwell Steele sat at the head of the long, rectangular table that dominated the Situation Room. His national security staff and the Joint Chiefs were arrayed to his left and right. General Winston Chung, Chairman of the Joint Chiefs, was just finishing up his summary of the radiation data collected from flyovers of Manhattan by unmanned aerial vehicles. Those readings were shown as overlays in a spectrum of colors on a satellite photo of the island, which was displayed on the giant video wall at the end of the table.

"This next set of images was taken by a Marine reconnaissance squad that Admiral Adams dispatched to do a ground survey of Lower Manhattan this morning," Chung concluded. "I'll let him describe them for you, sir."

Admiral Harlan Adams, the Chief of Staff of the Navy, accepted the remote control from Chung.

"Mr. President," he said, his deep voice rasping, "this first shot was taken from the World Financial Plaza, looking approximately northeast toward the remains of the World Trade Center."

The digital photograph showed the "pass" between the mountains of rubble that had been the World Financial Center and Three World Financial Center towers, with the figure of Lt. Roger Young, otherworldly in his bulky MOPP 4 suit, climbing the unsteady pile of debris.

"I'm not familiar enough with that part of Manhattan to understand what I'm looking at," Steele complained.

"For comparison's sake, Mr. President," Adams clarified, "here's a Google Earth image of approximately the same view, as it would have appeared two days ago."

The image of Lt. Young climbing the ruins was replaced on the big screen with a view across the Plaza. It showed the intact Freedom Tower soaring in the distance, behind the low dome of the Securities and Exchange Commission Building, which squatted in the foreground. The towers of the World Financial Center skyscrapers loomed on either side of the SEC headquarters.

"Jesus fucking Christ," said Steele.

Intellectually, he had known that the destruction the nuclear bomb had wreaked on Lower Manhattan had been devastating. The contrast between the two images made the concept horrifyingly real to him on an emotional level he had not previously experienced. For a long moment, he sat dumbstruck. The room was quiet around him, as the others surrounding the table absorbed the impact, as well.

"Let me see the previous one again," Steele said, in a shaken voice.

Adams manipulated the remote control. The photo of Lt. Young climbing the pile of rubble reappeared on the big screen.

"Jesus!" Steele repeated.

There was another long moment of silence, as he got his emotions under control.

Then the President said, "Proceed, Admiral," in a voice as devoid of emotion as his reaction to the two contrasting images had vibrated with it.

"Yes, sir," Adams said. "This next photo is of Ground Zero itself. It was taken by Lt. Roger Young, whom you saw climbing the remains of the SEC Building in the previous photo."

The Google Earth image briefly flashed on the big screen, followed by a picture of the melted-looking stub of the Freedom Tower and the rubble-strewn, glassy crater that surrounded it. All of the skyscrapers around One World Trade Center appeared to have collapsed. They formed a nearly-continuous ring of smoldering wreckage, surmounted by a still-dense cloud of smoke, with the misshapen base of the Freedom Tower at its center. What had been the National September 11 Memorial was now buried in debris. The effect was that of a Moonscape: barren, lifeless, alien, and somehow unreal.

"Unbelievable," Steele said. After a moment, he asked, "Are there more?"

"Yes sir," said Adams, summoning the next image.

It had been taken from the same position, but angled towards what had been the Goldman Sachs Building and 101 Barclay Street. Both were now just part of the ring wall of shattered skyscrapers, with Midtown Manhattan invisible behind the obscuring columns of smoke from their still-burning remains. After a moment, Adams brought up the following photo. It looked southeast toward the ruins of 5 World Trade Center and the Equitable Life Building. Again, nothing but devastation was visible.

"Is there a closer view of Ground Zero?" Steele asked.

"No sir," replied Adams.

"Why not?" Steele demanded.

"Mr. President," Adams said, "the levels of radiation in, and immediately around Ground Zero are extremely high – high enough that they interfere significantly with both the imaging and control systems of our unmanned aerial vehicles. As it turned out, this task was one which men could do, while robots, unfortunately, could not. I say 'unfortunately', because, in the process of obtaining these photographs, Lt. Young absorbed what will probably turn out to have been a fatal dose of radiation. I feel I should also add that, in my view, he went well beyond the call of duty in doing so. The other members of his squad took very high doses of radiation, as well, although none of them was nearly as heavily irradiated as Lt. Young. Had he attempted to get any closer, he probably would not have survived to bring us the pictures you've just seen."

"You're saying that man's a hero," Steele observed.

"Yes sir," agreed Admiral Adams. "They all are."

May 2, 2020, 4:31 pm EDT

Clay St., Hackensack, NJ

Nakeesha Gramble dreamed she was an angel.

She had been lying huddled in her bed, when, all at once, she started floating up into the air. The ceiling disappeared, and she rose high into the sky. Nakeesha looked down on her house, and spotted her Big Wheel sitting in the driveway. That made her smile. Her Big Wheel always made her happy.

She hadn't been happy at all, for what seemed like days and days now.

The last time Marq had come into her room, he had grabbed her by her braids, like he always did now, to use her mouth as if she were some kind of appliance – a mere object for him to gratify himself with. But her braids had pulled right out of her scalp in Marq's hands. With them had come patches of her burning scalp, revealing to her molester's horrified eyes the raw bone of her skull.

Shaken, her Mama's boyfriend had fled from Nakeesha's bedroom, leaving her to sink back into the stupor from which he had roused her. That slowly-deepening coma had protected her for the last several hours from having to experience her own suffering.

But that was in the past.

Now – right now – Nakeesha was flying way up high in the sky. Her neighborhood was all spread out below her, like a map. There was the Center for Food Action. Across the street was the funeral home, with the big, showy trees in front of it. And there were her Mama and Donell, somehow together again, and walking hand-in-hand along 1st Street.

Nakeesha waved to her Mama and Donell.

They smiled, and waved back at her. Nakeesha was so happy her Mama and Donell were back together that she felt like she would burst. Now they could be a family, and the Po-Po could never, ever take Donell away from them again.

She was flying very high, now

Hackensack was so tiny below her that she had to laugh at how absurd and toy-like it looked. Above her, she saw a bright, white light beaming down, setting her wings gloriously aglow. Nakeesha just wished her Mama and Donell could see her now. Her angel wings suffused with radiance, her white robe rippling in the air, she joyfully flew higher and higher.

Into the light.

May 2, 2020, 5:46 pm EDT

Wooten Rd., Sandston, VA

Richard Wayne Lee hadn't gotten much sleep.

Then again, he never got much sleep any more. That was all right. After tonight, he'd never need to sleep again. In the meantime, there was an awful lot for him to do.

He'd just finished unloading the five plastic, five-gallon gas cans, steel funnel, and 22-quart Tramontina stock pot he'd purchased at the Mechanicsville Walmart Supercenter. Now, he was transferring a double armload of styrofoam cups and plates to the insides of his garage.

He hadn't been able to locate any benzene, but that wasn't too big a problem. The recipes for homemade napalm he'd found on the Internet had made it clear that benzene just made the stuff more flammable. With its wings full of avgas, his little Cessna was going to make a pretty good ignition source. The whole point of the napalm was simply to make sure the fire couldn't be extinguished easily. He figured 25 gallons of it ought to accomplish that pretty well.

R. Wayne whistled, as he dumped the plates and cups on the floor of the garage, and headed back through the rain to his gleaming F150 for another load. Thunderstruck, he suddenly realized that he was actually *happy*. It was an unfamiliar sensation – he hadn't been truly happy in quite a long time. In fact it had been decades, now that he thought about it.

- There's nothing like having a purpose in life to make a man feel good about himself. –

R. Wayne savored the wisdom of the insight.

Dumping the final load of supplies on the garage floor, he went back outside to lock the tonneau cover on his truck bed. Re-entering his garage, he pulled the door down behind him.

- Nosy damned neighbors can kiss my wrinkled, gray ass. -

The image made him laugh out loud.

Lord almighty, he felt good! Dilaudid kept him from feeling bad – at least, most of the time – but today he felt like his old self. Better than his old self. In fact, he felt fan-fucking-*tastic*. Nearly as good as the first time he'd flown solo, all those years ago, by God!

Still whistling, he hoisted the stock pot up onto his sturdy wooden workbench, then heaved one of the sloshing gas cans up beside it. He'd made it a point to fill each of the cans at a different gas station on the way home from Walmart. No point in setting off alarms with DIS. He'd paid in cash for four of the fill-ups, too. Unscrewing the knurled plastic cap, he manhandled the gas can up onto his shoulder, and began pouring its contents into the stock pot. The fumes from the hi-test gasoline made his head swim.

- Use only in well-ventilated conditions. –

The last of the gas gurgled into the pot.

He set the can back on the garage floor. Then he put the cap on the work bench, and started towards his kitchen, to fetch the long-handled spatula he used for barbequing.

- Tonight in Hell, they'll be serving barbequed tyrant. -

Lord, he felt good!

May 2, 2020, 7:28 pm EDT

Yale Farm Road, Romulus, NY

"Goddamnit!" shouted Sean Halloran, Sr., pounding on the steering wheel of his Chevy Sierra pickup truck, "this fuckin' traffic hasn't moved for a fuckin' *hour*!"

As usual, the 8-year-old truck ignored his rage, while his wife could not. Fiona cowered against the passenger's door. She knew better than to think anything she could say would calm her husband, when he was in this black a mood. Better to simply take what cover she could, and try to weather the storm, than to risk re-focusing his wrath on her.

Strapped into his car seat behind them, Sean, Jr. began crying lustily.

"Aw, for fuck's sake," said Sean Sr. "Fiona …"

"I'm sorry, Sean," his wife told him, "he's just scared … and prob'ly hungry, too."

"What the *fuck* am I suppos'd to do about that, huh?" demanded Sean, Sr. "What the *fuck* am I suppos'd to do?"

"I know it's not your fault, Honey," Fiona hastily assured him, in her most sympathetic tone. "But little Sean's just a baby. He can't understand, like I do."

Suddenly contrite, Sean Sr. reached across the cab to gently squeeze his spouse's knee.

"I'm sorry, Sweetheart," he told her. "It's just that we're almost outta gas – and it's gonna be dark, soon. I'm just worried, is all."

A sudden surge of affection for her husband swept Fiona. He really was a good provider, and she had no doubt that he loved both her and their son with all his heart. It really wasn't his fault. He just had a little problem controlling his temper, when things didn't go exactly his way. That was all. Sean was just trying to protect them.

Sean, Jr. abruptly stopped crying. He began to hiccup, instead.

Fiona decided to unbuckle her seat belt, so she could turn around and fish Sean Jr.'s bottle out of the cooler beside him on the rear seat. She hoped a little apple juice would make him feel better.

"Why don't ya turn the engine off, Sean?" she asked, as she rummaged in the cooler. "Ya know – to save gas?"

"Fuck, Fiona," Sean Sr. replied, "ya know the line's gonna move the second I do."

"But isn't that what ya want?" Fiona asked.

Sean Sr. opened his mouth to respond. Then he thought better of it. When she was right, by God, Fiona was fuckin' right.

He turned the truck off, but left the ignition switch in the utility position, so they could listen to the radio. The temporary plastic signs, positioned every 100 yards or so along Yale Farm Road, instructed drivers to tune to 710 AM for instructions. Mostly, those instructions consisted of telling those drivers to remain in their cars, and to be patient. All applications for temporary housing would be processed in the order of the applicant's arrival.

- That's just fuckin' fine – for the assholes who got here early. -

Halloran thought his family would be among them, but he hadn't counted on the sheer number of his fellow Boston-area exiles. All of them, it seemed, had set out at once on Interstate 90, headed west from Schenectady. By the time the Hallorans turned south on highway 96 toward Romulus, traffic had already slowed to the pace of an arthritic turtle. It was now painfully apparent to Sean, Sr. that they weren't the only ones in need of FEMA's "temporary housing". Ever since a state trooper stationed at the intersection of 96 and Yale Farm Road waved them off the highway – along with everyone else who couldn't show an ID proving they lived in the area – they'd been stuck creeping along the narrow country road, at well under a mile per hour. Their only diversion had been the occasional Humvee or six-by-six truck, roaring by in the otherwise-vacant opposite lane.

Frustrated, Sean Sr. fished in his pocket for his pack of smokes.

- Only four left. -

Given his luck so far, there was a good chance that, even when they eventually reached their destination, cigarettes were likely to remain a scarce commodity for at least the next day or two.

- And I prob'ly won't be able to find any beer there, either. Goddamnit! -

Once again, Sean Halloran, Sr.'s knuckles turned white on the steering wheel.

May 2, 2020, 8:02 pm EDT

Clay St., Hackensack, NJ

Sprawled across her daughter's bed, Latonya Gramble lay weeping. Her shoulders heaved with sobs, her shaking arms desperately clutched Nakeesha's still, cold corpse.

Latonya had awakened from her heroin-induced daze only minutes earlier. She had gone stumbling through the rented duplex in search of her lover, Marqus Collins, and the promise of another fix. Instead, she had found only silence and gloom, until she had entered the bedroom where her mutilated daughter's corpse lay. It was already stiffening in death.

She had wailed like a lost soul. Falling to her knees, she gathered her precious baby's lifeless form to her, in an agony of loss and loneliness.

Nakeesha had been everything to Latonya. At least, she had been everything, until Latonya accepted heroin into her life. Then Nakeesha, along with every other aspect of Latonya's old existence, faded into insignificance next to her all-consuming passion for her new best friend forever, smack.

Her most recent boyfriend had introduced her to brown sugar.

Marqus had come into her life after Donell Jackson had been arrested while breaking into a house on the other side of Hackensack. Donell was convicted of violating his parole, and sent to finish out his original five-year term in Newark. That had been a terrible event in the life of Latonya Gramble. Donell had been so good to her, and to Nakeesha, that his loss had sent Latonya into an emotional tailspin. Even after Marqus, with his suave good looks, had insinuated himself into their lives, his frequent compliments about her fine booty and DSL hadn't really affected her depression. Nakeesha had never really warmed to him, either, so Latonya's relationship with Marqus had been a strictly casual thing – until H entered her life.

"Just try it, Baby," Marqus told her, "Ain't no big thing."

So she had tried it, using a rolled-up dollar bill to snuff up a small pile of the stuff off a hand mirror from the bathroom.

The horse made her feel all warm and drowsy. More importantly, it made her troubles seem to fade away into nothing. Donell's absence no longer hurt so much. Latonya no longer felt so alone and helpless. And the relentless financial pressure of being the single mother of a pre-schooler retreated safely behind the cozy blanket of well-being that first hit of scag had given her.

Naturally enough, after that initial, blissful experience, the next time Marq – he was Marq, now, rather than the more formal Marqus – offered her a snort, she eagerly accepted it, disappearing into the snug, wooly insulation from her problems it provided. Not too long afterward, she began skin popping.

"It's better, Baby," Marq had assured her. "You'll see."

And she had. And it was. And one thing led to another. Inside of a month, she was mainlining.

Now the all-consuming comfort of her last hit was wearing off. Marq was nowhere to be found. Her beautiful, sweet baby Nakeesha was dead in her bed, her beautiful braids ripped out of her blood-soaked head. Latonya was all alone in the dark.

And starting to jones.

Mourning the loss of her daughter, her lover, her fix, and her future, Latonya Gramble gave voice to an extended, wordless, animal cry of primal pain.

Outside, it began to rain.

May 2, 2020, 9:08 pm EDT

The White House Living Room, Washington, DC

"Excuse me, Mr. President," said Special Agent Richard "Dick" Wright, head of William Orwell Steele's second-shift Secret Service detail.

Steele looked up from the report he had been skimming on Iranian *Quds* Force covert activities in the Republic of Central Iraq, the Sunni-dominated fragment of the sundered Islamic Republic of Iraq.

"Yes, Dick?" the President asked.

"I'm sorry to interrupt you, sir," Wright said, "but the Vice President's security detail reports that Mrs. Hunter left Walter Reed ten minutes ago. Her ETA at the east gate is six minutes."

"Thank you, Dick," Steele replied.

He closed the red Top Secret folder, and placed the *Quds* Force report on top of a two-inch stack of similar red folders on the coffee table in front of him. Sitting next to it was a second, three-inch stack of unread reports, most of them also enclosed in red folders. Steele knew that, by nine o'clock the next morning, there would be another five-inch stack of reports waiting for him. Only some of them would be holdovers from the current "pending" pile. He envied President Kennedy's purported ability to speed-read 2500 words per minute. Even skimming the text for key passages, his own pace was considerably slower – and the flow of new information the President was expected to absorb was never-ending.

Steele stood, and stretched.

"Tell Mrs. Hunter's detail I'll meet her at the North Portico," he instructed.

The President stopped to use the restroom, and spent a moment scratching his Great Dane behind the ears. Accompanied by Agent Wright and his beloved dog, he started for the second floor elevator. Two minutes later, he was standing on the gray marble steps of the North Portico, flanked by uniformed Secret Service members. Wright and two other Special Agents stood in front of him.

Duke, sitting beside the President, whined in anticipation. He recognized the signs of an impending visitor – someone who would inevitably want to pet and praise him.

It was raining heavily, and the infamous North Portico winds were cutting. Steele, determined to greet the Vice President himself, refused to retreat into the glass vestibule that separated the front door to the White House from the Entrance Hall within. To his surprise, he felt like a schoolboy awaiting his first date; nervous and unsure of himself; filled with anticipation, but looking forward to Diana Hunter's arrival. Luckily, the Vice President's limousine pulled up the driveway only a minute or so later.

The President, descended the six steps to the curb, as Hunter stepped out of the car.

"Hello, Mr. President," she greeted him. "Lovely weather we're having, isn't it?"

"Madam Vice President," Steele replied, "it is not."

Offering her his arm, he added, "Shall we run for it?"

"That," she responded, "would not be very dignified, would it?"

"Nope," agreed the President.

Detouring around the delighted Duke, whose frantically-wagging tail shook his entire hindquarters, the executive couple made tracks for the vestibule. They were chased by a uniformed Secret Service agent trying desperately – and ineffectively – to shield them from the downpour with an umbrella. The First Dog crowded in after them. As he vigorously shook himself dry, Duke sprayed them both with second-hand raindrops.

Hunter laughed, forestalling Steele's apology.

"There went our dignity," she observed.

"Dogs," Steele nodded. "You gotta love 'em."

"And I do," the Vice President replied.

Suiting action to words, she took Duke's massive head in her hands, and energetically scrubbed him behind the ears.

"Who's a good boy?" she cooed. "Who's a good boy?"

The overjoyed animal responded by laving Hunter's carefully-made-up face with his handkerchief-sized tongue.

"Oh, God, Diana," the President told her, "I'm sorry."

"Don't be," Hunter replied. "Doggy kisses are always welcome."

"Your diplomacy is showing," Steele observed. "I see you're flying solo tonight."

Hunter nodded.

"I thought one freeloader at the President's table would be plenty, so I gave my staff the night off," she said.

"You're a very considerate guest, then," Steele replied. "I don't usually have that pleasure."

"Thank you for the kind words," Hunter said. "But I'm simply being selfish. Tonight I wanted your undivided attention."

"That you have," the President affirmed, smiling. "So, can I buy you a drink, or would you rather eat first?"

"Food before alcohol, always," Hunter replied. "And, frankly, I'm famished. But first," she gestured to her slobber-covered face, "I need to make a few cosmetic repairs."

Sandy Wilkerson, the White House night usher, approached the two executives.

"Pardon my interruption," he inquired, "but would the Vice President care for a moist towelette?"

"Thank you," Hunter said. "And then a quick trip to the powder room, perhaps?"

Steele grinned. "You're in good hands with Sandy, Diana. Shall we plan on meeting at the Family Dining Room in, say, five minutes?"

"That works for me," agreed the Vice President. Turning to follow Wilkerson, she looked back over her shoulder and favored the President with a warm smile.

May 2, 2020, 9:28 pm EDT

Hanover County Municipal Airport, VA

Richard Wayne Lee turned right off rain-slicked Air Park Road into the Hanover County Municipal Airport parking lot. At the entrance, he turned left, and pulled up to the secondary gate that extended from the airport perimeter fence to the HOVA aircraft maintenance and repair shop. Leaving his immaculately-maintained F150 pickup running, Lee got out of the vehicle to inspect the gate. As expected, he found it secured with a padlocked chain.

- Not a problem. -

Lee walked around the passenger side door of the gleaming red pickup truck. He leaned into the F150, and pulled out the pair of heavy-duty bolt cutters he'd brought along for just such a contingency. Moments later, there was a snapping sound, and the lock and chain fell away from the gate. R. Wayne slid the chain-link gate aside.

He got back behind the wheel of his truck, drove onto the tarmac, parked, and returned to slide the now-unlocked gate closed. He cut around the engine and airframe shop, and drove the short distance to the end of the second row of tie-downs, where his beloved Cessna was parked.

Lee backed his pickup in next to the passenger door of the little fabric-winged aircraft. Getting out, he went around to the rear of the F150, and unlocked the tonneau cover. He dropped the pickup's gate to give himself easier access to his homemade napalm. Then he unlocked the airplane's passenger door, braced it open with a tieback, and folded the passenger seat down.

- No sense in making the job any harder than it has to be. -

"What the Hell you think you're doing, Mister?" demanded a gruff voice behind him.

A flashlight beam threw his shadow, sharp and black, against the maroon-and-cream-painted fuselage of the Cessna.

"Well, hello, Curtis," Lee said cheerfully, recognizing the voice.

He turned to face Curtis Suggs, the air park's night watchman, carefully shielding his eyes from the blinding light of Suggs's torch.

"Mind pointing that flashlight somewhere other than my peepers?" he requested, mildly.

"R. Wayne? That you?" demanded the elderly African-American security guard.

Suggs lowered the powerful light, to throw a pool of illumination at Lee's feet.

"What you doin' out here this time of night?" he demanded.

"Just wanted to put my hands on the old girl," Lee told him. "You know how it is – couldn't sleep – and hurt too damned much to just sit at home. Besides, I'm overdue to turn her over. Got to keep that Lycoming lubed, y'know."

"How'd you get in here, anyway, Mr. Lee?" asked the watchman. "I know the gates is all locked. I done locked 'em myself."

R. Wayne shrugged.

"Well, the one by the shop wasn't," he told the elderly guard. "Maybe you missed it."

"Uh huh," replied Suggs, doubt plain in his voice.

Lee sighed.

"Tell you what, Curtis," he said, "since you're here, can I get you to turn the prop for me? You'd really be doing me a big favor."

"You cain't fly that airplane, you know," the guard told him. "The President done said so."

"I know that, Curtis," R. Wayne said, his tone appeasing. "Of course I know that. I just want to fire the engine up, and maybe taxi the old girl up and down the runway one time. You know – just to make sure her engine is properly lubricated. I don't want it to rust, while I'm waiting for the President to let us start flying again is all. Think you could give me a hand?"

"Well, I don't know," replied Curtis Suggs.

His brow furrowed in thought.

Lee kept a friendly smile firmly pasted across his face. He and Suggs had known each other for years, and he had no reason to expect his request would be refused.

At length, the elderly watchman grudgingly allowed, "I guess I might could. Don't you go tellin' nobody, though."

R. Wayne's smile became genuine.

"Cross my heart," he promised, suiting action to words, "and hope to die."

"Well, alright then," Suggs said.

Lee led the guard through the drizzle to the nose of the Cessna. He had Suggs face the double-bladed Sensenich propeller, and instructed him to "give that sucker a good yank" once he himself threw the ignition switch. The gray-haired watchman nodded his comprehension of the task.

"You're gonna need to use both hands," R. Wayne told him. "She'll be a little stiff."

Suggs nodded. "I kin turn it," he predicted, turning off his flashlight, and slipping it into its holster on his belt. "Just you wait and see."

"I believe you can, at that," Lee said in a sincere and encouraging tone.

He unlocked the right-hand door, and hoisted himself into the pilot's seat. Centering the rudder, he pumped the primer three times, put his hand on the throttle, and turned the ignition switch.

"Hit it!" he called.

Suggs put both hands on the prop blade, and gave a mighty heave. The Lycoming O-235-C1's magnetos spun. Lee fed it fuel. With a cough and a sputter, emitting a blast of blue smoke, the horizontally-opposed four-cylinder motor roared to life. R. Wayne gave Suggs a thumbs-up, and a broad grin. He checked to be certain the Cessna's brakes were set, and then hopped back out of the aircraft.

"Good job, Curtis," he shouted in the guard's ear.

"See," the watchman yelled back, "I told you I could do it."

Richard Wayne Lee nodded in agreement, and shouted, "I knew you could."

Then he shot Curtis Suggs twice in the chest, at point-blank range, with the Smith & Wesson .44 Stealth Hunter he had pulled from the waistband of his fatigue pants.

The elderly black guard, a look of utter shock on his face, toppled backwards onto the glistening tarmac like a felled tree. His skull hit the blacktop with a soggy thunk. Lee leaned over him, and put a final shot from the Stealth Hunter through Suggs's forehead, one carefully-aimed inch above his eyes.

"Sorry Curtis," he told the corpse. "Every revolution has its casualties. I guess you get to be the Crispus Attucks of this one."

Then, whistling cheerfully, R. Wayne set about loading his five cans of homemade napalm into the cargo space behind the Cessna's seats.

May 2, 2020, 9:58 pm EDT

Port Authority Bus Terminal, New York, NY

To her sheer astonishment and profound delight, Eydis Finnursdottir was happy. Utterly, deliriously happy, in a way she had never before experienced. True, she was still a foreigner in a foreign land, dirty, tired, and surrounded by radioactive death. But she was no longer alone in her predicament. And – because the Terminal's food vendors had decided that afternoon to give away the swiftly-defrosting contents of their non-functioning freezers – she was no longer quite as ravenously hungry as she had been before she met Gregory Alan Shergold.

- Greg Shergold. -

She savored the syllables.

Just thinking his name made Eydis nearly swoon with joy. He had been her constant companion since ... forever, it seemed. Although it had been only hours ago that he had inquired whether she needed help, it seemed to her now as though they had somehow always known each other; had always been together.

They had spent the intervening hours talking endlessly, telling each other everything about themselves. She told him about her girlhood in Reykjavik; about her training as a *Róverskátar*; about her study of architecture at the Academy of the Arts; about the along *Laugavegur*, and the night life that never really got going until after midnight; about her father's work and her mother's career; about her older brother's job; her younger brother's love of football; her dog Snorri; her dreams, hopes, and ambitions. He had regaled her with tales of growing up on the Upper West Side of Manhattan; of his lawyer father, and socialite mother; of his rebellion against their predetermined plans for his life; of his little sister Cissy and her dedication to all things Barbie; of his childhood collection of postcards from around the world; of his classes in fine arts and design at Parsons; of his dog Colonel Mustard; of his hopes, dreams, and ambitions.

They had discussed music; talked politics; spoken of travel, philosophy, and literature. Finally, they talked themselves out. Now, like two ancient souls who had at last found one another again, lifetimes after their last parting, they simply stood, leaning together.

Each had a hand in the other's back pocket. Her head rested on his shoulder, as they looked out through the glass windows of the Terminal at the formless darkness. Spellbound, they listened to the roar of the rain, and the howl of the wind, watching as the full fury of Tropical Storm Beth clawed, and bit at Manhattan.

For the moment, it was more than enough for happiness.

May 2, 2020, 10:22 pm EDT

Over the Potomac River

R. Wayne Lee wiped his sweating palms on his khaki cargo pants: first the left, then the right, careful to keep one hand on the control yoke at all times. He was proud of the flying he'd done this night – although he was acutely aware that the most demanding part of the journey still lay ahead. Nonetheless, R. Wayne thought he'd done better than most pilots could have.

He'd kept the little Cessna barely high enough to clear the treetops and power lines, flying parallel to Interstate 95 from Richmond to just beyond Fredericksburg, then cutting over to the Potomac below Quantico – all by Visual Flight Rules. At night. Through pounding rain that would have kept most VFR pilots grounded. Buffeted for the past half-hour by frighteningly-powerful horizontal gusts of wind and stomach-churning vertical shear. All without the aid of GPS; navigating strictly by dead reckoning; using only his compass, wrist chronograph, and airspeed indicator to find his way.

- Damned fine flying, if I say so myself. -

He was feeling lightheaded. The wooziness was not just from the extra Dilaudid he'd dry-swallowed 20 minutes or so earlier, but also from the gasoline fumes emanating from five open containers of homebrew napalm jostling in the cargo space behind him in the cramped little cabin. He had deliberately left their caps lying back on the tarmac at ODT, alongside his abandoned F-150 pickup truck.

- When I hit the White House, it's not just me that's going to splash. -

Looking to his left, Lee realized with a start that the ghostly mansion he saw perched on a hilltop must be Mount Vernon, home of George Washington.

- You'd be proud of me, General. I'm battling tyranny in my time, just as you did in yours. -

His radio was on, and tuned to 121.5 MHz, the general aviation distress frequency. So far, there had been no attempt to contact him. Of course, he was flying with his transponder turned off. Without running lights, the little Cessna was nearly invisible to ground observers. Likewise, the howling rainstorm through which he'd been flying covered the plane's engine noise, and helped cloak him from the extensive radar coverage inside the Washington Air Defense Information Zone. Just as importantly, he was flying right down on the deck. That was extremely dangerous, given the devilish turbulence he'd been fighting – not to mention the Potomac's penchant for generating fog. But he'd made it this far. Now he was actually inside the Restricted Flight Zone for the Washington ADIZ West Sector, with no one in Washington's officialdom seemingly the wiser.

- *Surely the Lord is my shepherd – and, soon enough, I'll be lying down in His green pastures.* -

He chuckled.

- *Yea, though I fly through the Valley of Death, I shall fear no evil.* -

May 2, 2020, 10:21 pm EDT

The White House Living Room, Washington, DC

"So," the President said, raising both his cut-crystal whisky glass and his eyebrow, "is this the moment of truth?"

"I suppose it is," the Vice President replied.

She raised her own glass.

"To truth," she toasted.

"To truth," William Orwell Steele repeated.

He knocked back a healthy slug of Lagavulin.

Diana Hunter took a swallow of Maker's Mark. She set her half-filled glass down on the coffee table, next to Steele's stack of unread Top Secret folders. Taking a deep breath, she looked Steele directly in the eye, her gaze steady, her expression serious.

"First of all," she began, "I want to apologize to you for all the mean, vicious – and untrue – things we said about you during the 2016 primary."

"Please," Steele replied dismissively, "That was just political rhetoric. Everyone does it."

Hunter reached for his hand. Her tawny eyes flashed.

"No," she contradicted. "Everyone doesn't. You didn't."

Steele set his drink down beside hers, to give himself cover while he formulated a response.

"Di, I assure you that was purely a matter of strategy," he said.

Hunter shook her head.

"No it wasn't," she insisted. "I have it on very good authority that Andy Philips tried to persuade you to go negative, and you overruled him. Not once, but over and over again. Will, I've observed you more closely than you think, not just during the campaign, but during the past four years, as well. I've seen that you can make the hard decisions when you have to, but at heart, you're still very much a Boy Scout."

- Am I blushing? It sure feels that way. -

Aloud, he said, "Courteous, kind, thrifty, brave ... I forget what all else a Boy Scout is supposed to be ... but I'm not really very many of those things. A President can't be."

Hunter took both of his hands in hers. Her grip was fierce.

"I'm deadly serious," she said. "Please don't make light of this!"

Steele was instantly contrite. "I'm sorry, Di," he said. "Speak your piece. I'll shut up."

"I mean what I say," Hunter insisted. "I'm sincerely apologizing to you for those attack ads. I'm ashamed that they were products of my ambition ... and, yes, of Benjamin's guidance. But I gave in to his pressure to go negative, while you refused to give in to Andy's pressure to do the same to me." She looked down for a moment at her lap, where her fists lay clenched in embarrassment, before continuing, "As far as I'm concerned, that's a measure of the difference in our characters. You had the strength to follow your ethical compass, regardless of your own campaign manager's advice. I didn't. And now, four years later, after watching how you've handled yourself in office, I've come to truly admire that quality in you, both as a man and as a President."

"Di ..." Steele began.

Hunter shook her head emphatically.

"Please let me finish," she insisted, gripping his arm to punctuate her plea.

"You've been a good and effective President, so far, despite our pitiful excuse for a Congress," she told him. "Now, suddenly, you've been presented with the opportunity to become a great President. Yes, the circumstances are unthinkably bad ... but surely you're familiar with the cliché that the same Mandarin character means both 'danger' and 'opportunity'?

"I think … no, I *know* … you have the makings of one of the greatest leaders this country has ever known. I've seen in you the qualities it will take to pull America through this crisis: your ability to lead by example, your determination to hold to the right, and the *vision* your predecessors have for so long lacked. I'm convinced that you – and perhaps *only* you – can change this country in the ways it so desperately needs to be changed … to return it to the greatness it once had. I'm equally convinced that, because of the opportunity this crisis presents, you *will* accomplish those things." She looked directly into his eyes. "I want to help," she said.

"Well, of course …" Steele responded.

"Up until now," Hunter interrupted, "I've been very much the traditional Veep: the warm body in waiting, a heartbeat away from relevancy. I've chaired task forces. I've been your political bird dog with Congress. I've done all the standard tricks that Vice Presidents do: sit up, beg, roll over, play dead."

She shot a look at Duke. The President's Great Dane was lying upside down on his dog bed, all four paws in the air, blissfully unconscious.

"None of that has been meaningful," she said, dismissively. "None of it has *mattered* – because none of it *had* to matter. But now …"

The Vice President looked down at her lap for a long moment, before continuing.

"Will," she said, at last, "this country is either going to rise to greatness again, or it's going to collapse. Which of those alternatives happens will, in large measure, depend on the leadership *you* provide. I know the pressure you'll face in the process will be enormous. To do what must be done, to guide our country back to greatness, you will need all the help you can get. I want to provide some of that help. My purpose in asking for this meeting is to persuade you to let me share the burden – and the responsibility – of leadership with you."

She put a finger to the President's lips, forestalling his reply.

"This evening at Bethesda, Benjamin's medical oncologist told me it's time to think about transferring him to hospice," she told him.

"Oh God, Diana!" Steele said. "I'm so sorry to hear that!"

"I know, Will. I know," she assured him. "Despite the fact that Benjamin masterminded those attack ads, I'm convinced you sincerely mean that. That's a sign of your character in itself. For you, bygones really are bygones. For me? Less so ... at least, up until recently. But, now that Benjamin is passing, I want to master that art of forgiveness. I want to put all that selfishness – that focus on ambition for my personal political future, rather than on the future of this country – behind me. I want to learn to forgive ... because I, too, want a chance at achieving greatness."

She watched his expression change to one of distaste. Clutching at his hands again, she spoke quickly and earnestly.

"Please don't misunderstand, Will," Hunter implored. "My husband is a wonderful, warm, witty, *loving* man – and one of the great political minds on the planet. I owe him so much more than I will ever have the opportunity to repay – not just because I literally would not be here, now, in this room with you, if it were not for his guidance and wisdom, but because he has always been so very, very *good* to me. He has truly been my rock, my anchor, my one true love. But his cancer has robbed us of all of those things. All that's left now is a Benjamin-shaped husk, incapable of doing anything but suffering, and longing for death."

She paused for a moment, and blinked back tears, before continuing, "Earlier this evening, Dr. Ellison informed me that, once he goes into hospice care, they'll put Ben into a medically-induced coma to control his pain. He'll die that way, never again having regained consciousness. You *do* see, don't you? The truth is that, in every important way, my husband – the man I love with all my heart and soul – is already dead."

"Diane, I'm so sorry," Steele said helplessly.

He was beginning to regret his initial revulsion at her confession.

"Believe me, I know that," Hunter replied. "Your compassion is so much a part of what makes you the man you are that it could hardly be otherwise. If you will only give me the chance, I hope, by apprenticing myself to you, to develop in myself that greatness of character – greatness of, for want of a better term, 'soul' – that you have in such abundance. Please, I beg of you: won't you give me the chance at that kind of greatness?"

Her gaze implored his belief.

"I ask only that you let me work beside you," she told him. "Test me. Delegate *real* responsibility to me ... and let me prove to you what I have to offer. It needn't be a public role. I don't care about getting credit, or about building political capital. I swear to you that I'm not seeking glory. Will, what I'm looking for is ... call it 'redemption'. Let me earn that ... and I swear to you that I will try my very best to be worthy of the trust you place in me. Please, Will, let me be your partner in greatness ... and let us do great things together."

She placed her hand upon his arm in supplication.

A long moment passed, as the President and his Vice President gazed into one another's eyes. Steele felt a surge of admiration and respect for Hunter's candor sweep through him. That ... and something more: a stir of emotions he had not experienced in nearly four years. Perhaps because of those feelings, he sternly suppressed the quiet inner voice that urged him to caution, insisted he consider her past history, and warned him to guard himself against the possibility of betrayal or disappointment.

Having bared her political soul to Steele, Hunter herself experienced an inner wave of neediness. It was swiftly followed by an equally strong swell of determination not to submit to her weakness. Grimly, she braced herself for his rejection of her plea.

"Diana ..." Steele began.

He was interrupted by an urgent knock at the door. Agent Wright burst into the short hallway between the outside corridor and the Presidential sanctum.

"Mr. President, Madam Vice President," he announced, his expression grim, "I need you to come with me right now. The White House is under attack."

May 2, 2020, 10:31 pm EDT

Over the National Mall, Washington, DC

R. Wayne Lee banked left, away from the brightly-illuminated spire of the Washington Monument. His tiny aircraft crossed Constitution Avenue, and began flying over the Ellipse, at treetop level. Coordinated, low-intensity laser beams from several different building tops began sweeping his cockpit with a continuous, repeating pattern of red, then red, then green flashing light.

From his flight radio, an urgent voice blared, "Attention unidentified aircraft! You have violated a Restricted Flight Zone! Turn around *now*, or you will be fired on!"

R. Wayne laughed in exaltation.

- Too late, traitors! The tyrant's time has come! Lord, let me smite him in Your name! -

He was right down on the deck, now.

The Cessna's wheels almost touched the manicured lawn of the Ellipse. Behind him trailed a cloud of turbulence-whipped water droplets from his wing vortices. R. Wayne was pushing the little aircraft's throttle to its maximum, and the Lycoming engine roared like a wounded beast in response. His airspeed indicator was pegged at over 140 knots – well above the Cessna's "never exceed" speed.

Ahead of him, tiny flashes of light winked from the ground, as uniformed Secret Service officers began firing at him with handguns. He pulled up slightly, to give himself maneuvering room, and began jinking left and right, to make the Cessna a harder target to hit. There was an audible crack, and the windshield in front of the folded passenger seat suddenly had a thumb-sized hole, surrounded by a spider web of crazed fractures.

- Yea, though I fly through the Valley of Death, I shall fear no evil, for the Lord is my shepherd! -

He pulled back lightly on the yoke, long enough to gain sufficient altitude to clear the wrought-iron fence around the White House. He passed the

Presidential basketball court, and began banking slightly to his left. R. Wayne aimed the Cessna at the far end of the mansion, where, according to the Internet, the Tyrant had his private quarters.

At that instant, flame lanced from the top of the Eisenhower Executive Office Building.

The Avenger anti-aircraft battery installed there for close-range defense had fired a single, Stinger missile at the intruder. In the driving rain, the Avenger's integrated radar targeting system had trouble acquiring the little fabric-winged craft, but its Forward-Looking InfraRed sensors easily locked on the Cessna's straining, overheated engine. The FLIR unerringly guided the Avenger battery's Stinger to intercept R. Wayne's little aircraft. The two flying objects met, while the 140 was still over the South Lawn.

The Stinger detonated.

A bright, red fireball lit up the night sky. Sheer momentum carried the flaming wreckage forward, raining flaming blobs of jellied gasoline as it came, to impact against the trees in front of the Map Room on the mansion's ground floor, setting them furiously ablaze. Two uniformed Secret Servicemen standing directly in the path of destruction were splashed with R. Wayne's homemade napalm. Both instantly turned into screaming human torches.

The rain-drenched night filled with the earsplitting screech of air raid sirens, the shriek of fire alarms, the urgent shouts of uniformed and plainclothes Secret Service personnel, and the swiftly-dying screams of burning men.

May 2, 2020, 11:31 pm EDT

Seneca Temporary Housing Facility, Romulus, NY

Sean Halloran, Sr. was angry, and getting angrier.

He had spent hours inching along a country road to get to this so-called "temporary housing facility", looking forward to an opportunity for his little family to spend the night under an actual roof, sleeping in real beds. Instead, he had discovered – now that his 2012 Sierra crew cab was nearly out of gas – that all he'd managed to secure was a parking space in the middle of nowhere.

That the man in military fatigues who was currently asking him a bunch of damn-fool questions insisted on remaining cool, calm, and polite in the face of his righteous anger only made him angrier. Halloran longed for a good shouting match. He wanted nothing more than to roar his resentment and outrage, until his opponent cowered in surrender. But this middle-aged soldier, with his clipboard and flashlight, steadfastly refused to oblige him.

"Listen, pal," Sean, Sr. snarled, "I got a wife and baby here. You're tryin' to tell me there's no place they can sleep *inside* tonight?"

"Yes, sir," replied the man with the clipboard, "I'm afraid that's correct."

"What the *fuck*!" Halloran insisted, "How can ya stand there ..." he peered at the stripes on the soldier's sleeve, "... Sergeant ..."

"Corporal," the soldier said, patiently.

"I don't give a flyin' fuck what rank ya are!" Sean, Sr. responded. "I don't give a good goddamn if you're a fuckin' *general*! All I care about is my wife and baby need a fuckin' roof over their fuckin' heads ... *now*, goddamnit!"

"Yes, sir," the corporal replied, his voice betraying no emotion. "I understand your concern. What I'm telling you is, there are no more indoor housing facilities available at this location, at this time."

"How in fuckin' Hell can that be?" Halloran demanded, face mottled with rage. "The radio said this was s'posed to be a 'temporary housin' facility' for refugees from the Fallout Zone. *We're* refugees from the fuckin' Fallout Zone! Where the Hell is the temporary housin' we were promised?"

"Sir," the soldier said, "as I explained to you earlier, the existing structures at this facility are already full. FEMA is bringing in a supply of cabin tents tomorrow, but, for tonight, there is simply no additional housing available. I'm sorry, but there's nothing I, personally, can do to change that situation."

"Yeah?" Sean, Sr. shot back. "Well, I bet you, personally, are gonna sleep indoors tonight, aren't ya?"

The corporal's mouth tightened momentarily.

Then he replied, "As a matter of fact …" he briefly consulted his clipboard, "… Mr. Halloran, I'm on duty until 0800 hours. So, no, sir, I won't be sleeping indoors tonight."

"But ya would be if ya weren't scheduled to work tonight, wouldn't ya?" Halloran insisted.

The soldier shook his head, raindrops glittering on his wet, curly hair.

"No, sir, I wouldn't be," he demurred. "My unit has donated its tents to refugee families like yours. If I weren't on duty, I'd be sleeping under the stars tonight."

Sean, Sr. opened his mouth to continue his tirade, then closed it with a snap. He peered at the patch over the corporal's right breast pocket. This annoyingly-polite Corporal Smith had sandbagged him. There was nothing he could say to turn the tables on him. Deprived of a suitable target for his rage, Halloran abruptly deflated. Suddenly, he was just a very tired, hungry, unwashed man, whose family was going to have to spend the night in his truck. Again.

Defeated, Sean, Sr. asked Corporal Smith quietly, "I don't s'pose there's any place to buy smokes around here, is there?"

"No, sir," Smith confirmed. "Not yet, at any rate. Word is, they'll be setting up a canteen sometime tomorrow, if that's any consolation."

Halloran slumped in his seat. No cigarettes.

"Fuck," he said. "What about food?"

Corporal Smith consulted the police-style radio he wore clipped to his lapel.

"The mess tent is scheduled to open tomorrow morning, sir," he reported. "Chow should be available by 0600 hours."

"For Christ's sake, is there a bathroom available, at least?" Sean, Sr. pleaded.

Smith pointed down the line of bunkers and parked vehicles.

"There are port-a-potties located at the end of this crossroad, Mr. Halloran," he replied. "I'm afraid that's all we have to offer in the way of bathroom facilities, for now. I believe they're planning to set up field showers sometime tomorrow, though."

Halloran glanced across the pickup's cab at his wife Fiona. She gazed back at him with an expression halfway between resignation and despair.

"Okay," Sean, Sr. said, his voice nearly inaudible. "If that's how it is, I guess that's how it is."

"Yes, sir," Corporal Smith confirmed. "That's how it is."

He offered Halloran the clipboard.

"Can I get you to sign here, Mr. Halloran?" he requested.

Sean, Sr. shrugged. He scrawled his name on the line Smith indicated. He didn't even care to inquire what he was signing for. He just wanted the corporal to go away, before he, Sean Halloran, Sr., broke down in front of him, and bawled like a baby.

"Thank you, sir," Corporal Smith said.

He regarded Halloran for a moment, noting the way his lip trembled

In a surprisingly warm, and reassuring tone, he added, "Don't worry, Mr. Halloran. Things will get better tomorrow. Wait and see."

As Smith turned, and marched away toward the next carful of Fallout Zone refugees, tears of frustrated helplessness began to trickle down Sean, Sr.'s cheeks.

May 3, 2020, 01:13 am EDT

Copley Square, Boston, MA

Copley Square was devoid of human life. A fine layer of ash and dust filtered from the cloud-choked sky onto the palette cradled in the left arm of the bronze statue of John Singleton Copley. His only companions in the square of greenery and parquet brickwork were the bronze sculptures of the tortoise and hare, near the corner of Boylston and Darmouth streets.

Behind Copley's statue loomed the brilliantly-lit mass of the Fairmont Copley Plaza hotel, its glittering Beaux-arts façade proudly displayed to the deserted neighborhood. Even most of the homeless had been rounded up; coaxed onto free shuttle buses that had taken them West, away from the Fallout Zone. Only the scavengers – sleeping squirrels, roosting pigeons, prowling alley cats, scuttling brown rats, and a handful of their human counterparts – remained behind in the normally-bustling Back Bay district.

Ryan Patrick Cohan scratched absently at the scabrous back of his left hand, as he contemplated the haul he had collected from the Fairmont Copley Plaza.

Piled beneath the red canopy that extended between the pillars of the luxurious hotel's St. James Avenue entrance were dozens of microwave ovens and flat-screen TVs. There was also a considerable heap of travel-sized liquor bottles he had looted from dozens of mini-bars. It had been a back-straining chore to drag the swag this far, despite the assistance of the luggage trolleys that absent bellmen had thoughtfully abandoned for his use. Now, he faced the additional labor of hauling his hoard to the ancient, decrepit Econoline van parked at the curb.

- *Well, shit. Might as well take a little break first.* -

He bent to grab a half-dozen miniature bottles of vodka.

- *Smirnoff.* -

He nodded, approvingly.

Shoving most of them into a capacious pocket of his ratty pea coat, he unscrewed the top of one, and tilted it down his throat.

"Ahh," he said aloud. "Good stuff."

Cohan wiped his lips on his sleeve, and rummaged in his coat for a pack of cigarettes. He lit one with a butane lighter, and appreciatively inhaled the fragrant tobacco. It was a Marlboro – a brand normally well out of his price range. This particular pack, however, had cost him nothing other than the effort involved in breaking into the Seven-Eleven from which he'd stolen it.

- From now on, it's nothing but the good stuff for Ryan P. Cohan. -

Cohan stumped out to the van, and pulled open its sliding door. He turned around to sit in the doorway, so his feet rested on the sidewalk, pulled out, opened, and drained another miniature liquor bottle. He belched reflectively, and took a long, luxurious drag on the Marlboro, paying no attention to the tiny particles of fallout that filtered down from the darkened sky onto his balding head, his jacket, and the glowing tip of the cigarette on which he was sucking.

May 3, 2020, 02:35 am EDT

Off The Peninsula at Bayonne Harbor, Bayonne, NJ

- The Old Man has gone completely batshit. –

Chief Petty Officer Curtis Simmons attempted to peer through the pounding rain and spume blowing off the heaving seas around him. To be out at night, in surging seas as rough as the ones surrounding him and his crew, in a dinky, little Zodiac inflatable boat was nutty enough in Simmons's book. But to be out at night, in high seas, in a Zodiac, wearing Mission Oriented Protective Posture Level 4 suits was sheer, raving insanity – straightjacket, rubber-room, full-fledged funny farm crazy.

- The kind of crazy that gets men killed. -

Nonetheless, here he was – him and his three-man detail. They had orders straight from the XO: locate, board, and commandeer any and all available tugboats. Commodore Collins had made it clear that by "commandeer", he meant the tugs' crews, as well as the boats themselves. That worried Simmons more than he wanted to admit. Tugboat crews had a reputation for being ornery and independent – and he had only three squids and their side arms to employ as convincers, should those swabbies take exception to being shanghaied.

- Jesus jumping Christ on a cracker. I hate the fucking Navy. -

It was a standard swabby's complaint, he knew: frequently made, seldom meant seriously.

- Except sometimes. Sometimes I mean every word. -

Even the powerful electric torch he carried was largely ineffective in cutting through the gloom of the heaving seas and lustily-blowing salt spray. Still, Simmons thought he saw the suggestion of a promising outline to his left.

"Ten degrees to port!" he shouted to Darnell Johnson, the E-5 who was acting as coxswain. When Johnson put his free hand to his ear, indicating he couldn't hear Simmons's order over the howl of the wind and the buzz of the outboard engine, the CPO pointed emphatically to his left. Then he held up his right hand, with his thumb and finger held an inch apart. Petty Officer Johnson nodded his understanding of the Chief's sign-language order, and altered the Combat Rubber Reconnaissance Craft's course accordingly.

Simmons noted with satisfaction that the hazy shape he'd spotted through the storm quickly resolved into a stubby hull. Her gunwales were well-fendered with heavy-duty truck tires. As the Zodiac approached the tug, he made out the name "Iron Maiden" painted in weathered, foot-high, black letters on her prow.

Johnson brought the Zodiac smoothly to a halt alongside the pitching tug. Seamen Zawinsky and Buehl hooked the Portal boarding ladder to her railing, and swarmed up onto the tug's deck, mooring lines in hand. Sweating in his MOPP 4 suit, Simmons followed them aboard the tugboat.

"Ready side arms," he ordered, unbuttoning the flap on his own holster.

Instinctively maintaining his balance, despite the wildly-pitching deck, Simmons made his way toward the little boat's wheelhouse.

Unsurprisingly, he found the wheelhouse door closed against the elements. When he tried the handle, it refused to budge.

- *Aha!* -

He pulled his Beretta 92FS service weapon from its holster, and used the butt to hammer on the door. When there was no immediate response from inside the wheelhouse, he pounded on the door again, with greater force. A few seconds later, the door opened a crack. The gale-force wind caught it, and slammed it wide open, revealing a quartet of suspicious, unshaven faces, each gripping an improvised cudgel.

For a second, the four tugboat crewmen stood frozen in confusion. Simmons was amused to see that three of them wore expressions of terror. The fourth – he would bet anything it was their captain – seemed more puzzled than frightened at the sight of the CPO in his shiny, wet, black MOPP suit.

"Aren't you going to invite me in?" Simmons shouted, pointedly holstering his sidearm. "It's fucking nasty out here!"

Two of the crewmen looked in astonishment from the CPO to one another, then back to Simmons again, in a perfect, natural double-take. The third merely goggled at Simmons. Meanwhile, their captain lowered the large crescent wrench he had been brandishing, and stepped back into the confines of the tug's wheelhouse.

"Come in, if you're coming," he shouted, "but close the damn door behind you!"

Simmons stepped inside. He turned to secure the door behind him, then pulled off the MOPP suit's hood with one hand, and his gas mask with the other. He turned back to face the tugboat's crew, revealing his round face, shaven head, and toothy smile.

"Greetings, Earthlings," he said. "I come in peace."

The man he'd identified as the tug's skipper grinned at his sally.

"Just don't ask me to take you to my leader," he replied.

"Roger that," Simmons responded.

Tucking the gas mask and hood under his arm, he offered his hand.

"Chief Petty Officer Curtis Simmons, USS John F. Kennedy," he stated.

Taking the CPO's hand, the grizzled seaman responded, "Jake Cordell, skipper of this tub. Pleased to make your acquaintance, Chief."

"Likewise," Simmons said.

Nodding toward the other two sailors, Cordell told him, "That's Vasily Cukor, first mate, and this is Harvey Wilkerson, our engineer. The newb with his chow hatch open is Silvio Fanucci, our deckhand."

Simmons nodded at each man, in turn.

"Pleased to meet you," he said.

"So, what can we do for the Navy?" inquired Cordell. He added, "I put it that way, because, what with the weather being so pleasant, and all, I have a feeling we wouldn't be having this conversation, if you didn't need something from us."

"Funny you should ask," Simmons replied.

Swiftly he outlined for the Iron Maiden's crew the rescue mission to which the JFK had been assigned.

"The problem is," he continued, "the Kennedy can't dock at mid-town without help from tugboats like yours – and it'll need lots of help. So not only do we need your boat, we need to round up as many more like it as we can. The hope is you'll be willing to help us with both those things. You know as well as I do there's a whole lot of stranded New Yorkers who're depending on us to do the right thing."

The Chief thought it politic not to mention – at least, as of yet – that he was empowered to commandeer Cordell's tug, as well as his crew.

- Carrot first. Then stick – and only if necessary. -

Captain Cordell rubbed his bristly chin.

"Well, since I can't really ask our owner for permission right now, by rights I suppose I should refuse your request until I can," he said. "But fuck him. The Maiden's yours, if you can get her running. We sure as hell haven't been able to."

"What's wrong with your boat?" Simmons asked.

Cordell shrugged.

"Everything electrical, and all her electronics are dead as doornails," he replied. "Batteries, NavNet, radios, everything – it's all just ballast, now."

"EMP from the bomb," Simmons told him.

Cordell nodded.

"That was my guess," he said. "Of course, the fact that everything was working fine right up until we saw the flash was kind of a major clue."

Simmons nodded, in turn.

"Yep, EMP," he replied, confidently. "Well, back on the Kennedy, we've got all kinds of spare radios, marine batteries, and whatnot. I'm pretty sure we can get you back up and running by morning."

"That'd be good," Cordell told him. "So, after you're all loaded up on landlubbers, any chance we can hitch a ride with you, when you're ready to ship out?"

Simmons eyed him soberly, before he replied.

"That decision is above my pay grade, Skipper," he confessed. "I'm afraid you'll have to take it up with the Old Man. But I can promise you and your crew fresh chow, a hot shower, and clean clothes, at the very least. That, and vouchers for the use of your boat and your crew."

Cordell waved the offer away.

"Fuck vouchers," he said. "But the grub and the shower sound mighty good to me. When do we get started?"

"Well," Simmons said, "now seems as good a time as any. Listen, though, is there any chance you can help us locate more tugs? Because we're sure as hell gonna need 'em."

Cordell shrugged.

"If they're berthed? No problem," he said. "But if they were working when the bomb went off? That, my friend, is a whole 'nother thing. Any of 'em that survived the blast will be adrift – and New York Harbor is a mighty big place."

May 3, 2020, 3:32 am EDT

Clay St., Hackensack, NJ

Latonya Gramble lay twitching on the cool linoleum of the only bathroom of her rented duplex apartment. Compulsively, she brushed away armies of imaginary insects that crawled over her skin. Her mouth, her chin, and the front of her blouse were befouled with vomit, and a miasma of diarrhea hung in the still air of the lavatory.

Helpless tears leaked from beneath her tightly-closed eyelids.

- I wish I was dead. Dead like my precious baby. Lord help me, I'm so sorry, Nakeesha. I'm so, so sorry, baby. -

Self-pity enfolded her like a scratchy blanket. Latonya never had imagined herself having to kick a heroin habit, much less going cold turkey in her own, dark, empty home, with the body of her mutilated daughter cold and stiff in the tiny bedroom where she had died. She had always assumed she would, instead, be a good mother to her only daughter. A conscientious mother; a mother who would one day watch her daughter walk down the aisle on her wedding day. Someday, a grandmother, spoiling her grandbabies, and reveling in their love.

Not a junkie with a dead child, involuntarily detoxing on a bathroom floor.

Sudden nausea wrenched at her. She was too weak to raise herself up enough to hang her head over the toilet rim, so the surge of bile simply drooled out of her open mouth onto the floor beneath her. When the spasm passed, too exhausted to move, Latonya let her head loll.

Her cheek rested in the swiftly-cooling puddle.

May 3, 2020, 5:27 am EDT

Port Authority Bus Terminal, New York, NY

Eydis Finnursdottir awoke in the arms of her lover. She urgently needed to urinate, but the sensuous intimacy of Greg Shergold's embrace, the feel of his skin on hers, and the sensation of his breath stirring her curls, was irresistible. For the moment, she was content merely to bask in the comfort of his physical presence.

They had kissed, chastely and tentatively, at first, then with increasing urgency and hunger. By unspoken mutual assent, they broke their embrace, to search, hand in hand, for a private place in which to consummate their love. Eventually, they found their way to this broom closet, in the bowling alley on the second floor of the Port Authority building. Here, in profound darkness, they had eagerly stripped one another of their clothing, plunging into a timeless state of shared exploration that lasted for what seemed like an eternity.

She had reveled in the feel of him: in her hands, in her mouth, in her sex. He had tasted every part of her body – licking, kissing, nibbling, sucking. Between them, they composed an improvised ballet of erotic positions; flowing from one to the next like magical dancers. They had taken, and given pleasure with utter abandon: tenderly, fiercely, instinctively; with passion, and purpose, and total dedication. Four times she made him explode in ecstasy – once in her hand, once in her mouth, twice deep inside her. Drowning in pleasure, she lost count of the orgasms he had given her with his skillful fingers, his talented tongue, and his exquisitely thrusting cock.

Eydis considered herself something of an expert on sex. She had lost her virginity at 15, and considered it a burden well shed. Since then, she taken half a dozen lovers, some of them quite skilled, patient, and attentive. But what had happened between her and Greg Shergold last night had been so extraordinarily more intense an experience than any of her previous assignations, every sexual encounter that preceded it receded into insignificance. Compared to Greg, the most highly skilled of her prior lovers had been as fumblingly incompetent as her first.

Eydis sighed, wriggling in delight against Greg's nakedness. Still sleeping, he reacted instinctively by drawing her closer to him. It was heavenly.

- But, even so, I must urinate. -

Sighing again, this time in resignation, rather than contentment, Eydis sat up in the darkness. In the process, she woke Greg.

"Come back here, you," he said, reaching for her.

His voice was like buttered honey to her ears. Nonetheless, she lightly slapped his hand away.

"I must urinate, Greg," she told him.

"Damned biology," he replied.

Eydis giggled, and playfully slapped his flank.

"Come, help me to find my clothing, will you?" she asked. "We can always return here afterwards."

"That," he predicted, "will definitely happen."

He pinched her bottom, making her shriek in false outrage, and added, "Wench."

May 3, 2020, 7:49 am EDT

Seneca Temporary Housing Facility, Romulus, NY

Followed by his wife Fiona, who was carrying their son Sean, Jr. in her arms, Sean Halloran, Sr. waded through the mud toward the patch of grass where his 2016 Chevrolet Sierra crew cab pickup truck was parked. He wished desperately for a cigarette. He had smoked the last of his supply while waiting for the shuttle bus outside the mess tent, just 20 minutes earlier. Now his craving was all the keener, knowing the prospect for another one any time in the next few hours was dim.

His Timberlands were covered in rich, black muck by the time he reached the Sierra. Halloran stood in the rain, debating whether to remove his boots, so as not to muddy the interior of his truck. The alternative was simply to get in, and accept that mud would be a fixture in his life for the foreseeable future.

"Nice truck," a man observed, as the squelching noise of approaching footsteps came to a halt.

Sean turned to face the voice's owner, frowning at the interruption of his gloomy deliberations.

"Thanks," he replied, automatically, looking over the newcomer.

Well over six feet in height, with a shaven head, and what looked like tribal tattoos peeking out of the collar of his military-surplus, fatigue jacket, the stranger stood, hands on hips, beside an ancient, battered, white Chevy Suburban. On the other side of the Suburban's hood, a thin, dark-haired woman with a beaky nose waited patiently, shielding her face from the rain with one hand. She was surrounded by three tow-headed pre-teen boys, all dressed alike in jeans, heavy-metal tee-shirts, and tour jackets bearing the logo of Hammerhand, a popular death-metal band.

The big stranger stepped forward, and extended his hand.

"I'm Adam Manson," he said. "Pleased to meet ya, bro."

"Sean Halloran, Sr.," Sean responded, accepting the handshake.

He was startled at the power of Manson's grip, and increased the strength of his own in response. The big man merely grinned, and bore down harder still. Sweat popped out on Halloran's brow, as he exerted his maximum power. Manson's smile never wavered, as he effortlessly crushed the bones of Sean's hand together.

"Ow!" Halloran yelped. Manson immediately released his grip, still smiling pleasantly.

"That's some handshake ya've got there," Sean admitted ruefully, rubbing his aching hand.

"Thanks," replied Manson, adding, "You've got a pretty good grip yourself."

"Ah … thanks," said Halloran, somewhat consoled.

"That's Ruby," Manson told him, indicating the dark-haired woman with a toss of his head, "and those are the boys: Jacob, Caleb, and Moses."

Sean waved at Manson's family, feeling foolish.

"That's Fiona," he said, mirroring Manson's head gesture, "my wife. And Sean, Jr., our son."

Manson coolly studied Fiona, taking in her curly red hair – frizzy now, in the high humidity – and her green eyes, then pointedly lowering his gaze to her bust for a long, uncomfortable moment.

"Good-looking kid," he said, at last.

"Thanks," said Halloran, unsure whether to take offense at Manson's lengthy inspection of Fiona's figure.

"It looks like we're gonna be neighbors," Manson observed.

Sean shrugged. "I guess so," he admitted.

While his wife and children remained standing in the rain, Manson pulled a purple, draw-string bag and a small, flat, tin box from one of his jacket's capacious pockets. Opening the latter, he extracted a cigarette paper. He filled it with shag tobacco from the former. Bending forward to shield both from the downpour, he proceeded expertly to roll a cigarette.

Sticking it between his lips, the big man returned his makings to the pocket from which he'd extracted them, pulled out a much-worn Zippo lighter, and fired up his hand-rolled cigarette. He sucked in a lungful of tobacco smoke, and exhaled it in Halloran's face, sighing contentedly.

Sean inhaled the blue, second-hand cloud with profound envy. His eyes were hungrily fixed on the cigarette dangling from Manson's lips.

"Want one?" the big man asked.

Halloran nodded, helplessly.

"Yes I do," he replied.

"You shoulda said so," Manson commented, reaching into his pocket again.

"That's very kind of ya," Sean told him.

His eyes were fixed on the bigger man's hands. Manson manipulated the tobacco and rolling paper, producing a tightly-rolled cigarette as if by magic.

"Think nothing of it," the big man instructed, handing the hand-rolled smoke to Halloran. "After all, that's what friends are for, right?"

May 3, 2020, 8:43 am EDT

One Observatory Circle, Washington, DC

Diana Hunter critically examined her face in the vanity mirror of her dressing table. She sighed unhappily at the puffiness of the skin beneath her famous tawny eyes.

- Another Preparation H morning. I simply have *to cut back on this late-night lifestyle. -*

She smiled wryly at the private jest. Normally, she was in bed by 10:00 pm. Last night, however, the Secret Service herded her, the President, and a dozen or more White House staffers into the Presidential Emergency Operations Center – the bombproof redoubt located deep beneath the East Wing. The Secret Service feared a follow-up to the light plane's attack on the Presidential mansion. The agents had also insisted the presence of so many firefighters on the grounds – the wreckage of the Cessna and the trees in front of the Residence had burned for nearly an hour, before the fire crews brought it under control – presented an unacceptable security risk, as well. Acquiescing to security considerations, they had remained virtual prisoners in the Presidential bunker until nearly one o'clock in the morning.

Unfortunately for Hunter's plans, the circumstances of their confinement did not give them the privacy she felt she needed to continue to press the President to make her his full partner in ruling the United States under martial law. She had instead been forced to settle for watching the 24-hour news cycle wallow in the hazy, public details of the failed attack on the White House.

With electricity restored to the northeastern grid, both the cable news channels and the broadcast networks had given over their entire schedules exclusively to round-the-clock wallowing in coverage of the aftermath of the nuclear attack on Lower Manhattan. MSNBC was calling its reportage "America in Crisis". Following last night's attack, the baying packs of correspondents collectively had switched to a non-stop, endlessly-repetitive focus on what Fox News trumpeted as the "Assault on the White House". Cooped up in the PEOC, surrounded by low-level staffers whose presence kept them from resuming their private conversation, it was fascinating – if more than a little creepy – to watch.

Only toward the end of their internment in the PEOC had any of the news operations come up with actual video –grainy, low-resolution footage from a cell phone camera, at that – of the little aircraft exploding. Most of the night, the bulk of their coverage had consisted of studio anchors, alternately grilling hastily-assembled panels of "experts" on their analysis of events, and conversing in breathless tones to field correspondents. Those worthies, standing outside in the driving rain, were stuck no closer to the action than the middle of the Ellipse. There they endlessly reviewed their fragmentary and confused summary of the evening's attack, over shaky zoom shots of firefighters milling around the burned foliage and ugly, black smoke stains disfiguring the South side of the White House. Nuclear terrorism, the horrific loss of life in Lower Manhattan, and fear mongering in general were temporarily relegated to 30-second news summaries at the top and bottom of the hour.

It was well after midnight before the Secret Service had finally agreed to release them from their fortified prison. Because of the ongoing noise and activity beneath the Presidential bedroom, Steele had decided to spend the night at Blair House – the official Presidential guest quarters, across Pennsylvania Avenue from the Eisenhower Executive Office Building. He had graciously offered her the use of a guest suite there, as well, but Hunter had declined, claiming she preferred to sleep in her own bed.

In fact, under more propitious circumstances, she would have jumped at the chance to continue their private conversation on more-or-less neutral ground. But she had been physically and emotionally exhausted by the day's events, and simply didn't feel up to continuing her campaign of persuasion at that late hour. Too, she had not wanted to seem over-eager to take advantage of the new intimacy of their relationship. Diana Hunter had long ago learned to trust her instincts when it came to men. Those instincts practically shouted at her to hang back, play it cool, and give Steele time and space to consider her proposition.

- Besides – I really didn't bring a thing to wear. -

May 3, 2020, 9:25 am EDT

Massachusetts Avenue, Washington, DC

Arleigh Solomon loved newspapers.

He loved their columnar layout; their mix of news, features, and ads; their editorial pages; their comics; their puzzles, horoscopes, and advice columns. He cherished the size of their pages, the feel of them, the smell of them, even the ink stains they left on his fingers. He understood that he was a dinosaur, but didn't much care. The Secretary of the Department of Internal Security maintained subscriptions to a half-dozen different newspapers. Each morning, he read them all religiously.

That he was currently forced to forego the twin pleasures of both the New York Times, and the Wall Street Journal Sunday editions offended his sensibilities. As much as anything, that deprivation sharpened his thirst for vengeance on the perpetrators of the May Day bombing. Resentful, therefore, and sulking, Solomon took solace in studying the Washington Post's Sunday edition with a level of concentration even more ferocious than usual.

Perusing the Metro section, Solomon came across a brief article about a minivan with New Jersey plates that had crashed into the Pakistani Embassy, sometime early Saturday morning. Washington Metro Police reportedly had discovered two bodies inside – one of them, the car's owner, dead of a gunshot wound, the other an unidentified male, deceased from unknown causes. The story set Solomon's internal alarm bells ringing at deafening levels.

- As the man said of the haddock in the punch bowl, 'There's something fishy going on here.'" -

The Secretary reached across the sadly-truncated stack of Sunday papers at his elbow to pick up his smartphone. Brushing its screen with his thumb to awaken it, he ordered, "Get me John Clune."

"Which number shall I try first," the phone inquired, in a lush contralto voice, "office, car, home, or ...?"

"Cell," Solomon interrupted.

"Dialing," responded his phone.

There was a three-second pause, while the connection was made. Then the Secretary heard the ringing of the other man's cell phone.

"Clune," came the voice of the Director of the FBI.

He would not have been Solomon's first choice for the office, when his predecessor had unexpectedly died of a heart attack, two years earlier. Somewhat surprisingly, Clune had proven to be both effective, and well-liked by the Bureau's senior staff. Solomon now cheerfully admitted that he had been the right man for the job, after all.

"John? Arleigh Solomon here," he told the Director.

"Mr. Secretary," replied Clune. "What can I do for you?"

"Have you seen today's Post?" Solomon asked.

"I have it around here somewhere," Clune admitted.

"Metro section, page three, bottom of the page," Solomon informed him. "Article about a car crash at the Pak embassy."

"And?" Clune asked.

"Suspicious, John," rumbled Solomon. "Very suspicious. I don't understand how we missed hearing about it until now."

"Well, sir," Clune replied, "we've all been a little distracted for the past few days."

Solomon snorted in response.

"And," the FBI Director continued, "that power outage messed communications up pretty badly, as well."

Ignoring Clune's explanation, Solomon commanded, "Have your people round up all the evidence: the minivan, the bodies, forensics, everything. Analyze the Hell out of it. I want a preliminary report by 0800 tomorrow."

"Yes, sir, Mr. Secretary," Clune replied.

"Good," said Solomon, "And, speaking of distractions, what have you got so far on last night's interloper?"

"The pilot appears to have been the owner of the plane," Clune told him. "Fellow by the name of Richard Wayne Lee."

"You're sure about that?" Solomon asked.

"Fairly certain, Mr. Secretary," Clune replied. "Hanover County sheriff's deputies found his truck parked on the apron, next to the body of the county airport's night watchman – a man named Curtis Suggs. Suggs was shot with .44 magnum slugs that Ballistics will almost undoubtedly match up to a gun we found in the wreckage of the plane. We sent a field team to Lee's home. It was rigged with booby traps. And, to put a bow on it, he left a note."

"I see," Solomon rumbled.

After a moment, he added, "Good work, Mr. Director."

"Thank you, sir," Clune said, sincerely.

"Anything else I should know?" Solomon demanded.

"Let's see," Clune said. After a short pause, he continued, "Lee was a member of Merlin Friend's organization, the Sons of Fallen Patriots. And he had stage four lung cancer."

"So," Solomon said, "an extremist militia-type with nothing to lose."

"That's about the size of it," Clune affirmed.

"Good to know," Solomon said, terminating the call.

Dismissing the matter for the moment, he returned his attention to the Metro section. He was determined to at least finish reading that much of the Sunday Post, before he had to get ready for the emergency Cabinet meeting at ten.

May 3, 2020, 10:03 am EDT

Northern State Prison, Newark, NJ

Donell Jackson felt surprisingly good for a man who'd had the living shit beat out of him just over a day earlier. His face was swollen, and still felt hot to the touch. He had a split upper lip, two black eyes, and lumps all over his head. Even so, things could have been worse. He still had all his teeth, and nothing actually seemed to be broken – although his ribs ached every time he took a breath.

He had spent most of the past 24 hours asleep, recovering from his all-night round of shuttle diplomacy on behalf of Big Sugar Washington – and the gang initiation that had followed it. Awakening, he found himself with a new cellmate, Charles "Chuckie D" Dickens. He counted that as a major improvement in his circumstances. His old cellie, Luther "Ugly" Congreve, had been a spun-out con who never showered, and masturbated constantly. Jackson understood that Congreve's deplorable personal hygiene was a strategy to make himself a less desirable target for sexual exploitation. Nonetheless, it had made him a distinctly unpleasant cellmate. Donell was deeply grateful to be rid of him.

Obeying the boss's summons, Jackson was on his way now to see Big Sugar.

As he made his way among the tiers, Donell was pleased to see that the *détente* he had helped to broker between the inmate gangs and the prison's authorities seemed to be holding. The cell doors all were open, and the prisoners mingled freely with one another. He saw no guards. Most importantly, the sense of tension, and imminent violence was gone. The cons he passed appeared calm, even cheerful – lounging, playing dominoes, chatting, smoking cigarettes, and drinking pruno – and determinedly ignoring their own imprisonment.

- We did that. Big Sugar and me. –

Jackson's chin lifted, and he had to consciously keep from strutting.

Considering the alternative – the population locked down in their cells, guarded by men whose nerves were stretched to the breaking point, with the whole prison on the verge of an orgy of violence – it was, in Shakespeare's phrase, "a consummation devoutly to be wished."

Donell was amused by the notion. Of all the inmates in the joint, perhaps only he and Washington would recognize the quote. Together with their joint ambassadorial efforts, it gave him a gratifying feeling of affinity for his new capo.

As he entered the boss's cell, Jackson found Big Sugar seated in his throne-like recliner, studying a chess board. Donell glanced at the layout of the pieces. The positions of both sides were well-developed, but he couldn't immediately tell which one had the advantage.

"Game 6 of the classic Fischer-Spassky match," Washington explained. "As I am certain you have noticed, it is currently Spassky's move. Do you know the game?"

Jackson shook his head.

Big Sugar pointed to the board.

"In the match in Reykjavík, Spassky pushed this pawn, thus," he explained. "He thereby lost a game he could have won, had he only moved his Queen's bishop *here*, instead. Do you see the difference?"

Donell again shook his head.

"I'm sorry," he said, "I know the moves, but I've never really studied chess."

"That is unfortunate," Washington replied. "It is a game that repays deep study – the only game in which luck plays absolutely no part."

"So I understand," Jackson told him. "Sorry."

"Well," Big Sugar said, sitting back in his chair, "no matter. Would you care for some pruno, brother Donell?"

"Uh, no thank you," Jackson demurred. "I could go for some coffee, though."

"Of course," Washington replied. "How thoughtless of me. I forgot you have only just wakened."

He turned to "Little Boy" Shabazz, his hulking chief enforcer, and requested, "David, would you be so good as to make Donell a cup of instant?"

"Sure thing, boss," Shabazz assented.

Big Sugar returned his attention to Jackson.

"So, Donell, how are you feeling?" he asked.

Jackson shrugged. "It only hurts when I laugh," he responded.

Washington smiled broadly.

"Stout fellow," he commented, approvingly. "It's good to see that you have not lost your sense of humor. I feel increasingly certain I have not misjudged you."

Donell waved the compliment away. But it made him feel good inside.

- Praise from Caesar. -

Big Sugar leaned forward in his chair, his expression once again serious.

"I imagine you're wondering why I've summoned you," he said, making it a statement, rather than a question.

"Yes, sir," Jackson replied.

"Are you aware that it is now raining rather heavily outside?" the mob boss asked.

"Uh ... no," Donell confessed, "I didn't realize that."

"That is hardly surprising," Washington commented, "considering the thickness of these walls. There is also the fact that you have been unconscious for most of the past 24 hours, as well."

Without interrupting their conversation, Little Boy handed Jackson a steaming mug of instant coffee.

He accepted it with a murmured, "Thanks."

"In fact," Big Sugar continued, "we are approximately in the middle of the passage through this area of Tropical Storm Beth. According to the

National Weather Service forecast, Beth is expected to drop between six and nine inches of precipitation before it passes. Does that suggest anything of interest to you, Donell?"

Jackson took a reflective sip of the scorching coffee before replying.

"Mmm ... it might," he said.

"Go on," Washington invited.

"Well," Donell said, "that much rain should wash away a lot of the fallout, not just here, but all over the area."

"Just so," Big Sugar agreed, nodding in approval. "Please be so kind as to extrapolate."

Jackson frowned, and took another sip. Suddenly, the light dawned.

"You're planning an escape," he stated.

Washington beamed.

"You really have quite a remarkable mind, Donell," he said. "Yes, I am indeed planning an escape. I have, in fact, been planning an escape for several days now."

"That's why you worked so hard to convince the Warden to let you arrange this," Jackson exclaimed, sweeping his arm around to encompass the prison's peaceful, unguarded condition.

"That is correct," Big Sugar said.

"You wanted to convince him he could trust you," Donell continued, "so that he wouldn't just lock us down, and wait for reinforcements."

"Exactly so," Washington agreed. "*Exactly* so."

He looked around the cell at Little Boy and Chuckie D.

"Now do you see why I asked Donell to join our organization?" he asked. "He sees as obvious what others entirely miss."

He turned back to face Jackson.

"Yes, Donell," Big Sugar said, "I am indeed planning an escape. The destruction of New York presents us with a singular opportunity. Not only does it permit us to escape, but it allows us to leave our old lives behind, as well. In effect, we have been given the chance to disappear altogether from the authorities' view."

"This is what I propose," Washington explained. "Tell me whether you perceive any issues with my strategy ..."

May 3, 2020, 10:32 pm EDT

The Cabinet Room, Washington, DC

The President had gotten very little sleep the previous night. As a result, he felt irritable and fidgety. He sat, drumming his fingers impatiently, shifting uncomfortably in his chair at the center of the long, oval, Cabinet table.

Arleigh Solomon was relating the details of the FBI's investigation of Richard Wayne Lee, and outlining the sequence of events that led to his spectacular, fiery end.

"Mr. President," the Secretary of the Department of Internal Security concluded, "I think the key capture here is that Merlin Friend is clearly guilty of having incited the late Mr. Lee to attempt your assassination. I'm convinced that, unless we make a prompt and public example of Mr. Friend, we can expect more such incidents in the coming days. His broadcasts go far beyond the Pale. Merlin Friend has, in fact, been actively fomenting armed insurrection against the United States government. That's treason, in anybody's book."

"Mr. President," Evan Spitzberger, the Attorney General, cut in, "I have to agree with Secretary Solomon. Friend has crossed the line. He needs to be stopped."

Steele shook his head, frowning.

"No," he said. "Absolutely not. I regard my declaration of martial law as an unavoidable and strictly temporary evil. However, crisis or no crisis, I took an oath to preserve, protect, and defend the Constitution of the United States. And, by God, that is what I intend to do. I will not discard the First Amendment in the service of mere expediency."

He aimed a forefinger at the Secretary, and shook it for emphasis.

"That is a slippery slope on which I have no intention to set foot," he insisted. "Is that clear to everyone? Regardless of what Merlin Friend, or anyone else may say to the contrary, I am not a tyrant, and I categorically refuse to behave as one."

Solomon, his expression stony, spent several long seconds carefully, and unnecessarily, squaring up the papers on the conference table before him.

"It's your call, Mr. President," he rumbled, at last, clearly unhappy with Steele's decision.

"So it is," Steele agreed. "And, now that we've disposed of that issue, let's pass on to the status of the relief effort, shall we?"

May 3, 2020, 11:43 am EDT

40°46'01.16" N, 74°00'16.53" W, New York Harbor, NY

Chief Petty Officer Curtis Simmons felt like someone had gone over his eyeballs once, lightly, with fine-grit sandpaper. He had been awake for more than 24 hours, with only a couple of light naps – both taken while sitting upright in the driving rain in a jolting Zodiac, on his way to or from the USS John F. Kennedy – to lessen his fatigue.

- I'd give my left nut for a solid 40 winks, right now. And I could spare it, too. After all, neither of my nuts have seen much action recently. -

The self-deprecating joke brought a grin to his round face, despite his weariness.

Simmons, and his three-man crew – along with other, similar details – had spent the past nine hours shuttling electrical supplies to tugboat crews across New York Harbor. Starting with Captain Jake Cordell and the men of the Iron Maiden, they had located, contacted, and provided water taxi services to six of the powerful little ships. All six had been incapacitated by the EMP from the nuclear explosion in Lower Manhattan. Now, at last, all six were fully operational, and preparing to maneuver the JFK from the New York Harbor ship channel to dock at the West 48th Street Freight Station's Pier 88.

- It was damned well worth the effort. -

The nuclear aircraft carrier would soon be in position to actually begin carrying out its assigned mission; rescuing stranded New Yorkers from the radioactively-contaminated death-trap into which their city had been transformed. In his estimation, that prospect justified his exhaustion several times over. Pride in his detail's accomplishment was reward enough in Simmons's book, but it hadn't hurt at all when, a couple of hours earlier, Commodore Collins, the Kennedy's Executive Officer, had stopped to personally pat him on the shoulder, and say, "Well done, Chief," .

Now that his assignment was completed, he could have opted to get some much-deserved sack time. Nobody would have criticized him for it.

Instead, as a guest of Captain Cordell, he stood gripping the bow rail of the Iron Maiden, as it cautiously bellied up to the looming hull of the JFK. He would have preferred to be on the bridge, of course, but space there was at a premium. The CPO was unwilling to provide even a slight distraction to Cordell, as the tugboat captain performed the delicate task of maneuvering the carrier into its berth.

Standing on the Maiden's deck, Simmons was glad, indeed, that he'd been able to ditch his MOPP suit hours earlier. A thorough radiac scan of the tug determined that the thunderous rain of Tropical Storm Beth's passage had scoured the worst of the fallout from her decks. Beth's thorough flushing of the Iron Maiden's deck left him free, now, to stand protected only by his duty uniform and a reefer that kept him dry, despite the constant downpour.

- Odds are, that's gonna make it a lot less dangerous for all those civilians, too. -

The tugboat's whistle emitted one short shriek.

Simmons heard Captain Cordell holler, "'Ware contact!" just before the Maiden's line of truck tire bumpers thumped the JFK's bow.

The deck lurched beneath his feet, and the CPO reflexively bent his knees to absorb the shock, not even consciously aware that he was doing so. 30 feet further astern along the carrier's hull from the Iron Maiden, a second tugboat nosed into the Kennedy. Another 30 feet down, a third tug eased up against the CVN-79. Simmons knew that, on the JFK's other flank, three more tugboats were pressed against the carrier's stern.

Simmons heard the Maiden's powerful diesels rev to a deafening, full-throated roar, as the tugboat began pushing the carrier's bow to starboard. The tug shuddered from its engines' terrific torque, and its deck transmitted that pulsation to the CPO. The intensity of the vibration made his teeth chatter. A huge fan of spume sprayed out from the Iron Maiden's stern, as her dirigible propellers churned the harbor's water to froth.

- Damn! This is one helluva *boat! -*

Until that moment, Simmons had never really appreciated how much power a tugboat captain commanded.

Slowly, the USS John F. Kennedy began to pivot toward Manhattan Island.

May 3, 2020, 12:37 pm EDT

Washington National Cathedral, Washington, DC

Diana Hunter, seated next to the President in the first pew of the Cathedral Church of Saint Peter and Saint Paul, fought desperately to control the tears that threatened to flood from her tawny eyes.

Until this very moment, the Vice President had not allowed herself to grieve for the uncounted victims of the May Day nuclear bombing. Somehow, the combination of the Senate Chaplain's good, gray, Episcopalian sermon, with its measured cadences and mournful reassurances of divine succor, combined with the hovering specter of her beloved husband and mentor Benjamin's impending death to rob her of her detachment. She felt her lower lip tremble, afraid it betrayed her struggle for self-control to the worldwide audience watching the service on television. The mental image of mascara running in ugly rivulets down her cheeks appalled Hunter. She knew that, should she allow that to happen, the resulting image would define her for the rest of her career – an inescapable element of her every future campaign, every biography, every news story.

As the Reverend Hiram Dunwiddie, Chaplain of the Senate, gave way to his House counterpart, Hunter rummaged in her clutch purse for a tissue, as insurance against the failure of her self-discipline.

The Reverend William J. "Billy Joe" Barker, current Chaplain of the House of Representatives, was accustomed to an audience of the powerful. Today, though, here at the National Cathedral, he was preaching not just to a great nation's leaders, but to the nation itself – indeed, to the world. Trading places with Dunwiddie at the pulpit, he felt the power of the Holy Spirit possess him.

Reverend Billy Joe had taken more than one sip of decidedly secular spirits before the service began. He knew that to have been a sin in the sight of his Lord. He figured, though, that his personal Savior would forgive him for this minor trespass. Jesus, in his omniscient fashion, surely had to know that he, Billy Joe Barker, secretly suffered from chronic, near-crippling stage fright. A drop or two of Johnny Walker helped lubricate his throat, and free his tongue to preach the Word, despite that handicap.

It was inconceivable to Billy Joe that Jesus would want His consecrated shepherd to risk becoming tongue-tied and incoherent, in the face of such a vast audience of potential converts. Why, the Fox News channel had estimated the world-wide TV audience for this national memorial service at as many as 1,000,000,000 people, with 120,000,000 of those being his fellow Americans. How then could Christ, in His mercy, not forgive him for consuming what, after all, was only a modest dose of purely medicinal whiskey, given the huge number of souls at stake?

The medicine was doing its job well. Never had Reverend Barker felt more eloquent. Never had his audience been more rapt. He felt the power of the Scripture course through him as he assumed his place at the pulpit.

"Brothers and sisters," he thundered, gazing out at the row upon row of dignitaries seated in the magnificent neo-Gothic cathedral's nave, "we are all beholden to Gawd – and to His only-begotten Son, Jay-sus."

The North Texas twang in Billy Joe's delivery was not an affectation. He had been born and reared in Crockett, smack-dab in the middle of the driest, most Christian county in the state. He had continued to cultivate his North Texas accent as a mark of authenticity. Reverend Barker was as proud of his Lone Star State heritage as he was of his unwavering faith in the Good Book.

Let others – like his Senate counterpart – take pride in their sophistication of speech, if they would. Billy Joe reveled in being a simple, country preacher, who espoused the most rock-ribbed, fundamental, and literal interpretation of Holy Scripture possible. He was determined to seize this golden opportunity to spread that glorious Word – along with the promise of Hellfire and damnation to those who denied its truth – with all his evangelical might and main.

"Far, far too many of us have, in our pride, our arrogance, and our profound foolishness, turned our faces away from Gawd," he declared, spreading his arms to stand as if representing his crucified Savior before his rapt listeners. "We have turned away from Jay-sus, turned away from faith in the inerrant Word of the Gospels! Why then should we be surprised when Gawd turns His own face away from us?"

A disapproving murmur ran through the congregation. But Reverend Billy Joe was on a roll. He ignored the ripple of disquiet, raising his booming voice to still more grandiose heights of passion and power.

"Can we truly blame Him for visitin' this terrible tragedy on us? For punishin' our lack of faith in Him with truly Biblical vengeance?" Billy Joe cried.

The murmur of unrest became a chorus of disapproval. The crowd began to boo. Some shouted, "Shame!" The call was picked up, and repeated.

Billy Joe Barker stood there, blinking, with the television lights revealing the cold sweat of fear to all the untold millions, as it popped out all over his bejowled face. He mopped at his streaming brow, and opened his mouth to try as best he could to regain control of the situation. But his throat was suddenly dry as the dust of Crockett, Texas, and he could manage no more than a weakly-croaked, "Wait ..."

It was already too late for Reverend Billy Joe. The outraged crowd was on its feet, howling for his blood. Barker took to his heels, and fled in panic.

Still seated in the first pew, Diana Hunter – striving mightily to keep from bursting into laughter at Billy Joe Barker's indecorous exit – offered silent thanks to the luckless evangelist for saving her dignity, if not her soul.

May 3, 2020, 1:44 pm EDT

Commonwealth Avenue, Boston, MA

Ryan Patrick Cohan awoke disoriented, unsure of where he was. This was not an uncommon occurrence in Cohan's life.

He felt terrible. His head hurt, his mouth tasted of vomit, and the frilly canopy above him seemed to spin gently before his sleep-encrusted eyes. This was also a routine occurrence in Ryan Cohan's life – one for which he had long ago discovered a reliable and trusted remedy.

- Booze. I need more booze. -

Sitting up, propping himself on his elbows, Cohan took in the rich wood paneling, elaborately-sculpted moldings, and gilt-framed artwork on the walls. Woozily, he contemplated the massive four-poster canopy bed in which he lounged, and the size, and sumptuous furnishings of the room it occupied. He belched appreciatively.

- Nice. Ritzy, even. A guy could get used to this, easy. -

He was still fully dressed, right down to his ragged, dumpster-scavenged Nikes and ratty pea coat. That, too, was a familiar state of affairs.

Slowly, hazily, the previous night's events came back to him. He had clear memories of looting the Fairmont Copley Plaza Hotel. He recalled sitting in the doorway of his van, rewarding himself for his hard work by downing bottle after miniature bottle of Smirnoff vodka. He smiled fondly at that recollection.

He remembered much less clearly driving the few short blocks to Commonwealth Avenue, and searching for an unlocked door. He hazily recalled throwing something large and heavy – perhaps a big-screen TV he had stolen from the Fairmont – through the frosted glass door of one of the towering mansions that lined Commonwealth. After that, though, his memory rapidly faded.

Cohan was ragingly thirsty. He also desperately needed to urinate, so he levered himself up off of the deliciously soft mattress, and onto his unsteady feet. He felt a little nauseous. That was unusual for him –

typically, he felt sick to his stomach only much earlier in his drinking cycle – but he shrugged it off as an artifact of having had consumed even larger than usual quantities of alcohol the previous night. Instead he focused on searching for a bathroom.

The one he found, after a brief detour into the master suite's generous walk-in closet, was a revelation to him.

- *A shower* and *a bathtub!* -

He marveled, as he urinated copiously into a black marble toilet.

- *Now* that's *class!* -

Cohan reached into the voluminous pockets of his pea coat, coming up with a pack of Marlboros and a butane lighter. Gratefully, he sucked in a lungful of smoke from the day's first cigarette, as he studiously inspected the lavatory's bidet – a device whose purpose mystified him.

Then he turned to look at himself in the wall-to-wall mirror above the twin, black marble vanities.

Staring back at him was a balding, middle-aged figure, with a grimy, unshaven face, a noticeable stoop, and a distinct pot belly. Peering more closely at his reflection, he saw a scatter of what appeared to be pin-point burns across his nearly-hairless pate. There were more such angry red dots all down his nose and on the tops of his cheeks. Rubbing at the spots on his face spread thin, black smears from the center of each one, like a set of pencil marks across his nose and cheeks.

- *Oughta wash my face. But … fuck it. Booze first.* -

So, leaving his face covered in smudges of highly radioactive fallout, Ryan Patrick Cohan went in search of more alcohol.

May 3, 2020, 2:13 pm EDT

The Kennedy Center Concert Hall, Washington, DC

William Orwell Steele did not feel like a man who had recently survived an assassination attempt. That was an experience with which he was all-too-intimately familiar. The memory of his beloved wife Julia literally dying before his eyes, struck down as she impulsively threw herself into his arms before a stadium filled with his wildly-enthusiastic supporters, haunted his dreams virtually every night. The assassin's armor-piercing, high-caliber round easily had pierced the two-inch-thick "bulletproof" Lexan barrier around the podium. It hit her squarely between the shoulder blades, fracturing her spine. When the fragmented bullet slammed into Julia Steele's heart, it exploded. She had died instantly, as hydrostatic shock pulped her brain.

Steele would never forget the sight of her loving smile turning, in a single instant, to a terrible, slack vacancy. The shining joy in her eyes extinguished in the space of a heartbeat. Her flaccid body suddenly slumped in his arms, a wife-sized puppet, with its strings cut. He had had only the briefest of moments for that vision to sear itself into his memory, before his Secret Service detail gang-tackled him, and hustled him to safety. Nonetheless, it was branded on his soul, dominating his every memory of Julia.

No, last night had felt nothing like that awful September morning in Cleveland. Despite the urgency of Agent Wright's warning, regardless of the fact that only the Avenger anti-aircraft battery had prevented that deluded fool from flying his napalm-laden Cessna into the Presidential living room, he had never felt any immediate sense of danger at any time. He had, in fact, never felt personally threatened at all. For William Orwell Steele, the ex-postal worker's attack on the White House had had all the emotional impact of a fire drill.

By contrast, his conversation with Diana Hunter, in the moments leading up to the aerial assault, had stirred emotions in him that had lain dormant for nearly four years. As profoundly different as they both were in terms of personality, there was something about Diana that reminded him of Julia. They shared some essential quality upon which he could not place his mental finger, but that resonated on a profound level within him. His exchange with Hunter had awakened the almost physical sense of loss that so terribly plagued him throughout the final six weeks of his Presidential campaign. That renewed grief contributed significantly to the inner turmoil that had kept him nearly sleepless last night.

Now, as he waited in the wings of the Kennedy Center's Concert Hall, Steele felt numb, and sad, and very, very tired.

"Ladies and gentlemen," the announcer's voice boomed, "the President of the United States."

Straightening, automatically squaring his shoulders, and lifting his chin, William Orwell Steele strode out onto the stage of the vast hall, to face his country and the world.

"My fellow Americans, and citizens of all nations, around the globe" he began, reading from the teleprompter, "we come together today, not to grieve, but to remember. To remember, and to celebrate the lives of those whom we have so recently, so tragically lost. We shall probably never accurately know just how many of our fellow citizens, our friends and family, our visitors, and our guests fell victim to Friday's attack. But the precise number of the fallen is not what matters. What matters is that, regardless of the tally, far too many lives – each of them unique and irreplaceably individual – were lost on May Day.

"It is important that we who witness this historic concert understand that those who will perform here today do so not to entertain us, but to honor them: the ones that we – all of us – have lost. Humbly, knowing how inadequate my words are, I say to those lost ones: 'We miss you. We shall always miss you. We will never forget you. We wish with all our might that you were still here, with us, alive and whole. But you are gone, now – taken untimely from we who cherished you. The burden of life has passed to us, whom you have left behind. We will carry on in your memory, because we know that is what you would have wanted us to do. But, whatever we do, wherever our own paths may lead, our thoughts will always be with you.'

Steele's voice cracked, as he concluded, "Farewell.'"

Beneath the giant chandeliers, the audience surged to its feet, applauding the President.

He stood before them, alone, blinking in the spotlight.

May 3, 2020, 3:31 pm EDT

Clay St., Hackensack, NJ

Gasping for air, Latonya Gramble struggled free of her rank, sopping-wet bed clothing.

Less than an hour earlier, she had burrowed into that same bed, mounding the covers over her freezing body. Huddling beneath them, she had curled herself into a tight ball for warmth. Her fingers and toes were icicles. Unable to bear the touch of her own hands, she had kept them clasped, as if in prayer, tucked beneath her pillow.

Now, though, she rivered sweat, as her body tried desperately to substitute its own endorphin production for the external supply of opiates to which it had become so accustomed. Latonya was ragingly thirsty. The parched tissues of her throat felt as if they were trying to glue themselves together. Her nose ran so copiously she could barely breathe.

Wearily, Latonya climbed out of the queen-size bed she had, until yesterday, shared with Marqus Collins. She felt shaky, and unsteady on her feet. Her arms and legs twitched convulsively, but her overwhelming thirst drove her to the duplex's tiny bathroom for water.

It was dark in the bathroom and throughout the house. The sky was still filled with black storm clouds, the curtains drawn, in classic junkie style, against prying eyes. With electrical power to Hackensack still out, the interior of the duplex was gloomy, even in mid-afternoon.

It was therefore perhaps not surprising Latonya failed to realize her sweaty palms were still covered in the greasy, black fallout that had killed her daughter. It had been transferred to them as she had cradled Nakeesha's forlorn corpse, the previous day. Cupping her hands beneath the cold water faucet, to catch the flow, she drank from them again and again. Consumed with thirst, she did not even notice the bitter, metallic taste of the radioactive sludge she ingested with every swallow.

When at last her thirst was slaked, Latonya urinated, then returned to her bedroom. The now-cold and stinking sweat that soaked her sheets and blankets repelled her.

Too exhausted by her ordeal to summon the energy to change the bed clothing, she retreated to the hallway. Her shoulders slumping in resignation, she shuffled into Nakeesha's bedroom. Despairing, she collapsed on her daughter's single bed. She molded herself to her daughter's tiny, cold, stiff body, pressed her face against the corpse's cornrows – still soaked with the virulently poisonous fallout that had killed her child – and let her tears stream into her dead baby's hair.

Eventually, she drifted into uneasy sleep.

May 3, 2020, 5:53 pm EDT

Wisconsin Avenue, Chevy Chase, MD

Diana Hunter was a jumble of conflicting emotions. Sadness and resignation underlay them all. Sadness at the orders she was on her way to Bethesda to sign: orders to transfer her beloved husband Benjamin to home hospice care, and not to resuscitate him when his heart inevitably stopped. Resignation to his inevitable, impending death. At the same time, she felt a sense of exaltation and pride, in the afterglow of the national memorial concert at the Kennedy Center she had just left.

It had been an unexpectedly uplifting experience. Elegiac, yes, but inspiring at the same time.

The acts had built, one upon the next, throughout the event. It had begun with the President's brief, but moving speech, and concluded three-and-a-half hours later with folk-hop superstar Ne-on Glowbaby's syncopated, soulful, *a cappella* rendition of America The Beautiful, sung as counterpoint to the National Choir of Men and Boys' lush arrangement of Swing Low, Sweet Chariot. The combination had been so sublime, so fraught with emotion, that Glowbaby's whispered, "Good night," at its conclusion left the audience in a stunned silence for seconds. When, at last, its members had recovered sufficiently, they rose, as one, for a standing ovation that lasted nearly ten minutes.

Hunter had slipped away during that ovation. No camera recorded her escape. All eyes had been on the stage, where Ne-on Glowbaby had reacted to the acclaim by turning his back to the crowd, and vigorously applauding the members of the choir. No one had recorded the tears Hunter unashamedly had allowed to flow down her elegant cheeks, as she exited from the Presidential box.

Once safely ensconced in her limousine, Hunter took the opportunity to repair the damage to her makeup, while her motorcade wended its way along Potomac Parkway toward Bethesda.

Cosmetic armor restored, she sat, sipping a bottle of spring water. Hunter gazed absently out the tinted windows of her limo, attempting to sort through the confusion of her emotions, and gird herself for the coming emotional ordeal. She was determined that the tumor-riddled husk of her beloved husband would come home to die in the vice-presidential mansion they had shared for the past four years. But she realized her decision to have him transferred from Walter Reed – where she could at least pretend there was still hope he could recover – to One Observatory Circle, was a final acknowledgment that his passing was inevitable. Her only remaining hope would be that his death would be painless and relatively dignified.

- Oh, Ben! How will I ever get through this without you? -

Hunter gazed out the window at the lush, green, drizzle-misted landscape of the Chevy Chase Country Club passing by on the right. Unexpectedly, the Sun broke through the late afternoon clouds. A spectacularly bright rainbow suddenly sprang into being above the golf course's back nine.

- How beautiful! -

Unheeded tears cascaded from the corners of her tawny eyes, again ruining her makeup.

May 3, 2020, 6:37 pm EDT

Seneca Temporary Housing Facility, Romulus, NY

Sean Halloran, Sr. arrived at his new tent-cabin home tired and sweaty, but otherwise cheerful. Happy, even. Shortly after he and his family had returned from breakfast at the hastily-erected camp mess hall – an open-air field tent with a propane-fueled kitchen – a mud-spattered six-by-six truck pulled up in front of his Sierra crew cab. The driver of the six-by-six honked its brassy horn, leaned out, and motioned for him to roll down the window of his pickup truck.

"You Halloran?" he hollered over the rumble of the six-by-six's engine.

"And whaht if I am?" Sean responded, suspiciously.

The driver of the six-by-six had brandished a clipboard.

He shouted, "Says here you're a licensed contractor. That true?"

"I am – in Massachussetts," Halloran replied.

"That's good enough for Uncle Sam," the driver of the six-by-six yelled. "There's work for you, if you want it."

"What kind, and how much does it pay?" Sean asked, interested despite himself.

"Construction work," the six-by-six driver called. "Lots of it. $17.50 an hour, paid by the day."

Rolling up his window and climbing out of the Sierra, Halloran replied, "Okay. I'm int'rested."

Turning to his wife, he told her, "We need the money, Fiona. You and Sean, Jr. will be safe enough here, I reckon. Be sure to lock the truck, when ya go to supper."

"I love ya, Sean," Fiona responded, in a small, forlorn voice.

"I love ya too," Sean assured her, already turning away.

Slamming the crew cab's door, he asked the six-by-six driver whether he should bring his own tools.

"I don't think so," the other replied.

He hooked his thumb at the truck's bed.

"Climb in back, if you're coming," he instructed. "We're running late."

"Hey!" called Adam Manson, owner of the ancient, battered Chevy Suburban parked next to Halloran's Sierra crew cab, "Need anyone else?"

The six-by-six's driver frowned at the question.

"Ain't nobody else from this stretch on my list," he replied. "You got any construction experience?"

Manson nodded. "Two years as a hod carrier, four more as a general construction worker. So, yeah."

"Climb in back, if you want to risk it," the driver told him. "If they don't want you, you'll have to walk back, though."

"I'll risk it," Manson agreed.

"Fair enough," the other said. "Let's go."

That had been more than 12 hours ago. In the meantime, Sean, Sr. and Manson had been transported to a staging area. There they'd each been given a small mountain of paperwork to fill out. Halloran had not seen his new neighbor since. He himself had gotten plenty of work, though, mostly as a carpenter.

His principal task had been to erect showers at more than a dozen locations throughout the camp. One of them was just a couple of hundred yards from where Fiona and Sean, Jr. waited for him in the Sierra. But the crew he was on took its lunch break on the other side of the camp, too far for him to walk back to check in with his wife. He'd been fully occupied constructing the facility's infrastructure ever since.

Half an hour ago, they'd finally knocked off for the day. Sean, Sr. had been given a pay voucher for eight hours of straight time and three-and-a-quarter hours overtime. The overtime pay came as a pleasant surprise.

- I guess there are some good things about the government, after all. -

Halloran had persuaded the driver of the six-by-six that returned him to his campsite at the end of the work day to swing by the newly-constructed camp canteen, so he could buy a pack of smokes. He was in a cheerful mood when the truck pulled to a stop in front of his Chevy. His mood improved still more when he realized that, looming behind his truck and the Manson's Suburban, was a freshly-erected cabin tent, complete with a neatly pegged-out rain fly.

He swung down from the six-by-six's bed. Then he banged on the side of the truck, to let the driver know he was clear.

"See you tomorrow, Sean," the driver said, waving to him.

"Yeah – thanks, man," Halloran replied.

The six-wheeler roared away. Sean had to step lively to keep from being splattered by the mud its tires threw up behind it. He turned to face his new home. There, in the opening of the cabin tent, was his wife, with Sean, Jr. in her arms. Halloran could not help but break into a jaw-cracking smile.

"Fiona, darlin'," he called, slogging toward her and his son, "I'm so happy to see ya! And you, too, Sean, Jr.!"

"Oh, Sean!" Fiona cried, her eyes filling with tears.

"Theah's nothin' to cry about, darlin'," Halloran said, as she rushed into his embrace. "Things are finally lookin' up!"

"Oh, Sean!" his wife repeated, burying her face in his shoulder.

Halloran held her at arms length, frowning.

"What's the matter, Fiona?" he demanded. "What's wrong, darlin'?"

Fiona shook her head vigorously, but refused to meet his eyes. "It's nothin'," she said. "Really, Sean."

As they stood in the rain, Adam Manson appeared in the entry of the tent. With a start, Halloran realized their families had been assigned a shared living space.

Manson was stripped to the waist. After a moment of incomprehension, Sean realized that his tent mate's torso, neck, and arms were completely covered, not in tribal tattoos, but in venomously racist ones. They included variations on the swastika, stylized SS double lightning bolt insignia, *Sturmabteilung*, and the stylized, snarling wolf's head of the Aryan Revolutionary Front, along with racist, xenophobic, and anti-government slogans. These were overlaid on lurid background images of naked, bound, writhing women, entwined with fang-baring rattlesnakes and cobras.

"Hey, bro!" Manson boomed cheerfully. "Are you morons gonna stand in the rain all night?"

May 3, 2020, 7:43 pm EDT

West 48th Street, New York, NY

"What are we to do, now, Greg?" asked Eydis Finnursdottir.

She was shivering in the downpour, despite the protection of Greg Shergold's coat draped over her shoulders.

"I'm not sure, Eydis," Shergold admitted.

They stood at the outer fringes of a vast multitude. The throng of survivors completely filled the street before them, rendering it impassable. Every one of the tens of thousands crammed into 48th Street had Pier 88, where the JFK lay docked, as their common goal.

Circling helicopters had spent the afternoon announcing the carrier's presence.

"The USS John F. Kennedy has arrived to evacuate you from Manhattan," their loudspeakers had blared. "Proceed to Pier 88 to board the Kennedy. Bring nothing with you! No pets or luggage of any kind will be permitted!"

That had not been the only warning the Navy choppers had provided.

"Avoid all green spaces!" they had thundered. "They are heavily contaminated with radioactivity!"

That had seemed counter-intuitive to Greg and Eydis, but they had assumed that the voice of authority, thundering from on high, knew whereof it spoke. Like everyone else, they had stuck religiously to the center of the street, since they left the shelter of the Port Authority Terminal. Now, though, the press of the crowd forced many of its members onto the sidewalks, into contact with the street trees that lined West 48th, even as thousands of additional refugees advanced toward them from the east.

"Maybe we should turn back, Eydis," Greg suggested.

"But Greg," Eydis protested, "we are so close!"

Shergold shook his head

"Actually, no," he told her, "we're not. There must be close to 100,000 people between us and Pier 88, already, Eydis. There's no way one aircraft carrier can accommodate that many of us, in one trip. We have to face facts. We're going to be stuck here for a while."

Eydis clapped her hands to her mouth, her green eyes huge.

"But, what are we to do, Greg?" she implored. "Where are we to go?"

Shergold's eyes narrowed in thought. He looked around at the steadily-thickening crowd, and again shook his head.

"We can't stay here, that's for sure," he observed.

He looked up at the darkening sky, then back at the shivering redhead beside him.

"I take it you don't want to go back to the bus terminal?" he asked.

Eydis shook her head, trembling in his borrowed black jacket. Leaving the Port Authority Terminal felt like a release from prison to her. She had no desire to return there.

"Okay," said Greg, "then I think we should probably try to make it to my parents' co-op. We'll be out of the weather, and there are comfortable beds there. Does that work for you?"

Eydis nodded. She pulled Greg's jacket more closely around her.

"Then that's what we'll do," Greg said.

He smiled at her, reassuringly.

"Don't worry, Eydis," he said. "It's kind of a hike, and it'll be dark by the time we get there ... but I'll get us there, I promise."

Eydis took his arm and briefly buried her face in his shoulder. Then she looked up at him. Her tone betrayed her total faith in him.

"I believe you, Greg," she told him. "Lead on. I shall follow wherever you go."

May 3, 2020, 9:03 pm, EDT

The White House Situation Room, Washington, DC

William Orwell Steele turned to Anderson Connaught IV. "What's the situation, so far, Andy?" he asked.

"As you know, Mr. President," the Treasury Secretary replied, "Asia is across the International Dateline, so it's already Monday there. Yesterday, the Indian government announced the NSE – that's their National Stock Exchange – would be closed today, so we won't learn anything from them. The Congress Party has obviously decided to adopt a wait-and-see policy toward world markets. They may not permit the NSE to open at all this week."

Steele nodded.

"Okay. So, India's out of the picture," he summarized. "Go on."

"The Australian Stock Exchange opened two hours ago, sir," the Treasury Secretary continued. "It closed, just over an hour later."

"Oh?" said the President.

Connaught nodded. "Yes, sir," he confirmed. "ASX got clobbered. It was down more than 90 percent, when its governing board suspended trading for the day, about an hour ago."

"*90* percent?" Steele repeated in disbelief.

"Yes, sir," the Treasury Secretary replied. "More than 90 percent, actually."

"That's – a little disconcerting," the President commented.

"Yes, sir," Connaught agreed. "It's not exactly encouraging."

After a momentary pause, he went on, "In Japan, the Nikkei didn't open at all, today. We think the Liberal Democrats saw what happened to the Aussies, and panicked. So they're opting to keep their heads down, and hoping the storm will pass them by."

"And you don't think that's going to happen," Steele suggested.

"No, sir, we don't," the Secretary agreed.

"I think he's right about that, Mr. President," senior White House economist Jebediah Springer put in.

"Thank you, Jeb," Steele responded.

He held up a hand to forestall further interruption.

"Go on, Mr. Secretary," he instructed.

"The Singapore stock exchange opened a few minutes ago," Connaught responded. "I'm afraid the picture there is equally grim."

He turned to his executive assistant.

"What's the current situation in Singapore, Miss Winston?" he queried.

"Down 94 percent, Mr. Secretary," Emily Winston replied.

"But still open?" Connaught asked.

"Yes, sir," she affirmed, "still open."

The Treasury Secretary turned back to face Steele.

"So Singapore is a write-off, Mr. President," Connaught summarized. "Meanwhile, the Shenzhen and Shanghai in China are due to open in a few minutes. While the ASX and Singapore are important indicators, how China reacts is our real concern. A major downdraft there would be a strong indicator that the rout will be global."

Steele snorted.

"I'd say that's already pretty much a foregone conclusion, wouldn't you, Mr. Secretary?" he observed.

Connaught shrugged.

"Perhaps so, Mr. President," he conceded. "Anyway, we think China will tell the definitive tale. They are still America's largest debt holder. If they sense a market opportunity in our misfortune, it's possible their exchanges may actually experience an upswing."

"'Possible,'" Steele quoted. "But not likely."

"No, sir," the Secretary conceded, "Probably not."

May 3, 10:15 pm EDT

Clifford Street, Newark, NJ

Donell Jackson was in awe of Arun "Big Sugar" Washington's seemingly limitless ability to find and exploit talent. Washington seemed easily able to formulate, and implement ingenious strategies, as well. He could recognize, and seize opportunities that were invisible to everyone else.

Their escape from Northern State Prison had provided Donell with fresh reasons to admire Big Sugar.

Washington's plan evolved out of the relationship the gang boss had long cultivated with a "duck" named Carter Hawley. Their friendship was based on their mutual love of chess. In the excitement of an end-game Big Sugar purposely allowed him to dominate, the loose-lipped correctional officer casually revealed that the understaffed and overstretched guards no longer manned the prison's watchtowers. Hawley confided that they were convinced the prisoners feared the radioactive fallout outside the fence more than they hated confinement within it.

On learning of that gaping hole in Northern State's security, Big Sugar quickly arranged a conference with Warden Lundegran.

The topic of their meeting was the prison's rapidly-diminishing food supplies. Washington pointed out that, with no prospect in sight of fresh supplies being delivered, rationing was inevitable – and it would be best if it were implemented sooner, rather than later. Lundegran immediately grasped the truth of Big Sugar's observation. Washington added that resentment and unrest among the population at the prospect of having to tighten their belts was inevitable. The mob boss had then volunteered to break the news to the prisoners himself, at that evening's meal, in exchange for a list of modest additional privileges for his crew. The Warden agreed to the plan, relieved that Big Sugar had offered to make himself, rather than the prison's staff, the target of the population's animus.

Upon returning from their conference, Washington immediately instructed William "Big Willie" Dixon, who worked in the motor pool, to steal a bolt cutter.

That evening, in the dining hall, the gang boss – surrounded by his crew for protection – made his calm and reasoned case for rationing to four shifts of just-fed prisoners. Afterwards, Big Sugar invoked one of his crew's new privileges; requesting he and his men be permitted a half-hour of time in the exercise yard.

The bulls, confident that Washington and his gang had proven themselves trustworthy, had left them unsupervised. With no one observing them from the deserted watch towers, it had been a simple matter for Big Willie to cut through the triple fences. Once on the outside, they made their way north across the neighboring rail yard, into the Ironbound district of Newark proper. True to Big Sugar's prediction, no one had followed them.

"The population are not the only ones who fear the fallout," he observed.

Looking at the row of narrow, clapboard, two-story houses across the street, Jackson asked, "What now, Boss?"

"An excellent question, Donell," Washington replied, "I believe our first priority must be to obtain civilian clothing."

"So, we find a department store, and get some fresh threads?" Jackson asked.

Washington shook his head.

"Donell," he said, "I am gravely disappointed in you. Think it through. This is a working-class, residential neighborhood, is it not?"

Jackson nodded.

"And when did the bomb detonate?" Big Sugar queried.

"Friday noon," Donell replied.

"That is correct," Washington agreed. "Think, then: where are working-class people most likely to be, at mid-day on a Friday?"

Donell recognized he was being tested. Suddenly, the answer Big Sugar was looking for occurred to him.

"At work," Jackson said. "They're at work."

"Exactly correct," Washington beamed. "They are at work. Therefore, their residences are most likely vacant. By contrast, a department store would undoubtedly be open for business on a Friday, at noon. In fact, it would be crowded with customers, shopping on their lunch hour. Therefore, while a department store would indeed offer us a superior selection, it would also be filled with ...?"

"Witnesses," Donell replied. "Witnesses who could identify us and our brand-new duds."

"Precisely," Big Sugar said approvingly, "Consider, as well, that the customers and staff will now have had some two-and-a-half days to become familiar with one another. Thus, they would undoubtedly immediately recognize any new faces that suddenly appeared among them. On the other hand, a private residence will most likely be deserted. It is, therefore, the superior alternative for our purposes."

"Damn, Boss" Jackson said, shaking his head in admiration. "I have to admit that makes all kinds of sense."

"Indeed it does, brother Donell," Big Sugar told him. "So, would you not agree that now is a propitious time and place to engage in a modest bit of unauthorized entry?"

"You know, Suge," Jackson pointed out, "that's what got me jugged in the first place."

Washington nodded agreement.

"I do, indeed, Donell," he concurred. "That makes you the most qualified man for the task, does it not?"

Jackson sighed in resignation.

"I guess it does, at that," he admitted.

May 3, 2020, 11:03 pm EDT,

Seneca Temporary Housing Facility, Romulus, NY

Tired as he was, try as he might, Sean Halloran, Sr. could not sleep.

Things had been tense enough in the crowded cabin tent before darkness descended, and the lights had gone out. It was clear that Fiona was terrified of Adam Manson and his collection of racist tattoos, although Manson had said nothing directly threatening to either of them. In fact, he had been conspicuously and deliberately cheerful, and friendly towards both Hallorans in the hours since Sean Sr. had returned from his labors.

Mostly ignoring his three sons' complicated, three-way wrestling match and non-stop chatter, Manson regaled Halloran with the tale of his unsuccessful application to the camp's authorities for employment. Sean Sr. could not help but notice that the big man had conspicuously omitted mentioning the exact reason why he'd been turned down. Manson's narrative concluded with him slogging through the mud to return to his family, who were still huddled against the rain in their ancient Suburban.

The tattooed giant had arrived in time to help erect the cabin tent one of the ubiquitous six-by-sixes had delivered to their campsite. He spoke scornfully of the food the mess hall had served them for dinner, claiming that his wife Ruby was "ten times" better than the Seneca cooks. He then attempted to convince Halloran to play poker with him. When Sean, Sr. demurred, Manson asked if he wanted to smoke some marijuana.

In the absence of a six-pack of cold beer, Halloran would have welcomed some doobage. However, he was unwilling to become further indebted to Adam Manson. It was bad enough that he already owed the big man for the cigarettes Manson had rolled for him the previous day. The big man casually waved away Sean Sr.'s offer of a Marlboro, claiming he preferred his own – so that was a debt Halloran considered still unsatisfied. He was determined not to add to it. As a result, Sean Sr. had been forced to sit enviously by, tantalized by the delicious aroma, as his tent mate shared a joint of sinsemilla with his hook-nosed wife Ruby.

With Halloran politely rebuffing his every overture, Manson eventually turned to roughhousing with his sons. That had kept him occupied until night fell, and the time came to put out their FEMA-supplied lanterns. Separated from each other only by a thin, Army-surplus blanket hung from a rope to divide the tent into halves, the two families bedded down for the night.

Since then, Manson and his beak-nosed wife had been engaged in noisy, energetic, non-stop sex. The two of them were still going at it with undiminished enthusiasm.

"That's it," Halloran heard the big man tell Ruby, his voice hoarse with lust, "suck my nuts, bitch! Come on – use your tongue … just like that. Yeah, baby, suck those balls! God, what a slut you are!"

Sean, Sr. was as embarrassed by the abusive language Manson employed towards his spouse as he was by the explicitness of his instructions to her. When he thought of how their young sons must feel, listening to their father employ such degrading language to their mother, he was nearly overcome with outrage and resentment. Still, tempted as he was to voice his objections to his hulking tent mate, he simply could not bring himself to speak up.

Halloran desperately wanted to believe it was not physical cowardice that made him hold his tongue, but inhibition, instead. He felt certain it would be as humiliating for him to intrude on the Mansons' copulation as it would be if it were his own coitus that was interrupted. Even so, despite his furious, silent disapproval, their continuing display of unrestrained carnality had given him a painfully throbbing erection.

He was grateful for the darkness that hid his unwanted excitement from his beloved Fiona. He assumed she must find the spectacle as shameful as he did. All he could do was seethe with resentment and envy. He saw no choice but to grit his teeth, and pray that the lovers rutting on the other side of the blanket wall would exhaust themselves after – please, God! – not too many more orgasms.

- *First thing tomorrow, I'm gonna make 'em give us new roommates. I swear I am.* -

"Yeah, bitch!" Adam Manson ordered hoarsely. "*Suck* me, you fucking slut!"

May 3, 2020, 11:52 pm EDT

Clay St., Hackensack, NJ

Thrashing convulsively in her delirium, Latonya Gramble fell off her daughter's narrow bed onto the hardwood floor of Nakeesha's room. The impact jolted her awake. For a few seconds, she lay where she had fallen, confused and nauseated. As the clammy fingers of nightmare withdrew, and the horrors of reality asserted themselves in their place, her feverish brain slowly sorted out where she was, and why she felt so dizzy, sick, and disoriented.

Latonya was sufficiently conscious now to feel the demands of her raging thirst. Her body was like a dried piece of kindling, ready to burst into flame at the slightest spark. Her face felt flushed, hot, and painful, particularly on its left side – almost as if it had been burned in a fire. She reached up with a shaking hand to touch her cheek, and encountered tight, swollen blisters, all along her jaw, cheek, and temple, where they had lain against Nakeesha's fallout-encrusted cornrows.

- Sweet Jesus! What the fuck *happened to me?"*

That she herself had fallen victim to the same malignant poison that had slain her only child did not occur to her.

May 4 2020, 12:27 am EDT

1 Park Avenue West, New York City, NY

Eydis Finnursdottir desperately wished that she believed in a God who intervened in human affairs. Then she could pray for deliverance from her agonizing ordeal – for rescue or for death. She wanted so badly to be able to pray for help for her beloved Greg, whose beautiful face was now so disfigured from the savage pistol-whipping her tormentors had inflicted on him.

Shergold lay on his side, in the ante room of his parents' co-op, where the looters he and Eydis had surprised dragged him, after first beating him unconscious. His nose was flattened against his face. His features were swollen and mottled with ugly, purple and green bruises. There was a visible dent in the left side of his skull. Occasionally, a fat, lazy bubble of blood would form between his lips. Eventually, when his shallow breathing overcame its surface tension, it would pop.

Eydis was in agony.

Her captors had been raping her for what surely must be hours. At first it was all three of them, pumping their erect phalluses into her in unison; using her mouth, her rectum, and her vagina simultaneously. Now, though, they had switched to taking turns. One violated her, while the other two drank from the Shergold's well-stocked liquor cabinet. Occasionally, one or the other would use her bleeding mouth to stimulate himself, as he waited his turn at her other orifices, both of which were well-lubricated by a mixture of their semen and her blood.

Eydis knew without having to be told that she would not survive her experience with the three dark, Spanish-speaking looters. She was certain they would kill her, once they tired of violating her – and they would enjoy doing it.

Whether they would also bother to murder Greg, or simply leave him comatose, to die or recover on his own, was another question. If she were forced to wager, though, she would bet that they would not bother killing him. There was, after all, no enjoyment to be had in murdering an unconscious man. If he did not know his death was imminent and unavoidable, he could not experience fear. Merely ending his existence would be nothing to such men as these. Only the suffering of other humans – spiced with their victims' mortal terror, and garnished with their fruitless pleading – seemed to bring them joy.

Eydis was grimly determined to deny them the pleasure of hearing her beg for her life. However, she was honest enough with herself to wonder whether, when her time came, she would have the courage to remain silent in the face of impending death.

Greg choked noisily on his own blood, then groaned softly.

The one with the big belly – the one they called Luis – roused himself from his sprawl on the gold-and-white brocade couch. He staggered over to prod the unconscious Shergold with his foot. Seeing no reaction, Luis casually kicked him in the face. Then he lurched over to the liquor cabinet, to search for more rum.

The one with the pock-marked face – the others called him "Angel" – grunted and swore atop her. Maniacally he rammed himself into her ravaged vagina, as he shuddered in orgasm. Spent, he collapsed on top of Eydis, his full weight pressing her into the bloodstained, white carpet on which she lay.

"Hey, Angel!" called Luis. "Get up, mang – *İno esa ojete!* She's *my* turn!"

"*¡Chingate, Luis!*" snarled the third man – the one called Diego – who had three crudely-tattooed teardrops beneath his left eye. Heaving himself up off the couch, he declared, "Is *my* turn, *ese!*"

Luis shrugged indifferently. "Hep yourself, mang," he replied. "That *puta*, she's all stretch out, anyway."

"*Si*," agreed Diego, with an evil smile. "But her *ojete*, she's still nice an' tight."

May 4, 2020, 1:34 am EDT

Commonwealth Avenue, Boston, MA

Ryan Patrick Cohan gazed blearily down at the gleaming marble toilet bowl into which he had just finished puking.

- *It should be me floatin' in there, 'cause I sure do feel like shit.* -

The *vomitus* Cohan was contemplating was opaquely black and stringy-looking. That seemed unusual to him. Cohan was quite familiar with his own vomit. He saw it on a regular basis. It was typically a kind of light, greenish-tan color. This new tint and texture seemed wrong, but he couldn't quite put his finger on exactly why.

- *Prob'ly the caviar.* -

Two hours earlier, when his growling stomach had alerted him that he needed food, Cohan had found a five-pound tin of the delicacy, while rifling the mansion's refrigerator. He immediately decided it was something he had to try. He had always heard that only rich people ate caviar. Given his new motto, "Only the best for Ryan Cohan," Beluga seemed like just the thing.

His first bite left him feeling bitterly betrayed and disappointed. It turned out that caviar tasted *nasty*. Its consistency made him want to upchuck. It was way too salty. It tasted exactly like the cod liver oil he remembered his mother inflicting on him as a young child. It felt grainy and deeply unpleasant on his tongue.

- *I can't believe rich people* eat *this shit!* -

He spit his first and only mouthful of the horrid glop into the kitchen sink.

He dumped the rest of the blue tin into the disposal, as well.

Cohan had returned to rummaging through the fridge for something more palatable. Eventually, he settled on a package of blueberry Pop Tarts he found in a cabinet next to the refrigerator. Now *they* were delicious – toasted to a golden brown, they made a meal fit for a king – or a Cohan. The pastries tasted even better chased with three of the tiny bottles of Smirnoff from his still-significant stock.

After that modest feast, Cohan had passed out again.

Nausea wakened him. Now, as he weaved unsteadily above the marble toilet, he felt feverish and more lightheaded than usual. His face and scalp were painful, too, as if they had been burned. He turned to look at himself in the wall-sized mirror above the twin bathroom sinks, and saw that his face and head were inexplicably covered with small, round, angry-looking blisters.

- What the ...? What the fuck happened to me? -

Cohan coughed. His chest felt congested and rusty, as if he had a bad cold or a case of the flu.

- That's it. -

He eyed his collection of pinpoint blisters doubtfully.

- The flu. That's all it is – just the flu. -

May 4, 2020, 2:43 am EDT

One Observatory Circle, Washington, DC

In the guest bedroom of the Vice Presidential Mansion, Diana Hunter dozed in a satin-upholstered, Victorian-era arm chair. Even asleep, she listened for the sound of her husband Benjamin's shallow breathing.

For a moment, it stopped. Its absence jolted her fully awake; the momentary silence blaring like a klaxon in her ears. Instantly she was on her feet beside the hospital bed occupied by her dying spouse, her hand reaching for the call button tied around the raised rail.

Gasping, Benjamin began to breathe again. Hunter jerked her hand away from the lipstick-shaped call button, as if it might bite her.

She looked down at her beloved husband; at his wasted body, so shrunken and caved in. Her eyes filled with tears.

Benjamin was almost unrecognizable to her, now.

His cheeks were sunken from the wasting effects of his cancer and the chemotherapy that had failed so utterly to stop its ravages. His skin, grayish-yellow from jaundice and poor circulation, was parchment-thin. It was stretched over the jutting prominences of his cheekbones. Nonetheless, his face was puffy from the effects of chemo, despite its emaciation. The swelling had smoothed his features, removing all but the myriad of tiny wrinkles that chronic pain had incised around his eyes. Not a single hair remained on his face and head – the chemical poisons that had failed to save him had taken them all: beard, eyelashes, and eyebrows included.

- He looks ... otherworldly. -

She reached down to lightly caress his cheek with her fingertips. He did not react. Benjamin Hunter was too profoundly unconscious from the continuous fentanyl drip that insulated him from his agony even to know she touched him.

Hunter sighed.

Benjamin – her darling Benjamin – would never awaken again. He would never know she had watched over him in his final hours. He would pass from life, unaware of the moment of his own death. The prospect filled her with a sadness so profound it was like a physical weight: encumbering her every limb; burdening her heart; bowing her very shoulders under the load of her grief.

Hunter knew there was a private-duty hospice nurse on duty in the hallway. There would be one on duty around the clock, until the end. She knew, too, that she herself should try to get some sleep. The call of her official duties in the hours and days ahead would demand every bit of her strength, and the keen edge of her considerable intellect. And yet ... and yet, she could not bring herself to abandon even this pitiful remnant of her beloved husband, confidante, guru, lover, and partner. Not while he still drew breath.

With a sigh of resignation, the Vice President resumed her vigil in the antique arm chair beside her husband's bed.

In time, she dozed.

May 4, 3:28 am EDT

Clifford Street, Newark, NJ

- It's just luck. That's all it is – pure, dumb luck. -

He, Donell Jackson, was alive and David "Little Boy" Shabazz was dead. It was sheer, blind luck that it wasn't the other way around. Luck alone kept him from lying dead on the floor, with a bullet in his brain. It could just as easily have been Little Boy, standing with his hands in the air, hoping to God that the agitated old cracker with the gat in his hand wouldn't decide to shoot him, too.

Things had been going so well, too.

At the first house they'd tried breaking into, he checked the lintel above the back door, to see whether the owner had stashed a spare key there, as they so often did. That hadn't panned out. When he cased the bushes on either side of the back steps, however, he spotted a glaringly obvious, artificial rock. Sure enough, it held a key. Seconds later, they were inside.

Big Sugar Washington had sternly cautioned his gang not to ransack the place.

"We are in search of replacement clothing," he told them. "Nothing more. Ideally, when the owners of this residence eventually return, they should have no reason to suspect we were ever present."

"What about jewelry, gold, cash?" Kendall "Wide Load" Broadus asked. "You know: loot. C'an't we take none of that?"

Washington shook his head firmly.

"No, Kendall, you may not," he said. "We must remain as invisible to the authorities as possible, once order returns to Newark."

"You really think that gonna' happen, Boss?" asked William "Big Willy" Dixon.

"Indeed I do," Big Sugar replied. "In point of fact, I anticipate the arrival of National Guardsmen or other Federal military forces as early as daybreak."

"You do?" Big Willy asked, doubtfully. "How come?"

"Were I Commander-in-Chief, brother William," Washington responded, "it is what I would do. I have no doubt President Steele has come to the same conclusions as I, given the exigencies of the situation."

"The *what*?" Dixon demanded.

"The fact that there is such a large number of voters in such dire and immediate need of rescue, and succor," Big Sugar explained. "Given a disaster of such unprecedented scope and severity, combined with the obvious inability of – and lack of sufficient resources for – local authorities to cope, the need for military intervention must be as obvious to him as it is to me."

"Oh," Big Willy responded.

"Now, assuming none of you have further questions regarding my orders," Washington concluded, "let us focus on the task of obtaining civilian clothing. It is critical that we be able to greet our nominal rescuers without arousing their suspicion."

In accordance with their capo's instructions, the gang concentrated on searching closets and dressers, looking for garments with which to replace their prison uniforms. They found suitable attire for Donell, and Dante "Smoove" Woodruff, before Big Sugar called a halt.

"It would be foolish to take more than a few items from each residence," he told them. "The owners are unlikely to miss a mere sample of their clothing. However, should a significant percentage of their wardrobe disappear, they could not help but notice. There are other houses on this block. Let us move on to them."

They had done so. Donell even relocked the door behind them. He carefully replaced the key in its hiding place, and restored the fake stone to its position by the rear steps.

At the second house they visited, his search of the lintel above the back door produced a spare key. The gangsters were able to scrounge nondescript outfits for Big Willy and Wide Load. In a nightstand by the queen-size bed in the master bedroom, Big Willy also found a gun.

"Put that back where you found it, William," Big Sugar told him.

"But, Boss ..." Dixon objected.

"Do not force me to repeat myself, William," Washington warned. "Think! Are you so short-sighted as to believe the owners of this house will fail to notice the disappearance of a firearm they keep by their own bed?"

"I guess not, Boss," Big Willy admitted.

"Put it back, William," Big Sugar demanded.

"Yes, Boss," Dixon meekly replied. "Sorry, Boss."

At the third house, Donell was unable to locate a spare key.

"You want me to break a window, Big Sugar?" he asked.

Washington shook his head.

"No, Donell," he replied. "Let us pass on."

At the fourth house, Big Sugar stopped Jackson from stepping forward.

"Let us see whether anyone has benefitted from the lessons you have provided, Donell," Washington proposed.

Turning to the rest of the gang, he asked, "Who among you would like to demonstrate what he has learned from Donell about the gentle art of night entry?"

"Yo, Boss!" Little Boy volunteered, raising his hand. "I'll do it."

"By all means, brother David."

Big Sugar gestured to the wrought-iron gate in the fence around the back yard.

Confidently, Shabazz stepped forward, grasped the brass knob on the gate, and tried to turn it. It didn't budge. Frowning, Little Boy tried again, with equally unsatisfying results. Stepping back, he put his fists on his hips. Eyes narrowed in concentration, he inspected the gate.

After nearly a full minute of examination, Shabazz abandoned his study of the wrought-iron gate. Instead, he stepped back still further, and critically examined the front of the house. When he spotted a blue, ceramic, garden gnome beside the concrete walk, a wide grin split his dark brown face, revealing a prominent gold incisor. He bent to lift the sculpture, revealing the key beneath.

Donell showed his approval by applauding.

Little Boy bowed in acknowledgment. He used the key to unlock the gate. Stepping through, he held it open for the others to pass into the back yard. Once the last of his fellow gang members entered the rear yard, the spring-loaded gate noisily clanged shut behind them.

Shabazz located the key to the back door in the mouth of a cheerful, green ceramic frog, which squatted five feet from the rear steps.

"We in," he announced triumphantly, flinging open the door.

"Well done, brother David," Washington said, approvingly.

The gang followed Little Boy into the kitchen.

Donell, who brought up the rear, was just closing the door behind them, when a single shot rang out. In the confined space, it was deafeningly loud. The muzzle flash threw their looming shadows on the door.

Startled, heart hammering in his chest, Donell spun around just in time to see Shabazz pitch forward in the gloom. The hulking gangster's body slammed face-forward into the linoleum floor. It sprawled, unmoving, where it fell. Little Boy's fall revealed a whiskery, old, white man with a sparse crew cut, dressed in pajamas and a plaid bathrobe. He held a large revolver in one rock-steady hand and a flashlight in the other. The elderly householder crouched in the doorway to the living room, in a classic combat stance.

"Freeze," the gunman ordered, in a flat, hard voice.

Jackson looked wildly around the cramped, crowded kitchen for an escape route, but found none.

Slowly, Donell raised his hands above his head.

- Bad luck That's all it is. Just bad fuckin' luck. -

May 4 2020, 4:16 am EDT

1 Park Avenue West, New York City, NY

Eydis Finnursdottir slowly, carefully eased herself up off the pelvis of the snoring fat man passed out beneath her. As his shrunken penis fell out of her vagina, a stream of blood and semen followed it, coating the thicket of wiry hair surrounding his genitals. Eydis froze in an uncomfortable, spraddle-legged crouch, and held her breath, willing him to remain asleep.

The recumbent Luis Diaz, sprawled on the white carpet, continued blissfully to snore.

With great deliberation, Eydis rose to her feet, and stepped to one side. For a long moment, she stared down at Diaz, her expression stony. At length, she turned to survey the other occupants of the luxurious co-op.

Her lover Greg, whose parents owned the apartment, lay in the ante room, ominously still. He had been dragged there after Diego Colón, the leader of gang, savagely pistol-whipped him, long hours ago.

Colón himself was passed out in a massive off-white recliner. A half-empty bottle of Patrón Reposado tequila lay on its side on the carpet to his right; a half-smoked cigarillo had burnt an ugly hole in the white shag on his left. Lolling on the nine-foot, cream-colored sectional couch was her third rapist, the hatchet-faced, pockmarked Angel Santiago. Santiago twitched and mumbled in a drunken dream.

It was very dark in the parlor.

Eydis was almost happy about that, because it meant she could not clearly see the bite marks, burns, and bruises that covered her body. She could feel them well enough, though. She was certain, for instance, that her nose was broken. She had to breathe through her mouth, because of it. Her left eye was swollen almost shut, a souvenir of the many times all three of the men who had spent the night raping her had cuffed her with an open hand, or punched her. They had struck her, not because she was in any way failing to perform every degrading action they demanded of her, but purely for the sadistic pleasure of hearing her whimper, as she worked desperately to gratify them.

Without question, it had been the single most horrible and terrifying ordeal Eydis had ever had to endure. She would carry its scars for a long time, she knew – and not all of those scars would be physical. But now, at too long last, there was a slim opportunity to escape her torment. She was determined not to waste it.

Eydis tiptoed over to the recliner where Diego Colón dozed. For a long moment, she merely stood beside him, holding her breath so as not to wake him. Mentally, she rehearsed the actions she must take. So very much depended on her ability to execute them correctly the first time, without error or hesitation. There would be no possibility of a second chance should she fail.

Slowly, she raised her right hand level with her aching breasts. Eydis felt a glacial calm descend over her. Her hand neither trembled, nor wavered, as it slowly descended towards the Glock pistol thrust into Colón's belt. For the briefest of moments, her hand hovered above its target. Then Eydis swooped. She yanked the weapon free, and swiftly skipped backward to evade Colón's grasp, as he sprang from his seat.

"*¡La puta!*" he snarled. "*¡Dome la pistola!* Give me the gun, bitch!"

Eydis shook her head. Her right hand steadily pointed the big, square gun at Colón, her left hand steadying her right.

"Be quiet," she told him, her voice emotionless, "or I will shoot you."

"You don' have the *coraje, gringo puta*," Colón sneered. "Besides, you can' shoot me. The safety she is on."

He reached out towards her, radiating confidence.

Eydis shook her head once more.

"There is no safety," she told him.

She pulled the trigger twice, putting both rounds into the center of Diego Colón's chest. He fell backward. Eydis pivoted on her heel to cover Angel Santiago, who had shaken off his slumber, and was getting up from his repose. As he came to his feet, Eydis shot him twice, as well. His face frozen in surprise, he fell back onto couch, then toppled over sideways and was still.

Eydis turned to face the naked Luis Diaz He had rolled over, and was trying to scramble to his feet. Diaz froze, caught trying to get his feet under him. He looked at her with terror in his eyes.

"*Por Dios* ..." he began.

Eydis shot him twice in the face. He collapsed onto the carpet. An ugly stain began to spread around his shattered head.

Coolly, Eydis stepped over to the unmoving Colón, and shot him once in the forehead. Turning to Angel Santiago, she did the same to him. Then, with all her strength she threw the Glock Model 17 – the exact, NATO-issue model with which her father had drilled her in the fundamentals of gun safety and marksmanship when she was 16 years old – toward the furthest corner of the room. Turning, she ran to her beloved's side, before the overwhelming emotional reaction to the stress of her narrow escape stormed through her.

Eydis fell to her knees. Sobbing, she began to quiver like a spider web in a hurricane.

"Oh, *Greg!*" she cried.

May 4, 4:28 am EDT

Clifford Street, Newark, NJ

Donell Jackson had never been so petrified with fear.

Not when his 14-year-old uncle Deandre James wrecked the car in which they were joyriding. Not when he had been arrested for the first time. Not even when he had initially entered the New Jersey prison system, three years earlier. Never before had he felt the arctic edge of the Reaper's blade so close to his neck. Never before had he realized that the phrase "it scared the shit out of me" could have such literal meaning.

Jackson's profound dread made Big Sugar Washington's calm self-assurance seem all the more remarkable by contrast. While Donell cowered in anticipation of the whiskery old cracker's next shot, Washington stood erect. He seemed unfazed by the sudden, violent demise of David "Little Boy" Shabazz. As the gang boss engaged their elderly captor in conversation, Big Sugar's tone was serene. He did not raise his voice, nor did he allow it to betray any hint of anxiety.

"We appear to be trespassing in your domicile, sir," Washington said. "For that, I apologize. We believed it to be unoccupied. Obviously, we regret that our brother David lost his life in the process of discovering our mistake. I assure you that we had no intent to disturb you. If you will be so good as to permit it, we shall immediately vacate your premises. And, again, I apologize for our intrusion."

"Shut yer yap, nigger," the old man ordered. "You and yer convict buddies ain't goin' nowhere."

"Excuse me, sir," replied Big Sugar, "but are you seriously proposing to hold my friends and I hostage?"

"You talk real fancy for a coon," the man responded, maintaining his combat stance. "You don't listen so good, though. I told you to shut yer fuckin' yap. Now shut it!"

There was steel in the old man's voice. Jackson could tell that, at some point in his life, he had commanded men in uniform – military, police, or both.

Washington regarded their captor, unruffled.

"We do not intend to harm you, sir," he told the old man in the plaid bathrobe, "but we will not voluntarily permit ourselves to be re-imprisoned. Surely you can understand our position."

"Mebbe I should just shoot your black ass," replied the gunman. "You don't shut the fuck up, mebbe I just will."

Big Sugar slowly shook his head. "That would be the gravest possible error on your part, sir."

"Oh yeah?" the oldster replied, amused. "How do you figure?"

"The firearm you are wielding is a Smith & Wesson Model 500, is it not?" Washington inquired.

The gunman nodded slowly, suddenly wary.

"That it is, sonny boy," he confirmed. "Most powerful handgun in the world."

"Indeed," agreed Big Sugar. "If I recall correctly, it holds five, .50 caliber magnum rounds of ammunition, does it not?"

"So?" challenged the old man.

His eyes flickered from one to another of Washington's gang, as he silently totaled the crowd facing him.

"So," Big Sugar told him, "you have already expended one of them on our late brother David. That leaves you with four remaining bullets. You will note that there are six of us still alive. You may well kill three or four before you expend your remaining ammunition, but the survivors will surely overwhelm you."

"You'll be the first to die, big boy" the oldster assured him. "Count on it."

Washington shrugged.

"Everyone dies," he observed. "At least for me it will be quick. Given the stopping power of the .50 caliber magnum round, it may well be all but painless, as well. On the other hand, should you be so foolish as to fire on me or any of my men, I strongly suspect your own demise will be anything but quick and painless."

"You got a goddamn lotta gall to threaten *me*, sonny boy," the old man said.

Big Sugar shook his head.

"You misapprehend me, sir," he explained. "My statement was more of a prediction, than a threat. Should you begin firing on us, I fully expect to be your first victim. However, I then will be unable to dissuade my men from taking vengeance upon you. I think we both realize it is beyond question that they will do so. Thus, you have everything to gain, and literally nothing to lose by continuing our conversation."

"I will be go to fucking Hell," the gunman said, admiration creeping into his voice. "All right, speak yer piece."

"As I said," Washington told him, "we truly had no idea that your home was occupied. Had we known, we would simply have passed it by, and our brother David would still be among the living. I assure you – and you may believe me, because I have nothing to lose by speaking the truth – our intention was not to loot your residence, but merely to obtain suitably-sized civilian clothing in place of our uniforms."

Big Sugar made a production of looking their captor up and down.

"Considering the disparity in our sizes," he continued, "it is clear that your clothes would not be suitable for me. Since brother David's frame was similarly large – and we two were the only members of our band who had yet to obtain civilian clothing – upon inspecting your closet, we would have left your residence and possessions undisturbed, and simply continued our search elsewhere."

"Okay," said the old man with the gun, "Suppose you're tellin' the truth. Now what?"

Washington shrugged, spreading his hands in an almost Gallic gesture of resignation.

"I propose that we do exactly that," he responded. "Leave here, and continue our search elsewhere. If you wish, we will even take poor

David's remains with us, to save you the inconvenience of disposing of them."

The gunman laughed.

"You got more brass than a marching band," he observed. "I swear. You break into my house, I kill your little pal, and now you expect me to just let you waltz away to go break into my neighbors' places? Them's some mighty big balls on you, nigger, I'll give you that."

"Consider the alternatives," Big Sugar invited, "either you begin firing – in which case you and I will both join our brother David – or you attempt to hold us at gunpoint until the proper authorities arrive. That is a proposition which I must tell you my men are likely to resist. How long do you expect to be able to go without sleep, Mr. ...?"

"Fout," the man replied. "Jeremiah Fout."

"Realistically, then, Mr. Fout," said Washington, "both alternatives are unappealing in the extreme. The first is a particularly messy route to mutual suicide, the second is simply unworkable, and would undoubtedly end in tragedy, as well. Why risk a bloodbath that neither of us will survive, when we can simply walk away into the night, and you can continue your vigil until the cavalry appears to save the day."

"Right," said Fout. "I let you go, and you just walk away? Seems unlikely. What's to keep you from burning my place down with me in it?"

Big Sugar again shrugged.

"You will simply have to trust me," he told Fout. "Should you allow us to leave, I give you my word that no harm will come to you as a result."

Fout snorted, derisively.

"The word of a criminal," he sneered.

Washington shook his head.

"No sir," he replied, "the word of a Marine."

Fout's eyes narrowed. "You expect me to believe you were in the Corps?"

"Second Division," Big Sugar told him, "Regimental Combat Team 2. I made Gunnery Sergeant before I mustered out."

"No shit," Fout responded. "What was your specialty?

"Combat rifleman," Washington replied.

"Every Marine," Fout observed.

"Yes, sir," Big Sugar agreed. "But some Marines more than others."

"Combat Team 2, eh?" Fout said. "You see any action?"

"Nasiriyah," Washington replied, "Fallujah, Al Anbar. The usual."

He shrugged.

"Those are some ragged-ass desert shitholes, Sergeant," Fout said.

"Indeed," Big Sugar agreed.

"So, how'd you come by the fancy talk, anyway?" Fout asked.

Washington shook his head.

"With all due respect, sir," he replied, "I have a duty to my men. Rather than further exploring my admittedly fascinating biography, I must insist we focus on resolving this impasse without further casualties. And, to be honest, it would not be to my long-term advantage to reveal to you any more about me than I have already disclosed."

Fout regarded him in silence for a long moment.

Then he said, "Remind me not to play poker with you, Sergeant."

"I trust that situation will never arise," Washington told him.

"All right," Fout said. "You give me your word as a Marine you won't retaliate for me plugging your friend there," he nodded toward Little Boy's corpse, stretched out on the floor in front of him, "and I'll let you and your men walk away."

"You have my solemn oath," Big Sugar assured him.

Fout stuffed the big Smith & Wesson into his belt. He extended his right hand to Washington. Solemnly, Big Sugar stuck out his own massive paw. The two men shook hands.

"Good luck, son," said Fout. "You're gonna need it."

"Thank you, sir," Washington replied. "The same to you."

He turned to face his men.

"Big Willy, Smoove, kindly remove brother David."

He stepped aside to allow "Big Willy" Dixon and Dante "Smoove" Woodruff to pick up Shabazz's body. When they lifted him from the floor, his pulped brain fell out. It squelched noisily on the tile floor.

"Sorry about the mess, sir," Big Sugar apologized.

"Kitchen needed cleaning anyway," Fout observed.

Donell turned to open the back door. He stood aside as Dixon and Woodruff, struggling with the massive body, hauled Little Boy's remains outside. The other gangsters followed Big Willy and Smoove, leaving only Washington and Jackson inside. Donell was therefore the only witness to the final exchange between Big Sugar and Jeremiah Fout.

"I would appreciate it if you would be as circumspect as possible regarding our encounter," Washington told the old man.

"I ain't gonna rat you out, son," Fout told him. "Us Marines gotta stick together."

"Thank you, sir," Big Sugar said. "You will not have cause to regret your decision."

He turned to leave.

"*Semper Fi*, Sergeant," Fout said to Big Sugar Washington's retreating back, "*Semper Fi*."

May 4, 2020, 5:13 am EDT

Treasury Building, Washington, DC

Secretary of the Treasury Anderson Connaught IV was seated at his office desk, in front of a 28-inch widescreen computer monitor. On it, the images of Bernard Lord Silkington, Right Honourable Chancellor of the Exchequer, and Sir Ellston St. John, Chief Executive of the London Stock Exchange Group were displayed in separate windows.

"Good morning, Lord Silkington," Connaught said. "And good morning to you, Sir St. John. Thank you both for taking this call."

Connaught glanced over his shoulder at the man standing behind him.

"I think you both know Rajiv Mehta, my Director of Policy Planning?" he stated.

"Good to see you, Rajiv," Silkington responded.

"Hello, Rajiv," said St. John.

"Gentlemen," Connaught began, "we don't have a lot of time to spare, so you'll forgive me for getting straight to the point. Given the carnage in the Asian markets, the President has asked me to urge you – in the strongest possible terms – to consider declaring a one-week exchange holiday. It might be best if you were to order a halt to private trading, as well. We've already spoken with Geert de Graaf, and he has agreed to our proposal on behalf of ICE. The President hopes you'll also see the wisdom of giving the markets a breather, as Geert has."

St. John snorted dismissively.

"You sodding Yanks think you run the bloody world," he sneered. "We've done perfectly well on our own for the past 1,000 years, and we don't need you yobs telling us how to run our economy, thank you very much."

"Now, Ellston," Silkington admonished, "keep a civil tongue. The Yanks are our friends, after all."

"With friends like them ..." St. John commented.

"Enough, Ellston," Silkington demanded. "Mr. Secretary, what Ellston is trying to say is that we've taken that decision on our own initiative, just minutes ago."

"Thank God," Connaught said fervently.

"And what of your own markets?" Silkington inquired.

"Well, the NYSE, AMEX, and the Nasdaq are all down, of course," Connaught replied. "I'm sure you've seen the satellite photos."

Both Silkington and St. John nodded.

"Terrible thing," Silkington said.

"As for the Pacific Stock Exchange, BATS, Chicago Merchantile Exchange, Chicago Board of Options Exchange, and so on," Connaught continued, "the next calls on my list are to BATS, in Lenexa, Kansas, and the Chicago exchanges, with San Francisco next."

Silkington nodded.

"Good show," he said. "If you don't mind my asking, have you a feel for how the dark pools intend to handle the crisis?"

"Well," Connaught told him, "Instinet and NYFIX are gone, of course. The same goes for Posit/MatchNow."

Silkington nodded. All three companies had been headquartered in New York City.

"Smartpool, as well," Connaught went on. "BlockCross appears to be down – we're attributing that to the evacuation of Boston, of course ..."

"And what of next week?" St. John interrupted. "And the weeks ahead? Surely you aren't proposing we keep our markets shuttered indefinitely?"

Connaught sighed.

"No, of course not, Sir Ellston," he replied. "In the long run, globally speaking, the exchanges will just have to deal with the downdraft as best they can. In the short term, though, we may or may not choose to keep our own exchanges closed for some additional time. Thankfully, that's not a decision we have to make immediately."

He ran a hand across the top of his very expensive, white toupee. He had been up all night, and now he felt old and tired

"We're just going to have to see how things go – and hope this breathing space gives sanity a chance to prevail," he said.

"Given the worldwide economic balls-up this thing has caused," St. John demanded, "I'd like you to explain just what you would bloody well consider a 'sane' response?"

"I wish I could tell you," Connaught responded. "I really do. But I know one thing: simply standing by, and wringing our hands, while a combination of panic and automated trading cause a bloodbath in the world's equity markets isn't it."

"Hear, hear," Silkington agreed.

May 4, 2020, 6:37 am EDT

Pier 88, West 48th Street Freight Station, New York, NY

Chief Petty Officer Curtis Simmons had been on duty for only a little over seven minutes. Already he was running out of patience.

In the wan light of the cloud-crowded dawn, Simmons stood at the base of a hastily-rigged gangway that ran from the edge of Pier 88 to the deck of the aircraft carrier USS John F. Kennedy. In addition to his Navy working uniform, he wore a MK-7 Naval Battle Helmet, with a Beretta 92f service pistol holstered at his side. In his left hand he held a clipboard with a stack of forms. In his right was a Navy-issue ballpoint pen. In front of him a line of civilians stretched in a series of S-curves up the dock to West 48th Street. There, a temporary gate and chain-link fence acted as a chokepoint to restrain the crowd that filled the street as far beyond as the eye could see.

At the head of that line was a woman of late middle age. The gray roots of her brunette-dyed hair were just beginning to show. She wore a Navy blue, thoroughly rain-soaked, Burberry trench coat. In one hand she carried a Navy Davek umbrella, in the other a Hermes Blue Roi Crocodile Birkin. The furry face of a blue-dyed Yorkshire terrier peeked out of her handbag. A royal azure Mandalay evening dress showed through the open front of her coat. Her fingers, throat, and ears all displayed blue emerald or sapphire jewelry. For the past five minutes, CPO Simmons had been attempting without success to explain to the lean, perfectly-manicured socialite that refugees were not permitted to bring pets aboard the Kennedy, regardless of their size.

"Ma'am," he told her for the fourth time, "if I made an exception for you, I'd have to make an exception for everyone else. Do you understand?"

"Certainly not!" the patrician woman replied. "My Cassie isn't any bigger than a minute. As you can see perfectly well, young man, she fits nicely in my bag – where I assure you she is quite comfortable. Are you trying to tell me I can't bring my handbag aboard your great, big boat?"

"No, Ma'am," Simmons responded. "I'm telling you, 'You can't bring your dog aboard.'"

"Why not?" she demanded. "My bag takes up no more space with Cassie in it than without her. So, what difference does it make to *you*?"

"The difference is that I have my orders, Ma'am," said Simmons, "and those orders are very clear: 'no pets on shipboard'."

"And you're such a simpleton that you can't see that making an exception for a tiny, little thing like Cassie will make absolutely no difference?" the woman demanded.

"As I've told you – repeatedly – I have my orders, Ma'am," Simmons replied. "I'm not at liberty to make exceptions to those orders. *Any* exceptions."

"Then I demand to see your Captain!" the socialite told him. "Tell him that Elizabeth Shergold wants to speak with him!"

The line behind her rumbled with discontent.

"Ma'am," said Simmons, gritting his teeth, "that's not going to happen. Captain Plein is too busy to speak to you, or anyone else in this line."

He gestured to the long queue of people behind her.

"You've already taken up far more of my time than you're entitled to," he continued, "and I owe it to all these other people to get on with screening them. So, either ditch the dog, or stand aside. It's your choice."

"How dare you speak to me that way!" huffed the socialite. "The sheer, unadulterated *nerve* of you! You are, without a doubt, one of the rudest, most self-important little men I have ever had the misfortune to encounter!"

"Right back at you," Simmons commented. "Ma'am."

"Make no mistake," she threatened, peering at the name stitched above Simmons's left breast pocket, "Mr. Simmons. My Congressman will hear about this! I assure you, he will see to it that you will regret it."

"With all due respect, Ma'am," Simmons told her, "I already regret it. Now, for the last time, scupper the dog, or stand aside."

"I shall do neither, Mr. Simmons!" Elizabeth Shergold declared. "I know my rights!"

"And I'd like to give you my left," Simmons muttered under his breath.

He turned to the sailors who stood at parade rest behind him, flanking the gangway.

"Spud, Shorty," he ordered, "kindly move this battleaxe out of these good people's way."

Seamen Samuel "Spud" Zawinsky and Farrell "Shorty" Buehl grasped the socialite firmly by her upper arms. They lifted her off her feet, and carried her to one side. The line of refugees behind her erupted in cheers and raucous laughter.

May 4, 7:18 am EDT

Delancy Street, Newark, NJ

Donell Jackson stood dejectedly in the steady, early-morning drizzle. He and his fellow gangsters watched the remains of David "Little Boy" Shabazz burn inside a Kia Sedona they had found crashed into a street light.

"Farewell, brother David," Big Sugar Washington said solemnly. "You were a good man and a good soldier. We shall miss you."

There was a general murmur of agreement from the other members of the mob, gathered in a circle around the burning car.

"And now, gentlemen," Big Sugar advised, "I suggest we remove ourselves from harm's way, before the flames reach this vehicle's fuel tank."

He turned, and began walking briskly toward Pacific Street. His subordinates promptly fell in behind him.

As they trekked toward the intersection of Delancy and Pacific, Jackson caught up with Washington.

Pitching his voice low to keep their conversation private, he commented, "I didn't know you were in the Marines, Boss."

Big Sugar shook his head in amusement.

"I was not, Donell," he replied.

"But ..." Jackson began, flabbergasted, "what about all that shit you told the peckerwood?"

"The biographical details I supplied to Mr. Fout in actuality belonged to our late brother David," Washington told him. "I myself would never have considered joining that brotherhood of courageous fools, Donell. Nor, had I done so, would I have found myself assigned to combat, I assure you."

"How do you figure?" Jackson asked.

"I am far too intelligent and well-educated for the leaders of the Marine Corps to be willing to waste my potential as mere cannon fodder, Donell," Big Sugar replied. "The rank-and-file are, for the most part, noble idiots – but that is less true of their senior officers. I have no doubt that I would have served my theoretical enlistment in a clerical position, rather than in a combat role, like that of our late brother David. Again, however, given my personal predilections, such a situation would never have arisen in the first place."

Behind them, there was a muffled boom, as the Kia's gas tank exploded. As one, they stopped, and turned to look at the inferno that was the funeral pyre of David Shabazz.

At length, Dante "Smoove" Woodruff asked, "So, what now, Boss?"

"Our first priority must be to put as much distance between ourselves and the scene of our late brother David's incineration as practicable," Washington replied. "We must give the Federal authorities no grounds to suspect a connection between it and ourselves."

"That's thinkin', Boss," commented Smoove.

"Thank you, Dante," Big Sugar replied. "However, I suspect your question concerned our somewhat longer-term strategy, did it not?"

Woodruff nodded.

"That's right," he affirmed.

"Then I must tell you, I think we have no choice but to temporarily part company," Washington responded.

"What for?" asked Wide Load Broadus.

"Think, Kendall," Big Sugar replied. "Should we encounter the authorities as six black men together, what is likely to be their immediate reaction?"

Broadus looked doubtful, so Donell spoke up. "They'll think we're a gang."

"Indeed they will," said Washington, nodding approvingly. "Therefore, it is in our best interests to make contact with them as individuals. Under those circumstances, they will be more likely to regard us as refugees – and to treat us accordingly."

"We meet up again, later – right, Boss?" Broadus broke in, eagerly.

"Precisely so," Big Sugar said.

May 4, 8:07 am EDT

Seton Hall University, South Orange, NJ

Second Lieutenant Dolores Anunciacion de la Madonna Pena, commander of 2nd Platoon, 69th Infantry Regiment, 42nd Infantry Division, stood at parade rest in the parking lot of Xavier Hall. The lieutenant surveyed the thin ranks of the National Guard platoon which stood at attention before her. There were far too many faces missing from her New York City-based unit for Pena's peace of mind.

Mentally, she shrugged off her concern for the missing.

- We have a job to do. I need to focus on my part in it. -

Pena lifted her chin. She purposely forced her voice to a low pitch, to imbue it with a tone of command.

"Three days ago, we were all civilians," she began. "Today, we are proud members of the Fighting 69th – a regiment with one of the most glorious records of service in the entire U.S. Army. In recognition of that tradition, Brigade HQ has tasked us with a critically important mission."

Lieutenant Pena paused for effect. She sneaked a glimpse at her platoon sergeant out of the corner of her eye. Sergeant First Class Justin "Kit" Carson's face was impassive. Pena couldn't tell if he approved of her approach to rallying their troops or not. His opinion mattered to her, because today was her first command under active-duty conditions.

- The first time I've been anything other than a pretend soldier. -

Her palms were damp, but she refused to allow her expression and demeanor to betray her apprehension.

"Our orders are to conduct a door-to-door search of the Fallout Zone. Our specific mission is to locate survivors," she continued. "Recon teams have preceded us into the Zone. They have marked safe areas with green flags, and unsafe areas with red flags. It is vital that you be aware of those flags at all times while carrying out your mission. Do not, under any circumstances, stray into red-flagged areas. If you encounter civilians trapped in those areas, instruct them to come to you. If they are shielded within a structure, advise them remain there pending the arrival of a decontamination team.

"In either case, mark the location on your tac map, and call in the location and situation to Brigade HQ. Test all civilians you encounter with your portable radiac units. If you encounter a civilian who is radioactively contaminated, order him – or her – to remain where you find them, pending arrival of a decontamination team. Mark their location on your tactical map, and radio HQ with their location and situation. HQ will send transport for any and all civilians you encounter, so, regardless of circumstances, do not attempt to evacuate them yourselves."

Lieutenant Pena paused again to gauge her troops' reaction to her speech. They seemed attentive. She regarded that as a hopeful sign.

"Remember: your own safety is paramount," she told them. "You are an asset to your country. Don't allow yourself to become a liability."

Pena paused again, before continuing, "Colonel Mabry has also tasked us to be on the lookout for looters. In the course of the current operation, you may encounter civilians who are taking advantage of the lack of police presence to appropriate goods which do not belong to them. It is the policy of the United States government to regard such persons as criminals. Basically, if they're stealing consumer electronics, guns, jewelry, or other valuables, you are to treat them as looters. Take any such criminals you may encounter into custody, mark the location of the encounter on your tac map, and call the incident in to HQ.

"However – and I want to stress here how important it is that you exercise good judgment in this regard – if the goods in question are necessary for survival, such as food, water, lanterns, basic medical supplies, and so forth, you are *not* to treat those persons as looters. If all they've appropriated is food, or water, or other necessities for survival, you are to treat such persons as refugees, not looters. You are to insist they leave those goods behind, but otherwise you are to treat them exactly the same as any other refugees you may encounter."

She let her gaze travel slowly from one end of the formation to the other.

"Are there any questions?" she asked.

No one spoke up.

"All right then," Lieutenant Pena said. "I want you to make those who have preceded us as members of the 69th proud of us, and of what we accomplish here, today and in the days to come. Those who fought, and died at Bull Run, at the Marne, and in Iraq are watching you. Those who were killed securing Ground Zero on 9/11 are counting on you to carry on the tradition of service to civilians in need that they established. And *I* am counting on you to make *me* proud. Remember your heritage as soldiers of the Fighting 69th, and make sure that your actions reflect only credit upon that record."

Pena paused a moment to gauge her troops' reaction to her speech. It seemed to her that, perhaps, they stood a little straighter, a little taller, a little prouder.

"Dismissed," she told them.

She turned to "Kit" Carson, and ordered, "Move 'em out, Sergeant."

May 3, 2020, 8:57 am EDT

Commonwealth Avenue, Boston, MA

Ryan Patrick Cohan coughed, and coughed again. His coughs were shallow, breathy, bubbling things; bare gasps, in comparison to the deep, purgative explosions he had experienced just hours ago.

He felt like weeping at the unfairness of it. This was supposed to be his time of glory; the time when he was at his absolute peak. This was the time when he expected all good things to come to Ryan Cohan.

- Nothing but the best for me. -

Except here he was, dying on the floor of a stranger's bathroom, instead.

Dying. There was no escaping that. Cohan could tell his lungs were filling with fluid. Somehow, he had managed to contract some kind of galloping pneumonia. He knew the symptoms all too well. He knew, too, that only a well-equipped hospital – Massachusetts General, for instance, where he had spent nearly a week in intensive care during his second, and worst bout with the disease – could save him.

Except that Mass General had been completely evacuated on Saturday, along with the rest of his hometown. Even if he could somehow get himself there before his lungs filled up completely, before his air supply shut off for good, there would be no doctors to treat him. He would find no orderlies to intubate him, no paramedics to do chest compressions, no nurses to monitor his vitals, no candy stripers to sponge his forehead, and smooth his sparse hair.

He was, in a word, fucked. Royally, utterly, perfectly fucked.

And the worst thing about it – the thing that most made him want to cry at the unfairness of it all – was that his throat was raw as fresh liver, and his stomach was in full, Bunker Hill-style rebellion. That meant he couldn't even enjoy one last swig of vodka from the supply of miniature bottles he had stolen from the Fairmont Copley Plaza Hotel.

He could only lie there on the floor and die, one increasingly-shallow cough at a time.

May 4 2020, 9:23 am EDT

1 Park Avenue West, New York City, NY

In that moment of twilight awareness when Eydis Finnursdottir began to wake, muzzily suspended in the interstice between dream and reality, she was snuggled spoon-fashion against her beloved Greg Shergold. Comforted by the warmth of his body and his now-intimately-familiar smell, she sighed, and wriggled in pleasure at their physical closeness.

Then, abruptly, she came fully awake. Every appalling detail of the nightmarish ordeal she had so recently undergone came back to her. Her bliss instantly transformed into panic. She sat bolt upright, the pain in her breasts, vagina, and rectum instantly reasserting itself. She barely noticed. Her entire concern was focused on Greg, whose wounds appeared even more hideous now than they had in the pre-dawn gloom.

Her lover's nose was a ruin, smashed flat against his face. The flesh was torn and black with coagulated blood. His eyes were swollen and surrounded by purplish-black bruises. His left zygomatic arch had been crushed by the barrel of Diego Colón's Glock, and there was a visible dent in his skull above his left ear. His breathing, too, was labored and apneatic.

Eydis sprang to her feet. She flew across the parlor to fling wide the window drapes, letting in the light of a clearing sky. Ignoring the lovely view across the expanse of Central Park, she raced back to where her beloved Greg lay unconscious, in the apartment's ante room. She crouched, and bent to gently peel open his eyelids – first one, then the other. As she had feared, his pupils were of distinctly different sizes: the left contracted almost to a pinpoint, the right dilated so far that the iris had all but vanished.

The training she had received as part of the *Slysavarnarfélagið Landsbjörg* – the Scouting-based search-and-rescue organization to which she belonged from the age of 17 until she had graduated college as a *Róverskátar*, at 22 – told her Greg had sustained a serious concussion. There was a strong possibility he had suffered brain damage, as well. It was clear he needed immediate medical attention, and that he would require surgery for the injuries that Diego Colón had inflicted on him.

She longed to surrender to tears, and to the overwhelming wave of hopelessness their situation evoked. Impatiently, she shook off that temptation. Instead, her desperate need to help Greg galvanized her into coldly logical action.

She rose to her feet, and went to the guest bathroom, barely sparing a glance at the trio of corpses that littered the parlor. Soaking a towel, she returned to Greg. Gently, she sponged away the crusted blood that caked his face. She bound a second towel around her lover's head, to compensate for his shattered zygomatic arch.

Eydis took a quick shower, to wash the stench of her rapists off her skin. Feeling better physically and psychologically, she had gone rummaging through Greg's mother's walk-in closet and Chippendale dresser for clothes to replace the ones Colón and his companions had shredded during the long night.

Catching sight of herself in the full-length mirror on the wall of the master bedroom, she could not help but stare. The elegant Navy skirt and Egyptian blue blouse she had appropriated seemed somehow to complement the collection of greenish-purple bruises visible on every exposed surface of her skin.

- What a beauty I am! -

Eydis surveyed her puffy black eyes and crushed nose.

Still driven by the necessities of her predicament, she rifled the kitchen. All she came up with was a half-full box of cinnamon Pop Tarts and a jar of raw honey. Every other foodstuff she found required cooking – and the kitchens' cook top, oven, and microwave all ran on electricity that might never be restored to Manhattan's thoroughly-ruined grid. Grimacing at the surfeit of sugar, Eydis nonetheless forced herself to consume both the pastries and the honey, recognizing the need to replenish her body's energy for the task that lay ahead of her.

Then she re-examined the bedrooms, looking for materials with which she could build a travois. She discovered the bed frame in what had been Greg's little sister Cissy's room could be taken apart without the use of tools. Silently thanking its unknown designer, she had disassembled Cissy's bed. She used the frame's rails, the bed clothing, and her considerable knowledge of knots to construct the transport. In a stroke of good luck, a quick scan of the room's closet turned up a My Little Pony backpack, which provided her with the basis of a shoulder harness for the device.

Gently, Eydis rolled the comatose Greg onto the completed transport's frame. She tied him securely onto the travois with belts taken from his father's closet, and covered him with a layer of coats. Then, thinking about the distance they must travel, she filled as many plastic bottles as she could find with water from the kitchen tap, and tucked them in around her beloved.

Finally, she was ready to bid farewell to the luxuriously-appointed co-op she and Greg had hoped would be a refuge from the cold, wet streets of Upper Manhattan – that had, instead, turned out to be a deadly trap. Eydis tucked Diego Colón's freshly-reloaded Glock 17 into the waistband of her borrowed skirt. Shrugging into the shoulder harness of her improvised travois, she spent a long moment gazing at the grievously-injured Greg.

"I shall save you, my love," she told him. "I promise this."

Squaring her thin shoulders, Eydis Finnursdottir began her painstaking descent of the building's northeastern staircase.

May 4, 2020, 10:07 am EDT

The House Chamber of the Capitol Building, Washington, DC

The Honorable Alvin Spreckels, Speaker of the House and Florida's 16th Congressional District Representative, banged the gavel on the top of his desk.

"The Clerk will give her report," he ordered, lowering himself into his wing-backed chair.

"Mr. Speaker," replied Clerk of the House of Representatives Mina Tollins-Choate from the desk below the Speaker, "the Clerk of the Senate sends word that the Senators have passed by voice vote Senate Resolution 199, this House concurring, declaring a continuing emergency session of the Senate and of the House, which shall not adjourn until Monday, May 21, 2020, unless the leadership of both Houses shall agree to adjourn in the meantime."

"Thank you, Madam Clerk," Spreckels responded. "The Chair recognizes the Member from the 1st District of Idaho, for the purpose of a one-minute speech."

"Mr. Speaker," requested Representative Easau Piltch, speaking from the front row of seats on the Republican side of the chamber, "I ask unanimous consent to address the House for one minute, and to revise and extend my remarks."

"Hearing no objection," the Speaker responded, "the Member is granted one minute to speak."

"Thank you, Mr. Speaker," Piltch said.

Standing, he made his way to the podium in the Well of the House.

"Mr. Speaker," he announced, "I rise to demand the impeachment of the Tyrant William Orwell Steele, and to offer particulars of a resolution to that end."

The gallery above the floor, which was crowded with visitors, instantly exploded in hisses, catcalls, and outraged shouts of disapproval. Alvin Spreckels pounded his gavel repeatedly, and with increasing force.

"Order!" he demanded. "Order! There will be order in the gallery, or the Chair will have it cleared!"

Slowly, reluctantly, the hubbub subsided.

The Speaker turned his glowering focus to Piltch, still standing in the Well. With his chin thrust out, Spreckels's cascade of wattles and extra chins was even more imposing than usual.

"Representative Piltch," he grated, "you are out of order. The Chair will not tolerate incivility in any form. I remind you that this House has rules which forbid the use of insults in referring to the Chief Executive."

"Mr. Speaker," Piltch responded, "with respect, I wish to point out that the term 'tyrant' is an objective description of the President's current status. I therefore respectfully refuse to withdraw my remark."

Furious, Spreckels pounded his gavel.

"I repeat: 'The Member is out of order,'" he barked, purpling with rage. "Your time has expired, Mr. Piltch. The Member will remove himself from the Well."

"Again, with respect," Piltch countered, "I beg leave to have the substance of my charges against the Tyrant William Orwell ..."

"*You are out of order!*" the Speaker thundered, as he rose from his seat.

He pounded his gavel.

Turning to his right, he ordered, "The Sergeant-at-Arms will display the Mace to the Member!"

Atticus Martial Freed, Sergeant-at-Arms of the House of Representatives, rose from his chair to Spreckels's right.

He hoisted the ceremonial mace from its pedestal, behind and to the right of the Speaker's desk. Using his right hand, he grasped the bottom of the shaft of 13 ebony rods bound with silver bands. With his left, he steadied the heavy construct, holding it near the globe and eagle at its top. Carrying the symbolic weapon, he advanced from the upper level of the rostrum toward the podium in the Well, where Piltch stood, defiant.

"Mr. Speaker," Piltch insisted, "I object to this heavy-handed and unseemly attempt to silence a member of this House! I will be heard, Sir! I will be *heard*!"

Carrying the heavy mace, Freed approached Piltch. The Sergeant-at-Arms presented the ceremonial bludgeon to the fractious Representative.

"Congressman, the Chair has ruled you out of order. I am therefore compelled to ask you …" he began.

"Get that thing out of my face!" Piltch demanded.

Vigorously, with the strength of a lifelong outdoorsman who split firewood for relaxation, he shoved the offending object back at Freed.

Surprised by the Representative's assault, and off-balance from the awkward weight of the mace, the Sergeant-at-Arms tripped, and went down, falling over backwards. His head hit the floor of the Well with a sickening crack. The 15-inch-wide, solid-silver eagle atop the four-and-a-half-inch silver globe that together formed the head of the mace fell from his nerveless hands. It smacked into his dark face with an audible thump.

Piltch screeched in shock, and jumped back from the podium.

Spreckels angrily pounded his gavel.

"Guards!" he shouted. "Arrest that man! *Guards!*"

The Capitol building had been crawling with police since the May Day bombing. Now two of them sprinted from the Cloakroom down the aisle toward the hapless Representative.

Piltch mumbled, "But … but … I didn't mean …"

Atticus Freed lay very still. A pool of blood began forming around his head, staining the peacock-blue and gold carpet dark red.

May 4, 2020, 11:12 am EDT

Seneca Temporary Housing Facility, Romulus, NY

"Now, let me get this straight," asked Sean Halloran, Sr., "You're askin' me to inform on Adam Manson for ya?"

"Exactly," FBI Senior Field Agent Howard Klinger replied.

Halloran shook his head, frowning. "I don't like the idea," he said.

"Before you say 'no', you should really think it over," urged Klinger's partner, Timothy O'Reilly.

"I don't have to think about it," Halloran told him. "I'm no rat, regardless of what I think of Adam."

"Mr. Halloran," Klinger responded, in a placating tone. "May I call you Sean?"

Halloran shrugged.

"Call me Peggy, if ya want," he said. "I'm still not goin' to change my mind."

More than two hours of bureaucratic runaround had left Halloran than a little bit on edge.

After returning from breakfast at one of the Seneca Facility's giant mess tents, he set off on his quest to obtain new quarters for his family – quarters they wouldn't have to share with the shaven-headed, sex-crazed, heavily-tattooed Adam Manson and his submissive, hook-nosed wife Ruby, or their three, energetic, tow-headed boys.

He'd first encountered a harassed-looking schlub of a man named Aldon Quarleman, whose office door had proclaimed him to be the FEMA facility's Housing Director.

Quarleman patiently explained that the only other choices available to the Hallorans were to move to a barracks tent – which they would share with a 120 other refugees – or to accept relocation to another temporary housing facility in Nevada or Arizona. And, no, regretfully, Sean Sr.

Thom Stark

would be able to take with him neither his pickup truck nor his expensive collection of tools, currently locked in the Titan toolbox bolted to the Sierra's bed.

Halloran didn't care for either alternative.

He tried to explain to Quarleman about Adam Manson's collection of racist tattoos, and his proclivity for prolonged and noisy sex with Ruby. The Housing Director remained politely, but unwaveringly firm on the subject. He refused to create a precedent, by allowing the Hallorans to swap assignments with some other couple that had been lucky enough to draw one of the prized cabin tents as their temporary housing.

"Look, Mr. … Halloran, was it?" Quarleman had told him. "I understand you don't like your tent mates. I really do. But, from what you've told me, Mr. … I believe you said his name was Manson? Mr. Manson has not physically threatened you or your wife in any way. Is that correct?"

Halloran grudgingly allowed that it was.

"Then I'm afraid my hands are tied," Quarleman said. "If I approve your request to switch assignments, merely because you dislike your tent mates, I'll be forced to allow everyone who complains to do so – or else lay myself open to charges of favoritism. Either alternative would be bad for the residents' morale. And, frankly, it would cause me, personally, a considerable amount of unnecessary stress and superfluous additional paperwork. I neither need the one nor want the other. Now, if you don't mind, I have many urgent matters to attend to. I'm sorry, but this interview is over."

Frustrated and defeated, Sean Sr. left Quarleman to his overflowing desk. To demonstrate his displeasure, he deliberately slammed the bureaucrat's office door on his way out.

To his surprise, as he stalked toward the entrance of the state police academy FEMA had taken over as its headquarters, he was intercepted by Klinger and O'Reilly. The FBI agents had invited him to join them for a cup of coffee, and "a little chat."

That had been nearly two hours ago. Since then, Klinger and his partner had been by turns encouraging, demanding, and flattering. In the process, they elicited from Sean Sr. everything he knew about Adam Manson.

"Listen, Sean," Klinger continued, "I want you to think of this, not as us asking you to rat Manson out, but inviting you to help us keep an eye on a man with links to a dangerous domestic terrorist organization."

Halloran folded his arms across his chest.

"Yeah, okay," he said, in a tone of profound disinterest.

"This is important," Klinger told him. "Adam Manson is a long-time member of the Aryan Revolutionary Front. They're a neo-Nazi group that advocates race war and revolution. We have reason to believe they're planning to take advantage of the disruption caused by Friday's bombing to conduct acts of armed insurrection."

He paused to gauge Halloran's reaction. Sean Sr. kept his best poker face in place, giving away as little as possible.

"We need your help to stop them, Sean," Klinger continued. "Right now, you're in a position to render a unique service to your government and your country. We're asking you to do the right thing. You need to step up, and accept your responsibility to help us make America a safer place."

Halloran remained expressionless.

"If you won't do it out of patriotism," Klinger added, "at least do it for the sake of your wife and son."

Sean Sr. made a wry face.

"I'm serious, Sean," Klinger insisted. "Manson and his crowd are bad actors. The worst. If we don't stop them, they're going to make this country an even scarier and more dangerous place than it already is. You – Sean Halloran, Sr. – can help us do that. And, if you do, I assure you that your country will be eager to demonstrate its gratitude."

"Yeah?" Halloran said, showing interest for the first time. "And what do ya mean by, 'demonstrate its gratitude'? How, exactly, is it gonna do that?"

The two FBI agents exchanged glances.

After a moment, Klinger answered, "You understand I can't make any specific promises, until we see what kind of intelligence you're able to develop, right?"

"Uh huh," replied Halloran.

His expression was once again remote.

"But," Klinger continued smoothly, "the least you can expect is to be relocated to a nice, little house in the suburbs, somewhere far away from here, where nobody will recognize you. We'll give you the house, of course. There'd also be a modest stipend to cover your expenses."

"I'm listenin'," Sean Sr. grudgingly admitted.

"Naturally, we'll pay you for your time and trouble."

"Yeah?" Halloran asked. "How much?"

Carefully controlling his excitement, Klinger replied offhandedly, "Well, once again, that would depend on the quality of the intelligence you provide. Let's say, a couple of thousand dollars a week, to start off. Then up or down from there, depending."

Halloran's poker face remained in place.

"And how about my family's safety – can ya guarantee that?" he asked.

Once again, the agents exchanged a look.

"Insofar as that's possible?" Klinger responded. "Absolutely."

"'Insofar as that's possible,'" Sean Sr. repeated. "Ya know, I'm just not sure what that means. What does it mean to *you*?"

Klinger spread his hands, temporizingly.

"We'll extract you and your family from any threatening situation you might encounter – by force, if necessary," he explained. "And, of course, we'll put you in the witness protection program, once you've gotten as much information from Manson as possible. But we'll need you to wear a wire."

Halloran shook his head.

"I don't think that's ah good idea," he said.

"Why not?" Klinger asked. "It would be for your own protection."

"I'm no kinda actor," Sean Sr. told him. "If ya make me wear a wire, Adam will know somethin's up, for sure."

Klinger and O'Reilly both seemed unconvinced.

He added, "I'm just tryin' to be honest with ya. I don't think I can pull off wearin' a wire. What else ya got?"

The FBI agents put their heads together, and conversed briefly, in low, urgent tones.

Then Klinger replied, "What if we gave you a ... I dunno ... let's say, a boombox? You can tell Manson you bought it at the canteen – and we'll make sure the same model is stocked there, in case he checks. Can you pretend it's just a boombox?"

"Even though it's not really a boombox, ya mean?" Halloran asked.

"Oh, it'll be a boombox, all right," Klinger assured him. "It'll play CDs ... have a radio, do Wi-Fi streaming. You'll be able to plug your phone into it – all that stuff. It'll all work."

Halloran nodded.

"I could prob'ly get away with that," he told them.

"Then we have a deal?" Klinger asked, extending his right hand.

"Yeah," Halloran said, shaking on it, "I think we do."

May 4, 2020, 12:03 pm EDT

Clay St., Hackensack, NJ

Donell Jackson had a bad feeling, the moment the unlocked front door of Latonya Gramble's rented duplex swung open. A now-familiar, sickeningly-sweet, yet repulsive odor greeted him as he entered. The interior was shrouded in gloom, shades drawn and curtains closed against the rapidly-increasing brightness of the first day since the passage of Tropical Storm Beth.

Jackson had taken leave from Big Sugar Washington some hours earlier. Before they parted, he revealed to Big Sugar his intent to rescue Latonya Gramble and her sweet, lively, young daughter Nakeesha from Hackensack.

"Donell," Washington told him, "I must assume you realize that Hackensack will have experienced much heavier fallout than has Newark. You may find that your woman and her child have already fallen victim to radiation poisoning. If that is the case, you will be risking potentially lethal exposure to yourself in what may well be a fruitless attempt at their rescue."

"I know that, Boss," Jackson admitted, "but I have to try."

He felt compelled to explain his determination to Big Sugar.

"Latonya, she's … she's not a strong woman," he said. "But she's been good to me. Real good. And her daughter Nakeesha? When you meet her, you'll understand what a special little girl she is. It's hard to explain."

Washington regarded him in silence for a moment. His expression was sober.

Then he observed, "Donell, it is clear to me that you care for this woman and her child."

Jackson nodded. "Yes I do," he said.

Big Sugar reached out, and put a gigantic hand on Donell's shoulder.

"Then do what you must," he instructed. "Should you survive, I will see you in Asbury Park."

"I'll be there," Jackson promised. "All three of us will be there."

"I wish you good luck," Washington told him.

"Thanks, Boss," Donell replied.

He and Big Sugar turned in opposite directions, to go their separate ways.

Donell started out for Hackensack on foot, but he quickly realized he needed transportation. Without it, just getting to his destination would take most of the day. He knew little about the hazards of radiation exposure, but it seemed obvious that the longer he spent in the area immediately downwind from Manhattan, where the fallout had been heaviest, the greater would be his exposure. Dying nobly was no part of his plan. What he intended was to rescue Latonya and Nakeesha, and get the three of them away from Hackensack as quickly as possible.

As soon as he was out of Big Sugar Washington's sight, he began trying garage doors, hoping to find one that had been left unlocked. It took nearly two hours before his search was rewarded. That particular garage was empty, except for one delirious, clearly terminally-ill, homeless man of indeterminable age. Donell had passed on, leaving the man to his misery.

- Huh-uh. Can't save the whole world. Can't even try. -

An hour later, in full daylight and lightly-drizzling rain, Jackson came upon a second garage with an unlocked side door. Inside it, he discovered a half-disassembled Harley-Davidson Fat Boy motorcycle and a pink, Huffy 20-inch girl's bicycle. With a regretful glance at the gutted Harley, he rolled the Huffy outside, awkwardly mounted it, and began to pedal East.

He stuck to freeways as much as possible, both to avoid the hassle of navigation and to limit his exposure to radiation. He figured the pounding rains of the past two days would have washed asphalt and concrete mostly free of fallout. By contrast, areas of dirt or vegetation, and cracks in sidewalks and along curbs would tend to collect it. Surface streets, Donell decided, were likely to be much more dangerous than the

Interstate – assuming he stayed away from the highway's shoulder and median strip.

The New Jersey Turnpike was a sea of dead automobiles and trucks. Jackson passed myriads of vehicles that had been abandoned by their drivers when the EMP from the bomb fried their electronic fuel injection systems. It had been a long, weary ride for a man so long unaccustomed to pumping pedals. That the bicycle was several inches too short for his long legs did not help.

After several hours of increasingly-exhausting exercise, Donell crossed over to the Expressway, at Ridgefield Park. A little while later, just north of Teterboro, he took the Polify Road exit. He was at last back in Hackensack.

Cycling along Polify was an eerie experience. A deathly quiet lay over the city. No birds sang. In the light breeze, under clearing skies, only the trees moved. Here and there along the street lay the corpse of a dog, or cat, or pigeon, just beginning to bloat.

The smell of decay was omnipresent. He crossed Essex Street into downtown Hackensack, and Polify Road became 1st Street. The profound silence of what should have been a bustling cityscape began to wear away his courage.

Every synapse in his brain screamed at him.

- This is wrong! Run from this place! Death is here! -

Pedaling along 1st Street, his knees aching from the strain, Jackson wrestled with his fears. Only stubborn determination, and loyalty to Latonya and her sweet, young daughter kept him on course for Clay Street.

Passing Hackensack High School, Donell's spirits began to rise. He knew he was only three short blocks from Clay Street, as the school's ball fields passed on his right. His reunion with Latonya and Nakeesha, about which he had spent so many long, lonely nights fantasizing, was only minutes away. Then he made the turn onto Clay Street. Seconds later he was in Latonya's driveway.

Stepping into the darkness of Latonya's rented duplex, Jackson automatically flipped the light switch. He was momentarily surprised when the gloom persisted. From sheer habit, he flipped the switch again before realization struck.

- Oh, yeah – power's out, dummy. -

"Latonya?" he called.

There was no answer. Donell heard the sound of running water coming from the unit's tiny bathroom.

"La-*ton*-ya?" he repeated.

His tone was demanding now.

Still there was no answer.

"Nakeesha?" he called.

Jackson's query was met with an anguished wail. It was a sound of loss and grief so profound, it raised the hair on the back of his neck. As the cry of anguish continued, the backs of his arms pebbled with goose pimples.

Heedless of obstacles, Donell raced toward the dwelling's tiny bathroom. As he reached the narrow doorway, his eyes – still adjusted to the brightness of daylight – strained to pierce the shadows. The shower was running.

"Latonya?" Jackson asked, his voice breaking.

"D ... Donell?" came her response.

"I'm here, baby," Jackson told her.

In two swift steps, he reached the bathtub, bent, and scooped Latonya's unresisting body into his arms. He barely noticed the cold water hammering on his back, as he lifted her shivering form out of the tub. Tenderly, he carried her into the living room.

Laying her trembling form on the couch, Donell ran to sweep back the curtains. Outside light filled the room for the first time in three days. When he turned to look at her, he caught his first glimpse of the ugly mass of blisters that covered the left side of Latonya's face.

"Fuck, Latonya!" Jackson cried, repulsed by her disfigurement.

Love and pity overcame his revulsion. He dropped to his knees beside her.

"What happened to you, girl?" he asked, tenderly. "And where's Nakeesha?"

Immediately, Latonya Gramble again began to keen her loss, grief, and guilt. A terrible sense of foreboding gripped Donell.

"Latonya!" he demanded, shaking her roughly, knowing what her answer would be, yet unable to resist the compulsion to ask, "Where's *Nakeesha*?"

May 4, 2020, 1:08 pm EDT

The White House Situation Room, Washington, DC

William Orwell Steele leaned back in his chair, and threw the red Top Secret folder onto the long, rectangular table. He looked around the table at the assembled members of his National Security council. Keenly aware that her husband lay comatose and dying in the Vice Presidential Mansion, he was somewhat surprised to see Diana Hunter among them.

The President turned to his Secretary of Internal Security.

"All right, Arleigh," he ordered, "walk me through it. What does this," he tapped the red folder in front of him, "mean?"

"Well, Mr. President," Arleigh Solomon replied, "as nearly as we can determine, the pieces fit together like this: Friday night, around midnight, a stolen Toyota mini-van crashed into the gate of the Pakistani embassy. The embassy's security people called DCPD to report it – and to complain about the quality of American security. That tells us they weren't expecting visitors."

"Go on," Steele invited.

"Inside the van were two bodies," Solomon continued. "One was the van's owner, a woman named Elsa Jean Brophy. She had been shot twice at close range, by a gun belonging to the second fatality. According to his driver's license and passport – both of which were found on the body – he was one Timothy James Hilliard of Long Island.

"Sir, here's where it gets interesting. It turns out that Mr. 'Hilliard' died of severe radiation poisoning. In fact, his body was so radioactive that the assistant Medical Examiner who did the preliminary autopsy had to be hospitalized. So have the ambulance attendants who transported Mr. 'Hilliard' and Mrs. Brophy to the morgue."

"Really," the President said.

His tone made it a statement, rather than a question.

"Yes, sir," Solomon confirmed. "And it gets better. When the FBI took charge of the case on Sunday, they checked the validity of Mr. Hilliard's passport with State. It's a forgery. A very good forgery, but a forgery, nonetheless."

"That's interesting," Steele observed.

"Yes, sir," Solomon agreed, "Also interesting is the fact that Mr. Hilliard had some $10,000 in Krugerrands, sewn into the waistband of his trousers."

The President frowned.

"So it's the Pakistanis, then," he stated.

"I hesitate to jump to any conclusions, sir," Solomon cautioned, "but, yes, it's starting to look that way."

"Nail it down, Arleigh," Steele said. "I want this airtight."

"We're working on it, sir," Solomon assured him.

He turned to John Clune, Director of the FBI, who sat across the table from him.

"Director Clune," he said, "why don't you take it from here?"

"Thank you, Arleigh," Clune replied. "Mr. President, Mr. 'Hilliard's' drivers license appears to be genuine, as far as we can tell. Our assumption is that he was a deep-cover agent – which would mean he assumed the identity of an American infant who died around 35 years ago. As you might expect, doing a records search in New York State is a little problematic, at the moment, but we have made checking into Mr. 'Hilliard's' background a priority. I expect a comprehensive report within the next 24 to 48 hours. Our genetics staff suggested we also run a comparison of Mr. Hilliard's DNA against the National Geographic Society's international database, and we're doing that now. That should give us a pretty good idea of Mr. Hilliard's ethnic background. We expect to have the results of those tests within 24 to 48 hours, as well."

"Why? What will that tell you?" Steele asked.

"Mr. President," Clune responded, "Mr. 'Hilliard' had green eyes and blond hair. Ordinarily, that would be enough to deflect suspicion from Pakistan, in and of itself. However, it turns out there's a Pakistani tribe called the Kalash. Some of them have green eyes and light brown or blond hair."

"Really?" President asked.

"Yes, sir," Clune said. "Apparently they claim to be descended from soldiers who invaded Pakistan with Alexander the Great's army. However, the National Geographic's genetic database doesn't seem to bear that assertion out."

"Now that *is* interesting," Steele commented.

"Yes, sir," Clune agreed, "it is."

"Director Murdock, would you give us the foreign intelligence perspective?" Arleigh Solomon asked.

"Gladly," replied Christopher Murdock, Director of the Central Intelligence Agency. "Mr. President, we're currently attempting to acquire a high-value asset in Islamabad. Assuming we succeed, we hope to discover from him whether the ISI was involved in Friday's attack, and, if so, to what degree."

"What do you mean by 'attempting to acquire a high-value asset'?" Steele inquired.

"Sir," Murdock said, "believe me when I tell you that you don't want to know."

The President paused. He gave Murdock a long, thoughtful look, before responding.

"In this case, I believe I do want to know," he replied. "Forget deniability for the moment – in plain English, we're talking about your operatives kidnapping a high-ranking member of the ISI, are we not?"

Murdock glanced at Ken Watanabe, the Presidential Counsel. The President's lawyer pursed his lips, but remained silent. Murdock returned his gaze to Steele.

"Yes, Mr. President," he admitted. "We are."

"Who?" Steele demanded.

Murdock licked his lips, then responded, "General Rashid Omar Sheikh, the Director of ISI's Joint Intelligence Miscellaneous Department. Mr. President, if the Paks were responsible for the bombing, it would have been his shop that planned it, and carried it out. Sheikh himself would've had to sign off on every aspect of planning and operations. If the Paks did it, he's the guy who's responsible."

"Mr. Director," Steele asked softly, "do you recall the circumstances under which you became Director of the CIA?"

"Vividly," Murdock replied. Then he hastily added, "Sir."

When the CIA's attempt to eliminate the Director General of Pakistan's Inter-Service Intelligence Directorate had gone badly – and very publicly – awry, his predecessor had deservedly taken most of the blame. Murdock had inherited command of an agency that was widely considered to be completely out of control. The blowback from the botched assassination caused a massive rupture in relations between Pakistan and the United States. It also had led directly to a Congressionally-mandated, major reorganization of the Department of Homeland Security, including renaming it as the Department of Internal Security.

"With that firmly in mind – do what you have to do, Chris," the President told him. Then, eyes narrowed and voice stern, he added, "And, whatever you do, don't fuck this up. If we're wrong about Pakistan being responsible, things could get very, very ugly, very, very quickly. Do I make myself clear?"

"Yes, sir," Murdock assured him. "Crystal. Our people in Islamabad are very aware of the risks involved, so they're using only native Pak assets for the … acquisition. If they blow it … well, let's just say there are contingency plans in place to cut any links back to the Agency."

"These aren't the same people who fucked up the Shirani hit, are they?" Steele demanded, sharply.

"Oh no, sir," Murdock replied. "Those officers were terminated."

The President looked aghast.

"You don't mean … ?" he asked.

"No, sir," Murdock hastily assured him. "I only meant they were immediately fired from their posts – and retired from the Agency. We don't do ... the other thing ... unless there's actual treason involved."

Steele took a deep breath.

"All right," he said. "Keep me informed on your progress – and by that I mean all three of you."

There was a chorus of "yes sirs" from the three intelligence community Directors.

"So, what's next on the agenda?" the President asked.

"Sir?" Diana Hunter responded. "If I may?"

"Please do, Madam Vice President," Steele replied, mindful of her plea for greater involvement in the Administration's leadership and decision making.

"In view of the fact that you've scheduled your first news conference since Friday's bombing for this evening," Hunter pointed out, "I suggest we address the issue of whether we had any warning of the attack. If so, you'll need to be able to address the source or sources of that intelligence, its quality, and so on."

Solomon looked as if he had bitten deeply into a lemon. Murdock's features tensed.

"Mr. President," Hunter added, "you know the press is going to ask the question. It won't just be Fox, either. Given the Bush administration's history of disregarding CIA warnings about Al Qaeda in advance of the 9/11 attacks, the media is automatically going to assume incompetence on our part, at best. We need to be prepared for that."

Steele nodded. "You're right, of course," he replied.

He looked first to his right, at Solomon, then left at Murdock and Clune.

"So," he asked, "what did we know, and when did we know it?"

May 4, 2020, 11:14 pm PKT (2:14 pm EDT)

Street 58, Sector F-7/4, Islamabad, Pakistan

Bashir Qadir Durrani let the gray Mercedes E550 sedan – a car so commonplace on the streets of Islamabad that it was practically invisible – drift to a stop. It came to rest in front of a wide, wrought-iron gate in the stucco wall that enclosed a tile-roofed, Mediterranean-influenced mansion. The house was nearly invisible in the shade of the spreading, paper mulberry trees surrounding it.

Guards in camouflage-pattern, Pakistan Army duty uniforms and black berets stepped toward the Mercedes. The soldiers' faces were hard, in the light of the gibbous moon. Durrani rolled his window down, stuck his head out, and smiled sheepishly.

In Pashto, he said, "A thousand apologies, brothers, but we seem to have lost our way. Might I trouble you for directions to Street 58, in Sector F-8/4?"

The older of the two guards stepped forward, still frowning, but with noticeably less hostility in his expression His chevrons identified him as a *naik* – the Pakistani equivalent of a corporal.

The *naik* replied, "You must show me your papers."

His companion, a lance *naik*, stood back, his Heckler & Koch MP5K submachine gun held ready.

"Of course, of course," Durrani said.

He pulled his head back, and rolled his body slightly towards the window as he reached for his waist. In the passenger seat behind him, Hameed Rehman Davi rolled down his own window.

The *naik* flinched in alarm, and quickly stepped back.

"Hands up!" the *naik* barked. "You must step out of the car!"

"Of course! Certainly," Durrani told him, his hands still below the level of the window. "I am opening my door now, you see?"

Both guards' eyes flicked towards the driver. In the back seat, Davi smoothly pulled, aimed, and fired his silenced Glock 17, downing the lance *naik* with two shots to the chest. He then turned his fire on the remaining soldier, as the senior guard's finger tightened on the trigger of his own MP5K. Durrani, who had his own pistol raised by then, fired twice. The silenced, 9mm rounds caught the *naik* in the throat and mouth. He fell over backward, fountaining blood.

The street was once again quiet. The four men in the Mercedes, shawls wrapped as masks around their faces, leaped out of the car. Two of them dragged the bodies of the soldiers into the shadows by the iron gate.

Davi began scaling the portal. Durrani unzipped the fanny pack he wore under his *kameez* and *achkan*, and pulled out a three-ounce, spray can of flat black enamel. He handed it up to Davi, who methodically covered the lens of the surveillance camera above the gate with paint.

Durrani returned to the Mercedes, closing the other three doors before getting back behind the wheel of the still-running automobile. He turned off the headlights, and lit up a Diplomat filter-tip cigarette. Then he pulled a map of the city out of the glove box, and pretended to study it.

Meanwhile, Davi and the other two passengers – Fahad Abbas Afridi and Younis Masood Khakwani – climbed over the wrought-iron gate. They quietly made their way up the concrete driveway toward the sprawling house in the center of the grounds.

Ten minutes later, Durrani's cell phone rang. He glanced at the caller ID to confirm it was Davi calling, then pressed the talk button.

"Yes?" he answered.

"We have acquired the packages," Davi told him. "We are wrapping gifts now."

"I await your delivery," Durrani replied.

He was relieved to hear that Davi, Afridi, and Khakwani had located, and subdued all the residents of the mansion. According to Davi's coded message, they were now busy securing their captives with zip ties, and silencing them with ball gags. He turned in his seat, as if to try to better see his map in the moonlight. Durrani kept a careful watch on the house's driveway over the top of the document.

In less than five minutes, he heard a distinct clack as the wrought-iron gate was unlocked remotely from the house. Shortly afterward, a black Mercedes GL550 SUV, its lights off, eased through the open gate. Durrani put his own vehicle in gear, and let it roll forward far enough to allow the SUV to exit onto the street behind him. He shifted back into park, then reached under the dashboard, and unlocked the E550's trunk.

The SUV pulled onto the street, and parked at the curb behind the sedan, facing the opposite direction. Fahad Afridi and Younis Khakwani leaped out, and raced to the back of the car. They swiftly transferred the trussed, unconscious body of General Rashid Omar Sheikh, Director of the ISI's Joint Intelligence Miscellaneous Department, from the GL550's cargo compartment to the E550's trunk. Afridi then climbed into the front passenger seat of the GL550, while Khakwani slid into the E550 next to Durrani.

Going in opposite directions toward the ends of the block-long, tree-lined street, both automobiles pulled away from the curb at the same instant.

May 4, 2020, 3:10 pm EST

8th Avenue, New York, NY

Eydis Finnursdottir was utterly exhausted.

Straining against the straps of her improvised travois, she weaved from side to side, like a drunk on the wrong side of a three-day bender. Her neck and shoulders were on fire with the strain of almost six hours spent pulling the unconscious body of Greg Shergold along the eerily-silent streets of Manhattan.

When she had set out from the co-op that belonged to Greg's parents', she knew she would be facing a severe test of stamina and determination. Even so, she had not been prepared for such agonizingly slow progress. The steel bed-rails that made up the legs of the travois screeched, and gave off sparks, as they dragged over the rough concrete of New York's streets. Their unpadded ends dug into the tops of her shoulders, like blunt knives. In the past few hours, she had repeatedly considered abandoning her construction, and carrying Greg on her shoulders, instead – but logic and common sense had always prevailed.

- As bad as this is, surely that would be worse, yes? –

The only answer was obvious.

- Yes. Surely it would. -

Eydis had pulled the improvised travois along 8th Avenue, through a city that reeked of death. Her route was littered with the corpses of pigeons, dogs, and the occasional homeless person, huddled in a doorway. All were victims of the fallout that had blanketed the city, until Tropical Storm Beth's pounding rains washed the worst of it away.

No one she encountered had offered to help her with her burden. Twice she had been compelled to pull the late Diego Colón's Glock 17 out from its hiding place, to warn men with ragged clothes and hungry eyes to stay away.

She had been forced to stop often, to rest. At first, it had been every couple of blocks, but her pauses had steadily increased in number as the hours wore on. Lately, she had been left with no choice, but to halt two or three times for each block she traveled. She knew that she had utterly exhausted her reserves of energy. For the past hour or more, only determination and willpower had kept her going. Both were now swiftly failing.

Turning the corner onto 48th Street, Eydis spied a vast crowd of refugees, filling the street ahead. Most of its members faced toward Pier 88, the USS John F. Kennedy, and the promise of rescue.

The guttering flame of hope flared anew. With renewed determination, Eydis pulled against the shoulder straps she had fashioned from Cissy Shergold's My Little Pony backpack.

- Just a little farther, my lov. Just a little farther. -

Leaning into the straps across her shoulders, she exerted every remaining scrap of willpower. Eydis forced herself to move one foot forward, to drag her load another precious few inches. Then another. Then the next.

"Just a little farther," echoing in her head like a mantra, Eydis Finnursdottir inched along.

She had long since exhausted her supply of bottled water. Now her thirst was an elemental thing. Her dehydrated body had stopped even sweating, despite her superhuman exertion. The jungle-like humidity and 80-degree weather colluded to cause her core body temperature to soar to feverish heights. Nearing collapse, Eydis tottered on.

She tried to call out for help. All she could manage was a strangled whisper.

After what seemed like hours, she drew close enough to the crowd of refugees that the fingernails-on-a-blackboard screech of the steel bed rails on concrete penetrated the hum of a thousand simultaneous conversations. Heads began to turn in her direction.

The last thing she remembered seeing was a dozen or more men running toward her and her beloved Greg. Then blackness engulfed Eydis Finnursdottir, the pavement rose up to strike her in the face, and consciousness fled.

May 4, 2020, 4:36 pm EDT

Seton Hall University, South Orange, NJ

Second Lieutenant Dolores Anunciacion de la Madonna Pena knocked politely on the door of what had been the Seton Hall University Athletic Director's office.

Major Hilton Morris Burke, Executive Officer of the 1st Battalion, 27th Infantry Brigade, 42nd Infantry Division, looked up from his borrowed desk. With an impatient wave of his hand, he beckoned Pena to enter.

"What is it, Lieutenant?" he asked, as Pena stepped into the office.

"Sir," she replied, "my platoon picked up a civilian who claims to have been in downtown Hackensack this morning. I thought you'd want to know about him."

Burke nodded.

"Damn straight, Lieutenant," he agreed. "Who is this civvie?"

"According to the report," Pena replied, "he gave his name as ..." she glanced down at the clipboard she cradled in the crook of her left elbow, "Jack Donnellson. He wasn't carrying ID. African-American. Male, obviously. Mid-twenties."

"Where did your people encounter him?" Burke inquired.

"I-280, sir. At the Garden State Parkway checkpoint," Pena said.

"And he's where, now?" Burke demanded.

"He should be just about done with decon, sir," Pena told him. "Shall I have him brought to you?"

"By all means, Lieutenant," Burke said. Then, after a moment's reflection, he asked, "What kind of shape is he in? Will he be up to debriefing?"

"Yes, sir," Pena affirmed. "he should be. He was physically exhausted when my guys encountered him, but he seems healthy enough, otherwise. Apparently, he just wore himself out pedaling a bicycle all the way from Hackensack – and towing a kid's wagon, with his girlfriend in it."

The Major's eyebrows lifted toward his hairline.

"'Towing' his girlfriend?" he replied. "I take it *she* wasn't in very good shape?"

"No, sir," Pena said. "My people tell me their radiac went off the scale when they scanned her. I understand she's delirious, and pretty badly debilitated, physically."

"What do the medics say about her?" Burke queried.

Pena shook her head.

"I understand decon is having trouble decontaminating her sufficiently to permit the medicos to safely examine her," she told him.

Burke nodded, soberly.

"Hmm," he mused. "If she's so badly contaminated that it's unsafe for the medics to even come in contact with her, she's probably not going to be able to provide any useful intelligence."

"No, sir," Pena agreed. "From what my people tell me, she's probably a goner."

"Sorry to hear that," Burke said.

"Yes, sir," Pena replied.

May 4, 2020, 5:44 pm EST

Seneca Temporary Housing Facility, Romulus, NY

Sean Halloran, Sr. swung down off the shuttle bus, whistling Ne-on Glowbaby's hit song "Expose Yourself (To Love)". That sticky piece of ear candy had dominated the pop charts for weeks, and Halloran had recently encountered it while testing the radio function of the chunky boombox hanging from his right hand. Now he couldn't get it out of his head. Dangling from his left hand was a cloth shopping bag containing a six-pack of Bud Dry – a lager aged over dry ice to make it extra fizzy – and a full carton of Marlboro cigarettes. With his vices well-supplied, Sean, Sr.'s mood was as sunny as the lyrics to Glowbaby's song.

He strode along the paved access road to the spot where his Sierra crew cab pickup and Adam Manson's decrepit Suburban were parked. Their vehicles flanked the entrance to the cabin tent their families shared. Halloran turned off the pavement, and squelched through the clutching, ankle-deep mud to the tent.

"Sean!" cried his wife Fiona, as he entered the dwelling.

She ran to him, threw her arms around him, and buried her face in his chest.

"Easy, Darlin'," he told her, gently grasping her by the shoulders, and moving her to arms' length. "My boots are caked," he explained. "Let me get 'em off, and I promise ya all the hugs and kisses ya can stand."

Fiona nodded, silently beaming. Her cheeks were wet with tears.

"Let me take those for ya," she offered, reaching for the boombox, and the grocery bag.

"Thanks, Darlin'," Sean, Sr. said.

As he bent to unlace his Timberlands, the towering figure of Adam Manson thrust aside the blanket that divided the tent cabin.

"Well, if it isn't Sean the Elder!" he boomed.

His voice was loud, in the enclosed space.

Welcome home, bro!" Spying the boombox, Manson inquired, "What's with the sound machine?"

Hoping he sounded appropriately offhand, Halloran replied, "Oh, just somethin' I picked up at the canteen."

Manson's sharp-eyed gaze followed Fiona – one of his least-endearing habits, as far as Sean, Sr. was concerned – as she unpacked the grocery bag.

"Beer, too?" he observed. "You must be flush, bro."

Halloran shrugged.

"Looks like there's gonna be steady work, at least for the time bein'," he explained. "Seemed safe enough to treat ourselves a little."

"You like music, huh?" Manson asked.

Sean, Sr. rolled his eyes.

"Who doesn't?" he responded.

Manson permitted himself the suggestion of a smirk.

"How do feel about death metal?" he inquired.

Halloran again shrugged.

"Not my fav'rite," he answered. "Fiona hates it."

"Too bad," Manson commented. "How about speed metal? Or metal in general?"

"Same answer," Sean, Sr. told him.

It was Manson's turn to shrug.

"Oh, well," he said. "How about punk?"

"Three for three," Halloran replied.

"Don't tell me you're into dinosaur rock," Manson sneered.

"I like classic rock," Sean, Sr. replied, defensively. 'And indie. We're both into indie."

"Ugh," Manson commented.

"Well, it's our boombox, so ..." Halloran began.

"Yeah," Manson said, interrupting him, "but we have to listen to it, too, right?"

Sean, Sr. shrugged. "We can keep tha volume down," he offered.

"How do you feel about talk radio?" Manson countered.

Halloran opened his mouth to respond with a contemptuous, "Ugh."

Before the syllable could leave his lips, it occurred to him that yielding on this issue could help establish a bond between him and Manson. That, in turn, might help him persuade Manson to disclose information the FBI would find valuable.

"I ... uh ... I dunno," he said, groping for the appropriate response. "I've never really listened to much of it. Why do ya ask?"

Manson's eyes glowed with eagerness.

"There's this program I like to listen to, weeknights," he replied. "It's called 'Merlin Friend, live from Patriot Studio 1'. Ever heard of it?"

May 5, 2020, 3:17 am PKT (May 4, 6:17 pm EDT)

Jinnah Road, Rawalpindi, Pakistan

General Rashid Omar Sheikh, Director of the Inter-Service Intelligence Directorate's Joint Intelligence Miscellaneous Department, awoke naked, bound, blind, and soaking wet.

The effects of the sedative he had been given when he was kidnapped from his bed had not yet entirely worn off. For several seconds, he was completely disoriented. His drug-fogged brain found it difficult to grasp how and why he found himself strapped tightly to a hard surface, tilted so that his feet were higher than his head, blindfolded, and dripping cold water.

"See if he's awake," said a familiar voice.

He recognized it as belonging to John O'Brien, who had arrived in Islamabad as Deputy Commercial Attaché for the American Consulate. Within hours, the ISI had identified him as the new CIA Deputy Chief of Station for Islamabad.

Sheikh felt a sudden, stabbing pain in the sole of his left foot, exactly as if someone had viciously jabbed him with a hat pin.

"*Akh*!" he yelped, taken by surprise.

"He's awake, all right," observed a different voice.

"Good morning, Rashid," O'Brien said. "I've been looking forward to this moment for quite a while."

"*Za na poheegum,*" Sheikh replied, shaking his head.

"Oh, but you do understand," O'Brien contradicted. "In fact, you read, write, and speak English perfectly – which is hardly surprising, considering your Oxford education."

In an obvious aside, O'Brien directed, "Again, please."

Once again, something stabbed him painfully. This time, it was in the sole of his right foot.

"*Akh!*" he exclaimed. Then, "Yes, you spawn of *Shaitan*, I understand!" Sheikh admitted.

"Good," said the CIA man. "Now that you understand our respective roles in this conversation, I'm hopeful our discussion will be ... productive."

It came to General Sheikh that he would not leave this place alive – and that his death would be neither pleasant nor quick. There would be no one, save unbelievers, to witness his courage, no one to testify to his resistance to the torture that he was about to undergo.

- Only Allah. -

There was no question about whether they would break him. Sheikh knew that no man can hold out against a determined and skillful torturer. He himself had sought answers from far too many men – and inevitably gotten them – to delude himself into believing he would react any differently. Courage had not helped them. Nor had stubbornness. Sooner or later, their ability to resist had deserted them.

So it would be with him. The time would come when his defiance would end. When it did, he would desperately seek to appease his tormentors. He would promise them anything to make the agony end, even if that ending was in death. His captors would not shrink from mutilation, from the infliction of shame and humiliation, from the worst kind of physical degradation. This he knew. No, the question was not whether he would break, but only how soon his surrender would come.

- Ah, Fairuzah! My precious, precious gem! May Allah keep you always! Insha'Allah, I shall see you again in Jannah! -

Rashid Omar Sheikh sighed, resigned to his fate.

"What do you wish to know?" he asked.

May 4, 2020, 7:40pm EDT

Pier 88, New York City

Eydis Finnursdottir groggily awoke. She found herself strapped to a gurney, with a strong wind beating down on her. A man in blue surgical scrubs, wearing headphones, was inserting a needle into the back of her hand. The roar of powerful engines was overwhelming. The medic was silhouetted in crimson light by the setting sun shining in through the open doorway.

"What ... where ... where am I?" she demanded. "What are you doing to me?"

"Relax, ma'am," the medic shouted, his mouth close to her ear.

Even though he was yelling to be heard over the engine noise, his voice was somehow kind.

You're being evacuated to a hospital," he hollered. "I just gave you a sedative to keep you calm."

"Where is my boyfriend?" Eydis demanded, nearly screaming. "Where is Greg?"

"You mean the man you were with when you were brought in?" the medic asked.

"Yes!" Eydis cried. "He is my boyfriend. His name is Greg Shergold. Where is he?"

"He'll be on the next flight," he shouted, patting her shoulder reassuringly. "You're both going to the same hospital. Do you understand?"

Eydis nodded, blinking back tears.

"You're safe now," the man in scrubs yelled. "Don't worry – everything's going to be all right!"

He slid the helicopter's door shut, and banged on the hull. The chopper lifted off, just as the sedative took effect. The world went gray, and consciousness again deserted Eydis Finnursdottir.

May 4, 2020, 8:15 pm EDT

East Orange Golf Course, Short Hills, NJ

Donell Jackson was angry and frustrated. He had spent hours being interrogated by men in uniform, answering the same questions over and over again. It felt as if his questioners were trying to catch him in a lie.

Of course, he *had* been lying to them about some things. His name, for instance. And how, and where he had spent the weekend. The funny thing was, his inquisitors hadn't seemed particularly interested in that aspect of his story. No, they had accepted at face value his assertion that his name was Jack Donnellson, and that he had been part of a crew remodeling a house in Nutley on Friday. Claiming he had spent Friday, Saturday, and Sunday holed up there, living on canned goods he and his co-workers had found in the home's pantry hadn't seemed to stir their suspicions in the slightest. Nor had they expressed any skepticism when he explained the bruises on his face as the product of a fight over a can of ravioli between himself and another member of the construction crew.

What they had focused on, what they had made him repeat the details of, again and again, was his journey by bicycle into the heart of Hackensack and back. They seemed to want to know every tiny detail of what he had seen along the way. What was the color and condition of the trees, for instance? Had he seen, or heard any birds or insects? What signs of life, in general, had he observed? Had he noticed any hand-printed signs in the windows of the buildings he passed? What had it *smelled* like?

That last one had been easy. It smelled like death.

When one group of interrogators finished with him, they'd turned him over to a new bunch. The new team insisted on covering the same ground, asking the same questions, going over the same details as the old one. They kept at him, giving him no time to think, until, finally, he had lost his temper.

He refused to answer any more of their queries, until he got some answers of his own. What had they done with his girlfriend Latonya? What were they going to do with him? And when was he going to get something to eat and drink?

That last question resulted in his questioners backing off, shamefaced, for nearly half an hour. They sent for a sandwich and a tepid can of generic cola. Wolfing down the one, and guzzling the other improved Donell's temper somewhat. It also stiffened his resolve to put an end to their inquisition.

"That's it," he told them. "You've asked me the same questions about 100 times, 100 different ways. You're so fuckin' curious about Hackensack? Go take a look for yourself. I'm done talking. Now, what the fuck have you done with my girlfriend?"

The brown-haired man with the silver eagles on his collars replied. "Ms. Gramble is in intensive care, Mr. Donnellson. I assure you she's getting the best possible care."

Donell demanded they let him see Latonya.

"I'm sorry, Mr. Donnellson," the brown-haired man, whose name patch read Silverman, replied, "but that's not possible right now. They don't allow visitors in the ICU. Not now."

Donell insisted they tell him when he would be allowed to visit her.

"As to that, I can't say," Silverman told him. "It depends on when they release her from intensive care."

"Well, then," Donell demanded, his frustration growing, "what the fuck happens to *me*? You gonna let me go on my way, or what?"

Silverman exchanged glances with the other three men in uniform around the wooden table, in the bare room where Donell had spent the past three hours.

"Mr. Donnellson," he had said, at last, "legally, we could compel you to remain here as long as we want. You understand? This country is now under martial law and your constitutional rights have been suspended."

Donell folded his arms across his chest and stared defiantly at Silverman.

"You can keep me, I guess," he replied. "It doesn't mean I'm gonna answer any more of your damn-fool questions, though."

Silverman sighed.

"You're right, of course, Mr. Donnellson," he admitted. "But the most important thing is, I'm convinced you've told us everything you know about conditions in Hackensack. Keeping you here any longer would serve no useful purpose – and we all have other duties to attend to. So ..."

"So you're gonna cut me loose?" Donell asked.

"Not exactly," Silverman told him.

Donell soon found out what the colonel meant. Armed soldiers escorted him out of the Regan Recreation and Athletic Center. They put him on a shuttle bus, along with a dozen other refugees. He was still dressed in the surgical scrubs he'd been given, after the soldiers who had conducted his radiac scan determined that his shoes and clothing were contaminated. The other passengers on the bus wore similar garb.

The bus drove west, under crimson skies, into the forested Short Hills district. A bare sliver of sun remained above the western horizon by the time it left the road. The shuttle turned into the parking lot of the East Orange Golf Course.

"End of the line," the driver announced. "Everybody out."

Soldiers with flashlights directed the new arrivals toward the clubhouse. There, they were given billet assignments. Uniformed men driving golf carts took them to their new quarters.

Donell found himself standing in front of a tent big enough to host a revival meeting. The guard outside the door glanced at his assignment sheet. After determining that his paperwork was in order, the soldier stood aside. He entered the canvas structure.

Jackson found the place crowded with cots, each of which had a metal footlocker at its foot. The beds were aligned in rows, three across, running almost its entire length of the tent. Near the door and at the opposite end of the structure, were open areas, each with a scatter of tables and chairs. From the centerline hung bright fluorescent light fixtures, one every ten feet. The space inside was crowded with people.

A guard standing inside the door again examined Donell's assignment sheet. The soldier directed him to a cot against one wall of the tent. It was most of the way to the other end of the structure.

Jackson made his way to his assigned bed, feeling dazed. He was at something of a loss for what to do next. Was he tired enough to sleep? He was exhausted – but far too keyed up to simply lie down, and close his eyes.

Merely to burn off excess energy, Donell got up, and strolled over to the common area nearest his cot. He examined the people congregated there. Most of them seemed to be engaged in games of one sort or another. At one table, they were playing cards, at the next, Monopoly. The third hosted a game of dominoes. At the fourth ...

"Brother Jackson!" boomed a delighted Arun "Big Sugar" Washington.

He stood up, and turned from the chessboard in front of him.

"What an unexpected pleasure to see you again!" said the delighted mob boss.

May 4, 2020, 9:01 pm EST

The White House State Dining Room, Washington, DC

"Ladies and gentlemen," announced Yvonne Clevinger, "the President of the United States."

William Orwell Steele strode into the State Dining Room, followed closely by the Vice President. He moved briskly to the podium in front of the room's marble fireplace. Flanked by free-standing American and Presidential flags, with Healy's oil portrait of a pensive, seated Abraham Lincoln looming over him, the President began to speak.

"My fellow Americans, and members of the White House press corps," he announced, "I thank you for joining me here, tonight, in the historic State Dining Room of the White House. I know the media representatives are eager to begin asking questions, and I promise we will get to them in a short while. However, let me begin with a few important announcements."

Steele paused to survey the room's occupants.

To his immediate left stood Diana Hunter. Beyond her were key members of his Cabinet and national security team, who had followed them into the room. To his right was Yvonne Clevinger, Deputy Press Secretary Clayton Reynolds, Science Advisor Clayton Dawkins, and Steele's Chief of Staff, Andover Philips. Beside them in the corner of the room was a camera operator, standing behind a bulky HDTV camera. In the rear, in front of the massive, gilt-framed mirror, was another camera and its operator. A sound engineer in a bulky headset and a similarly-accoutered floor director flanked the camera's dolly. Most of the space in the room – save for a four-foot-wide aisle left open in the center – was taken up with rows of chairs, in which the members of the White House Press Corps were seated. At each corner of the audience stood a massive light tree, blazing with high-intensity Klieg lights. A sturdy lighting scaffold, partially disguised with dark-blue draperies, rose above and behind the podium to provide backlight for the President. Secret Service agents stood as sentries in front of each doorway and each of the tall windows in the South wall.

Returning his gaze to the teleprompter, Steele resumed speaking.

"First, I'd like to update you on the USS John F. Kennedy's mission, and the status of the Manhattan rescue operation, in general," he stated.

There was a buzz of interest from the media representatives in the room. It quickly became a hush of rapt attention.

"Due to the overwhelming number of survivors who responded to the Kennedy's arrival, its mission has changed. As you know, the JFK was originally dispatched to Manhattan with the idea that it would act as a kind of shuttle. The plan was for it to physically transport survivors of the attack to safety in New Jersey. That proved to be impractical. There were far too many refugees for the Kennedy, alone, to make more than a small dent in their numbers. In response to this unanticipated circumstance, the Kennedy is now, instead, acting as the Manhattan terminus of an air bridge. This air bridge is using heavy-lift Navy helicopters to evacuate more than 4,000 survivors from Manhattan, every 12 hours."

The President paused, before continuing.

"I want to emphasize that this is good news," he said. "Had our original plan remained in effect, the Kennedy would only have been able to evacuate about 4,000 refugees every two days. This new strategy allows us to rescue four times as many survivors from Manhattan, in the same amount of time. In addition, I'm happy to announce that we expect elements of the Merchant Marine and additional Navy assets to arrive on-scene within the next 12 hours. By the end of the week, we should see a significant number of foreign vessels arriving, as well.

"I'll have more to say about that in a moment. First, however, I wanted to take the time to thank Captain William Plein and his crew for their flexibility, ingenuity, and outstanding effort in ensuring the success of the Kennedy's rescue mission. When the full story of their heroic actions is told, the entire nation – and especially the people of Manhattan – will realize how large a debt of gratitude we owe them."

"Mr. President," shouted Reed Bullock, the Fox News White House Correspondent, "why wasn't that the plan in the first place?"

Steele responded firmly, "I am still talking, Mr. Bullock. Please contain yourself, until I'm done."

The room erupted in raucous laughter.

"Next," Steele continued, "I want to address the effect Tropical Storm Beth has had on our predictions about conditions in the fallout area. Once again, I'm pleased to say that I have good news."

A murmur of excitement rose, and swiftly fell, as the information-starved journalists in the room leaned forward, keenly interested in the President's statement.

"Because of the extremely heavy rains that accompanied Beth, the residue of fallout on the ground throughout the Fallout Zone is considerably less than our original models predicted. I understand that the rain washed most of it off surface streets, and into storm drains. What this means, most importantly, is that the number of people we expect to survive the fallout cloud has dramatically increased. We now believe that there may be as few as a million fatalities, in total. That number includes both those killed by the blast itself, and those who have died, or will die from the effects of fallout."

The room hummed with excitement. The correspondents scribbled furiously, or whispered into their smartphones.

"What this does *not* mean," the President added, "is that the Fallout Zone is in any way safe for human habitation. Nor should we expect it to be, any time in the near future."

The audience fell silent, taken aback.

"The reason for that, is what is known as 'residual fallout'," the President explained. "There is still a considerable amount of radioactive dust soaked into the soil of lawns, parks, and other green areas. Additionally, because much of the fallout consists of radioactive metal particles, enough of it may still be present in such places as cracks in sidewalks, streets, gutters, and any other surfaces where rainwater normally collects to cause a significant ongoing health hazard. Storm drains and many of the reservoirs that service the Fallout Zone are – and will continue to be – heavily contaminated. Likewise, rivers and coastal waters in the fallout zone are also badly contaminated. We cannot pretend that scrubbing this huge number of surfaces, and dredging all these waterways and coastal seafloors will take anything short of decades."

Steele paused to take a sip of water. The reporters took advantage of his pause to scribble, type, or murmur notes.

"Because of the enormous challenges we face – and will continue to face – in rescuing and caring for victims of the May Day attack and refugees from the Fallout Zone," the President continued, "I am today calling on Congress to pass the May Day Relief Act. The legislation my administration is proposing would provide free medical care for survivors, low-interest-rate, direct-assistance loans to refugees, and block grants to the states that are most directly affected by the attack itself – and that are carrying most of the financial burden of providing for its refugees. In addition, the May Day Relief Act will fund the very high costs of decontamination and reclamation of the Fallout Zone. As you all know, our nation was already facing a debt crisis, before the events of last Friday. Because it is not unreasonable to ask that those of us who can afford it to lend a helping hand to their countrymen who have – through no fault, or action of their own – lost everything, we are proposing a 10% Federal surtax on businesses and individuals with more than $500,000 in adjusted gross income, to partially fund these unprecedented national expenses."

The hubbub that greeted his announcement was nearly deafening.

"I ask you to keep in mind," the President added, "that we, as a nation, have suffered nearly incalculable losses. My economic advisors estimate the physical damage to Manhattan, alone, amounts to several trillion dollars. That figure does not include the loss of income for tens of thousands of businesses, nor does it even begin to account for the toll in human suffering and lost lives. Make no mistake about it: this is the greatest single crisis this country has ever faced. Its final cost will undoubtedly exceed that of any war we have ever experienced."

He paused again, to let his audience absorb that statement.

"Having said that," Steele continued, "I am pleased to be able to tell you that we will not have to bear the burden entirely alone."

The roomful of correspondents was rapt.

"From the time that power was restored to the Northeastern Grid, on Saturday morning," the President told them, "both the State Department and the White House have been flooded with messages of condolence and support, and with offers of assistance from other countries. As you know, Secretary of State Thornton was in Brussels, last Friday, representing our country at a meeting of the European Council. The heads of all of the EU member-states have assured her that, despite their own financial difficulties, they stand ready to provide low-interest loans and grants-in-aid to us in our time of trial. Many of those countries, and others around the world have already dispatched to our shores freighters filled with food, medicine, portable shelters, blankets, and other supplies. Those relief shipments should begin arriving in American ports by the end of this week. We have also been assured that they stand ready to send doctors, nurses, and rescue specialists, as soon as we lift our present restrictions on air travel.

"Closer to home, Prime Minister Yves Prudhomme has offered the use of Canadian troops to provide security at refugee centers and temporary housing facilities. This will free additional American troops for Fallout Zone rescue and patrol duty. Prime Minister Prudhomme has also volunteered to supply us with Canadian search-and-rescue teams, as well as medical personnel, and supplies. Keep in mind that he has made this generous offer, despite the fact that the Fallout Zone extends to Canada's own Maritime Provinces."

Once again, the audience's reaction was electric. The muted hum of conversation mounted to a near-roar.

When it began to subside, Steele added, "Because our troops have been spread so thinly in the effort to rescue as many survivors as possible, I have gratefully accepted the Prime Minister's offer of help. Our military expects to be able to turn over the job of policing our temporary housing facilities and refugee centers to their Canadian counterparts within the next couple of days."

"Mister President!" came a chorus of voices, accompanied by frantically-waving hands.

"Just let me add one more observation," the President said, "before I open the floor for questions."

He paused for another sip of water.

"This disaster – what everyone is now calling the May Day attack – is literally without precedent in our country's history," Steele told them. "Even the nature of the explosion – which we now know was actually detonated inside the Freedom Tower itself – is fundamentally different from any nuclear test the United States, or any country has ever conducted. As a result, we have been forced to learn from, and adapt to conditions on the ground, as events were unfolding. The failure of the Northeastern power grid in the hours immediately following the bombing severely hampered both our ability to gather intelligence regarding the attack, and our ability to communicate with the affected area. Because of those limitations, we have, many times, been forced to make decisions on the fly, and to act despite often extremely limited information. Essentially, we have been forced to make guesses about what was needed, and how we should react. It's true that most of those guesses were educated ones. However, I have to tell you that the level of their education ... varied."

A scatter of chuckles greeted this sally.

"Over the past three-and-a-half days," Steele said, "I have been personally gratified at the way in which members of my administration, our military, and safety and medical personnel at all levels of government have stepped up to those challenges. As far as I can tell, not one of them has complained about the long hours, the lack of information, or the scarcity of resources with which they have had to contend. They have simply gone quietly and effectively about doing their jobs – doing what had to be done for the good of our country, and the benefit of their fellow Americans. They have not asked for praise, or even credit for their work. They have been simply magnificent. I am humbled by their dedication, and more proud of them than I can adequately express. I thank them all, from the bottom of my heart."

The applause was scattered when it began, but it built to a standing ovation. When, at last, it ended, the President spoke again.

"On their behalf, I thank you," he said.

He took another sip of water.

Refreshed, he said, "I'll take your questions, now. Mr. Bullock?"

May 4, 2020, 7:09 pm PDT (10:09 pm EDT)

University of California, Berkeley, CA

Herbert Richard Baumeister sat with his back against a lamp post, pretending to read the latest issue of The Daily Californian. He kept a covert watch on the westernmost rear entrance to the looming Valley Life Sciences Building. His Pro 29er mountain bike lay on its side, in the grass next to him. Baumeister wore a dark blue, Golden Bears sweatshirt, black, Lycra bike shorts, and a Nike-branded baseball cap, with the golden bear paw logo on the front. His garb made him virtually invisible among the student population of the University of California Berkeley campus. Despite the waning light, he also wore a pair of wraparound sunglasses.

The double doors at the rear of the Valley Life Sciences Building opened. A tall, very fit man in his mid-thirties emerged, pushing a mountain bike. He was dressed in a Cal sweatshirt, sweatpants, and baseball cap. He had on a UCB windbreaker, as well. The Secret Service agent was followed by Artemis Alexandra Steele, the estranged daughter – and only child – of President William Orwell Steele. She was tall, slim, and graceful. Dressed in a black track suit, she walked a Genius XL mountain bike. Behind her came two more members of her Secret Service detail. One was black, one white. Each maneuvered his own knobby-tired bicycle. Both dressed identically to the first Agent.

The little party paused at the bottom of the steps to strap on biking helmets. The lead Agent muttered briefly into a microphone concealed in his sleeve. Then they mounted their bicycles. In the same order in which they had exited the building, the little party set off toward West Circle and the setting sun.

Baumeister stood up, carelessly discarding his newspaper on the grass where he'd been sitting. He righted his bike, climbed on, and began following the First Daughter and her Secret Service retinue at a discrete distance. When he reached West Circle, he spotted Steele and her detail exiting the roundabout onto University Drive. Hanging back just far enough to reliably keep Artemis Steele's party in view, Baumeister turned right to follow it around The Crescent. They exited straight onto

University Avenue, and the long downhill slope toward the Berkeley Marina and San Francisco Bay.

Baumeister double-tapped the screen of the smartphone in the arm wallet strapped to his left bicep, then pushed the "on" button of his Bluetooth headset.

"Call Charlie," he instructed.

After a moment, he heard Charles Frederick Albright's cell phone ring. His call was answered before it rang a second time.

"Yo," Albright said.

"They're headed home," Baumeister told him.

"Sweet," Albright replied. "Hold on."

Baumeister briefly heard the sound of distant voices, made indecipherable by the noise of evening traffic along University Avenue. Then Albright spoke again.

"We're go," he said. "Be ready."

"Roger that," Baumeister responded.

Leaving his phone and headset on, Herb Baumeister stood on the pedals of his Pro 29er. He let it freewheel down University Avenue, less than a block behind Artemis Steele and her trio of Secret Service protectors.

May 4, 2020, 9:22 pm MDT (11:22 EDT)

Patriot Radio Studio 1, Athol, ID

"And we're back," announced Merlin Friend, speaking into the dangling Neumann microphone. "For those of you who are just joining us, we've been listening to William Orwell Steele lie through his teeth about everything that's happened since the CIA set off an atomic bomb in New York City on Friday."

Friend consulted the notepad on the console in front of him.

"Let's just review the deceptions, distortions, and outright lies the Tyrant has tried to cram down our throats over the past two hours, shall we?" he offered.

"Our socialist Tyrant continued to insist that Friday's attack – which we all know was a false-flag operation – was perpetrated by 'persons unknown,'" Friend continued. "When CBS's White House correspondent Katrina Ruth asked him what he knew about the attack beforehand, and when he knew it, our Liar-in-Chief had the audacity to claim there had been no advance warning at all – no 'chatter', as he called it! He even had the gall to say we should believe this supposed lack of 'chatter', somehow 'lends credence to the notion that a state actor may have been behind the bombing.'

"Of course, it's as obvious as the nose on the Tyrant's lying face that 'some state actor' was, indeed, behind the bombing – and that 'state actor' was none other than William the First, would-be Dictator-for-life of the Soviet Socialist Republic of America! There's no question in *my* mind that our home-grown Stalin ordered the CIA to bomb Manhattan. And his Jewish Svengali Arleigh Solomon and his hand-picked spymaster Christopher Murdock both conspired with him to make it happen!"

Friend's voice had risen to a near-shout. Now he lowered it to a stage whisper, as he leaned in toward the microphone.

"My fellow Patriots," he confided, "that was only the beginning of the Tyrant's nefarious plot to turn our country into a 'worker's paradise'. Believe it or not, he also called for Congress – which, with the shining exception of a handful of true patriots, such as our currently-imprisoned fellow Son, Representative Easau Piltch, is about as foul a collection of lickspittles, socialist fellow-travelers, and invertebrate tools as this once-great nation has ever burped up – to pass a bill redistributing the income of hard-working job creators to the long line of slackers, waiting for a government handout. Mark my words, Patriots, this is just the first, treacherous step toward the Tyrant's goal of replacing our capitalist economy with undisguised Marxism! 'From each, according to his ability, to each, according to his need' is the Tyrant's plan. In other words, stealing *our* hard-earned money, and giving it to the lazy, shiftless, welfare bums *he* cares so much about!"

Friend paused to finish off the nearly-empty highball glass of Tanqueray-and-tonic. It was his second of the broadcast, and it contained more gin than the first. Soon, he would start the third – the strongest of the night – which he would consume during the final hour of his show.

"But that is not the worst of the Tyrant's crimes against America we learned about tonight, Patriots," he confided, bending close to the microphone, as if disclosing a secret. "Just minutes ago, William Orwell Steele finally unveiled his true colors as the handmaiden of the New World Order, by announcing that he has invited foreign troops to take over as guards at his FEMA concentration camps! Imagine that! The Tyrant is going to give foreigners the authority to arrest, and detain – and shoot, and kill – American citizens, on American soil!"

Friend pounded his fist on the console, making the meters on his sound board jump.

"Listen to me, Patriots!" he demanded. "This is not the end of William Orwell Steele's evil agenda! It is just the beginning! Mark my words: the black helicopters are on their way! Soon, this filthy reptile – this dictator, this Tyrant – will turn the United States of America over to the direct control of the United Nations! If we allow that to happen, Patriots, you, and I, and everyone we love will forever be condemned to live our lives in chains, as slaves to the Bilderbergers, the Trilateralists, the Masons, the Rothchilds, and their godless New World Order!"

Friend lowered his voice, and once again leaned in towards the Neumann microphone.

"Patriots," he confided, "as you know, over the weekend, one of our courageous fellow Sons, retired postal worker Richard Wayne Lee, sacrificed his life, in a brave and audacious attempt to bring about an end to the odious reign of William Orwell Steele. Tragically, our brother Richard's heroic effort did not succeed. Instead, the Tyrant's thugs callously shot Richard Wayne Lee out of the sky. Now he has truly joined the hallowed ranks of Fallen Patriots."

Friend silently counted off three full seconds before allowing himself to continue.

"Fellow Patriots," he intoned, "Richard Wayne Lee – I'm told he preferred to be called 'R. Wayne' – died a hero. His sacrifice on behalf of our beloved country will never be forgotten, as long as a single Son of Fallen Patriots draws breath. But you and I must do more than simply mourn the loss of R. Wayne Lee. We must do more than merely pay tribute to his courage. We must – we absolutely *must* – follow his example! R. Wayne accepted his personal responsibility to help end the reign of the Tyrant. *He* may not have succeeded, but that does not mean that *we* should stop trying! Indeed, we *must not* stop trying, *ever*, until William Orwell Steele has been toppled from his throne, and our beloved country is once again free from the looming menace of the New World Order!'

Again, Friend paused for effect.

Then, his voice throbbing with emotion, he declared, "Only *you* can accomplish this noble goal, Patriots! Only *you* have the courage. Only *you* have the determination. Only *you* know what is required."

"Only you," he whispered.

Friend let the silence drag on a full five seconds afterward.

Then, briskly, he announced, "We'll be right back, after this message from our friends at Goldmine."

May 5, 2020, 12:03 am EDT

The President's Study, Washington, DC

"How the *fuck* did you allow this to happen?" the President demanded.

Secret Service Director Paul McConnochie looked grim.

"I'm sorry, Mr. President," he replied. "The particulars are still emerging. What I can confirm for you is, all but one member of your daughter's detail was killed. Special Agent Janese Johnson was the only survivor."

"How did she escape?" William Orwell Steele asked.

"As I understand it," McConnochie told him, "it was pure luck. Agent Johnson just happened to be picking up a take-out order at a restaurant near your daughter's apartment, when the attack took place."

"Jesus fucking Christ!" said the President. "How many dead?"

"15 agents, all together," McConnochie replied. "Plus your daughter's ... uh ... roommate, Bernadette Garcia."

"'Lover', you mean," Steele corrected. "Bernadette was Artie's lover."

Momentarily, his features twisted.

"Oh God – poor Bernie," he said.

He turned away from McConnochie.

After a moment, the President got his emotions back under control.

He turned back to the Secret Service Director, and said, "Paul, I apologize. I had no idea it was that bad."

"Yes, sir," McConnochie agreed. "It was bad, all right. Special Agent Johnson heard shooting on her way back to the apartment building, but the ... incident ... was over by the time she arrived on the scene. Again, the details are still unclear, but she reported that everyone at the Addison Street location was down when she arrived. With the cooperation of Berkeley PD, she's interviewing possible witnesses, as we speak. Madeline Czerwinski, SAIC of the San Francisco field office estimates the FBI will arrive on scene about ..." McConnochie checked his wristwatch. "... 20 minutes from now."

"And the agents who were with my daughter?" the President asked.

"Agents Schieffer, Conway, and Brown were all killed," McConnochie replied. "Berkeley PD has confirmed the identities of all three. Again, the exact circumstances are still unclear, but eyewitness accounts indicate at least one vehicle was involved, and there was gunfire at the kidnapping scene. Whether any of the agents were able to get shots off at the kidnappers, we have yet to determine."

"Kidnappers?" Steele asked. "There was more than one?"

"That's affirmative, Mr. President," McConnochie told him. "Preliminary eyewitness testimony indicates at least three perpetrators at the kidnapping scene – and we're assuming at least two more participated in the Addison Street attack. Possibly more."

The President shook his head in disbelief.

"So, there were two separate attacks?" he demanded.

"Yes, sir," McConnochie confirmed.

"It sounds as though they had to have been professionals." Steele observed.

"It looks that way, sir," McConnochie agreed. "Most likely ex-military. Possibly even ex-Special Forces."

"Jesus H. Christ," Steele replied.

He turned away. For a moment, he stared, unseeing, through the office's triple windows. Then he turned back to McConnochie.

"Have you received any demands for Artie's return?" he asked.

McConnochie shook his head.

"No, sir," he said. "Not so far. It's early, though. Your daughter was taken less than two hours ago. If they're holding her for ransom, it could be tomorrow morning before we hear from them. Possibly later."

"Goddamnit!" Steele snarled, pounding his fist on the oak desk.

He spun to face McConnochie, his expression bleak.

"I want you to find these motherfuckers, Paul," he demanded. "Find them, and kill them. Do you understand me?"

"Yes, sir," McConnochie replied, his face impassive. "I understand."

"And get my daughter back," the President added. "*Alive.*"

May 4, 2020, 10:15 pm PDT (May 5, 1:15 am EDT)

Alvarado Street, San Leandro, CA

Artemis Alexandra Steele awoke in utter darkness.

She felt herself floating. She could hear only a continuous surf of white noise coming from something clamped around her head. Earphones? Yes, earphones – the big, bulky kind that covered both ears. From the sensation of pressure around her head and across the bridge of her nose, she was wearing goggles, too. Her nostrils were pinched together with what felt like a diving clip. And there was something like an oxygen mask over her nose and mouth, feeding her air, as her body floated.

Experimentally, Artemis tried to move each of her limbs in turn. She discovered she could move them only an inch or two in any direction. It seemed obvious that her arms and legs were suspended between elastic restraints – bungee cords, perhaps?

She fought down a surge of terror.

- Panicking won't help You have to stay calm, and use your head, if you're going to get out of ... wherever you are. -

She tried to remember the sequence of events that led to her present predicament. She clearly recalled leaving the Valley Life Sciences building, surrounded by the members of her second-shift Secret Service detail. She knew that many presidential offspring before her had resented their government guardians. Some of them had gone to great lengths to evade them, in the name of personal liberty. Artemis Steele hadn't felt that way at all – not since that terrible day in Cleveland, when she'd watched her mother die.

Much as she resented her father, and the vaulting ambition that resulted in her mother's murder, Artemis Steele was grateful for the protection of her Secret Service detail. She made it a point to be as friendly towards the individual agents as possible. She bought them each birthday and Christmas presents, and frequently asked them about their spouses, and children.

It pained her to recall the nondescript, white van, whipping around the corner of University Avenue at Grant Street. It had deliberately mowed down Paul Schieffer, the Special Agent in Charge of her second-shift Secret Service detail. She would never forget the thump of the van's bumper hitting Schieffer, or the way his body sailed through the air, to land broken and bleeding in the middle of Grant Street. His death would be a part of her nightmares for the rest of her life, just as her mother's was.

She remembered the way her bike had slewed sideways, as she fought to stop it before she collided with the van. The way its side doors had burst open, to reveal two men in ski masks. How they had scrambled out of the van, one on each side of her, and how they grabbed her by the arms.

The sound of Lester Conway's dying shout, "Gun!" and Kevin Brown's "Mayday!" – both cut off in mid-syllable, as shots rang out behind her.

Bystanders and witnesses to the killings screaming, and running for cover. Trying to leap free from the encumbrance of her bike, shake off her captors, and run away. Being grabbed from behind. The way all three men had lifted her, and thrown her bodily into the van. The sound and feel of the vehicle accelerating down Grant Street.

One of the men had clapped a wet, foul-smelling cloth across her nose and mouth. The last thing she remembered was the sharp shift in her weight that accompanied the van's turn onto Berkeley Way, as it headed uphill. After that, there was only darkness – until she had awakened here.

- *Okay. That's how I got here. Now, how do I escape?* -

May 5, 2020, 2:19 am EDT

Monmouth Medical Center, West Long Branch, NJ

Eydis Finnursdottir awoke in the dimness of a hospital room. The white privacy curtain was drawn around the bed in which she lay. She could tell, however, that she was not alone by the gentle snoring, emanating from elsewhere in the room.

A movable table, on which stood a box of tissues and a squat, plastic glass of water sat to her left. An intravenous drip ran from a freestanding pole at the head of the bed to a cannula inserted into the back of her left hand. A blood-oxygen monitor was clamped to the end of her right middle finger. She was dressed in a light-blue hospital gown and socks, and, as she quickly discovered, her right arm was handcuffed to the bed rail.

Trying to sit up brought her neck a swift jolt of agony. Gritting her teeth against the pain, Eydis realized that, in fact, every part of her body hurt. She was weak as a newborn fawn, and very tired, despite the time she had recently spent unconscious. Still, she fought down the urge to surrender, and drift back to sleep. Instead, she searched the edges of the bed until she found a call button, which she immediately began to push, once every two seconds. After what seemed like an hour or more, an annoyed-looking, middle-aged, heavy-set nurse, whose nameplate identified her as Tammy Hildiger, RN, finally swept the privacy curtain aside.

"What do you need, sweetie?" Hildiger inquired, mechanically.

"Why am I restrained in this fashion?" Eydis demanded, holding up her right hand to the full extent her handcuffs permitted. "And where is my boyfriend, Greg Shergold?"

"Well, obviously, you're a prisoner," the nurse replied. "And I'm afraid I don't know who Greg Shergode is."

"Sher-*gold*," Eydis corrected. "His name is Greg Shergold. He is my boyfriend. I was told that he would be taken to the same hospital as I. Also, why am I a prisoner, please?"

Nurse Hildiger rolled her eyes.

"I have no idea why you're a prisoner, sweetheart," she told Eydis. "You just are. And I still don't know who Greg Sher*gold* is. Would you like me to see whether he's registered?"

"Yes, please," Eydis confirmed. "I would like that very much. Could you please also find someone to explain to me why I am a prisoner?"

"Oh, sure," Hildiger told her sarcastically. "I'll do that right away."

"Please," Eydis said. "I do not know what I have done wrong. I am just a visitor from Iceland."

Hildiger put her hands on her ample hips. She looked more closely at Eydis's battered features.

"What in Heaven's name happened to you, sweetie?" she asked.

"I was raped, and beaten by bad men," Eydis replied. "My boyfriend Greg also was beaten. I think he had a very bad concussion. I carried him ... a very long way. To find help, yes?"

She looked pleadingly at Hildiger

"Please, will you not help me find out what has happened to him, Miss Nurse Hildiger?" she begged.

"I'll tell you what," Hildiger replied, her indifference softened by the genuineness of Eydis's concern. "You try to get some sleep, and I'll see if I can find out whether your boyfriend is registered here. You said his name is Greg Shergold?"

"Yes, thank you," Eydis said, her eyes shining, "that is his name."

"All right," Hildiger promised. "I'll see what I can find out."

May 5, 2020, 12:27 pm PKT (3:27 am EDT)

Jinnah Road, Rawalpindi, Pakistan

General Rashid Omar Sheikh awoke gasping and sputtering.

He was blindfolded, freezing wet, and in agony. Sheikh doubted he had been unconscious longer than a few seconds. Surely his captors were not merciful enough to permit him to escape his torment any longer than was absolutely unavoidable. Had their positions been reversed – *Insha'Allah!* – he himself would certainly not have permitted it.

"Ah," said the voice of John O'Brien, "I see you're awake again, Rashid."

"Yes, *kafir*," Sheikh confirmed, through clenched teeth.

The throb of agony from his crushed fingers made it difficult for him to speak without screaming.

"Good," O'Brien said. "Shall we proceed?"

"What more do you want from me?" Sheikh asked, despairingly.

"Everything, of course," O'Brien replied. "Did you expect anything less?"

Sheikh shook his head.

"Of course not, *kafir*," he confessed. "And I have told you everything … but, naturally, you do not believe me."

"No," O'Brien agreed. "I don't."

Sheikh sighed. He had, in fact, held back as much information as he felt he could reasonably conceal. He had little hope, though, that he could keep any of it from them, in the end.

"We'll come back to 'Operation Sword of Allah' in a little while," O'Brien told him. "For now, let's turn our attention to June 2018. I want you to tell me how your people discovered the existence of Operation Playmate."

Sheikh involuntarily groaned. Soon, he knew, the torture would continue, even if he told O'Brien everything he wanted to know. Only death would allow him to escape.

- Perhaps I can manage to swallow my tongue. -

It seemed worth a try.

May 5, 2020, 4:33 am EDT

One Observatory Circle, Washington, DC

Hestia Argus, RN, had been lightly dozing in a sturdy chair in the second-floor hallway of the Vice Presidential Mansion.

She awoke to the sound of Diana Hunter's panicked call for help. Less than a second later, she was on her feet. She flung open the door to the guest bedroom, where the Vice President's husband lay dying. Argus flipped on the overhead light as she entered the room. Rapidly, the hospice nurse crossed to her patient's hospital bed, beside which Diana Hunter stood, trembling with anxiety.

"What's wrong, Mrs. Hunter?" the nurse asked.

"His breathing," Diana Hunter replied, fighting for calm. "He was hyperventilating ... gasping for breath."

Her tawny eyes were huge with fear.

"I ... it woke me up," she explained. "It ... it seemed like he was suffering."

Argus shook her head. "I doubt that, Mrs. Hunter," she said, reassuringly. "He's getting 1,000 micrograms of fentanyl per hour. Your husband may be having trouble breathing, but I don't think he's suffering."

Argus checked the urine collection bag hanging from the bed. It was empty, as she had suspected it would be. Bending over the bed, she unwrapped the stethoscope from around her neck, inserted the earpieces, and placed the chest piece over Benjamin Hunter's heart. She moved it around, checking his lung function, as well as his heart sounds. Checkup completed, she straightened up, and turned to face Diana Hunter.

"Your husband's body is shutting down, Mrs. Hunter," she told the Vice President.

She gestured at the empty urine bag.

"His kidneys aren't processing urine, " she continued, "his heartbeat is weakening ... and, if you'll notice, he isn't breathing, at the moment."

Diana Hunter's hands flew to her mouth.

"Oh, God!" she said, "Is he dead?"

Argus again shook her head. The short, processed curls beneath her nursing cap barely moved.

"No, ma'am," she said. "See? There …he's started up again."

As she spoke, Benjamin Hunter gasped loudly. He immediately began to hyperventilate, his chest moving convulsively.

Argus put a comforting hand on Diana Hunter's upper arm. The dark skin of her fingers contrasted vividly with the Vice President's pale complexion.

"It's natural, Mrs. Hunter," she said, "believe me. It's called 'Cheyne-Stokes respiration'. It happens to all my patients, at this stage in the process. Your husband will go through this cycle from now until …"

Diana Hunter's tawny eyes filled with tears.

"Then … there isn't anything you can do?"

Argus regarded her client with sympathy born of long experience.

"We could give him oxygen, if you like," she said. "Or we could put him on a ventilator, if you prefer. But, really, Mrs. Hunter, that will only delay the process."

She looked straight into the Vice President's anguished eyes.

"If he were my husband," she told Hunter, "and I was in your shoes? Knowing what I know, I wouldn't do either one."

"You wouldn't?" Diana Hunter asked.

Argus turned to look at Benjamin Hunter. His hyperventilation was slowing, now. She turned back to the Vice President, and shook her head.

"No, ma'am," she said. "I wouldn't."

Once again, she reached out to Diana Hunter. Argus stroked her arm reassuringly, as if the Vice President were a small, frightened animal.

"Close as he's getting, now?" she confided. "I wouldn't stand in his way."

May 5, 2020, 5:22 am EDT

Wedgewood Drive, Beavercreek, OH

The sound of breaking glass awoke Bhagat Singh. He glanced at the digital clock which sat on the nightstand beside the queen-size bed.

Singh frowned. He was not certain quite why he had wakened at this hour. Normally, he would not arise to begin his meditation for another 40 minutes, at this time of year. His wife Guneet Kaur lay beside him, still sound asleep.

As Singh lay, puzzled, his ears were suddenly blasted by the shriek of the downstairs smoke alarm.

"Guneet!" he shouted, springing to his feet. "Wake up! The house is on fire!"

His wife, normally slow to wake, sat bolt upright in bed. Her eyes were wide with surprise and fright.

"Quick! Quick!" Singh shouted, gathering up his curved *kirpan* in its gilded sheath from the nightstand.

His *dastaar* was draped over the back of the chair that sat next to the night table, ready for him to wind about his head, once his ritual, morning ablutions were complete. He reached for it, and swiftly hung it around his neck.

"We must get out!" he warned.

Guneet scrambled out of the opposite side of their bed. Singh pulled on his *kacha* – the flowing, knee-length shorts of a devout Sikh *Khalsa* – then ran toward the hallway.

Praying fervently to *Ek Onkar*, the omnipresent and infinite, he raced down the hall toward the bedrooms where their children slept. Singh threw open the door to his daughter Harjinder's room, just as the door across the hallway flew open. His six-year-old son Jagroop, eyes as big as an owl's, stood there, in his Star Wars pajamas, his *keski* askew on his head.

"Papa?" Jagroop asked, his childish voice still blurred with sleep. "What is going on?"

"There is a fire," Singh told him. "We must leave the house. Quickly, my son!"

Singh turned back to his four-year-old daughter's room. He took two, long steps to her bedside, and scooped her up in his arms.

Returning to the hallway, he saw that his son had gone back into his room to gather up his collection of action figures.

"Jagroop!" he commanded. "Come! Leave your toys, and follow me!"

He glanced behind him. Guneet was just emerging from their bedroom. Taking his son by the hand, Singh hurried towards the stairway. Together, they plunged down the steps to the ground floor of their home.

Reaching the landing, Singh saw the living room was engulfed in flames. The fire had already reached the entryway.

"Follow me!" he cried.

Guneet's footsteps padded close behind him.

Singh sprinted for the sliding doors that opened to the back patio, and the yard beyond. He had to let go of Jagroop's hand to open the slider. As he opened the door, he nearly lost the boy, who had spun around to watch the hungry flames clawing at the dining room ceiling.

Grasping his son by the shoulder, Singh dragged Jagroop out the door. He stopped short, at the unexpected sight of five shadowy figures arrayed along the outer edge of the patio. All were dressed in hunter's camouflage, and wore ski masks. Four of the five bore cudgels. As Guneet emerged from their burning house, Bhagat Singh instinctively stepped in front of her, shielding her from the menacing strangers.

"Hello, there, you rag head motherfuckers," greeted the man in the center.

He raised a Mossberg Chainsaw 12-guage shotgun to point at Bhagat Singh's chest.

"Payback's a bitch, ain't it?" he sneered.

May 5, 2020, 6:19 am EDT

Monmouth Medical Center, West Long Branch, NJ

Gregory Alan Shergold awoke, hurting, and confused.

His head felt as if it was being crushed in a giant vise. His face throbbed with pain. He couldn't breathe through his nose, at all. He could barely force his right eye open. His teeth felt loose in their sockets.

- Where am I? -

He tried to sit up, but a wave of dizziness swept over him. Head spinning, he fell back against the pillow. Wooziness abruptly became a surge of nausea. Still weak, he turned to the side, retching. Only a thin string of black bile came up.

After a while, the urge to vomit diminished somewhat. He fell back on his pillow, and tried to take stock of his situation. It was hard to concentrate. He could not seem to get his right eye to focus. His left was blind. It was covered by a thick pad of medical gauze, held in place by turn after turn of the same material wrapped around his head.

Trying not to move his spinning head, he looked down at himself. He was dressed in a light-blue-and-white-striped hospital gown. There was a needle in his left arm, connected, via plastic tubing, to an IV bag, which hung from a stand beside the head of his bed.

- Okay. I must be in a hospital. -

As lousy as he felt, that wasn't particularly surprising. Exactly what was wrong with him was a good question. It seemed clear that he had suffered some kind of injury to his face, at the very least.

- So, now the question is: 'How did I get here?' -

He tried to recall how he had come to be in this place, but he had no memory of his arrival, or its circumstances.

- All right. What's the last thing I remember? -

No recollection surfaced. The strain of trying to remember was exhausting. It was as if he had simply appeared there, in his bed, coalescing out of thin air, the product of a kind of spontaneous generation.

- The Phantom of the Hospital. -

The notion made him smile.

Smiling hurt, he discovered, so he stopped.

- Well, then. Now the question is: 'Who am I?' -

He discovered that he had no idea who he was. He did not know his name, nor his age, nor could he recall any incident from his past. He realized he had no idea what he looked like. As far as his biography was concerned, he might as well never have existed before he had come to consciousness, in this bed, only minutes ago.

His gaze fell on the plastic, patient ID bracelet around his wrist. Unsteadily, he raised it to eye level. It took fierce concentration to make out what was printed on it. He was forced to move it further and further away from his eye, before it finally swam into focus.

"Patient ID: 292846067, Name: Gregory Alan Shergold," he read. "Date: May 4, 2020."

- My name is Gregory Alan Shergold. -

It seemed unconvincing, somehow. It was as if the name belonged to a stranger, picked at random from the phone book.

Greg wanted to cry in despair. He found that required more effort than he could muster. His tiny reserve of energy utterly spent, he let his arm drop back to the bed, closed his good eye, and let the world go away.

May 5, 2020, 7:30 am EDT

DC Jail, D Street SE, Washington, DC

Esau Piltch awoke, squinting against the harsh brightness of fluorescent lights. They flooded the holding cell in which he had spent a lonely, frightened, and uncomfortable night. He sat up on the polished steel bench, where he'd tried with limited success to nap, and looked around the crowded chamber. It was filled with miscreants – most of them Negroes. One of the biggest and scariest-looking of those Negroes was staring directly at him, making no attempt to disguise his inspection.

Piltch was uncomfortable around black people. Idaho's 1st District included very few of them, and almost all of those were registered members of the wrong party. Here in the Capitol, his interactions with persons of color had mostly been confined to those who belonged to the Congressional Black Caucus – all of them middle-aged or older, well-educated, and well-spoken. Large, young black men scared him – and the man whose gaze was fixed on him at the moment was one of the largest young black men he had ever personally encountered.

His resolve stiffening, Piltch raised his own eyes to meet those of his observer.

"May I help you?" he asked.

His voice wavered only slightly.

"Yeah," the muscular, young man replied. "You that Congress-man, ain't you?"

"I beg your pardon?" Piltch responded.

"That Congress-man," his spectator repeated. "You know – the one what killed that dude."

Piltch's shoulders involuntarily hunched. His neck contracted, as if he were part tortoise, attempting to withdraw into his shell.

"It was an accident," he explained.

His tone was defensive.

"I didn't mean to ..." his voice trailed off.

The big man giggled. The sound was incongruous, coming out of such a massive frame.

"You in a heap of trouble, son," he told Piltch.

"But I'm a Congressman," Piltch protested, "not a common criminal!"

He immediately regretted his outburst.

Hastily, he added, "I mean no offense to you."

The man shrugged

"Ain't no thing," he said, offhandedly. "'A common criminal' is what I am."

His eyes glittered with amusement.

"And you a cracker," he added.

Piltch flinched.

"Ain't nobody no privileged character in here, dawg," the big man laughed.

"But I'm a member of Congress," Piltch complained. "I'd think they'd realize that – and treat me accordingly."

"Shee-it," the man commented, unfolding himself from the bench on which he sat. "You think they don't know that?"

He shook his head.

"'Course they do!" he continued, answering his own, rhetorical question. "They makin' an *example* of you, you know what I mean?"

"Wh-what?" Piltch responded, shaken.

"That dude you killed," the big man explained. "He a cop. Don't *nobody* kill no cop without they make an example of him. Everybody know *that*."

May 5, 2020, 8:15 am EDT

East Orange Golf Course, Short Hills, NJ

Donell Jackson was dreaming.

Nakeesha Gramble clung to him. She hugged him fiercely, crying, "I love you, Donell! Don't leave me! Please, don't leave me!" As he gazed down at the weeping child, the flesh melted from her bones, leaving only a small, white skeleton, with huge, brown eyes. Its skull was still improbably crowned with neat cornrows. Mingled horror and pity stopped his tongue, kept him from telling her ...

Suddenly, Jackson was awake. Revulsion and guilt, in equal measure, propelled him, shuddering, to a sitting position.

"I apologize for waking you, Donell," Big Sugar Washington said.

His deep voice was gentle with concern.

"It appeared as though you were experiencing a nightmare," he observed.

Jackson ran a hand over his forehead. It came away dripping, rank with sweat.

"You can say that again," he confirmed. "Ugh."

"It is just as well that you are awake, now," Washington told him. "Breakfast will only be available for another 15 minutes."

Donell rubbed his crusted eyes. He swung his feet off the cot, and reached for the Nikes he had stashed beneath it, the night before.

"is the grub here any good?" he asked.

Big Sugar shrugged.

"I regret to report that it does not quite measure up to the high standards of our alma mater," he replied.

Wrinkling his nose at his own aroma, Donell said, "Well, no loss, then. Right now, I need a shower more than I need powdered eggs.

Shoes tied, he stood up.

"Besides," he added, "I've got to see Latonya, anyway. I'll just pick something up at the hospital."

"I fear that is unlikely, Donell," Big Sugar said, shaking his head.

"What do you mean, Boss?" Jackson asked.

"Firstly," Washington responded, holding up a finger, "I doubt you would be permitted to see Ms. Gramble."

"Why not?" Donell demanded.

"Am I correct in my assumption that you two are not, in fact, husband and wife?" Big Sugar inquired.

"No, we're not married," Jackson admitted.

"Then standard hospital protocols will bar you from visiting her in an isolation ward," Washington explained. He added, "But that is actually beside the point."

"Why?" Donell asked. "What's the actual point?"

"The more cogent issue," Big Sugar told him, holding up a second finger, "is that, in all likelihood, you will not be permitted to leave these premises."

"What do you mean?" Jackson demanded. "I'm an American citizen. As far as these turkeys know, I got a right to go anywhere I damn well please."

Washington shook his massive head.

"I regret to say that you are incorrect," he replied. "As I predicted, the President has indeed declared martial law. In turn, the local military authorities have decreed that we 'refugees' are to be confined here, 'for our own protection', until they can arrange to transport us out of what they are calling the Fallout Zone."

His lips quirked, in a mirthless smile.

"You mean ... ?" Donell began.

"Yes, Donell," Big Sugar told him. "It appears that, once again, we are prisoners."

May 5, 2020, 9:13 am EDT

House of the Elect, I Street NW, Washington, DC

"Then we're agreed?" asked the Honorable Chester K. Chester, Representative of South Carolina's impoverished 5th District.

A chorus of affirmatives greeted his question. They came from his mostly-Southern and evangelical, Congressional brethren seated around the big oak breakfast table.

"We hold firm," responded Elvin Wheelwright, Georgia's 1st District Representative. "No tax increases. Period."

"Amen," agreed Bass Ransom, Republican junior Senator from Texas, the lone Senate member of the House of the Elect.

"What about the aid package?" inquired Joad Fungo, freshman Representative from Kansas' 1st District. "Are we gonna vote for that?"

"It's too popular," replied Chester. "We're gonna have to."

Ransom chuckled.

"Of course," he observed, "there ain't no way that bastard in the White House is gonna be able to pay for it, without a tax increase."

His fellow politicians made cheerful sounds of agreement.

"This is gonna be mighty entertainin'," Wheelwright observed.

"That it is," concurred Chester.

He looked around the table, at his fellow members of the House of the Elect.

"Gentlemen," he announced, "I believe a prayer is in order."

He turned to Fungo.

"Brother Joad," he requested, "would you be so kind as to favor us with a prayer?"

"I'd be honored," Fungo replied.

He put his palms together, closed his eyes, and bowed his head.

"Dear Lord," he intoned.

His voice throbbed with piety.

"We humbly beg You," he continued, "in the name of Your only-begotten Son Jesus, to bless us all and to guide us in the task You have set before us. Lend us, we pray, Your strength and Your wisdom, as we prepare to do battle with the godless monster William Orwell Steele. And Lord, please watch over and protect our beloved brother Esau Piltch, who even now languishes in the dark dungeons of the faithless. Your rod and Your staff, they comfort us. Our faith and devotion sustain us. May we always and only strive to do Your will. Amen."

"Amen," chorused his fellow believers.

Ransom pushed back his sleeves and picked up his fork

"Gentlemen," he said, "let's eat."

May 5, 2020, 10:24 am EDT

The Cabinet Room, Washington, DC

"*Poor Will,*" Diana Hunter thought, "*He looks even worse than I feel.*"

Dozing fitfully in the chair beside her dying husband's bed, the Vice President had managed little sleep. It was clear that the President had gotten even less. His features were haggard and bleary. The famous deep blue eyes seemed washed-out and faded from fatigue. Their lids were puffy and red-tinged, their sockets ringed with dark circles. He carried his leonine head low between his shoulders, like a prizefighter trying to present a smaller target to his opponent.

"... we're beginning to see a pattern of this kind of attack across the country," Secretary of Health and Human Services Ashley Conden reported. "This morning, persons unknown firebombed the house of a Sikh couple in Ohio. They beat the man to death, in front of his wife and small children."

Anger blazed in William Orwell Steele's deep blue eyes.

"Arleigh?" he demanded, turning to his Secretary of Internal Security. "What can you tell me about this incident?"

"Very little as of yet, Mr. President," Arleigh Solomon replied. "From all indications, it appears to have been an isolated event, rather than part of an organized campaign. But agents from the FBI office in Cincinnati only arrived on-scene a little over an hour ago, and evidence-gathering in the case obviously is still ongoing."

"I want an extremely public example made of whoever is responsible for this outrage," Steele ordered. "Do I make myself clear?"

"Perfectly, sir," Solomon agreed.

"We simply cannot allow hate crimes," the President continued. "We have an obligation to make that clear to even our most backward citizens."

"Hear, hear!" Diana Hunter responded, approvingly.

A mutter of assent ran around the long, oval table.

"All right, what's next?" Steele asked.

"Mr. President," responded Secretary of Commerce Marcy Collins, "we're getting widespread reports of price gouging in western New York, Pennsylvania, and Massachusetts – particularly for gasoline. Given the already-adverse economic impact of the evacuation on residents of the Fallout Zone, we think it's a legitimate concern."

"How widespread is 'widespread'?" asked Steele.

"Very," replied Collins. "And in some cases, the mark-up being demanded is downright piratical, sir."

"Such as?" the President demanded.

Collins consulted the report in front of her.

"Mr. President, we've had reports of prices as high as twenty dollars a gallon in places along Interstate 90," she told him.

"*Twenty* dollars a gallon?" Steele repeated, incredulous.

"Yes, sir," the Secretary confirmed.

"That's utterly outrageous!" the President fumed.

"Yes, sir," Collins agreed. "Unfortunately, there is a genuine supply problem in that area. Deliveries have understandably been disrupted. As a result, a substantial number of gas stations in the area have either gone to short hours, or they're limiting the amount of fuel any single customer can purchase at one time." She looked up from the summary she had been using as a reference. "Supply considerations aside, however, it seems clear that some dealers are taking unreasonable advantage of the situation."

Steele turned to Eric Forste, his Secretary of Transportation.

"Eric," he asked, "what impact would releasing oil from the Strategic Petroleum Reserve have on the problem?"

"In the short term?" Forste replied. "Probably none. Mr. President, those reserves are of crude oil, not refined gasoline. Theoretically speaking, in the medium run stuffing crude into the production pipeline should eventually bring down the wholesale price of gas. But that might or might not translate into lower prices at the pump – and it would still leave unaddressed the problem of constrained supplies in the Northeast region."

"Damn it," Steele demanded, "What can we do about this problem? Anybody?"

"You *could* declare a price ceiling on retail gasoline, Mr. President," suggested Secretary of the Treasury Anderson Connaught IV.

"Can I?" Steele asked, turning to Evan Spitzberger, the Attorney General.

Spitzberger nodded.

"Yes, Mr. President," he said, "you can. Keeping in mind that you have declared martial law, and that Congress has ratified that declaration, you'll find your powers in this regard are quite broad."

"In that case," Diana Hunter broke in, "Mr. President, why not just nationalize the oil industry?"

"Excuse me, Madam Vice President?" Steele replied.

"Forgive my interruption, sir," Hunter said, "but I think we may be missing a golden opportunity, here."

"Please explain," Steele invited.

"As you know, Mr. President," the Vice President responded, "ever since the Carter administration, Presidents have been trying to wean the American public off its oil addiction. Because of determined opposition from – and lobbying by – the oil patch, that effort has been a non-starter for more than four decades now. Despite greatly increased domestic drilling, our economy is still essentially a hostage of OPEC." Her eyes blazed with enthusiasm, despite her tiredness. " This could be the opportunity every president since Carter has been looking for: a chance to take the oil industry's money out of the equation. Given petroleum's profit margin, nationalizing the industry could even help fund the May Day Act."

"Mr. President!" protested Secretary of the Interior Joanna Muir. "Begging your pardon, but that's a ridiculous suggestion! Congress would never stand for such a move! The opposition would crucify us!"

"Congress wouldn't have much say in the matter," the Vice President riposted. "Sir."

The President held up a hand to forestall further argument.

"Okay," he said. "For the moment, let's declare a cap of … say seven dollars a gallon on regular, seven-and-a-half for premium, and eight bucks a gallon for diesel from the Ohio border East, effective immediately and until further notice. Failure to adhere to those limits to be punishable by forfeiture of all profits and confiscation of the business itself. Fair enough?"

He looked around the table for dissent and found none.

"All right," Steele said.

He turned to Diana Hunter.

"Madam Vice President," he offered, "if you'd be so good as to prepare a report on your proposal to nationalize the oil industry, I'll take it under advisement."

The smile with which Hunter greeted the President's request was positively feral.

"It will be my pleasure, Mr. President," she assured him.

May 5, 2020, 11:32 am EDT

Monmouth Medical Center, West Long Branch, NJ

Eydis Finnursdottir was sitting up in bed, staring out the window, when Lieutenant Rupert Griffin Stewart entered her hospital room. Stewart was attired in Navy dress uniform, carrying a soft-sided leather attaché case. Eydis turned to face him, as Stewart approached her. He flinched at the sight of her battered features and bruised flesh.

"Er … " the Lieutenant inquired, "are you one Eydis Finnursdottir, citizen of Iceland?"

"I am one, yes," Eydis replied. "Do you suppose there might be another one?"

Stewart scowled, unsure whether he was being teased.

"Please forgive my little joke, yes?" Eydis said. "My English is not good enough for making humor, I think."

She smiled at him, and Stewart's resentment evaporated.

"I've heard worse," Stewart confessed. "In fact, I've probably told worse jokes than that myself – and my command of English is excellent."

Eydis dimpled.

"You are very kind," she said. "How is it that I may help you?"

"I'm afraid it's the other way around," Stewart replied. "My name is Rupert Griffin Stewart, and I am, in fact, here to help *you*. The Judge Advocate General's office has appointed me as your counsel. I'll be defending you against the charges JAG has laid."

"Oh, my!" Eydis said. "Then I am confined in this way …" she lifted her right arm so that the handcuff attached to it clanked against her bed rail, "… because I am somehow a criminal? What is my crime, please?"

"Miss Finnursdottir … it is 'Miss', is it not?" Griffin asked.

Eydis nodded.

"Yes, I am unmarried," she confirmed.

"Miss Finnursdottir," Stewart said, "you are a foreign national who was found in possession of an unregistered handgun. Under civilian law that would be a felony in and of itself."

Eydis's free hand flew to cover her mouth. Her green eyes widened as far as their bruise-swollen lids allowed.

"However," Stewart continued, "the United States is currently under martial law, which makes it a matter for the military justice system. I'm sorry to tell you that, as a foreign tourist found in possession of an unregistered firearm, you have automatically been charged as an enemy combatant, as well."

"Oh, no!" Eydis cried. "But I do not wish any harm to the United States, Mr. Stewart! How can this be?"

"It's 'Lieutenant Stewart', Miss Finnursdottir," Stewart told her. "And pardon me for saying so, but just looking at you, I get the impression there may be what we would call 'extenuating circumstances' involved."

Eydis nodded timidly.

"Yes?" she said, uncertainly.

Stewart pulled the visitor's chair out from its place against the wall. He moved it to where he could sit facing Eydis.

"Why don't you explain to me exactly what happened to you," he suggested, "and how you came to be in possession of that gun?"

May 5, 2020, 12:04 pm EDT

The Senate Chamber of the Capitol Building, Washington, DC

Democratic junior Senator from Kentucky Delbert Aiden Dance, who had been appointed by the Majority Leader to serve as Acting President of the Senate *Pro Tempore*, sat down in the high-backed Presiding Officer's chair. He turned it to face the Senate floor. The Members and staff spread out before and below him were in the process of resuming their seats, as he picked up the hourglass-shaped, ivory gavel from its place to his right on the desk at the top of the dais.

"The Senate will be in order," Dance announced

He lightly tapped the gavel on the desk in front of him.

Vittorio Donofrio rose from his seat at the Majority's management desk in the well of the chamber.

"Mr. President," he said.

"The Chair recognizes Senator Donofrio," Dance acknowledged.

"Mr. President," Donofrio said, his Brooklyn accent unmistakable, "I ask unanimous consent to dispense wit' the morning business."

"Hearing no objection ..." Dance responded. Pausing no more than a heartbeat, he continued, "It is so ordered."

He brought the ivory gavel down, softly.

"Mr. President," Donofrio stated, "I move the Senate proceed to consider the matter to be known as the May Day Relief Act, under the terms of a unanimous consent agreement, that it be numbered SB 1141, and that it be considered to have been previously read twice before the Senate."

Christopher "Chris" Kohler, Majority Whip, and senior Senator from Oregon, half-rose from his seat beside Donofrio.

"The Chair recognizes Senator Kohler," said Delbert Dance.

"Mr. President, I second the motion," Kohler stated.

He resumed his seat.

"It has been moved and seconded that this Chamber proceed to consider the matter of the May Day Relief Act," Dance announced, lifting his gavel. "Is it the will of the Senate that it be brought to the floor?"

He paused momentarily before continuing.

"Hearing no objection," Dance said, "it is so ordered."

He again brought the gavel down, then turned to Marjorie Kern, the Senate's Legislative Clerk.

"The Clerk will report the title of the bill," he directed.

"SB 1141 shall henceforth be known as 'The May Day Relief Act: A Bill to provide financial assistance and relief for the victims of the act of nuclear terrorism that occurred on May 1, 2020 in New York City'," she stated.

"Thank you, Madam Clerk," Dance said.

He returned his gaze to the Majority Leader.

"Senator Donofrio?" he invited.

Donofrio raised a sheet of Senate stationery to his shoulder level, and shook it for visual effect.

"Mr. President," he announced, "it was my intention to ask unanimous consent in this matter – a bill, I feel compelled to point out, that is of critical importance to millions of our constituents and those of our colleagues in the House. Many of these voters now languish in FEMA's temporary housing facilities, bereft of their homes, their businesses, and the majority of their possessions an' property. However, per the Rules as adopted at the beginning of the 116th, I have received from Senator Ransom of Texas written notice that he objects to this bill as presented."

The Majority Leader turned to glare at Ransom. Ignoring Donofrio's disapproval, the Texan made an elaborate display of brushing an imaginary speck of lint off his immaculate shirt cuff.

"Therefore, Mr. President," Donofrio concluded, returning his gaze to the dais, "I am left with no choice but to move we proceed to consider this matter without preconditions on the terms of our debate, an' to ask for a second."

"Second," Kohler instantly responded, half-rising to his feet.

"Hearing no objection …" Dance repeated. "… it is so ordered."

He brought the gavel down, again.

"Mr. President," Donofrio stated, brandishing a new sheet of Senate stationery, "in accordance with Rule Twenty-two, I now present to the Clerk a petition, signed by myself and 15 of my distinguished colleagues, to invoke cloture in the debate on SB 1141."

Suiting action to words, the Majority Leader walked to the bar of the dais and handed the petition to Kern.

"The clerk will read the petition," Dance ordered.

Without rising from her seat, Kern read aloud, "'We, the undersigned, hereby petition to bring to a close debate upon SB 1141, and, *per* Rule Twenty-two of the Senate Rules and Procedures, to limit to no more than 30 hours *in toto* the time allotted for that debate.'"

She read aloud the names of the petition's signers, beginning with Donofrio's, and concluding with, "… and Senator Abby Cobelli of California."

Kern turned to look over her shoulder at Dance.

"Mr. President," she announced, "I count on this Petition the required sixteen signatures of Senators, duly elected, and chosen."

"The Chair accepts the petition," Dance said. "The Senate will vote upon the petition in two legislative days' time. Germane amendments to the underlying Motion shall therefore be offered no later than the stipulated deadlines of the next legislative day, and amendments in the second degree shall be offered on the second legislative day, no later than one hour prior to the vote to limit debate."

He banged the gavel.

"Senator Donofrio?" Dance prompted.

"Mr. President," Donofrio responded, "Let us now lay this matter aside, until the petition to limit debate shall have ripened, an' proceed to consider other matters in the meantime."

The Majority Leader consulted the schedule on the desk before him.

"Our next order of business will be to consider SB 1129, known as the Enhanced Federal Intelligence Surveillance Act, or E-FISA," he announced.

"Mr. President?" said Vincent Govan, the Vermont independent who was known as the conscience of the Senate. "I rise to speak in opposition to the bill."

"Senator Govan," Delbert Dance replied, "You have the floor."

May 5, 2020, 10:15 am PDT (May 5, 1:15 pm EDT)

Alvarado Street, San Leandro, CA

Adolph Ryan Wolf watched his underlings extract Artemis Steele's nude, unconscious body from the sensory deprivation chamber in which she had floated for the past 12 hours. The sight of her perfect, glistening form lying on the gurney, dripping Epsom salt solution on the floor of the warehouse that served as the clandestine headquarters of the Aryan Revolutionary Front, gave him an immediate, painfully-urgent erection.

- Mine. Physically now – and soon enough mentally and emotionally, as well. -

The prospect of breaking the President's daughter to his whim, of making her his willing – no, his *eager* – slave brought him more satisfaction than anything in his previous experience. However, the anticipation of possessing her physically, of taking her rumored maidenhead, of fucking the living shit out of her beautiful, athletic body was nothing compared to the excitement that gripped him at the prospect of her total surrender.

- I wish I could see the expression on that sonofabitch's face when she makes her first public announcement. -

He was transported with delight at the mental image of William Orwell Steele's furious, horrified visage. Wolf loathed the President. He despised Steele as a weakling, abominated his pandering, Socialist agenda, and hated still more the miscegenated mass of Takers who worshipped him. Bringing the man down was not enough for the secretive billionaire – he was driven to humiliate and torture his nemesis, to trample and obliterate him. Taking Steele's precious, lesbian daughter, and making her not only his panting sex slave, but the figurehead of the revolt against her father's misrule seemed to him an excellent beginning to that end.

Wolf turned to Dr. Increase Bright. Bright had been his friend and *confidante* since their days as roommates at Stanford University.

"How long will she be out?" he asked.

"Given her body mass," Bright replied, "at least another 45 minutes."

"And how long will your maintenance routine take?" Wolf demanded.

"Between 20 and 30 minutes, I expect," Bright told him. "If we skip the colonic, more like 10 to 20 minutes. Why do you ask?"

"I have to fuck her, Inky," Wolf confessed.

He stared down the long, luscious length of her legs, straight at Artemis Steele's irresistibly-beckoning, bare pubis.

"I have to fuck her right now," he added.

Bright shrugged.

"That shouldn't present a problem," he said. "She's shown about average tolerance for pentothal so far. If she starts to come around, I can always give her another 30 milligrams, and put her back under. You can rape her to your heart's content, Dolph. I assure you, she won't feel – or remember – a thing."

May 5, 2020, 2:21 pm EDT,

CIA Headquarters, Colonial Farm Road, McLean, VA

Director of the CIA Christopher Murdock looked up from the desk, in his office on the top floor of the Agency headquarters complex. Located in the unincorporated section of Fairfax County, Virginia, the Agency's home was known as Langley or McLean.

"Come in, Ty," he said to Tyrone James, Deputy Director for the National Clandestine Service. "What's up?"

"It's Rawalpindi, sir," James replied.

He strode across the blue-and-white patterned carpet to stand before Murdock's desk.

"And?" Murdock responded.

He closed the red Top Secret folder in front of him.

"What's the issue with Rawalpindi?" he demanded.

"They've completed their preliminary interrogation of General Sheikh," James told him. "Now they're asking for further instructions."

Murdock frowned. "Why?" he asked.

"Apparently, the Paks are all fucking over Islamabad and Rawalpindi," James explained. "They're putting a lot of pressure on their sources for information about Sheikh's kidnapping – a *lot* of pressure. O'Brien, the Deputy Chief of Station there, is concerned that one or more of his contractors will crack."

"I see," Murdock said. "Has he got something in mind to take the heat off?"

"Yes, sir," James said. "He'd like to dump Sheikh in the Swat, and make it look like the Taliban took him."

Murdock pushed his chair back from the desk, got to his feet, and turned to look out the window. It featured a view over the triple-canopied central courtyard of the Agency's headquarters complex. He stood there in silence for a long moment. Then he spoke, without turning around.

"I hate to throw away an asset as valuable as General Sheikh," he said.

"Yes, sir," acknowledged James.

He was aware the Director was thinking out loud.

"On the other hand," Murdock continued, "if O'Brien's people get caught with him … well, that would not be good."

"No, sir," James agreed, "it certainly would not."

Murdock turned around to face James. He gripped the back of his swivel chair with both hands.

"What have they learned from Sheikh, so far?" he asked.

"Well, sir, first," replied James, holding up his right index finger, "he's confirmed it was the Paks who bombed Manhattan. Apparently they've been working on it ever since the Shirani thing went South."

Murdock nodded.

He had inherited the job of DCIA in the aftermath of the disastrous failure of Operation Playmate – the CIA plot to assassinate General Mohammed Danish Shirani, then Director-General of Pakistan's Inter-Service Intelligence Directorate. Lives – and, more importantly, key intelligence assets – had been lost. Worse, the Agency itself had suffered a significant loss of credibility, not only with Congress, but with its assets and allies around the world. In addition, U.S.-Pakistan relations had been dealt a blow from which, it was now clear, they had never recovered.

"They code-named it 'Sword of Allah'," James added.

He raised his middle finger to join the first.

"Second," he continued, "he's confirmed that it was one of our assets named Darwish Sultan that blew Operation Playmate."

"Did he say how?" Murdock asked, his interest piqued.

The root cause of Playmate's failure had been a matter of Agency speculation for the past two years.

"Yes, sir," James said. "He asked them for money. And they gave it to him. A lot of it."

"Fucking contractors," Murdock said, with feeling.

"Yes, sir," James agreed.

He held up a third finger.

"Third," he continued, "he gave up two of our Pak assets he claims are doubles."

Murdock grunted. Known double agents could be especially valuable resources, if they remained unaware their status had been blown. On the other hand ...

"What level of confidence does O'Brien place in that item?" he asked.

James held his hand out, palm down, and wiggled it from side to side.

"Middling," he replied. "That's part of the conundrum."

"Of course," Murdock agreed.

James held up a fourth finger.

"Fourth," he added, "he's revealed the locations of a number of safe houses – Indian, Russian, and our own."

"That's interesting," Murdock commented.

"Yes, sir," James agreed. "What's especially interesting is that his intel on the Russian safe house, and the two Indian ones, matches information from other sources."

"That's *very* interesting," Murdock replied.

"Yes, sir," James said. He held up his thumb, folding the other four fingers into a fist. "Fifth: he gave up the names of a bunch of agents – Paks and others – there, here, and elsewhere."

"Anyone we didn't already know about?" Murdock asked.

"A few," James told him.

"Damn," Murdock commented.

Clearly, General Rashid Omar Sheikh had been an extremely valuable acquisition. O'Brien's problem was that the Paks obviously thought so, too. It was no wonder the ISI was determined to get him back – or to force his kidnappers to kill him, before he could reveal still more damaging information.

"All right," Murdock said, "O'Brien is the one whose ass is in the clamp. He knows how valuable Sheikh is to us, and he still wants to get rid of him. So tell him to get Sheikh's confession to this 'Sword of Allah' business on video. Have him get a signed, written confession, too – and video of him signing it. In the meantime, I'll kick this upstairs and ask for instructions."

"Are you sure that's a good idea?" James asked. "What about deniability?"

Murdock shook his head.

"Believe me," he told James, "POTUS has made it abundantly clear he's strictly hands-on for this operation. As for deniability ... there's been no paper trail, so far. As long as the White House hasn't been recording Security Council meetings – and I doubt they have – the President still has it, if he wants it."

James shrugged.

"Well," he responded, "he's the boss. Do you have any instructions for O'Brien, while we're waiting for orders from on high?"

"Tell him to get the video and the signed confession out in the next diplomatic bag," Murdock directed, "and to destroy any local copies the instant we confirm their arrival."

"Will do," James confirmed. "Anything else?"

"Yes," Murdock replied. "Tell him I said, 'Don't get caught.'"

May 5, 2020, 3:19 pm EDT

U.S. District Court, 3rd Street NW, Washington, DC

Representative Esau Piltch of Idaho's 1st District goggled at the swarm of photographers and cameramen, fighting to stick their lenses against the smoked glass of the stretch Cadillac Escalade in which he sat. Making his way through the press of paparazzi and media representatives, just moments earlier, had been one of the most intimidating experiences of his life. It had been nearly as daunting as the humiliating process of being booked into DC Jail the previous day, and the ordeal of his arraignment on charges of manslaughter less than an hour ago.

"What's wrong with those … people?" Piltch asked aloud. "They're like ants!"

"More like cockroaches," commented Jameson Matthew Peek, Esquire.

The attorney had appeared beside him, as if by magic, as he entered the courtroom of U.S. District Court Judge Joshua R. Lovett. Peek had entered a plea of "not guilty" on Piltch's behalf, and asked for and obtained his release on his own recognizance, as well. Seated next to his client in the back of the limousine, the barrister now leaned forward, and tapped the chauffeur on the shoulder.

Let's go," he ordered. "Get us out of here."

The driver raised both hands. He shrugged helplessly.

Catching Peek's eye in the rearview mirror, he complained, "They're blocking the road, sir."

"Blow your horn, and start edging forward," Peek told him. "They'll get out of the way quickly enough."

"Yes, sir," the chauffeur said. He began laying on the Escalade's horn.

"Idiots," Peek announced.

He made no effort to keep the driver from overhearing him.

"I'm surrounded by idiots," he complained.

Thinking the comment had been directed at him, Piltch quailed, and shrank back in his seat.

"Drink?" Peek inquired.

The lawyer flipped open the portable bar, and began rummaging in it for a suitable Scotch.

Piltch shook his head. "I'd better not," he replied. "I haven't eaten anything since yesterday morning."

Peek turned in his seat to look at his fellow passenger.

"They didn't feed you in jail?" he asked, his tone eager.

Piltch shook his head.

"No … that is … I didn't have much of an appetite," he explained. "It wasn't very appealing food, anyway," he added.

"Jail food never is," Peek assured him, losing interest. "Or, so I've repeatedly heard from my clients."

"I guess that's right," Piltch agreed, glumly.

He turned to look out the window at the Francis Perkins building, as the limo turned the corner onto Constitution Avenue NW. Peek busied himself with ice tongs, a bottle of Haig & Haig, and a lowball glass.

As Peek settled back to sip at his drink, Piltch asked, "Where are we going, anyway?"

"There's likely to be just as big a crowd of those parasites around your house in Arlington as there was at the courthouse, so I've taken the liberty of renting you a room at the Watergate," Peek responded.

"I'd rather stay at the House of the Elect, if it's all the same to you," Piltch requested, diffidently.

"Absolutely not," Peek replied, sternly.

"Wh … why not?" Piltch asked, bewildered.

"Because we're being followed, you fool!" Peek told him. "And because the very *last* thing the Party wants is to call the press's attention to your fellow nitwits at the so-called 'House of the Elect'."

"How dare you talk to me that way!" Piltch demanded, his dignity wounded beyond his ability to contain himself. "I am still a United States Congressman, you know!"

"Yeah," Peek replied, unimpressed. "You won't be for very much longer, Piltch – so enjoy it while it lasts."

"Wh ... what do you mean, I 'won't be for very much longer'?" Piltch inquired.

His dudgeon deflated in the face of Peek's calm certainty.

"I mean you're going to resign your office, in exchange for a slap on the wrist for your inexcusable stupidity in killing a beloved officer of the Congress you've so thoroughly disgraced," Peek snorted. "And then you're going to tuck your tail between your legs, high-tail it back to Bumfuck, Idaho, and keep your pointed, little head down until this whole, sorry mess blows over. That's what I mean."

His chin quivering in indignation, Piltch asked, "And if I refuse?"

"Then the Party is going to hang your dumb ass out to dry," Peek told him. "And, regardless of what the DC District Court does to you, they're going to impeach your sorry butt, and toss you the fuck out of Congress."

Piltch opened and closed his mouth. He managed to look rather like a feeding bass in the process, but no words came out.

"In which case," Peek added, "you'll lose your House pension and benefits – in addition to whatever the Court decides to do to you. Do you have any further questions, Congressman?"

His lips trembling, eyes filling with stinging tears, Piltch silently shook his head. Shame forced him to look away. He stared, unseeing, at the parade of government buildings flowing past the limo on Constitution Avenue.

After a while, he turned back to Peek. The Congressman still could not meet his lawyer's eyes.

"I think I will have that drink, after all," Piltch said, in a low, sad voice.

May 5, 2020, 4:26 pm EDT

Section 60, Arlington National Cemetery, Ft. Meyer, VA

William Orwell Steele struggled to master the grief that threatened to overwhelm him. He could not help but be aware of the crowd of media cameramen, just 100 feet away. The nation, he knew, desperately needed him to present an image of strong, confident leadership. He simply could not afford to give in to the flood of tears threatening to breach the dam of his self-control.

A sleepless night had left him exhausted and vulnerable. His concern for his kidnapped daughter's safety – his outright terror, to be honest – further undermined his ability to keep his emotions in check. Simply taking Artie had been a deliberate provocation by parties as yet unknown. Wantonly slaughtering her entire Secret Service contingent had been an act of deliberate terrorism: a statement of contempt for him, his administration, and the standards of civilized behavior. The message it sent seemed clear. It could only be a declaration of war; the opening gun in a conflict that promised to be savage beyond reason.

Beside him sat the widow of Secret Service Agent John Thomas Bailey.

Bailey was one of two uniformed agents who had died in that lunatic Richard Wayne Lee's quixotic assault on the White House. The prospect of more than a dozen such funerals over the next week or so was depressing enough. The distinct probability of many more to come before this latest challenge to the Republic and his Administration was overcome filled the President with despair.

To counteract the drain on his emotional reserves, Steele forced himself to focus on the minutiae of the occasion, rather than on its meaning. As a lifelong civilian, he had not previously had the chance to observe a funeral service with full military honors. The solemn pomp of the ceremony was a new experience for him.

Sitting beneath the plain, white canopy, the President watched in fascination as a military band approached the grave site at a slow march. It softly played a slow, mournful arrangement of The Battle Hymn Of The Republic. Behind the band marched an honor guard comprised of every off-duty Secret Service agent in Washington. Some were in the Service's own uniform, others in the dress uniforms of various branches of the armed forces in which the individual Agents had served, prior to joining the Treasury Department. Following them was the four-member color guard, carrying the flags of the United States and the Marine Corps. Bringing up the rear of the procession was the horse-drawn caisson, bearing its flag-wrapped burden. It was flanked on either side by solemn-faced pallbearers, their Officer in Charge following behind.

The funeral train halted on Marshall Drive, just beyond the grave site. Steele watched as the pallbearers carefully lifted the casket from the caisson. The two men at the rear of the carriage folded back the star field end of the American flag to reveal the coffin's head. Holding the casket above shoulder level, the pallbearers sidestepped in unison, until the coffin cleared the rear of the caisson. Then, lowering their burden to waist level, they turned 90 degrees in four short, coordinated steps.

The band began to play America The Beautiful, as the pallbearers slowly approached the grave site. Each synchronized pace was followed by a brief pause, until they reached the bronze bier over the grave. After carefully setting the casket down on the metal frame, the six pallbearers each took hold of the edges of the American flag. They stepped back, so that the flag was stretched taut between them.

The Officer in Charge of the rifle detail, whose members had been standing at attention 50 feet from the grave, shouted, "Present arms!"

Seven riflemen moved as one to comply.

"Ready!" commanded the OIC.

Seven riflemen raised their weapons to a 45 degree angle.

"Fire!"

Seven rifles spoke as one. Seven riflemen ejected spent cartridges, and returned to the ready position. Their movements were perfectly synchronized.

"Fire!"

Seven shots rang out. Seven cartridges hit the ground.

"Fire!"

Seven rifles fired. Seven empty cartridges were ejected.

"Present arms!"

The rifle detail complied. They stood frozen at attention, as the bugler raised his instrument. He began slowly, soulfully, and with great feeling to play Taps.

The final note of Butterfield's Lullaby lingered in the air for a long moment afterward.

Standing over the casket, the pallbearers began the elaborate process of preparing the flag for presentation to Agent Bailey's widow. It was first folded over twice, lengthwise. Then the two men at the foot of the coffin began to turn it into the classic, triangular bundle. As they worked, the other pallbearers passed the remaining length from hand to hand, until the final fold was made, and the remaining triangle of fabric was stuffed into the folded portion.

The Marine who was facing the mourners pressed the folded flag against his chest to flatten it, before he handed it across the casket to the soldier opposite him. The compacted flag was passed down the line of pallbearers, until it reached the Officer in Charge. The last man to have touched the folded flag saluted, as the OIC stood stiffly at attention.

At a quiet command, the pallbearers turned, and marched away. The OIC turned toward the mourners. He took four steps, went to one knee before the widow of Agent Bailey, and presented the folded flag to her.

"On behalf of the President of the United States," he recited, unable to keep himself from indulging in one swift, sidelong glance at Steele, "the United States Marine Corps, and a grateful Nation, please accept this flag, as a symbol of our appreciation for your loved one's honorable and faithful service."

As the OIC stood and saluted, Sarah Cowell, the Arlington Lady assigned to Agent Bailey's funeral, stepped forward.

She bent at the waist to murmur her personal condolences to his widow. Cowell presented Mary Bailey with a sympathy card from the Chief of

Staff of the Army and his wife, expressing thanks for Bailey's service. She also gave Mrs. Bailey a separate card from the Arlington Ladies themselves. Cowell then stood, to resume her place by her Old Guard escort.

As the chaplain spoke the words, "Dearly beloved ..." Mary Virginia Bailey broke down completely.

Her features a mask of agony, Agent Bailey's widow turned to the President of the United States. She buried her face in his neck. Anguished, heaving sobs racked her slim frame.

Steele's determination to preserve his own dignity dissolved in the face of her grief. As he gathered her in his arms, and began soothingly to pat her shoulder, William Orwell Steele at last let his own tears flow, unashamed.

May 5, 2020, 5:17 pm EDT

Northern State Prison, Newark, NJ

"I'm sorry, Warden, but I can't do that," said Second Lieutenant Dolores Anunciacion de la Madonna Pena.

"Why the hell not?" demanded Nathaniel Lundegran.

"Primarily because my people have been tasked with locating, and extracting survivors from the Fallout Zone," Pena replied, "not acting as substitute prison guards. I follow my orders, Warden. I don't have the authority to deviate from them."

Lundegran thrust out his lower jaw, and opened his mouth to respond.

"There is also the fact that my people are not trained as prison guards," Pena continued, cutting him off.

"'Corrections Officers'," Lundegran amended.

"Thank you for making my point for me," Pena said, nodding amicably.

As Lundegran again opened his mouth to complain, she clarified, "Which is that my command is so unqualified for that task, that I didn't even know the proper terminology for the job you want me to assign them to do."

Lundegran's expression spoke volumes about his unhappiness.

"All right," he conceded grudgingly, "I take your point. So, how do you propose to go about extracting *my* people and the inmate population?"

"I don't," Pena told him.

"What the fuck?" Lundegran barked. "Didn't you just finish telling me that your orders are to locate, *and extract* survivors from the Fallout Zone?"

"I did," Pena agreed.

"So, what the fuck are *we*?" Lundegran demanded. "House flies?"

"No, sir," Pena said.

Her tone was calm, her demeanor contained

"But I cannot in good conscience call for evacuation of your inmates, until I've had a chance to confer with my superiors regarding the situation here," she told him.

"Fuck!" Lundegran roared, slamming his fist down on his desk for emphasis. "Fuck, fuck, fuck, fuck, *fuck*! Do you have *any* idea how exhausted my CO's are, Lieutenant? Do you have any faint, fucking notion how piss-poor their morale is? *Do you*?"

"I'm sure conditions for you and your men are terrible," Pena told him. "Unfortunately, that doesn't change the realities of the situation."

She leaned forward. Her tone became sympathetic.

"Warden," Pena explained, "I honestly don't think *you* realize how chaotic conditions are outside these walls. According to the last official number I heard, there are currently more than 30,000,000 refugees from the Fallout Zone. The Federal government is strained to the limit, just trying to provide food, shelter, sanitation, and medical care for them. I realize conditions here suck – but *you* have to understand that it isn't any picnic on the outside, either. *Everyone* is exhausted, overstretched, and running on fumes – and my people are no exception. So, as hard as it is going to be for you to sit tight, and wait for relief, I'm afraid I have no choice but to ask you to do exactly that."

"And what am I supposed to do if my people refuse to stay put?" Lundegran asked. "I can't keep them here against their will, you know."

Pena looked him in the eye.

"In that case, Warden," she told him, "I suspect my superiors will just have to draft them into the Army – and assign them here as prison guar … excuse me, I mean 'Corrections Officers'."

"Is that a threat, Lieutenant?" Lundegran demanded. His eyes narrowed.

"No, Warden," Pena replied. "It's a prediction."

She continued unwaveringly to meet his gaze. At length, Lundegran looked aside.

"All right," he growled, "what the fuck *can* you do for us?"

"I think I can safely promise you fresh food and medical supplies within the next ... let's say 12 hours or so," Pena said. "As I have already promised, I will also speak with my superiors about providing relief for your staff, as soon as is possible."

"I'd appreciate that," said Lundegran. His tone was suddenly conciliatory. "And so would my men."

"I've given you my word, Warden," Pena told him.

"And I'll hold you to it," Lundegran replied.

"Before I contact HQ, is there anything else I need to tell them?" Pena asked.

Lundegran rubbed his chin. His five-o'clock shadow made a sandpapery noise.

"There is one thing," he said. "We had a breakout Sunday night. Seven prisoners escaped."

"Are they dangerous?" Pena asked.

"Extremely," Lundegran told her. "They're all members of a gang that's run by an especially violent – and smart – nigger named Arun Washington."

Pena recoiled at his casual use of the racial slur. Nostrils flaring, she frowned in disapproval.

Seemingly oblivious to her discomfort, Lundegran continued, "They call him 'Big Sugar'. He's sure enough big – six-eight, 290 pounds – all of it muscle. And he's one vicious motherfucker, believe me. I have video of him killing a man with his bare hands."

"I can alert my superiors to be on the lookout for the escapees," Pena offered.

She struggled to keep her distaste for Lundegran from showing.

It would certainly help," she added, "if you could provide photos and fingerprints, to go with their names."

"I'll have my secretary give you everything we have on them," Lundegran promised.

May 5, 2020, 6:34 pm EDT

East Orange Golf Course, Short Hills, NJ

"The time has come for us to decamp this facility, Donell," announced Big Sugar Washington.

He frowned at the glutinous mass of meat and gravy on the plastic sectional plate in front of him.

"I'm ready when you are, Boss," replied Donell Jackson.

Jackson was in a rebellious mood. He had spent a frustrating day at the East Orange Golf Course's clubhouse, working his way up the makeshift refugee camp's chain of command in pursuit of his request to visit Latonya Gramble. When he had finally obtained an audience with the commanding officer, his plea was flatly denied – as was his petition to appeal the CO's decision to higher authority.

"Me, too," chimed in Dante "Smoove" Woodruff, another member of Washington's mob. The gang leader had spotted him earlier in the day.

"I'm in," agreed Kendall "Wide Load" Broadus.

At lunch time, the *don* had been reunited with him in the giant mess tent.

"'Bout time," commented William "Big Willy" Dixon.

Smoove had encountered him while shoplifting cigarettes at the camp's canteen.

"Indeed, brother William," Washington concurred. "Should we overstay our welcome here, I fear we risk an involuntary return to our alma mater."

"Fuck that," Broadus opined, conversationally. "I ain't goin' back to no AdSeq, no how. An' you *know* that where Lundegran goin' to put us."

"That," Woodruff agreed, nodding, "or solitary, mos' like."

"Then we are of a mind," Big Sugar declared.

"So ... when, Boss?" Donell asked. "And how?"

"Tonight, I think," Washington replied, patting his lips with his paper napkin. "As the Bard observed, 'If 'twere done, when 'tis done …'"

"'… then 'twere well it were done quickly,'" Jackson quoted, completing Macbeth's line.

"Just so," Big Sugar said, nodding in approval. "As for 'how?', it seems reasonable to suppose that the National Guardsmen who are charged with patrolling the back nine of this facility will be less than maximally alert after midnight. It is certainly clear that they are overextended, and badly sleep-deprived. I suspect we need exercise only modest caution, in order successfully to make our way past their patrol, and through the woods. Once we reach Morristown, we should easily be able to acquire the transportation we shall need to take us far enough to escape the Army's reach."

"Sounds good to me," Donell commented.

He stood up and stepped over the bench where he had been seated.

There was a general mutter of agreement with Jackson's sentiment. The other gang members also got up from their shared table, leaving their plastic plates and cutlery behind. Flanking their leader, they ambled toward the exit, making small talk.

Conversation came to a sudden halt, as they left the huge mess tent.

They found themselves confronted with a long convoy of camouflage-pattern trucks. The caravan streamed into the parking lot of the East Orange Golf Course. As each vehicle came to a stop, it began disgorging squads of soldiers in urban battle dress. Each light-blue helmet was emblazoned with insignia of rank on the front and maple leaf decals on the side.

May 5, 2020, 7:27 pm EDT

The White House Family Dining Room, Washington, DC

"So, Vittorio," William Orwell Steele asked, a forkful of pan-seared Chilean sea bass paused halfway to his mouth, "do we have the votes for cloture?"

"No problem there, Mr. President," replied Vittorio Donofrio.

The Senate Majority Leader sat across the table from Steele.

"Some of the folks across the aisle even signed the petition," he added.

"Oh?" the President replied, intrigued. "How'd you manage that?"

Donofrio shrugged.

"The ones from the northeast got constituents who need the kinda help the Act'll provide," he said. "If they vote against it, they'll get murdered in the next cycle."

He swallowed the remains of his glass of Sauvignon Blanc.

"That's not what concerns, me, Mr. President," he confessed.

"What does concern you?" Steele asked.

"Amendments do, sir," Donofrio responded. "That Ransom bastard is a sneaky motherfucker – if you'll pardon my French, ma'am," he said, turning to address Diana Hunter.

The Vice President waved his concern away, with a smile.

"*Non è niente,*" she replied.

Donofrio's face lit up at her use of Italian.

"*Grazie mille!*" he told her.

The Majority Leader turned back to the President.

"Under the current rules," he explained, "once cloture is invoked, the other side gets to introduce two amendments in the first degree."

Andover Philips frowned. "'Amendments in the first degree?'" he interjected.

"Sorry, Andy," Donofrio responded. "I sometimes forget that not everybody understands Senate terminology. 'Amendments in the first degree' are amendments to the bill itself. Amendments in the second degree are amendments to the amendments."

"Hell's fucking bells, and tiny, little fishes!" Philips commented. "It's as if you people live on a completely different planet!"

Instead of taking offense at the implied criticism, Donofrio nodded in agreement.

"You ain't wrong, there, Andy," he concurred. "The Senate *is* another world. Yeah, I know it's hard for outsiders to understand our alien ways ..."

He worked his eyebrows up and down for comic effect.

"But understandin' those customs is the key to gettin' things done on the Hill," he explained.

"So," the President said, returning to the matter at hand, "exactly what has you worried, Vittorio?"

"I'll tell you, Mr. President," the Majority Leader replied. "The fact is, there's a lotta concern on our side about the funding mechanism for the Act. Our people're worried about raisin' taxes in an election year – and I have to say, they got reason to be. It won't do us any good to pass the bill, if it loses us the majority in November – and we both know the economy is already in a helluva mess."

"So, what would you suggest we do, instead?" Steele asked, reaching for his wine glass.

"I dunno, Mr. President," Donofrio said, placing both hands on the table and looking down to avoid the President's eye. "The thing is, that *chooch* Ransom is gonna have a lotta support to peel the surtax outta the bill – and some of it could come from our side of the aisle."

"Oh?" Steele queried. "I thought our caucus was solid on this matter."

"Well, sir," Donofrio responded, "it is and it ain't."

"Go on," the President prompted, setting his wineglass down and picking up his fork.

"Some of our members are up for re-election in deep-red states is what I'm getting' at, Mr. President," Donofrio explained. "If they don't have to go on the record as voting to increase taxes, it could make a big difference in their races."

Steele put down his fork, and sat up straight. He fixed Donofrio with an unwavering gaze.

"Mr. Majority Leader," he said.

His tone was flinty.

"We need those votes," he insisted. "I want you to tell your Blue Dogs that I said they're damned well going to vote with us ... or else."

"You're gonna have to be more specific about 'or else'," Donofrio replied, his face expressionless. "Mr. President," he added.

"Very well," the President replied. "How's this for specific? If they vote to approve the Act, the sky's the limit come November. The party will open its wallet as wide as necessary to give them absolute funding dominance in their races. I, personally, will stump for each of them – repeatedly, if necessary. And I'll twist the arms of every action hero, and country music star in my personal rolodex to campaign on their behalves, as well."

He paused, unblinking.

Then he continued, his voice becoming menacing, "But ... if they vote the Act down, not only won't they see a dime of party money – I will make it a point of pride to see that they are not re-elected, even if that requires me to campaign for their Republican opponents. You can tell them that's a solemn promise, regardless of how adverse the impact on our numbers in the Senate may be. Is that specific enough, Vittorio?"

"Yes, Mr. President," the Majority Leader replied, taken aback by his uncompromising fierceness. "That it is."

May 5, 2020, 5:15 pm PDT (8:15 pm EDT)

Alvarado Street, San Leandro, CA

Artemis Alexandra Steele could feel her sanity slipping away.

She was fairly sure that she had slept at least once since she had first found herself … here. She dreamed then, she thought. But the distinction between waking and sleep, between dream and hallucination, had been growing steadily less clear over time.

At first, the apparitions that appeared to her were simple things: geometric forms, patterns of color, flashes of light. Slowly, the white noise in her headphones had mutated, as well – at first, into whooshing swaths of sound, like the coming and going of so many helicopters. Later, it had become snatches of music, and of indistinctly overheard conversations.

Finally, aural and visual hallucination had merged into real-seeming, full-sensory experiences. She had been stalked, and chased. She had confronted monsters of hideous, shifting aspect that she could see only out of the corner of her eye. There had been long, accusatory exchanges with key figures in her life: her father, her dead mother, her lover Bernie, and Kevin Brown, the Agent in Charge of her second shift Secret Service detail. In each of those altercations, she had been tongue-tied, incapable of defending herself against their angry, incomprehensibly-vague tirades.

She desperately wanted to flee, to escape from the waking nightmare in which she found herself trapped – but she could find no exit, no refuge, no respite from the apparitions.

Then the Voice appeared. Faint at first – too faint to make out its exact words, regardless of how hard she strained to listen. But, unlike all the other voices that filled her head, this one was calm, reassuring, and confident. Slowly, slowly, the Voice's volume increased. After what seemed like an eternity, it finally grew loud enough for her to understand what it was saying:

"Trust me – I will rescue you. Love me – I will save you. Surrender to me – I will help you."

The Voice repeated the same, unvarying message, over and over again. Like a life raft bobbing on the dark sea of insanity, Artemis Steele clung to it with all her strength.

May 5, 2020, 7:00 pm MDT (9:00 pm EDT)

Patriot Radio Studio 1, Athol, ID

The red "on air" light lit up. The familiar sound of distant trumpets, and the echo of pounding hoofs passed from right to left, and on into the distance. Merlin Friend leaned close to the Neumann microphone dangling before him.

In his signature baritone, he announced, "Good evening, Patriots. This is your friend Merlin, coming to you, for what may be the last time ever, live from Patriot Radio Studio 1, in Coeur d'Alene."

Friend continued, "By now, I'm sure you've all heard that, last night, while the socialist Tyrant William Orwell Steele was lying to us out of both sides of his mouth, Patriots on the West Coast took his lesbian daughter into custody, right off the streets of the People's Republic of Berkeley. While they were at it, they took out a whole platoon of our Tyrant-in-Chief's Secret Service thugs, for good measure. Now, friends, let me say right up front that I have no idea who these unknown Patriots are … but I applaud their actions, nonetheless. In fact, not only do I applaud their actions, I applaud *them*. I'd love to shake each and every one of their hands, and personally congratulate them on a brilliant strategic move in our struggle against William Orwell Steele.

"You see," Friend explained, "by their actions last night, those heroes have gained real leverage over our socialist Tyrant. They have taken his only child away from him! Think about that. Even though she's a Lesbian, surely William the First will not dare risk his daughter's life by defying the just demands of our Patriot brothers. If those heroes are as sharp as I think they are, they'll force the Tyrant to resign – him, and that entire gang of crooks and incompetents he calls a Cabinet!"

Friend was nearly bouncing in his chair with enthusiasm, holding one finger aloft, like a cavalry saber. So as not to overload the delicate ribbon transducer in his microphone, he leaned back in his seat, before he unleashed the full oratorical resonance of his highly-trained voice.

"My fellow Patriots," Friend thundered, "*Now* is the time! The power resides with *us*, now, not with the Tyrant! *We* can bring him to his knees!

Now, while *he* is at his weakest, is the time for *us* to strike! Let the Bilderbergers, the Club of Rome, the Trilateralists, the Masons, and that whole, corrupt New World Order gang tremble before *us*, for *we* are about to unseat their champion: the Tyrant, William Orwell Steele himself!"

He let his voice rise almost to a scream. "The time has come to *rise up*, Patriots! Rise *up*, I tell you! Rise up, and *smite* this monster, hip and thigh!"

Friend paused, and took a sip from his ever-present Tanqueray-and-tonic. Setting the lowball glass down, he leaned forward until his lips almost touched the microphone.

"Only *you* can save this country, Patriots," he murmured, voice trembling with sincerity and conviction. "Only *you* have the courage, only *you* have the wisdom, only *you* have the faith in our country, our flag, and our precious Second Amendment."

He let his voice drop to a near-whisper. "Only you."

Friend sat back, eyeing the clock on the wall over the console in front of him.

He gave his audience three full seconds of silence, before he announced, in a brisk, businesslike tone, "We'll be right back, after these words from our friends at Goldmine."

May 6, 2020, 7:13 am PKT (May 5, 9:13 pm EDT)

Kota, Khyber Pakhtunkhwa, Pakistan

"We have not much further to go, brother," remarked Fahad Abbas Afridi, nervously.

He puffed on the latest in a continuous procession of Player Gold Leaf cigarettes, lighting it from the butt of its predecessor.

"*Insha'Allah*," replied Younis Masood Khakwani.

Khakwani had driven the Mercedes E550 sedan – now painted jet black – all the way from relatively cosmopolitan Rawalpindi here, to the tribal hinterlands of Northeastern Pakistan. Wrapped in plastic bags, the decapitated body of the late General Rashid Omar Sheikh was stuffed into the Mercedes's boot. Its head was tucked neatly under its right arm; its severed penis protruded from the general's blackened lips.

Squinting, Khakwani peered at the road ahead. He was tired. The N-95 highway was not in good repair, and the sun slanting down over the verdant shoulder of Sur Ghar stabbed directly through the dusty windshield, into his gritty eyes.

Over the course of many lucrative assignments they had undertaken together for John O'Brien, Khakwani had long since grown accustomed to his partner's chatter. He had learned to tune it out. Whenever responses seemed called for, he gave them automatically. Otherwise, he kept his own counsel.

- Each of us copes with fear in his own fashion. -

The CIA paid them well for their services – but they earned that money by gambling their very lives. Should any of O'Brien's many foes discover the nature of their employment ... well, that prospect did not bear thinking about. This assignment, in particular, was highly dangerous. The Swat Valley was still a Taliban stronghold, despite years of occupation by the army. Indeed, that was why they were here: to frame the Taliban for Sheikh's kidnap and murder, by leaving the sedan deep in their territory, with the General's body – mutilated in the manner characteristic of Taliban victims – in its trunk.

However, because of the entrenched nature of the Taliban presence in the Swat, the government forces in the area were in a constant state of high alert. Khakwani and his partner therefore risked discovery by both sides. Profitable as this assignment promised to be, it put them in a highly perilous position.

- Perhaps after this, I shall retire from life as a CIA asset. After all, wealth is of no use to a dead man. -

"Mingora is just a few kilometers ahead, brother," Afridi observed.

His nicotine-stained fingers removed the Player from his thin-lipped mouth just long enough to get the words out.

"Soon," he added, "we will be rid of this automobile and its cursed cargo."

As they rounded a gentle curve, passing the soccer grounds on the outskirts of the impoverished town of Kota, Khakwani's blood froze. Blocking the road ahead, was a temporary barricade. It stretched across the highway, from the local police station to the parking lot of the government primary school.

A bearded man dressed in tan trousers tucked into black combat boots, wearing the slate-blue uniform blouse and beret of the Khyber Pakhtunkhwa provincial police, held up a peremptory hand, commanding them to stop. Behind the barrier stood two of his fellows. All three men were armed with Kalashnikov rifles.

"Hold on, brother!" Khakwani cried.

He stamped the brake pedal, and spun the steering wheel.

The Mercedes slewed drunkenly across the road, in a semi-controlled skid. Its rear tires slid wildly on the badly-alligatored, asphalt surface. The sedan stalled, facing slightly away from the police roadblock, just past the still-shuttered Hamza book store. Khakwani heard shouts from the police. Then, almost simultaneously, there was the flat crack of a Kalashnikov, the plosive sound of the bullet penetrating the sedan's rear window, the hiss of the slug passing his head, and a second harsh kiss of its passage through the windshield.

Khakwani frantically yanked the gear selector into neutral. He twisted the key in the ignition, hunching over to present as small a target as possible. Two more police rounds tore through the Mercedes's cabin before the engine caught with a subdued roar.

"*Allahu akbar!*" Khakwani exclaimed fervently.

He slammed the car into gear, and gunned it down the narrow side road bordering the school's parking lot. His heart hammered in his chest.

"That was a narrow escape, brother!" Khakwani all but shouted in relief.

Fahad Afridi responded with a choked gurgle. Blood sprayed out of his mouth across the Mercedes's dashboard.

May 5, 2020, 10:16 pm EDT

Seneca Temporary Housing Facility, Romulus, NY

"You don't get it, bro," Adam Manson gesticulated.

Ash spilled, unnoticed, from the joint between his fingers.

"There's a war comin,' between the government and the people, whether you realize it or not," Manson insisted, "And, believe me Sean, you don't wanna be on the wrong side when the shootin' starts."

"I still say that's crazy talk," replied Sean Halloran, Sr.

The two men were outside, enjoying the balmy spring night. Inside the tent cabin their families shared, Sean's wife Fiona was feeding their infant son Sean Jr., while Manson's beaky spouse was putting their three sons to bed. In the background, Merlin Friend's tirade against the President blatted from Halloran's FBI-supplied boombox.

"How can you be so blind?" Manson demanded.

He paused for a long swallow of Budweiser Dry.

"Take a fuckin' look around you," he invited. "We're sittin' in a FEMA concentration camp, right this fuckin' second! And you say *I'm* the crazy one?"

He hit the stub of the jay fiercely, then pitched the roach into the darkness.

Halloran looked longingly after the remains of Manson's doobie. Politely refusing to share it, and its predecessors, got harder each day. But Sean, Sr. feared the loss of inhibition that went with getting stoned might inadvertently cause him to reveal his role as an FBI informant to his heavily-tattooed tent mate. The consequences of that kind of screw-up didn't bear thinking about, so Halloran quickly returned his attention to their debate, instead.

"You're just wicked paranoid, Adam," Sean argued. "Nobody's holdin' us here against our will. We can leave any time we want. We just don't have anyplace else to go, is all."

"And you think that's an *accident*?" Manson questioned. "Bro, you don't have any place else to go, because Steele had the CIA set off a fuckin' *atom bomb* in New York fuckin' City! *That's* why you've got no place else to go! Steele fuckin' *planned it* that way, bro! It was all fuckin' *planned*!"

"Oh, c'mon, Adam," Halloran protested. "Ya can't tell me ya really believe the CIA bombed New York! That's just fuckin' crazy."

He took a swig of his own beer, providing Manson with an opportunity to reply.

"Fuck yes, I believe the CIA bombed New York," Manson declared. "How else do you explain that commie fuck declaring martial law so goddamn fast? What'd it take him? An hour? Shit, bro, you *know* the CIA bombed New York! You think some rag head could've done it? *Hell* no! They got, like, radiation detectors all fuckin' *over* Manhattan. Ain't nobody can get a nuke past 'em, without settin' off at least *one* of 'em – unless they're the fuckin' CIA, that is!"

Halloran shook his head.

"It still sounds crazy to me," he said. "You're talkin' about the same CIA that couldn't even kill that Pakistahni fella, without fuckin' it all up, aren't ya? Seems unlikely to me."

"They got a new guy in charge of the CIA since then, bro," Manson told him.

Effortlessly, he rolled a cigarette.

"He ain't nearly as dumb as that clown LaPlace," the big man explained. "*He's* the one that fucked *that* operation up."

"I still say Merlin Friend is fulla shit," Halloran insisted.

He removed a pack of Marlboros from his shirt pocket, and shook one out.

"Steele is a good guy," he continued. "I voted for him last time, and I'll prob'ly do it again this November."

He took the cigarette between his lips, and fumbled for his lighter.

"Here, bro," Manson offered, flicking his battered Zippo alight.

"Thanks," Halloran said, accepting the light.

"You're welcome," Manson replied.

He lit his own hand-rolled cigarette, then snapped the Zippo closed with a practiced flick of his wrist.

"I still say you're wrong about Steele, though. If you ask me, he's a socialist asshole. The guy is planning to kill the Second Amendment, and turn this country into some kind of commie worker's paradise – except we're not going to let him get away with it."

"Who's 'we'?" Halloran asked.

The question was already out of his mouth before he realized that it was exactly the one whose answer his FBI handlers wanted to know. He started involuntarily at the realization.

A small, hard smile on his face, Adam Manson pulled his thumb and forefinger across his lips, as if zipping them.

"I could tell you, bro," he replied, "but then I'd have to kill you."

Manson laughed mirthlessly, but Halloran was chillingly certain his "joke" was nothing of the kind.

"I'm just sayin': there's a war comin'," Manson told him. "Soon. And, when it gets here, you're gonna have to pick a side."

He took a long drag on his cigarette before adding, "And, bro? For your family's sake, you'd best be sure it's not the wrong one."

May 5, 2020, 11:08 pm EDT

The White House Living Room, Washington, DC

Janese Meschelle Johnson tried to calm herself, as Special Agent in Charge Richard Wright knocked on the double doors of the Presidential living room. Wright opened the leftmost door to shoulder width.

"Special Agent Johnson is here, Mr. President," he announced.

Johnson heard POTUS reply, "Send her in, Dick."

Wright opened the dark oak doors wide. He stepped back into the White House's second-floor hallway, and gestured for Johnson to enter.

When she hesitated, Wright quietly told her, "The President's waiting, Agent Johnson."

Janese Johnson had seen the inside of the White House living room only twice before. For some reason, she was surprised to find it looked exactly the same as she remembered it. The large oil portrait of a smiling Julia Grey Steele still hung over the marble fireplace. The executive desk still occupied its place before the far window. The armchairs in front of the desk still faced the overstuffed loveseat, which Dr. Marcus Aurelius Clement currently shared with Duke, the President's Great Dane.

The brindle dog's big, square head flopped bonelessly onto the love seat's cushions, as Clement rose to greet her.

POTUS himself stood near the fireplace, one hand on the mantel, a lowball glass in the other. His expression was somber. Andover Philips, his Chief of Staff was seated on the chair nearest her, facing the Vice President, who occupied the wingback chair nearest the President.

"Please come in, Agent Johnson," the President said.

Philips turned to look at her. He half-rose from his seat, in greeting.

Taking a deep breath, Johnson replied, "Thank you, Mr. President."

She stepped into the room. Wright softly closed the doors behind her.

"May I call you Janese?" the President asked, as she approached the conversational furniture grouping.

"Mr. President," Johnson told him, her *café-au-lait* cheeks turning rosy at the unexpected familiarity, "you can call me anything you like."

"'Janese' it is, then," the President said. "Can I get you a drink, Janese?"

"No thank you, Mr. President," the Secret Service agent responded. "I'm fine."

"Have a seat," the President urged her. "I'm sure you must be tired, after your long flight."

"Actually, Mr. President," Johnson replied, "I am tired – of sitting down."

She smiled, hesitantly.

"I've been doing a lot of that for the past seven or eight hours," she explained. "Sitting down, I mean. If you don't mind, I'd rather stand."

"By all means stand, if you're more comfortable that way," the President acquiesced.

He gestured at his guests.

"Allow me to introduce these folks to you," he said, pointing to them in turn.

"I assume you know the Vice President?" he inquired.

"Ma'am," Johnson acknowledged, nodding.

Diana Hunter smiled, and offered her hand.

"Nice to meet you, Agent Johnson," she said.

"My pleasure, Ma'am," Johnson replied.

"Andy Philips, my Chief of Staff," the President continued.

"Sir," Johnson responded.

Philips executed a fractional, seated bow.

"Charmed, I'm sure," he said.

"And Dr. Clement, my personal physician," POTUS concluded.

"Doctor," Johnson acknowledged, with a small, nervous smile.

"Sister," Clement replied.

A warm smile split his dark face.

The President regarded Johnson soberly for a long moment.

"Janese," he said at last, "I assume you know why I sent for you?"

"As I understand it," Johnson replied, "you wanted to debrief me personally, Mr. President."

"That's one way to put it," the President agreed. "Why don't you start by bringing us up to speed on the progress of the investigation."

"My information on that will be a good eight hours out of date by now, sir," Johnson cautioned.

"That's all right," the President assured her. "Everything I've heard so far has been second-hand, at best. You're the only person I've talked to who's capable of giving me a first-person report. So – take your time, and tell me what you know."

"Mr. President," the Secret Service agent began, "I assume you've heard that we located the UPS truck, and the minivan that were used in the attacks."

The President nodded.

"Yes," he said, "I have. They were found near the Oakland Coliseum, were they not?"

"Yes, sir," Johnson confirmed. "Oakland PD located them on 88th Avenue, about an hour after the APB went out."

"Stripped clean, I understand?" the President asked.

"Yes, sir," Johnson replied. "They'd both been wiped clean of fingerprints, and bleached to eliminate DNA evidence."

"And the UPS driver was found in his truck?" POTUS queried.

"Yes, sir," Johnson said. "He'd been stripped of his uniform, and shot in the head, execution-style. The FBI doesn't consider him a suspect."

"So I understand," the President told her. "I also understand they've located a fair amount of video evidence."

"Yes and no, sir," Johnson said. "So far, the Bureau has located three cell phone recordings of all or part of the kidnapping and a half-dozen recordings of the van passing surveillance cameras. I don't believe they've found anything useful on the UPS truck, though."

The President nodded.

"That's pretty much what I've been told," he agreed.

He ran his hand through his hair. Agent Johnson was struck by how much gray had appeared in it in the past five days.

"I'm also told one of the agents got off a couple of shots at the perpetrators," the President added.

Johnson nodded.

"Yes, sir," she said. "The FBI says there were two rounds expended from the clip in Agent Harmoody's weapon ... and I saw two nine-mil casings on the floor of the C unit, next to his body."

"You were the first person on the scene at Addison Street, weren't you?" the President asked.

"Yes I was, Mr. President," Johnson confirmed.

"Suppose you walk us step-by-step through events as you witnessed them," the President suggested. "Start with whatever it was that first alerted you to the existence of an attack in progress, and take us through it at your own pace."

Johnson took a deep breath. She let it out slowly, girding herself for yet another unwelcome retelling of the nightmare on Addison Street. In the past 24 hours, she had told and retold the story at least a dozen times to various interrogators for the FBI and Berkeley PD, as well as to Paul McConnochie, the Director of the Secret Service. As a result, her memories remained vividly fresh and painful.

"Well, Mr. President," she began, "I had just picked up my detail's dinner order at Bangkok Thai – it's a restaurant just about exactly a block from the Addison Street location, as the crow flies. We order ... that is 'we ordered' ... from there all the time."

The President nodded. "Go on," he said.

"We use ..." she seemed to stumble over the phrase, then continued, "we *used* mountain bikes to get around Berkeley. I had mine with me at the restaurant. As I was leaving there, I heard two gunshots. I identified them as nine-mil rounds – which is the caliber of ammunition we use. I jumped on my bike, ran a red light at Acton, and got to the Addison Street location as quickly as I could."

"And what did you see when you got there?" the President asked.

"I observed a UPS truck headed west on Addison Street," Johnson replied. "It didn't seem to be driving unusually fast or erratically, so I didn't think much of it at the time. When I spotted the body of Agent Kellogg lying on the sidewalk in front of the A unit, that became my immediate focus."

"I understand," the President told her, encouragingly. "Go on – what happened then?"

"Well, sir," Johnson told him, "I checked Agent Kellogg for vitals, and determined that he was deceased. I stood up and knocked on the door of the A unit. We use ... I mean we *used* ... it as our CP, so there were always at least three agents in the room."

The President again nodded.

"There was no answer, so I pushed the door open. They were all dead in there," Johnson said.

She paused, transported by the remembered horror of the scene, and swallowed hard.

"Take your time," the President said gently.

Johnson shook her head, refusing to allow him to comfort her.

- *I'm a muthafuckin'* Secret Service *agent. I can* do *this.* -

"The agents in the A unit all had gunshot injuries – mostly headshots," Johnson continued.

She kept her eyes focused on the smiling portrait of the late Julia Steele over the fireplace.

"It was immediately clear to me that I could do nothing for them," Johnson said. "So I checked the B unit – the middle apartment. In it, I found the body of Bernadette Garcia, your daughter's roommate."

She glanced at the President, who did not bother to correct her. Johnson took another deep breath, willing herself not to cry.

"She was also deceased," Johnson continued. "So I checked the C unit – the apartment on the end of the building that we use … that we *used* … as a barracks. They were all dead in there, too. Except for Agent Cushing. She expired shortly after I arrived."

Agent Johnson's emotions spilled over at the memory. She and Alice Cushing had been more than co-workers – they had been friends. On those occasions when they both had the same day off, they delighted in doing girl things together: shopping, getting their hair and nails done, eating in Berkeley's abundance of ethnic restaurants, dancing at Ashkenaz. They had provided moral support for one another, when the testosterone-soaked atmosphere of their Addison Street station turned oppressive – as it did from time to time.

At Addison Street, too, she had cradled her friend's bleeding, bullet-riddled body in her arms. Helplessly, she had watched the life drain out of it, until, with one last shuddering breath, Alice Cushing died in her arms. It was literally the worst thing that had ever happened to Janese Johnson.

Tears began streaming down Johnson's face. She dug her nails into her palms so fiercely, they drew blood. The embarrassing flood continued, nonetheless.

"I'm sorry for your loss, Janese," the President said.

His tone was sincere – and she believed his sentiment was real.

Johnson had been prepared to be called on the carpet for the sin of survival. She had fully expected anger, bitterness, and accusations of incompetence, and dereliction of duty from the President. Instead, she had gotten empathy, concern, and what seemed like genuine caring. Like some kind of emotional judo, once she had set herself to resist a withering blast of disapproval, its absence left her collapsing, completely off balance.

The only child of the President of the United States was in the hands of men who had gone out of their way to demonstrate their utter ruthlessness and total disregard for human life. That he could express sympathy for *her* loss overwhelmed Janese. The accumulated stress of trying to conceal her grief and horror behind a façade of professional toughness had combined with her utter exhaustion – she had been continuously awake for nearly two days – to overpower the last of her defenses.

To her profound horror, Special Agent Janese Johnson broke down completely. She put her face in her hands, and helplessly surrendered to enormous, racking sobs. While she blubbered like a little girl, the President of the United States stroked her shoulder, and murmured soothing words of comfort and support.

After her crying jag passed its peak, William Orwell Steele took Janese Johnson by both shoulders. He held her at arm's length, and gazed intently into her face.

"You feel guilty to be alive," the President said. "Don't you, Janese?"

Johnson meekly nodded, without removing her hands to expose her face. She was merely sniffling now, rather than bawling.

"When Julia was killed right in front of me," the President told her, "I felt exactly the same way you do now."

"You did?" Janese asked, timorously.

"Yes I did," the President confessed. "I couldn't understand why God allowed her to die, but left me alive. It seemed so unfair. I felt it should have been me who was killed, not her."

"Mr. President," Johnson said, "I'm sorry. This is so unprofessional of me."

She stood awkwardly, shoulders hunched. Her hands were open before her, beseechingly.

"Nonsense," the President replied. "You've been through a horrific experience."

He looked at her appraisingly.

"And frankly," he added, "you look exhausted."

"I am very tired, Mr. President," Johnson admitted. "But … mostly I just want these feelings to go away."

"I'm sorry to say, if my own experience is any guide, they probably never will – at least not entirely," the President told her.

He turned to look at the portrait of his murdered spouse. A long moment passed before he spoke again.

"But you'll learn to live with them," he told her. "Eventually, you'll learn to live with them."

May 6, 2020, 10:02 am PKT (12:02 am EDT)

Embassy Road, Diplomatic Enclave, Islamabad, Pakistan

"Sir, I must request that you step out of the vehicle," the Pakistani Army *subidar* told John James O'Brien.

"Sorry, General," O'Brien replied, "but I'm afraid I'll have to decline."

"Sir, I must insist that you step out of the vehicle," the *subidar* repeated.

His tone was polite, but his expression was unfriendly. His right hand rested on his holstered Steyr M9A1 automatic pistol.

"I am going to reach into my jacket now, and bring out my identification papers," O'Brien told him. "I'd appreciate it if you'd refrain from shooting me when I do."

"Yes, yes," the *subidar* responded. "You must show your identification to me. You must also step out of your vehicle."

Slowly and carefully, O'Brien pulled his diplomatic ID and passport out of his inside jacket pocket. He passed them through the window of his Audi Q7 to the Pakistani officer.

"As you can see," O'Brien said, "I'm an accredited American diplomat. I work right over there."

He pointed through the windshield to the American Embassy complex that loomed less than a block away.

"I see that you are an American diplomat, sir." the *subidar* admitted. "Nevertheless, I must insist that you step out of the vehicle. Pakistani law requires that all people must cooperate with military authorities."

"Yes," O'Brien conceded, "of course it does. But I'm an accredited diplomat – which means I'm not subject to Pakistani law. So, again, I'm afraid I have to refuse your request."

"I must insist that you must step out of the vehicle, sir," the officer told O'Brien.

His voice was now as hard and unfriendly as his face.

"Otherwise, I must order my men to remove you from it," he threatened.

He stepped back and to the side, to allow O'Brien to better see the half-dozen heavily-armed soldiers who manned the barricade behind him.

"General," O'Brien began.

His tone artfully combined amusement and boredom.

"Do you really want to cause an international incident over this?" he asked. "Because, if you force me to step out of my car, that's what will happen, I assure you."

"I have my orders, sir," the Pakistani replied. "Now, will you step out of the vehicle, or must I order my men to remove you from it?"

O'Brien sighed. He glanced at the dashboard clock.

- The diplomatic shuttle should be coming down the road any moment now. -

"May I call my embassy, and explain the situation to them, first?" O'Brien requested.

The *subidar* shook his head, emphatically.

"No calls," he insisted. "There will be time for calling, later. Now, you must step out of the vehicle."

He unsnapped the restraining strap on his holstered sidearm, and placed his hand on the gun's butt.

"You must step out of the vehicle now, sir," he repeated.

O'Brien shook his head, ruefully.

"Okay, pal," he told the officer, "have it your way. But don't say I didn't warn you."

"Sir," the *subidar* said, "you must not threaten me."

"That wasn't a threat, General," O'Brien assured him.

He smiled, as he unfastened his seatbelt.

"It was a prediction," he said.

As slowly as possible, without giving the officer an excuse to order his soldiers to employ violence, O'Brien unlocked his door. He opened it, and stepped out of the Audi onto Embassy Road. Purposefully, he left his briefcase lying in plain view on the front passenger's seat.

The CIA officer understood very well what was in store for him. He would spend several hours as an unwilling guest of the ISI. Meanwhile, the Directorate's Miscellaneous Department would disassemble his automobile. It would also tear his briefcase to shreds, and expose his person to the equivalent of a decade's worth of medical and dental X-rays. Every effort would be made to discover some incriminating link between O'Brien and the kidnapping of General Rashid Omar Sheikh. When no such evidence was found, the ISI eventually would respond to the American Ambassador's stiffly-worded protest by releasing him, his Audi, and what remained of his briefcase, along with an apology for over-eager, low-level functionaries having detained him without authorization.

By the time O'Brien saw daylight again, Bashir Qadir Durrani – the driver and lookout for the General's kidnappers – would long since have completed his delivery of Sheikh's written and video-recorded confession to the American Embassy, and returned home to Rawalpindi.

As he stepped out of the Audi, O'Brien saw the diplomatic shuttle bus trundling down Embassy Road toward the Pakistani Army checkpoint. He knew Durrani and his fat, friendly wife were aboard the bus, supposedly on their way to the Embassy for a tourist visa interview. He knew this, because, 20 minutes earlier, Durrani had sent him a coded text from a "burner" cell phone telling him they were on their way.

O'Brien deliberately ignored the approaching shuttle, as he stood, facing the Pakistani *subidar*. Out of the corner of his eye, he watched as the bus pulled up to the barricade, and was waved through.

Cheerful, O'Brien asked, "All right, General, what now?"

"You will come with us, please," the *subidar* told him.

He pointed to the Mohafiz light armored personnel carrier, parked beside the checkpoint's closing gate.

"Why not?," O'Brien replied, watching the shuttle pull to a stop in front of the American Embassy. "It's not like I had other plans."

May 5, 2020, 10:17 pm PDT (May 6, 1:17 am EDT)

Alvarado Street, San Leandro, CA

"Damnit, Dolph," fumed Dr. Increase Bright, "you have to make up your mind. I can certainly sedate her, so you can fuck her again. But if you want her broken, she has to remain awake. I've told you repeatedly: knocking her out just delays the process."

"How long will I have to wait?" asked Adolph Ryan Wolf, impatiently.

"If you can refrain from raping her?" Bright replied. "To be safe, let's say around this time tomorrow."

"I don't know if I can hold out that long, Inky," Wolf confessed. "I'm so fucking horny ..."

"So? Why not just use your little fuck toy?" Bright suggested.

He gestured to the Chinese girl – naked but for a steel Cleopatra collar – who knelt submissively at Wolf's side.

Her name was Wang Jing-Wei. She was the daughter of Wang Chenglei, a Taiwanese technology sector investor. Her father had made the mistake of bidding against Wolf for a cash-starved Silicon Valley company that both tycoons coveted for its rich portfolio of exploitable patents. Wolf had the adolescent girl kidnapped, and turned her over to Bright for use as a test subject for his sensory-deprivation, brainwashing experiments. Jing-Wei had spent ten days in the same tank that now held Artemis Steele. When she finally emerged, the teenager was nearly catatonic.

Once she had been suitably conditioned, Wolf contracted with the Los Angeles-based Black Dragons to abduct, torture, and kill her father. The gangsters were instructed to force Wang Chenglei to watch a video of Wolf sodomizing his 14-year-old daughter, while they brutally emasculated the helpless Taiwanese investor. Since then, having Wang Jing-Wei fellate him as he watched the video of her father's castration and murder had become one of Wolf's favorite pastimes.

"Because she's a boring fuck. That's why," Wolf replied.

Bright shrugged.

"Well, it's up to you," he told Wolf. "Exercise a little patience now, and you can add Artemis Steele to your collection tomorrow. Or you can rape her now – but then it'll be Friday before she's fully broken."

Wolf gritted his teeth. Unconsciously, he flexed his hands, while conflicting impulses warred within him.

Finally, he grated, "All right, Inky, I'll wait. But she'd better be ready tomorrow."

"She will be," Bright assured him. "I've been giving her a milligram per hour of intravenous dextroamphetamine to increase her arousal – and to keep her from falling asleep."

"You know I don't give a damn about your methods," Ryan told him. "All I care about is results."

"You'll get them," Bright responded. "Just be patient."

"I'd better," Wolf snarled.

He snapped his fingers.

"Come," the billionaire commanded. He turned, and stalked away.

Head bowed, Wang Jing-Wei silently followed.

May 6, 2020, 2:23 am EDT

East Orange Golf Course, Short Hills, NJ

"Barbed-fuckin' wire? They done put up barbed-fuckin' *wire*?" objected Wide Load Broadus. "What the fuck is up with *that*?"

"Kindly keep your voice down, Kendall," Big Sugar Washington said.

His voice was low, but firm.

"I need hardly remind you that advertising our presence here is distinctly to our disadvantage," he told Broadus, reprovingly.

"Sorry, boss," Wide Load replied, in a stage whisper.

"So, what now?" Donell Jackson asked.

"I see little alternative, Donell," Washington responded. "For the moment, our only viable option is to retreat, before we are discovered."

"We're gonna try again, though, ain't we?" put in Dante "Smoove" Woodruff.

"Most assuredly so," Big Sugar told him. "However, before we can do so, we first must acquire the means to pass this obstacle."

He gestured to the roll of concertina razor wire that stretched out of sight in both directions. It blocked their way, just yards short of the tree line beyond the outside corner of the East Orange Golf Course's 11th hole dogleg.

"If we got to go back, then we got to go back, is all," observed William "Big Willy" Dixon.

"Fuckin' Feds," commented Wide Load.

He hawked and spat a wad of mucus at the wire.

May 6, 2020, 3:21 am

The Watergate Hotel, Washington, DC

When Jameson Matthew Peek, Esq. – the party's official messenger of his political doom – delivered Representative Esau Piltch to the Watergate Hotel, the lawyer had been merciful enough let the Congressman take with him to his room the bottle of Haig & Haig from the limousine in which they arrived. Now, some 12 hours later, Piltch poured the last remaining two fingers of tawny liquid into the plastic water glass on the night table beside the bed. He got unsteadily to his feet, and staggered to the bathroom, glass in hand.

Piltch discovered that the white plastic ice bucket sitting in a ring of condensation on the black marble vanity was filled only with icy water. Briefly, he considered making a trip down the hall to the ice machine. He decided, in view of his current notoriety, that he was just too drunk to risk being seen in public, even at three in the morning.

- Fuck it. Fuck everything. -

He put the plastic tumbler under the spigot, and sent a quick stream of water into it from the cold tap to dilute the scotch. Then he weaved his way back out into the hotel room. By the time he got to the queen-sized bed, he was overcome by a wave of dizziness. Suddenly, Piltch realized he was going to be sick.

- Air. That's what I need. Air. -

The congressman set the half-full glass of scotch and water down on the nightstand. He staggered to the sliding glass door that opened to a private balcony overlooking the distinctive double circle of the Watergate Hotel's outdoor swimming pool. Piltch opened the slider. Stepping outside, he stumbled, and barely managed to keep from tumbling over the railing to the plaza below.

- That'd be something, wouldn't it? Everybody would think I committed suicide! -

He chuckled hollowly at the thought of the headlines.

- Disgraced Congressman Dies in Fall at Watergate! Killer Congressman Kills Himself! Murdergate Suspect's Suicide! -

Abruptly, Piltch puked over the balcony's railing. He watched with dull fascination, as the vomitus twisted and spread out in its fall toward the pool deck, nine stories below. Faintly but clearly, he heard the splatter of its impact on the faux-stone pavement that surrounded the deserted pool.

- I need to be more careful. That really could have been me. -

He turned his head to look across the river at the lights of Arlington, Virginia. Their reflections twinkled on the dark expanse of the Potomac. It occurred to him that he was unlikely to see them in person – or any of metro DC's many other, unique vistas – very many more times.

His career in politics – in any aspect of politics – was well and truly over. That was now undeniable. He had no future in Washington, not even as a lobbyist. His disgrace would make him a pariah to his party and to his legislative peers alike, now and forever. There was a good chance he would even find himself expelled from the Idaho Bar.

- Idaho Bar Commission Rule 202.5. The Applicant ... must be a person of good moral character. In other words: 'Disgraced ex-Congressmen need not apply.' -

He was 47 years old and he was done. Finished. All the way over.

He could, if he chose, write a book, and pimp it on the talk show circuit. It might even be a bestseller. But law and politics – the only things he knew; the only things he truly *cared* about – would forevermore be closed to him. He would have to start again, from scratch, in some other field altogether.

Everywhere he went, people would surely whisper about him, "That's the Congressman who murdered that poor man."

They would turn away uneasy, when he approached them. Still worse, some of them would pump him for details of the incident, their eyes glittering with the same perverse interest with which they would devour news of the latest mass murder, or train wreck, or third-world atrocity. He would be *notorious.*

Piltch shuddered at the prospect.

- *My life really* is *over. It's a losing battle. Why even bother to fight it?* -

Piltch looked down again at the contents of his stomach, splattered across the pool deck 80 feet below.

- *That* could *be me.* -

Suddenly that prospect no longer frightened him.

May 6, 2020, 4:35 am EDT

Forest Drive, Beavercreek, OH

"Nine-one-one," the female operator announced, crisply. "What is your emergency?"

"I think someone is vandalizing the Sikh temple," replied Sandra Gale. She spoke into her cell phone in a quavering near-whisper.

"Can you be more specific, ma'am?" the operator asked.

"There are some men there," the elderly Gale said. "They're wearing ski masks. It looks like they're splashing some kind of liquid on the walls."

"How many men do you see, ma'am?" the operator queried. "Can you describe them to me?"

"I don't know," Gale replied. "At least four, I think. I can't see them very well. I'm afraid to get any closer."

"That's all right. Can I have your name and address, please, ma'am?" inquired the operator.

"No," replied Gale, "I'd rather not say – what with what happened yesterday, and all. Just please tell the police to hurry!"

"Can you give me the address of the ... did you say 'Sikh temple'?" the operator responded.

"Yes," Gale told her, "the Sikh temple! It's on Forest Drive, just off 142. Please, tell them to hurry!"

"I'm dispatching an officer now, ma'am," the operator assured her.

"Oh, my *god*!" Gale cried.

"What's the matter, ma'am?" the operator asked.

"It's on fire!" Gale replied hoarsely. "The whole place is on fire!"

May 6, 2020, 3:41 pm PKT (5:41 am EDT)

Daewoo Bus Terminal, Mingora, Khyber Pakhtunkhwa, Pakistan

Younis Masood Khakwani was nearing the end of his badly-depleted reserves of energy. It had been more than 24 hours since he last had slept. The stress and physical exertion to which he had been subjected since then had drained him almost completely.

His day had begun in Rawalpindi, with the distasteful task of beheading, and emasculating the late General Rashid Omar Sheikh. After he and his partner Fahad Abbas Afridi stuffed Sheikh's remains into the boot of the Mercedes E550 he would eventually abandon in Kota, they had driven it north, toward Mingora. The trip took several hours. They were fired on in Kota, at an unexpected police checkpoint. Afridi had been killed.

Khakwani had weaved through the village's dirt streets, to the edge of town. Trying not to panic, he concealed the Mercedes behind a dilapidated shack. He methodically stripped Afridi's corpse of its gun, cell phone, cash, and both his real and CIA-supplied counterfeit Smart National Identity Cards. As his final act before he abandoned the car, Khakwani moved his partner's body into the driver's seat.

He fled east across the ripening wheat fields, toward the looming shoulder of *Sur Ghar*. At any second, he expected to feel the mortal agony of a bullet in his back. Instead, to his surprise and gratitude, he made a clean getaway.

Carefully avoiding any contact with the farmers just filtering into their fields from dawn prayers, Khakwani made for the Swat River. There he washed his partner's blood off his hands. He also disposed of Afridi's SNICs, gun, and phone beneath the myriads of jagged, white stones that covered the banks of the river – swollen now to near maximum with heavy spring rains. There, too, he gathered a bundle of sticks to carry with him, hoping to be mistaken for one of the local *bazgarāno* collecting firewood.

Only then had he felt safe in returning to the N-95 highway. Khakwani plodded along its shoulder toward Mingora, largest city of the Swat district. He ignored passing traffic, acting the part of a local smallholder.

His ploy worked perfectly. It was a blessing that, here in the hinterlands, few peasants could afford to purchase the biometrically-based national ID card. Therefore few of them bothered to register their existence with NADRA – the National Database and Registration Authority. He passed through several police and army checkpoints along the way. Each time the stone-faced sentinels demanded to see his SNIC, Khakwani simply shrugged – and each time they had allowed him to pass through unsearched.

Eventually he reached Mingora.

There he abandoned his bundle of sticks, and continued on foot to the Daewoo bus terminal. There were other transportation choices available, but the Daewoo buses were well-known for being luxuriously comfortable and air-conditioned. Both amenities were powerfully attractive to a man as footsore and bone weary as Khakwani.

He stood, perusing the schedule mounted over the ticket window. Khakwani was dismayed to realize it would be nearly another two hours before the next bus to Rawalpindi was scheduled to depart. He looked again at the schedule board. There were only two buses to Rawalpindi per day. If he missed the 5:45 pm departure, he would be forced to wait until 10:00 am the following morning for the next bus.

Quite suddenly, the lure of a hot meal, a warm shower, and a decent night's sleep became nearly overpowering. As he stood there, irresolute, a well-dressed tourist tapped him on the shoulder.

"If you are not going to buy a ticket," the impeccably-groomed young man with the fierce mustache said haughtily, "kindly stand aside, so that others may do so."

Khakwani was struck by the man's unspoken, but unmistakable expression of distaste for what he obviously took to be a mere peasant – and a grubby one, at that – blocking the ticket window.

"Pardon me," Khakwani replied.

"Any time," the tourist shrugged.

Khakwani stepped aside.

The exchange convinced him it was imperative he improve his cover. The imperious tourist's tone spoke volumes about his assumptions regarding their respective social standings. His current, travel-stained appearance was out of place here. Khakwani was convinced he must, at a minimum, acquire clean clothing and a decent rucksack – or, better yet, a suitcase – before he returned to the Daewoo ticket window.

"The first rule of spy craft is: 'Blend in with your surroundings,'" as his CIA trainer had so often told him. "Ideally, you should appear so ordinary, and fit in so seamlessly with those around you that you become effectively invisible."

Weary and footsore, Younis Khakwani left the Daewoo terminal. On Landaki Road, he turned right, and began trudging toward central Mingora. His goal was the bustling shopping district surrounding the Green Chowk, and the promise of a meal, a shower, and a comfortable bed for the night.

May 6, 2020, 6:02 am EDT

Monmouth Medical Center, West Long Branch, NJ

Gregory Allan Shergold awoke to dazzling light. The rays of the fast-rising sun slashed through the window blind's slats, into his right eye.

He had been dreaming a wonderful dream. Its details now were fading more quickly than the daylight was increasing. All that remained was the memory of two huge, green, exotically-tilted eyes – and a smile so dazzlingly warm and loving it left his heart filled with tenderness and longing.

He sat up. Pain lanced through his head. A wave of sick dizziness made his stomach lurch. Bile rose in his throat. He turned swiftly to the side, and vomited noisily over the railing of his hospital bed onto the linoleum floor.

- I'm in a hospital bed. -

He desperately hung onto the rail.

- I guess that means I'm in a hospital. -

Falling back against his pillows caused the room to spin again. Briefly he closed his eye – but that made his vertigo worse. Trying to ignore his dizziness, he opened the eye again, and let his gaze wander the room, keeping his head as still as possible.

His trouble focusing did not prevent him from noticing the curtain pulled halfway around his bed. An identical drape concealed the bed across the room from him. There was a small television on a swing-arm to one side. He recognized an IV bag hanging from its stand on the same side of the bed as the TV. On the other side was the round-shouldered, blue cube of a diagnostic monitor, ticking quietly.

- Definitely a hospital. I must have been in an accident of some kind. -

He found it hard to breathe. His face hurt. It felt two sizes too large, despite the warm, comforting blanket of narcotics dripping through the needle in the back of his left hand. He didn't really care about that, though. The only thing that seemed important at the moment was holding on as tightly as he could to the memory of those incredible green eyes and the intoxicating smile that were all that remained of his dream.

Somehow he knew they were real. And the most important thing in the world was to find out who they belonged to.

May 6, 2020, 6:30 am EDT,

The President's Bedroom, Washington, DC

Julia – his glorious, radiant, beautiful Julia – was once again in his arms. His heart was full to bursting with love and gratitude for her presence. He broke their kiss long enough to look at her, eyes shining.

"Oh, Jules!" he exclaimed, "You survived, after all!"

But in Julia's brown eyes, he saw only an unfathomably deep reserve and sadness. Suddenly, he realized the truth.

- This is just a dream. -

William Orwell Steele opened his eyes. He was alone in the canopied bed in the presidential bedroom.

Duke, the Great Dane he and Julia had adopted six years ago as a gangling, adorable puppy, arose from his oversized dog bed. Standing by the bedside, he stretched his neck to nuzzle the President's cheek. The huge canine carefully laved Steele's face with his enormous, slobbery tongue.

Tears filled the President's eyes. Gratefully, he hugged his dog's big, square head.

"At least I still have you, boy," he murmured.

"At least I still have you."

May 6, 2020, 8:34 am EDT

The Executive Mansion, 138 Eagle Street, Albany, NY

"Good morning, ladies and gentlemen," John Bowditch, Governor of New York, said. "I welcome you to the Rose Garden. I want to thank you for coming, despite the early hour."

Bowditch paused to favor the assembled reporters with his engaging trademark grin.

"Let me begin by saying that I regret the necessity of holding this press conference," he continued. "But, despite the urgent demands of my duties as Governor of the great State of New York, I feel compelled to condemn the obstructionism of some members of my own party toward the May Day Relief Act. Tomorrow, this critically-important legislation will face a cloture vote in the United States Senate. I cannot stress strongly enough how vital passage of this Act will be to the people of the states most directly affected by this unprecedented act of terror. As Governor of New York, I cannot help but be aware that the Empire State has borne, and will continue to bear, the heaviest of those states' burdens."

Bowditch paused to consult his notes.

"As an example of what I mean, let me begin by telling you that I spent yesterday afternoon touring the Seneca Temporary Housing Facility, in Romulus, New York, some 200 miles east of Albany. As you know, the residents of the Seneca Facility are all refugees from the Fallout Zone. What you may not know is that most of them are not from New York. They are, instead, from Connecticut and Massachusetts. They have come to the Seneca Facility only because they have no other, viable choice.

"While it is true that the Federal government is picking up the bills, and providing many of the resources for Seneca's refugees, the impact of their presence on the citizens of our State nevertheless has been and will continue to be considerable. Every meal they eat, every watt of electricity they use, every gallon of gasoline the trucks that provide supplies to Seneca consume is a meal, a watt, and a gallon of gas taken from the permanent residents of New York."

Bowditch paused to survey the crowd.

"Do we begrudge them these essential supplies, despite the fact that their needs compete with those of our other residents?" he asked, rhetorically. "Of course not! They are our fellow Americans – and we Americans have always had, and must always have each others' backs in times of crisis. But the burden their presence places upon the citizens of New York is not a light one. We cannot continue to bear it unaided. We have no choice but turn to our fellow Americans for help, just as we ourselves are trying to help these new residents of our great state."

The Governor frowned.

"Yesterday evening, it came to my attention," he told them, "that certain members of the Senate are planning to filibuster the May Day Relief Act for purely partisan reasons. Apparently, they believe it will serve their own personal political interest in the upcoming November elections."

His jaw tightened.

"My friends," Bowditch said, "I come from a long line of Republicans. My father, Fred Bowditch, likes to say that, of all his memories, one of the proudest is of the day I checked the box marked 'Republican' on my very first voter registration form. As the progeny of a line stretching back to the Civil War, I sincerely believe that filibustering the May Day Relief Act is one of the most ill-advised initiatives senators of my party have ever attempted. Should it succeed, I fear it will spell the end of any possibility that a Republican will ever again be elected to high office in any of the states within the Fallout Zone – including this one.

"Let me be crystal clear on this point: I am convinced that this is a defining moment for our party. The Republican caucus *must* choose to place the good of our country above narrow, partisan interest. We *must* support the May Day Relief Act. To block its passage in order to avoid passing a purely temporary tax increase would be a suicidal act of partisan stupidity. It would fundamentally betray the people of New York and all the other States in the Fallout Zone."

The Governor again paused to survey the assembly.

"For the good of the country, for the sake of our posterity, for the tens of millions of May Day victims and refugees, for the sake of all our fellow citizens, I beg my party's Senators to do the right thing. Please, fellow Republicans, I implore you to do the right thing, simply because it *is* the right thing for everyone, regardless of political affliation. And, if you can't bring yourselves to do the right thing for the *right* reasons, I beseech you to understand that doing the *wrong* thing will mean the death of the Republican Party, as we know it. If you do not do the right thing – if you fail the people of the United States in their time of need – they will never, ever forgive you."

Governor Bowditch's eyes blazed with intensity.

"And neither will I."

May 6, 2020, 9:20 am EDT

Defense Service Office, Dalghren Hall, Annapolis, MD

"As you were, Lieutenant," ordered Clifford Fisk, Commander of the Annapolis Office of the U. S. Navy Defense Service Office North.

"Have a seat," he invited.

Fisk motioned to one of the wooden chairs, in front of his desk.

"Thank you, sir," replied Lieutenant Rupert Griffin Stewart.

He sat down and put his soft-sided, leather attaché case on the floor beside his chair.

"To what do I owe the pleasure of your visit, Lieutenant?" Fisk inquired.

"Sir," responded Stewart, "I wanted to talk to you in regard to the matter of one Eydis Finnursdottir, an Icelandic national who is currently being held under guard at Monmouth Medical Center per Public Law 107-40, sections 821 and 836 of title 10, and Presidential Directive 66 FR 57833."

"This person ... what did you say his name was, again?" Fisk demanded.

"*Her* name is Eydis Finnursdottir, sir," Stewart told him.

"Very well," Fisk said. "You say this Finnursdottir person is being held as an enemy combatant?"

"Yes, sir," Stewart replied, "that's affirmative."

"How the fuck did that happen?" Fisk asked. "Is she some kind of Al Qaeda sympathizer?"

"No, sir," Stewart responded, "I don't believe she is."

"Well, then," Fisk inquired, "What's the basis for her detention?"

"Apparently, sir," Stewart explained, "when she was brought to the JFK – unconscious, I might add – she was found in possession of an unregistered firearm."

"I see," Fisk said.

He frowned.

"I take it there's more to this story?" he asked.

Stewart nodded.

"Yes, sir," he confirmed. "I interviewed her in some depth yesterday. From what she told me, she and her boyfriend were attacked by gangbangers in his parents' Manhattan co-op. He was pistol-whipped and badly injured. She was tortured and repeatedly gang raped."

"Go on," Fisk urged.

He leaned back in his chair, toying with a fountain pen.

"Well, sir," Stewart told him, "Miss Finnursdottir maintains that, after several hours of being attacked by the gangsters – who she says were drinking heavily – they eventually passed out. She then took the firearm in question off of their leader. He woke up, and, long story short, she ended up shooting them all, in self-defense."

Fisk's eyebrows reached for his receding hairline.

"That seems pretty far-fetched," he observed.

"I agree, sir," Stewart said, "it does seem that way. Nonetheless, I believe Miss Finnursdottir is telling the truth about how she came to be in possession of the weapon."

"Oh?" Fisk responded. "Why is that?"

"Well, sir," Stewart explained, "first of all, her story actually seems pretty credible. She was admitted to Monmouth suffering from some pretty horrendous injuries. I went over her chart with the admitting physician. He tells me that, in addition to a badly-broken nose, multiple severe contusions, and numerous lacerations, an SAE exam revealed serious tearing of both her vaginal and anal tissues. Plus – and this is what convinced me she was telling the truth – she mainly seemed concerned about the effect the charges against her would have on her being separated from her boyfriend, rather than the consequences for her, personally."

"Do I take it this boyfriend is a U.S. citizen?" Fisk asked.

"That's affirmative, sir," Stewart said. "His name is Gregory Shergold. He's also currently a patient at Monmouth. I actually spoke with him yesterday, as well."

"And I suppose he confirms her story?" Fisk ventured.

"Well, sir," Stewart replied, "that's where it gets complicated. As I said, Mr. Shergold was seriously injured. In fact, he sustained a traumatic brain injury. The neurologist I spoke to said he was lucky to have survived it at all. It went untreated long enough that his memory has been pretty badly affected."

"Affected in what way?" Fisk asked.

"Well," Stewart said, "for one thing, he doesn't seem to be able to remember his own name. For another, he doesn't remember anything that's happened to him."

"You mean he doesn't remember being attacked?" Fisk suggested.

"I mean he doesn't seem to remember *anything*, period," Stewart replied. "His name, his age, his place of birth. Nothing."

"I see," Fisk said.

For several seconds, he sat, rocking slightly in his chair and tapping the fountain pen against his teeth.

Then he observed, "That's not much help to this Finnursdottir girl, is it?"

"No, sir," Stewart agreed, "it's not."

"So what do you propose I do about it?" Fisk asked.

"Well, sir," Stewart replied, "short of asking the AG to dismiss the charges against Miss Finnursdottir ..."

Fisk shook his head.

"Not gonna happen," he said.

"Then I'd like to see if we can get the FBI to investigate the scene of the crime, as it were," Stewart suggested. "I'd like them to determine whether the evidence supports Miss Finnursdottir's story. She's in a helluva fix otherwise, Major, and it seems to me that we might just owe her a little due diligence in that department."

"You understand that I can't make any promises in that regard?" Fisk warned.

"I realize that, sir," Stewart agreed. "To begin with, we have to get the FBI to agree to conduct the investigation. There's also the fact that, regardless of their sign-off, the final decision would be up to the Captain of the JFK."

Fisk nodded.

"Right on all counts," he concurred. "But I can at least put in the request. We'll see whether the Bureau is willing to play ball with us."

"I very much appreciate it, sir," Stewart told him.

Fisk waved the thank-you aside.

"All part of the service," he said.

He leaned forward, and stuck his fountain pen back in its holder.

"Was there anything else, Lieutenant?" he asked.

"Yes, sir," Stewart replied. "If it's okay with you, I'd like permission for Miss Finnursdottir to visit Mr. Shergold. She's clearly concerned about him. Who knows? Seeing her might even jog his memory."

Fisk frowned for a moment, then shrugged.

"I don't see how it could hurt," he responded. "Permission granted."

May 6, 2020, 10:14 am EDT

The Cabinet Room, Washington, DC

"All right, ladies and gentlemen," announced the President.

He seated himself at the center of the long oval table.

"Let's resume, shall we?" he ordered.

The hubbub of multiple overlapping conversations abruptly ceased. The occupants of the room sought their own seats. The Cabinet members were ranged around the table. Their senior aides sat behind them on the line of chairs along each of the long walls.

William Orwell Steele turned to Treasury Secretary Anderson Connaught IV.

"Andy, let's start with you," he directed. "Would you be so kind as to tell the rest of the Cabinet what you just told me?"

"I don't know that I'd characterize it as 'kind', Mr. President," Connaught replied. "About ten minutes ago, I received word that AIG has filed for bankruptcy."

The room went dead silent.

"Please tell me it's Chapter Eleven," begged Secretary of Commerce Marcy Collins.

Connaught shook his head.

"Sorry, Marcy, I'm afraid it's Chapter Seven," he told her. "They're throwing in the towel."

There was a collective gasp of horror from the assembled officials.

"You'll recall I predicted this would happen," Connaught reminded them. "Frankly, I'm surprised it took this long."

"How long do we have before the economy collapses completely, Andy?" the President inquired, quietly.

Connaught shrugged.

"If we're lucky?" he asked. "No more than a couple of days, at the outside." He sighed heavily. "Worst case? A few hours."

May 6, 2020, 4:37 pm BST (11:37 am EDT)

1 Lime Street, London, England

Sir Cyril Dunbar, Baronet Balfour of Sheffield, CEO of Lloyd's of London, reached out to the magnificent Newton's Cradle which sat on the opposite side of his massive, steel-and-glass desk from his office telephone. He lifted the right-most of its five steel balls, and let it swing downward, to impact upon its neighbour with a clack. Immediately, its impetus was transferred through the intervening globes to the left-most ball. It flew up in an arc, until, momentum expended, it descended again to strike its own neighbour. Then the ball on the right flew up once more, to what seemed like the same height from which it had originally been released.

Sir Cyril regarded the toy soberly. It had been a gift from the Chairman of Lloyd's – a token of the Board's appreciation for the sterling results the firm had enjoyed in Dunbar's first year as Chief Executive. The materials from which it was constructed made this particular version of the classic demonstration of Newton's laws of motion unique. The five steel balls were plated with iridium, rather than chromium. The wires from which they were suspended were titanium. The frame from which they hung was made of paladium, the surface of which had been exposed to a series of femtosecond laser pulses, turning it midnight black. Lines of two-carat rubies decorated the top of the frame, diamonds its sides, and emeralds the base. It was literally priceless – a one-of-a-kind *objet d'art* that had been made exclusively for him.

Sir Cyril spun in his chair, turning his back on his desk. The computer monitor displaying the screaming headlines of financial newsfeeds from around the world, and his swiftly-expanding email inbox, with its list of messages pleading for his attention both went unheeded. His desk phone's red, incoming-call lights, blinking their silent panic, and his smartphone, with its growing backlog of unanswered text messages, vanished from his view.

Instead, he gazed out over the vista of his firm's fabulously wealthy neighbourhood. Gloomily, he regarded the staid, square tower of the Deutsche Bank building, which loomed across Leadenhall Street to his left, and the giant, peculiar oval shape of 30 St. Mary Street – the infamous Gherkin – off in the distance to his right. He thought, not of Newton's Cradle, but of dominoes.

Dunbar envisioned those skyscrapers falling, tumbling into one another, bringing each other crashing to the ground – the ruin spreading out from Lloyd's in all directions, until it laid the entire world low.

- But we're not the actual centre, then, are we? -

No, the keystone of the financial universe's destruction was 180 Maiden Lane, in New York City, headquarters of American International Group. When it had toppled – rather too literally, in the wake of the nuclear explosion that had done for Lower Manhattan – the company that the Yank government once had deemed "too big to fail" had, nevertheless, failed. Spectacularly so.

For more than an hour now, Sir Cyril's phone lines, cellie, and email inbox had been filled to overflowing with messages, as the news of AIG's bankruptcy and forthcoming dissolution spread around the globe. Desperate for reassurance, Lloyd's Names, Members, brokers, and affiliates, along with myriad media and government officials, all demanded the answers they needed and feared.

Their questions were all the same, in the end: "What does this mean for *me* – for my family, my company, my future?"

- Ruin. It means ruin for us all. -

As complex as the insurance business often was, in the end, the reason for its forthcoming demise was dead simple. Reinsurance was the strategy of underwriting other companies' policies. It had been meant to spread risk as widely as possible, so as to lessen the chance that a single, major payout could ruin any one firm. Instead, it had so incestuously interconnected the whole industry that the abrupt and utter collapse of its biggest player could not help but topple the lot.

Reluctantly, Dunbar turned away from the window, back to his desk. The steel balls on each end of the gorgeous, incalculably-dear toy on his desk continued alternately to fly up and back, rhythmically clacking as they went. But, in the time he had spent staring gloomily out at London's doomed financial heartland, the heights each little globe reached had steadily diminished. Now, with each cycle they rose a mere fraction of the distance they had initially ascended.

- That's it then, isn't it? Eventually they bloody well stop. -

- Eventually it all *bloody well stops. -*

May 6, 2020, 12:31 pm EDT

The Oval Office, Washington, DC

As Senator John Parks of Ohio entered the Oval Office, the President stood up behind his ornate desk. A gift from Queen Victoria, it was made from the salvaged timbers of the HMS Resolute. With a smile, William Orwell Steele stepped around it, and strode toward the Senator. They came together near the tall window that looked out toward the Rose Garden.

"Senator Parks," Steele said, extending his right hand, "it's good to meet you."

"The feeling is mutual, Mr. President," Parks told him, giving his hand a firm shake.

"Have you had lunch?" Steele asked.

Parks was a shade under six feet tall, with thick straight black hair, beginning to gray. Beneath a high forehead, his deep-set black eyes were surmounted by bushy brows. His firm chin sported signs of a blue-black five o'clock shadow that looked like a permanent feature. The President found he liked the Senator's upright, almost military posture. Although he was aware that there were some key policy differences between them, Parks immediately impressed him as a man cut from different cloth than the typical Washington politician.

"No, sir, I have not," the Senator replied.

"In that case," the President told him, "I'd be pleased if you'd join me."

Parks cracked a brief smile.

"I try never to turn down a free meal, Mr. President," he confessed.

"Well, good," Steele responded, "because my stomach thinks my throat's been cut."

He motioned to the doorway directly across the Oval Office.

"This way, please," he said.

The two men crossed the Oval Office. They walked down a short hallway, past the door to the President's personal study, and into his private dining room. Inside, they found a table with two places already set. Steele sat at the head of the table, between the room's only two windows. The Senator took his place at the President's right.

As soon as they both were seated, a black-uniformed, Navy steward carrying a pair of covered plates stepped out of the tiny pantry next to the room's fireplace. He set the dinnerware before the President and his guest, and poured each man a glass of ice water from the pitcher on the table.

Removing the covers from the plates, the steward inquired, "Will there be anything else, Mr. President?"

Steele turned to Parks.

"Would you like something stronger to drink, Senator?" he asked.

Parks shook his head. "No thanks, Mr. President," he replied. "That's another one of my rules. Business or pleasure. Not both."

"Then that'll be all for now, Sam," Steele told the steward. "We'll let you know if we need anything later on."

"Very good, sir," the steward responded. "I'll be right outside, if you need me."

Quietly, he let himself out The door shut behind him.

"Dig in, Senator," invited the President.

Instead, Parks pushed his plate away.

He turned in his chair to face Steele directly, and said, "Mr. President, I appreciate your hospitality – and I surely am flattered that you've gone to all this trouble to butter me up. But, if you don't mind, I'd prefer not to waste either your time or mine on more of this ..." his sweeping motion took in the entire Oval Office suite. "What say we lay our cards on the table, instead?"

"Senator," Steele replied, "I appreciate your honesty – and your directness. So, by all means, let's show our hands."

"Thank you, Mr. President," Parks responded. "Let me start by saying I think we're both pretty clear on why you invited me here today. You want my vote on the May Day Relief Act."

"I do," Steele agreed.

He began spreading lemon chutney across wood-grilled salmon.

"But … I hope you don't mind if I eat while we talk," he added. "It really has been a long time since breakfast."

"I don't mind at all, Mr. President," Parks said. "You were saying?"

"Well, Senator," Steele responded, wielding knife and fork, "as I said, I'd very much appreciate your vote tomorrow. However, that's not the main reason I invited you to join me here today."

"That's – unexpected," Parks replied. "Why *did* you invite me here, Mr. President?"

Steele frowned.

"Before we get to that," he said, "I feel compelled to mention that I keep hearing your name mentioned as a possible candidate for this office in 2024 – assuming your man doesn't win this November, of course."

Parks made a disgusted noise.

"Please, Mr. President, we both know better than that," he replied. "Guy Prince is a clown. He's collected so much baggage in the primaries that … well, since that speech he made in Phoenix leaked onto the Internet, his chances against you in November have dropped to zero, and none. Given everthing that's happened since last Friday, he'll be lucky now, if he even carries his home state."

"Well," Steele conceded, "you may be right about that."

Parks snorted.

"You know I am, sir," he responded. "Prince is living proof that the Nixon strategy simply doesn't work in the 21st Century. Not with cell phone camcorders in everyone's pocket, and the Internet to keep a record of every blunder you make trying to pander to the base."

"So, what does that have to do with you, Senator?" Steele asked.

"Mr. President, there's not a chance in Hell that I'm ever going to win the Republican nomination," Parks confided. "All the talk you've heard on that score is just the media blowing smoke up the public's ass."

"I don't know about that," Steele replied. "You're intelligent, you're still relatively young, you have a lot of credibility on foreign policy and defense issues ..."

"And none of that matters a damn," Parks interrupted, "because ideological purity trumps every one of those points. At least, it does when it comes to my party's primary process. Mr. President, as things stand, were I foolish enough to speak my mind and vote my conscience, my future in GOP politics would be over. Oh, I'd serve out the remainder of my term, all right. Then, two years from now – because it will be a mid-term election, and what moderates we have left in the party will stay home – some bright-eyed zealot who thinks 'compromise' is a four-letter word will would whip the base into a frenzy about my 'treason', and I'd be out on my ass.

"Even if I can bring myself to keep toeing the Tea Party line, I'll still never be my party's presidential nominee. To be honest, I just can't stomach the prospect of spending the next four years pandering to a bunch of yahoos who think their goddamn faith matters more than the laws of physics. The real problem is, without their support, I couldn't get the nomination. And the horseshit I'd have to shovel to get their endorsement is such poison to the majority of voters that, even if I won the nomination, I'd find myself in the same fix Guy Prince is in right now. There's simply no way I could be elected President. It would be an utterly pointless exercise – and I'm not willing to waste time even considering it. End of dissertation."

The President had paused with his fork in mid-air as Parks's impassioned analysis reached its peak. Now he set it back down on his plate, and carefully wiped his lips with his linen napkin.

Well then, Senator," he asked, "since you've decided against running for President, what would you say, if I were to nominate you as the next Secretary of Defense?"

Parks sat back in his chair, thunderstruck.

The post of Defense Secretary had been vacant for the past ten days, ever since its previous occupant had dropped dead of a massive stroke on the seventh hole of the Burning Tree golf course. The late Kelvin Conable had sailed through his confirmation hearing. He had remained popular on both sides of the aisle throughout his tenure as Secretary. That made him a very tough act for anyone to follow.

On the other hand, Parks *was* the ranking Republican on the Senate Defense Authorization Committee. He felt he had proved his mettle as a junior member of the Intelligence Committee, as well. He was well-respected, by the majority of his peers. If Steele nominated him, there was no reason to think his fellow Senators would reject his confirmation. On the third hand, serving in this President's Administration in any capacity – much less at the Cabinet level – would truly be the kiss of death to any Presidential aspirations he might harbor. The Republican base would never forgive him for what its members would view as tantamount to political treason. In fact, given the base's propensity for holding grudges – and the ferocity of modern campaign tactics – the chances were high that he would never again be elected to office as a Republican.

And yet, the Secretary of Defense had real power and influence – more of both than any individual senator. Parks was certain he had the knowledge, the political skills, and the strength of character the position required. The only real remaining question was, did he want the job?

"Mr. President," Parks replied, finally reaching his decision, "I'd be honored to accept your nomination as Secretary."

"Well, then," Steele responded, "assuming nothing untoward comes up in the vetting process ..."

He looked Parks in the eye.

"Can I assume nothing will?" he asked.

Parks nodded.

"Yes, sir," he affirmed. "I'm not exactly a Boy Scout – but I gave up beating my wife weeks ago."

Steele grinned at the Senator's response.

Then, "No youthful peccadilloes?" he demanded. "No mistresses, no gambling debts, no substance addictions?"

"I have a three-cup-a-day caffeine habit," Parks admitted, "and I do like a good cigar from time to time. Luckily Cubans aren't illegal anymore, so ... no, sir. No dead hookers or live sheep. Plenty of unsavory companions, of course, but they're all either elected officials or denizens of K Street. I'm pretty sure I'll pass inspection."

"Good enough," the President said, extending his right hand. "Welcome to the team, then, Senator. Or should I say, 'Mr. Secretary-designate?'"

May 6, 2020, 1:17 pm EDT

VFA-47 Ready Room, USS John F. Kennedy

"As you were, Chief," said "Commodore" Barnaby Collins, Executive Officer of the USS John F. Kennedy.

He returned Chief Petty Officer Curtis Simmons's salute.

Simmons had just stepped through the doorway into the ready room normally used by the "Terminators" – one of two F-35 CV squadrons assigned to the JFK Battle Group's Carrier Air Wing. There were no fighter pilots currently aboard the Kennedy. They and their aircraft had flown off the carrier before it set out on its mission. The CPO had expected the room, usually crowded with fighter jockeys, to be empty.

Instead, the compartment's rows of airline-style chairs were now filled with men dressed in the distinctive MARPAT desert camouflage-pattern utility uniforms of Marine combat troops. Swiftly surveying the assembly, Simmons spotted a trio of familiar faces at the back of the room, standing with another swabbie he recognized as part of the JFK's crew. He turned back to the XO.

Collins was flanked on one side by a Hispanic-looking civilian. The man wore a dark blue windbreaker, tan cargo pants, shiny, black Florsheim dress shoes, and a black polo shirt with the letters "FBI" embroidered over the breast pocket. On the XO's other side stood a Marine officer, whose uniform bore no insignia of rank.

"Lieutenant Anthony Taylor," Collins said, turning to face the tall, hawk-faced man.

Taylor sported a shaved head and a three-inch, purple scar that ran from just above his right eyebrow to below his right cheekbone.

"Meet CPO Curtis Simmons, my go-to guy for oddball assignments," the XO continued.

"Pleasure," Taylor stated. He extended his hand, unsmiling.

"Likewise," Simmons assured him, clasping the Marine's hand.

Taylor gave him two firm, business-like shakes, then stepped back.

Collins turned towards the civilian.

"And this is Special Agent Roberto Guzman, of the FBI," he told Simmons.

The CPO and the FBI agent shook hands.

Introductions complete, Collins continued, "To bring you up to speed, Chief, Lieutenant Taylor and his platoon have orders direct from the President to extract Marilyn Selph, our UN ambassador, along with her staff, for transport to DC. They'll be commencing that mission in just under 20 mikes. In the meantime, we've received a request from the FBI to provide escort for Agent Guzman here," he nodded to the civilian. "He's investigating a former guest of ours. You may remember her – the redheaded girl who showed up dockside, carrying her boyfriend on her back?"

"Yes, sir, I do," Simmons replied.

He himself hadn't personally seen the girl carrying her boyfriend. However, he'd been on gangway duty when a group of men muscled their way through the throng of refugees, bearing the girl and her beau on their shoulders, and demanding they both receive immediate medical attention. None of those men had asked for any special treatment for themselves – only for the girl, and her man. Word of how she had appeared on the street, near death from exhaustion and dehydration, but determined to haul what was presumably her lover to safety had quickly spread all over the Kennedy. Her story swiftly became the stuff of legend.

"I don't understand, sir," Simmons continued, "what the ... heck ... could she be charged with?"

"I'm sure Agent Guzman will give you those details," Collins replied, "if you accept the mission."

"Yes, sir," Simmons acknowledged, his curiosity piqued.

"I'd like you, and your detail, to escort Agent Guzman to the scene of the alleged crime, and get him back safely to the JFK, once his investigation is complete," Collins told him. "I want to stress that this is a strictly volunteer mission. You're under no obligation to accept it, unless you do so willingly."

He cast a glance at the back of the room.

"That goes for the other members of your detail, as well," he added.

"Will it help that girl, sir?" Simmons asked the XO.

"Probably," Guzman responded for him.

"Then I volunteer for the mission, sir," Simmons said. "And so do my guys."

There was a chorus of agreement from the back of the compartment.

"All right then," Collins confirmed. "The assignment is yours. Lieutenant Taylor and his men, will provide escort for the first half of your mission. After that, you'll be on your own."

"Yes, sir," Simmons acknowledged.

"Now, this is important, Chief, so listen up," Collins cautioned. "You are to proceed with your mission, if – and only if – at the point where you and Lieutenant Taylor have to part company, it is safe to proceed to your own destination. If you feel the hazard to you and your men is in any way excessive, you are, instead, to accompany Lieutenant Taylor's unit to the UN and return with them to the Kennedy. Let me stress this point: the safety of you and your men – and of Agent Guzman – is paramount. We're doing this strictly as a courtesy to the FBI, and you're too valuable to the Kennedy to risk losing. If you can't do it safely, don't do it at all. Am I clear?"

"Aye, sir," CPO Simmons affirmed.

"All right then," Collins replied. "Draw weapons, brain buckets, and vests for you and your detail. You're to meet Lieutenant Taylor at the gangway in 15 mikes."

"15 mikes. Aye, sir," Simmons repeated.

"You're dismissed," said the XO.

May 6, 2020, 1:37 pm CDT (2:37 pm EDT)

Wells Fargo Bank, Bellevue, NB

"Hello, Mrs. Collinsworth? This is Angie Stomatopoulis at Wells Fargo. I'm fine, thank you.

"Listen, Mrs. Collinsworth, I'm calling about your mortgage application. I'm afraid I have some bad news – we're going to have to hold off on final approval ...

"What's that? Yes, I know you were expecting it to close today, but there's been a ... complication. Well, I'm getting to that. I'm sorry, but your insurance company has withdrawn their approval for your PMI policy ... it stands for 'Private Mortgage Insurance' ... and our mortgage lending standards require ...

"Excuse me? Yes, I'm sure you have an excellent record with them. It's just that ... I don't know if you've been watching the news today, but the insurance industry has ...

"Listen, I understand you've been waiting a long time. Believe me, I sympathize with you. I'm an Air Force wife, too, so I completely ...

"No, I'm sorry, but there's nothing I can do. No, I'm afraid Wells is not allowed to offer insurance on mortgages we write.

"Please don't cry, Mrs. Collinsworth. May I call you Barbara? Listen, I completely understand the fix this puts you in. Gary's tour at Offutt is up in November, and we'll be facing the same problem from the other side – we won't be able to sell our house, if the buyer can't get PMI.

"Where? Probably Ramstein. Look, Barbara, that's not important. What's important is that we're just going to have to give your application a little more time. Okay? I'm sure this freeze on PMI policies is just a temporary thing. In the meantime, we just have to have faith in the system ...

"I understand, Barbara. Don't worry, it'll all work out. You'll see. This is just a little bump in the road.

"Okay, I will, the moment I hear anything. I promise. Listen, I have to go – I have a lot of other customers I have to call about this same thing. Yes, all of them, I'm afraid.

"All right. You take care, too. 'Bye, Barbara."

May 6, 2020, 3:24 pm EDT

Monmouth Medical Center, West Long Branch, NJ

Dr. Theodore "Ted" Volberding, specialist in brain trauma at the Monmouth Medical Center Neuroscience Institute, knocked softly on the open door.

"Mr. Shergold?" he inquired, stepping inside. "I see you're awake. How are you feeling today?"

Gregory Shergold was sitting up in his hospital bed He turned toward the physician and shrugged.

"Okay, I guess," he replied. "My head hurts."

"I'm sure it does, Mr. Shergold," Volberding said, soothingly.

He snagged his patient's chart from its place on the end rail of his bed.

"You've sustained some very serious injuries," he observed. "We're hoping we'll be able to do something about the damage to your brain pretty soon. In the meantime, though, do you feel up to having some visitors?"

"I guess so," Shergold responded.

"You don't have to see anyone, unless you want to," Volberding told him.

"No, it's okay," Shergold said. "I don't mind."

"All right, then," Volberding said.

He turned, and gave a come-hither wave to the little group of people who were standing in the corridor, out of Shergold's line of sight.

The first to enter was Lieutenant Rupert Griffin Stewart, carrying his leather briefcase. His expression was serious.

"Hello, Mr. Shergold," Stewart prompted. "Do you remember me? I'm Lieutenant Stewart. I don't know if you recall, but we had a little conversation yesterday afternoon."

Shergold began to shake his head, and immediately winced in pain. "I ... ung ... I'm sorry, Mister, but I don't remember that, at all."

"That's okay," Stewart assured him. "It's not really all that important. May I call you 'Greg'?"

Shergold shrugged.

"Okay then," Stewart said. "Greg, there's someone who wants very much to see you. Would you like to see her?"

"I guess so," Shergold responded, apathetically. "Sure, why not?"

Stewart turned toward the doorway and beckoned.

A male nurse dressed in blue scrubs bent to release the brakes on the wheelchair in which Eydis Finnursdottir sat, hands cuffed in front of her. The nurse pushed her into the room. Volberding's attention was focused on his patient's reaction to her entrance. Seeing only polite interest, but no outward signs of recognition on Shergold's part, the neurologist scrawled a note on the chart he cradled in the crook of his left elbow.

"Oh, my poor Greg!" cried Eydis.

Her eyes filled with tears, as she realized the extent of her lover's injuries.

"Gregory Shergold," Stewart said, formally. "Say hello to Eydis Finnurs ..."

Before Stewart could complete his introduction, Eydis launched herself out of her wheelchair. Heedless of the agonizing pain that lanced through her neck and upper back at the sudden motion, she flung herself on Greg Shergold. Her arms tenderly surrounded his heavily-bandaged head; her tear-soaked cheek pressed gently against his own.

Sobbing in mingled grief and joy, Eydis' pent-up emotions tumbled out in a tangle of words.

"Oh, Greg," she wept. "I am so happy to see you! I have been so worried about you! It is like an eternity, since I last have seen you! Oh, Greg, I am so happy that you are alive! I was so afraid ..."

"Excuse me, Miss," Shergold asked, politely. "Do I know you from somewhere?"

His simple question halted Eydis' flow of murmured declarations in mid-tide. Confused and hurt, she pushed herself away from her beloved. With wounded solemnity, she gazed at him.

"Do you truly not know me, Greg?" she asked.

Her voice trembled.

"I am your girlfriend, Eydis Finnursdottir," she stated.

Greg looked carefully at her bruised and battered face, just inches away from his own. With its crushed, prizefighter's nose, its wealth of cuts and bruises, and the purple, swollen flesh surrounding its vivid, emerald eyes, it was the face of a complete stranger. Except ...

"Eyes ..." he muttered, concentrating fiercely, "... green ... green eyes."

He focused exclusively on them. Ignoring their puffy lids and the red bloom of a broken blood vessel in the right one, there was something about those particular eyes. A familiar something, like a vision or a half-remembered dream ... of eyes ...

"Eydis?" he asked, recognition dawning.

"Oh, Greg!" cried Eydis.

Her eyes shone, with tears of joy and gratitude.

"I knew that you could not forget me!" she told him.

Dr. Volberding's pen flew across Greg Shergold's chart.

May 6, 2020, 4:31 pm EDT,

The West Wing Press Briefing Room, Washington, DC

"Ladies and gentlemen," declared Yvonne Clevinger from the podium at the front of the Press Briefing Room, "I have a brief statement from the President. Afterwards, I'll take questions."

The murmur of correspondents' voices conversing and taking verbal notes suddenly gave way to attentive silence. Clevinger put on a pair of half-glasses.

"As you know," Clevinger continued, reading from the text before her, "this great nation – which is already coping with the greatest calamity in its peacetime history – now faces a fresh crisis, in the collapse of the insurance industry. I want you to know that this event was not unforeseen. Nor has it caught this Administration unprepared. My staff, working in close cooperation with the staff of the Secretary of the Treasury, is currently developing a proposal to assume the liabilities of the insurers who have filed for bankruptcy – including AIG. This plan will provide continuing coverage to their policyholders. We expect to be able to present the completed plan to Congress, no later than Friday morning, May 8th – the day after tomorrow. Until then, I ask for your patience, and your faith in my Administration's commitment to providing businesses and private individuals alike with the same protection your former insurers provided, and upon which you rely."

Clevinger took her glasses off, and placed them on top of the podium. She squared her shoulders, and took a deep, calming breath. Her hazel eyes swept the room.

"That concludes the President's statement," she announced. "I'll take questions now."

May 6, 2020, 5:22 pm EDT

Seneca Temporary Housing Facility, Romulus, NY

Feeling good about himself, Sean Halloran, Sr. swung down off the shuttle bus. He ambled down the roadway toward the cabin tent he called "home", a six-pack of Budweiser Dry dangling from his right hand. The contractor smiled, thinking about the money the FBI was paying him to do little more than engage his tent mate Adam Manson in conversation.

Sure, his family's living situation at the Seneca Temporary Housing Facility was a long way from ideal. They still had no running water in the tent, the porta-potties at the end of each line of bunkers, and tents frequently overflowed, and – worst of all – the loud, all-night sex marathons in which Manson and his hook-nosed wife Ruby constantly indulged kept him from sleeping more than a few hours.

- Still, things could be a lot worse. -

At least he, his wife, and child had a place to sleep, three, free hot meals a day – and a ridiculously large income, for a family that lived in a tent. Cigarettes, beer, and marijuana were all available at reasonable prices at the facility's canteen. And, ever since the passing of Tropical Storm Beth, the spring weather in upstate New York had been toasty warm.

- Although without air conditionin', it's liable to get brutal around here, by August. -

Halloran shrugged.

- Things change. -

His eyes were on the clear blue sky above him.

- We'll just have to wait, and see what happens. -

He shrugged.

The toe of his boot caught on the lip of an unpatched pot hole. He stumbled and almost fell.

- Watch where you're goin', ya zoof! -

Returning his gaze to the path in front of him, he was surprised to see his wife Fiona hurrying along the roadway toward him. She was carrying Sean Jr. on her hip, her face creased with concern.

"Fiona!" Halloran called. "What's the matter, darlin'?"

"Oh, Sean," his wife replied, "I'm so glad to see ya!"

Halloran held his arms wide. Fiona flung herself, trembling, into his embrace.

"What is it, sweetheart?" Sean, Sr. asked. "What's wrong?"

"Oh, Sean," Fiona replied, her face buried in his chest, "it's that awful Manson family! They're just so crude … I can't stand them, Sean! I really can't!"

Frowning, Halloran gently broke their embrace. He looked deeply into his wife's tear-filled eyes.

"What have they done to ya, Fiona?" he demanded. "If that sonofabitch has laid a goddamn finger on ya …"

Fiona shook her head.

"No," she said. "No, it's nothin' like that, Sean. It's just …"

"Just what?" Halloran asked, his tone bristling with suspicion.

His wife looked him directly in the eyes.

"They fuck all day, Sean" Fiona replied, defiantly. "*All* day. And they're just as loud about it durin' the day, as they are at night!"

Halloran could not help himself. He laughed aloud. He instantly regretted it, as his wife's eyes blazed with anger.

Fiona stamped her foot in frustration.

"T'isn't funny!" she raged. "I have to take Sean, Jr. for long walks every day, just to get away from them for a while. Fuck, fuck, fuck, fuck, *fuck*! That's all they do, the live-long day. Like *animals*! Just like *animals*! I can't take it anymore! I'm at my wit's end! Yh have to *do* somethin' about it! It's makin' me crazy, Sean! It's makin' me *wicked* crazy!"

"Okay, Fiona," Sean, Sr. pledged.

His sunny mood had entirely vanished. He'd never heard his proper Catholic wife use such deliberately vulgar language before. That she had done so now, and with such vehemence, was a measure of how upset she was – and of how seriously he was forced to take the issue.

"Okay," he told her. "I'll talk to Adam about it tonight, I promise."

"Ya will?" his wife asked, her expression timorously hopeful.

"I promise," Halloran repeated. "Don't worry, Fiona."

"Thanks, Sean," his wife murmured.

Once more, she buried her face in his chest.

"Thanks, so much," she repeated.

"Don't worry, Fiona," Halloran told her again, "I'll take care of it."

Unconsciously, he stroked her back to calm her. He stared down the road, to where his Chevrolet Sierra pickup truck and Adam Manson's battered Suburban sat, parked in front of the tent their families shared. Thinking about Manson's huge, muscular frame, his extensive collection of violently racist tattoos, and his mercurial temperament, he was already regretting his promise to Fiona – and dreading the conversation to come.

May 6 2020, 6:27 pm EDT

1 Park Avenue West, New York City, NY

"Chief!" hissed Seaman Farrell "Shorty" Buehl, "Bandits at six!"

Chief Petty Officer Curtis Simmons nodded acknowledgement of the warning.

"Ready weapons," he ordered, in a stage whisper.

"Aye, Chief," Buehl, Seaman Samuel Zawinsky, and Petty Officer Second Class Darnell Johnson murmured, approximately in unison.

Simmons turned to Hospital Corpsman Second Class Xavier Harmon. The Corpsman stood in the doorway of the apartment on the Northeast corner of the of the towering, Franco-German Renaissance-style co-op's fifth floor.

"Harmon," he said quietly, "go get Guzman."

"Aye, Chief," Harmon acknowledged.

The corpsman sprinted to the entrance to the apartment's parlor.

He stuck his head in, and said, "Visitors, Agent Guzman. Chief Simmons wants you."

"I was just finishing up," FBI Special Agent Roberto Guzman replied, zipping closed his soft-side black evidence bag.

He stripped off the Tyvek over-suit he had donned to prevent contaminating the scene. In less than 20 seconds, he had joined Simmons at the apartment's doorway. Guzmans' .40 caliber Glock 23 was in his hand.

Harmon, who was unarmed, hung back in the foyer, out of the line of possible gunfire.

In response to Simmons's hand signals, Buehl, Zawinski, and Johnson had taken firing positions. Buehl crouched in the landing's elevator doorway. Zawinski knelt in the entry to the other apartment off the Northeast fifth floor stairwell. Johnson sat on the flight of stairs leading up to the sixth floor. Between the five men's weapons, anyone coming up from the fourth floor would be the focus of a deadly enfilade.

They waited. The echo of footsteps climbing the stairs grew louder. The faint buzz of muttered conversation increased in volume to the point where it was possible to make out what was being said.

"... swear, blood, that booty so dime, I like to nutted, just *scopin'* it!"

"Halt!" boomed Simmons, in a commanding voice.

The first of the four men ascending the staircase had just reached the fifth-floor landing.

"Drop your weapons," the CPO added, "and raise your hands."

The leader of the quartet was dressed in a designer, fluorescent, orange-and-black sweat suit, a wide-brimmed, purple "pimp hat" with an ostrich feather stuck in its leopard-print band, and garish, very expensive Nike sneakers. He put his hands on his hips.

"Say, *what*?" he demanded.

"I said," Simmons responded, "put your hands *up*, or I will blow your dumb ass away. *Now*, punk!"

To underline his point, the CPO fired a round from his Beretta 92FS service weapon into the ceiling. The crack of the 9x19mm Parabellum round in the confined space was painfully loud.

The gangster on the landing reacted by immediately raising his hands over his head. His companions, however, pulled their own weapons from the waistbands of their sweatpants. Crouching, they took aim at Simmons, who was only partly sheltered by the doorframe of the apartment directly in front of them.

"Uh, uh, *uh*!" cautioned Darnell Johnson, from his perch on the stairs above them.

Three astonished heads swiveled to stare at up Johnson. He squinted back at them over the sights of his assault rifle, smiling beatifically.

"This is Special Agent Roberto Guzman of the FBI," the G-man announced.

He stepped into the apartment doorway, and assumed a two-handed combat stance, pistol leveled.

"Under the terms of Executive Order 14389," he continued, "I am authorized to use deadly force against you at my discretion. Lay down your arms immediately or I will open fire."

The three armed gangsters looked at one another, in a state of panic.

"Shee-it!" the one in green sweats said. "Popeye *and* the fuckin' Feds? You fuckin' kiddin' me?"

He bent to place his firearm on the lip of the landing, then raised his hands over his head.

"What you waitin' on?" demanded the gangbanger in the purple hat. "Lay *down*, muthafuckas!"

Reluctantly, the two sweat-suited men laid their weapons on the stair, where their companion in green stood. Then they stood up, and put their hands over their heads.

"Good doggies," commented Darnell Johnson, approvingly.

He was still sighting down the barrel of his weapon.

"Okay," Guzman ordered sternly. "You, in the pimp hat. Lie down on your face and cross your hands behind your back."

"Muthafuckin' G-man," the leader of the disarmed gangsters complained.

"No talking," Simmons commanded.

The grumbling hoodlum reluctantly dropped to his hands and knees. Then he stretched out on the floor of the landing and crossed his hands at the small of his back.

"You three," Petty Officer Johnson directed, "up against the wall."

Zawinsky advanced to the bottom step of the flight above them, and aimed his M-16A3 at the three men below.

"Shee-it," the gangster lowest on the stairway commented.

A moment later, he and his fellows were backed against the wall.

"Turn around, and face the wall," Johnson told them, sternly.

His aim was unwavering.

They complied.

Agent Guzman holstered his weapon, took two steps, and knelt to handcuff the gang's leader. He removed the hoodlum's gun from the waistband of his sweat pants, and skimmed it across the floor of the landing toward Simmons. The CPO stopped its slide with his foot.

Standing, the FBI man told Simmons, "Keep an eye on these punks."

He shouldered past the CPO into the apartment, where he had left his bag.

In seconds, Guzman returned, a bouquet of zip ties in his hand.

"You," he commanded, "green guy. Come up here – slowly – and lie down next to purple hat."

"Marlon," directed the gangsters' prone leader, his voice somewhat muffled, "do like he said."

"You heard him, Marlon," Guzman ordered. "Come up here, and lie the fuck down. We don't have all day."

Marlon turned, and trudged up the stairs, hands still raised. As he reached the landing, he paused.

"For a Fed, you got a dirty mouth, muthafucka," he commented, resentfully.

His observation produced a round of snickering from the Navy men.

"Fuckin' A," the FBI agent responded. "Now lie the fuck down – muthafucka."

Without further editorializing, Marlon joined his boss on the floor.

Guzman knelt, with his knee in the small of the green-clad gangster's back, and trussed his wrists with a zip tie. Then he zip tied his ankles together. Marlon complained steadily. Without rising, the FBI man turned to the gang leader on the floor beside him, and zip tied together the purple-hatted thug's feet, then his hands. Only once the hoodlum was secured with the plastic restraints did Guzman unlock and remove his steel cuffs.

Less than two minutes later, the remaining pair were laid out next to their fellow gang members. All four were securely bound, hand and foot.

"Shorty," Simmons ordered, holstering his Beretta, "round up their weapons."

"Aye, Chief," Buehl acknowledged. He slung his rifle over his shoulder and moved to comply.

Agent Guzman disappeared once more into the apartment where he had spent the past three hours collecting evidence. After a moment, he reappeared, black bag in hand.

"All right, ladies," he said, addressing the trussed-up gangsters, "this is your lucky day. Keep in mind that I could just shoot your asses right here, and nobody would say 'boo.' Instead, I left you a box cutter back there. Once we're gone, feel free to look for it. If I'm feeling extra-generous, we might even leave your gats at the gate."

He turned and nodded to Simmons.

"Okay, you swabbies," the CPO ordered, acknowledging the FBI agent's nod with one of his own. "Time to cut and run."

May 6, 2020, 7:43 pm EDT

1388 Research Park Drive, Beavercreek, OH

"Let me explain a few things to you, Mr. Stoat," offered Karl Mayther, FBI Agent in Charge of the FBI's Cincinnati Field Office. "You're under arrest as a suspect in the arson of the Sikh temple. Under normal circumstances, you'd have a right to the presence of an attorney during questioning."

Earl Harley Stoat, a big, balding, man in his late twenties with a substantial beer gut spilling over his jeans, nodded cautiously, his lower lip thrust out in a curiously childish expression of truculence.

"Yeah," he replied. "Like I said, I know my rights. You gotta give me a lawyer. It's in the Constitution."

"Don't interrupt me again, Earl," Mayther told him, harshly.

He leaned over to place both hands flat on the table between them.

"I'll gag your fat ass," he threatened. "Understand?"

Stoat blinked in surprise, and flinched. "You ... you ... !" he stammered.

"Shut! The *fuck*! Up!" Mayther roared, slamming his right palm on the tabletop with a loud bang.

Stoat cowered. He leaned back in his chair, as far as the staple in the melamine resin tabletop to which his handcuffs were attached would allow. Audibly, he swallowed.

"That's better," Mayther said, pushing himself upright again. "As I was saying, that's under *normal* circumstances."

He narrowed his eyes and stared directly into Stoat's.

"These are not normal circumstances," he stated.

Mayther continued to stare into Stoat's eyes, until the fat man in the sleeveless tee shirt dropped his gaze to the surface of the interrogation room's table.

"The United States is currently under martial law," Mayther continued. "Do you know what that means, Earl?"

"Yeah," Stoat replied sullenly, without looking up. "It means William Orwell Steele is a fuckin' dictator."

"That's right, Earl," Mayther nodded. "He is."

Stoat, who had been expecting the FBI agent to argue with him, raised his head. He gaped in astonishment at Mayther.

"And do you know what *that* means, Earl?" Mayther continued.

Open-mouthed, Stoat slowly shook his head.

"I'll tell you what it means," Mayther said. "It means that right now you don't *have* any Constitutional rights. Under martial law, the military is in charge – and the military doesn't even have to give saboteurs like you a trial. They can just stand you up in front of a wall and *shoot* your fat ass. Just like that."

The FBI SAIC snapped his fingers in illustration.

Rivers of sweat created dark half-moons under the armholes of Stoat's tee shirt.

"Tell me, you dumb, fucking briar hopper," Mayther continued, "did you know that almost all gas stations have surveillance cameras, now?"

Stoat started in surprise. His lower lip began to tremble.

"For instance, the station where you filled up those gas cans this morning has them," the agent told him. "And they got nice, clear video of you and your idiot pals incriminating yourselves."

Mayther spun the laptop around on the table, so that Stoat could see its screen.

"Would you like to see that video, Earl?" the FBI man asked.

Stoat shook his head. Beads of sweat cascaded off his glistening cheeks.

"We have credit card records of you purchasing that gas, too," Mayther said. "We have the gas cans you left in your garage. And you know what?

They still have traces of fresh gasoline in them. E-85, just like it says on the receipt you had in your pocket, when you were booked."

Mayther held Stoat's eyes. He leaned over the table and placed his palms flat on its top again, bringing his implacable gaze within two feet of the shivering suspect.

"And, before you try telling me you bought all that gas this morning for your fucking lawnmower, keep in mind that I know you spent the day at work, Earl. You fat, sad, sack of shit," the G-man warned.

Earl Stoat began to cry.

"So, here's the deal," Mayther told him, sternly. "Either you roll over on your domestic terrorist buddies, right fucking *now*, or I turn you over to the local National Guard Commander, and let him blow your stupid, worthless ass away. Because Earl? Your accomplices? We've got nice, clear video of them, too. Clear enough for TV news reports, clear enough for wanted posters – and plenty clear enough for facial recognition software to find their drivers licenses. So we don't really *need* you to cooperate. With or without you, we'll get them, and their asses will go up against the wall, too."

Mayther's voice softened.

"So, do yourself a favor, Earl," he insisted. "Tell us who your friends are. Give us a full confession – and I mean *everything*, including killing Mr. Singh – and I'll cut you a deal. Hold anything back – and I mean *anything* – and I call Colonel Strong."

The FBI agent pulled out his smartphone.

"*Decide*," he commanded, his finger poised over the dial icon.

May 6, 2020, 8:11 pm EDT

Seneca Temporary Housing Facility, Romulus, NY

"I got to admit, bro," Adam Manson confessed, in a tone of grudging admiration, "it took balls for you to bring that up. Especially to me."

Sean Halloran, Sr. shrugged, uneasy with Manson's words of praise.

"We're both adults here," he replied. "It wasn't that big a deal."

"Yeah, it was," Manson insisted, shaking his head. "'Cause I know you're scared of me."

"Am not," Halloran protested.

His choice of words immediately made him feel like a six-year old.

"Are too," Manson responded easily.

He took a long swallow of beer.

"Don't try to bullshit me, buddy," he told Sean, Sr. "I could tell you were scared shitless, the first time you saw me without a shirt on."

"It's Fiona I'm scared of," Halloran maintained, "not you. That's why I ..."

"I thought I told you not to bullshit me," Manson warned.

He frowned, and balled his fists. His thick biceps bulged, menacingly.

Halloran flinched, involuntarily.

"See?" Manson said. "What'd I tell you?"

The big man laughed convivially.

"I'm just fuckin' with you, bro," he confessed. "But, you're no more afraid of that little girl than I am."

He took another long swig of beer, casually crushed the empty can, and got up to rummage for a replacement in the cooler that sat between them.

"Even a complete retard could tell she worships you, Sean," Manson told Halloran.

He popped the tab on a fresh beer, and resumed his seat.

"It's just like the Good Book says," he quoted, "'Wives, submit yourselves unto your own husbands, as unto the Lord.'"

Halloran frowned.

"What's that?" he asked. "Somethin' from the Old Testament?"

Manson shook his head.

"Ephesians 5:22," he corrected. "Colossians 3:18 says pretty much the same thing."

He looked up from the cigarette he was rolling.

"You don't read the Bible much," he challenged, "do you, Sean?"

Halloran shrugged.

"Not really," he admitted. "Fiona's the religious one in the family. I'm just … well, I was raised a good Catholic boy, but …" his voice trailed off.

"Fallen away, huh?" Manson observed.

"I guess so," Halloran agreed.

Manson shook his head. He lit his hand-rolled cigarette with his battered Zippo.

"Back-sliding's as bad as not payin' attention when the President's wipin' his ass on the Constitution," he opined. "Maybe worse. Physical slavery only lasts a lifetime. Damnation's eternal. You gotta get right with the Lord, bro. The Rapture could come any time."

Halloran again shrugged.

"I'll take my chances," he replied. "Right now, I'm more concerned with this world than the next one."

He took a long swallow of his beer.

"So, whaht makes ya think we're in danger of bein' enslaved, Adam?" he asked.

"Listen," responded Manson.

He reached down to turn up the volume on Halloran's FBI-supplied boombox.

"... tell you *the time is at hand*!" the voice of Merlin Friend suddenly thundered. "Patriots, *arise*! The tyrant must be thrown down – *now*, before the jackboots of his UN masters reach our front doors! Rise *up*, Patriots! Rise up, *now*! Rise up, *tonight*! Only *you* can stop this monster! Only *you* can foil his evil minions! Rouse your militias! Take up arms! Hang the socialist tyrant William Orwell Steele from the nearest lamppost, before we're all trampled under the heel of the New World Order! *Revolt*, I tell you! *Revolt!*"

There was a long moment of silence, before Friend announced in a businesslike tone, "We'll be right back, after this message from our friends at Goldmine."

Manson turned the boombox's volume down to a whisper again.

"That's what," he told Halloran.

Sean, Sr. shook his head.

"I don't get it," he confessed. "What am I missin'?"

Manson gave him a long, calculating look. He took a swig of beer, then leaned toward Halloran.

"Only this, bro," he confided, "Merlin Friend is gettin' the militia boys all worked up. You heard him. And he's right – something's got to be done. One spark is all it's gonna take, and the Second American Revolution is *on*."

Manson inhaled a long breath of tobacco smoke, and exhaled a series of smoke rings.

"So, ya think the militias are really gonna rise up?" Halloran asked

"Sure as I'm sittin' here, Sean," Manson confirmed.

He tilted his beer and swallowed noisily.

"Only thing is," he added, "most of those militia dudes couldn't fight their way through a Girl Scout troop. They're just a buncha fat, old fools playin' at bein' soldiers."

Manson looked left and right, as if checking for unseen listeners.

Then, in a voice pitched just loud enough for Halloran to make out, he said, "But not all of 'em. There's at least one exception I know of."

"And I s'pose ya could tell me what it is, but then ya'd have to kill me, right?" Halloran replied.

"Well, that," Adam Manson nodded, "or else recruit you."

May 6, 2020, 9:038 pm EDT

The White House Living Room, Washington, DC

"I have to admit," confessed William Orwell Steele, "I feel bad about playing hooky, with the insurance bailout plan still incomplete."

He stood beside the room's fireplace, his elbow propped on its mantel. Above him, the face of the late Julia Steele smiled from its picture frame.

Dr. Marcus Aurelius Clement noted with concern the slight tremor in the hand in which Steele held his Scotch.

"Mr. President," he responded, "speaking as your physician, I think you urgently need this down time. Quite frankly, I've never seen a human being under as much pressure as you've been subjected to over the past week. In my professional opinion, I believe you can best serve the country at this moment by focusing on your own needs, at least for the next few hours."

"He's right, sir," Diana Hunter concurred. "You've delegated responsibility for the insurance bailout to Andy Connaught and Marcy Collins. They're both more than qualified to craft such a plan – and, if you'll pardon my saying so, you are not. Unless I'm mistaken, your degrees are in history and political science, rather than economics or finance."

Steele nodded acknowledgment of her observation.

"That being the case," Hunter opined, "if I were in your place, I'd let the experts do the heavy lifting, and worry about getting a decent night's sleep, instead."

"You're right, of course," the President admitted. "Both of you."

He lifted his glass, and took a long swallow of Lagavulin.

"It's just hard to turn it all off," he confessed.

Steele turned to Andover Philips, his Chief of Staff and longtime friend.

"Andy, would you be good enough to get me a refill?" he asked.

"Absolutely," Philips replied.

He stood, and moved to the sideboard.

"Speaking of delegating," Steele continued, "I was very impressed with the level of detail in your proposal to nationalize the oil industry, Madam Vice President."

Diana Hunter waved his praise away. Her immaculately-manicured nails clinked softly against her wineglass in passing.

"The credit really belongs to my staff," she said. "They did all the hard work. I just pointed them at the problem."

"Well, it's a fine job, regardless," the President told her. He frowned. "Given the debt we're about to take on with this insurance crisis, we may not have a lot of choice in the matter."

"You know, sir," the Vice President responded, "I've been thinking that we really ought to look at the entire fossil fuel industry. Not just oil, but coal, natural gas, and propane, too. It seems to me that ..."

She was interrupted by a discrete knock at the door. It opened, and Special Agent Richard "Dick" Wright entered, holding the President's personal smartphone.

"Excuse me, Mr. President," Wright apologized. "You have a call from Secretary Burke."

Steele crossed the room to where Agent Wright stood at the end of the short vestibule between the interior and the hallway outside. He handed his empty glass to Philips, as he passed the sideboard.

"Arleigh?" Steele inquired, accepting the proffered phone.

He turned away from Wright, with a wave of thanks. The Secret Service agent quietly left the room, closing the double doors behind him.

"What's up?" the President demanded.

There was a moment of silence as Arleigh Solomon responded to his query. Steele's guests watched for his reaction. They were not disappointed. The President suddenly straightened, and his eyes lit with interest.

"Arleigh?" he repeated. "I'm going to put you on speaker, so Andy Philips and the Vice President can hear this. Would you please repeat what you just told me?"

"Certainly, Mr. President," came Solomon's reply.

His rumbling voice was made tinny by the smartphone's tiny speaker.

"I said," the Secretary reiterated, "'The FBI has in custody the people responsible for the burning of that Sikh *Gurdwara* – that's what they call their temples – in Ohio.' Three of them have confessed, and rolled over on the ringleader. The SAIC tells me his agents have recovered solid evidence that the same suspects were also responsible for beating Mr. Singh to death."

"That's very good news, indeed, Arleigh" Steele told him. "My compliments to the agents involved."

"I'll pass those along, sir," Solomon promised. "I should mention that the SAIC has requested permission to turn the bunch of them over to the commander of the local National Guard unit, for trial before a military commission. He promised one of them a deal, but the others ..."

"No," the President said, interrupting. "I want you to have them, the Agent in Charge, and all the associated evidence and reports flown to the JFK, instead. We'll try them there, where there'll be no question whether a military commission has jurisdiction."

"As you wish, Mr. President," Solomon agreed. "And, sir? There's one more thing."

"What's that, Arleigh?" Steele asked.

"Mr. President," the Secretary of Internal Security told him, "we think we've identified one of your daughter's kidnappers."

May 6, 2020, 7:15 pm PDT (10:15 am EDT)

Alvarado Street, San Leandro, CA

Artemis Alexandra Steele had been trying forever to resist the confident, seductive, insistent voice that was her constant and only companion. With every particle of her will, she tried to ignore its insidious promises. She had employed every trick she could think of, attempting to block out its hypnotic rhythm.

At first, she focused on her work as a teaching assistant for her mentor, thesis advisor, and inspiration, Dr. Cassandra Cayce.

Cayce's bestselling book "The Permian Extinction, Global Warming, and You" had literally changed the course of her life. It had given her inchoate desire for a meaningful career direction and purpose. It had crystallized her ambition and provided her with a model upon which to base her academic trajectory. She had expected that, in time, she, like Cayce, would achieve one of the handful of doctorates in paleoecology. It would enable her to devote her life to studying the effect of global extinction events on ecologies and evolutionary trends, and help to spread the gospel of preparedness that Cayce had striven so tirelessly to evangelize.

Artemis tried to concentrate on the research she had been conducting in the Hetch Hetchy watershed, high in the Sierra Nevada. She struggled to recall her observations about the effects of regional drought on "blooms" of various life forms. Her tentative hypothesis was that such explosions in the numbers of particular species were harbingers of an impending, general ecological collapse. Most recently, the swarms of tarantulas carpeting the Sierra Nevada's high-altitude mountain meadows had added to the small mountain of statistical evidence she'd been accumulating.

It had not worked.

Like a sonic incubus, the voice wore down her will to resist. It wormed its way deep into her subconscious, promising her rescue and freedom in exchange for belief and surrender. As the endless, trackless hours slowly crept by, its constantly repeated message, "Trust me – I will rescue you.

Love me – I will save you. Surrender to me – I will help you," gradually, irresistibly eroded her will.

In the absence of every other sensation, the hypnotic mantra methodically depleted her deepest reserves of psychic strength. Slowly, relentlessly, it sapped her resolve. Iteration by iteration, it overcame her desperate determination to remain free. To remain whole. To remain *herself*.

Now, all too terribly clearly, she understood that she was being remolded against her will into a slave to the voice. Despite her desperate struggle, her transformation was inexorably progressing toward complete surrender and utter subjugation. She knew she would find no escape, no rescue from the mental shackles it was creating. Soon her bondage would be complete. There would be nothing of Artemis Steele left to save.

Knowing that – and recognizing she was helpless to prevent it – was the worst torture of all.

May 7, 2020, 9:21 am PKT (May 6, 11:21 pm EDT)

Daewoo Bus Terminal, Mingora, Khyber Pakhtunkhwa, Pakistan

Younis Masood Khakwani climbed out of the pedicab he had taken from the Green Chowk. He joined the queue that was already spilling out from the Daewoo Bus Terminal gate onto Landaki Road.

As each person in the line reached the entry, he or she was required to submit his Smart National ID Card to a hard-faced, black-bereted Army *naik*, The screener ran it through a portable reader, then scanned the card owner's thumbprint to compare it with the image stored on the card itself. The *naik* was flanked by a pair of equally tough-looking soldiers, both of whom were armed with Heckler & Koch MP5 submachine guns. Their presence insured that those waiting their turn stayed quiet and orderly, and promptly complied with the corporal's demands.

- Well ... it seems the government has succumbed to our deception. -

The thought cheered him.

It meant that his friend and partner Fahad Afridi's life had not been sacrificed in vain. Clearly, the Army believed the Taliban was responsible for the kidnapping and murder of Rashid Omar Sheikh. Just as clearly, it was conducting a province-wide crackdown, in response to the discovery of Sheikh's decapitated body in the trunk of the Mercedes E550 that Khakwani had abandoned in the village of Kota, some 27 hours earlier.

Khakwani was happy that he had gotten up at dawn, despite his exhaustion.

Bolting his breakfast, he had made a whirlwind expedition through the Green Chowk's markets. He bought the expensive, richly-embroidered, purple kameez and satin shalwar in which he was now dressed, as well as an assortment of other clothing in keeping with his cover as a rich tourist. He also purchased a leather, wheeled suitcase and a couple of expensive, hard-cover souvenir books that featured full-page photographs of assorted points of interest in the Swat Valley.

Back in his hotel room, he used his smartphone to rephotograph several dozen of those images. Then Khakwani used the phone's image editing software to crop those photos, subtly blur a few, and add pictures of himself to the foreground of half-dozen others. Leaving the books behind, he had returned to the street. There, he persuaded several different passersby to use his smartphone to snap pictures of him smiling, with the bustling Green Chowk marketplace in the background.

Just before checking out of his hotel, Khakwani had waxed his mustache ends into fierce points. He also trimmed, oiled and carefully combed his beard, in keeping with his cover as a wealthy tourist. All in all, he was certain his assumed identity was convincing enough to pass any foreseeable inspection – as long as his untested, CIA-counterfeit SNIC was good enough to fool the *naik*'s scanner.

The line continued to grow, as it inched toward the bus terminal's gate.

By the time Khakwani reached the *naik* and his portable SNIC reader, nearly two dozen people were lined up behind him. He was increasingly thankful he had arrived early. It was beginning to look as though, if he had waited much longer, all the seats on the 10:00 am bus to Rawalpindi would already have been filled. He would then have had to wait until 4:00 pm for the next departure. Given how quickly government troops were pouring into Mingora, it seemed best for him to leave the city as soon as possible. Remaining until the late afternoon could only increase the risk that he would be apprehended.

"Your card," the *naik* demanded.

Khakwani affected a bored expression. He handed over his counterfeit SNIC, without comment.

"Your right thumb, here," the *naik* instructed, betraying no sign of suspicion.

- Allahu akbar! -

He pressed the indicated digit against the scanner's rectangular glass surface. The *naik* glanced at the readout.

"Your card," the *naik* said, handing the fake SNIC back to Khakwani.

He nodded, distantly, like the upper-class tourist he was pretending to be, and passed through the gate into the Daewoo Bus Terminal.

May 7, 2020, 12:27 am EDT

Fort Monmouth Temporary Housing Facility, NJ

It had been a long day filled with loss, grief, humiliation, frustration, and anger for Elizabeth Shergold.

She awoke shortly after dawn, following a restless, intermittently-sleepless night spent huddled on the concrete surface of the 48th Street Pier. A thin, Mylar blanket covered her. Her wadded-up Burberry coat substituted for a pillow. Almost the instant her eyes opened, she realized her precious Yorkie Cassie, who had spent the previous two nights curled up in her arms, was missing.

It took two long hours of frantic searching, calling Cassie's name, and questioning indifferent or forthrightly hostile members of the crowd of refugees waiting to board the USS John F. Kennedy for Elizabeth to face the fact that her beloved dog was well and truly lost. Hard as it was to accept, the only conclusion she could reach was that Cassie had most likely been stolen by the same, resentful hooligans who so enthusiastically jeered her insistence that she be permitted to bring her little blue-dyed terrier aboard the giant aircraft carrier.

Elizabeth spent the next few hours mourning her loss: sobbing helplessly, wracked with guilt.

"Poor Cassie," she murmured, over and over again.

Slowly, grief turned to anger and bitterness.

- How can people be so heartless? How can people be so cruel? -

Eventually, a kind of emotional numbness set in. Her beautiful, loving dog – her constant companion for the past nine years – was gone. There was nothing she could do about that. Hard as it was to abandon hope, little as she wanted to face the prospect of going on alone, she had no choice. There was no sympathy to be found in the anonymous crowd, no pity for her loss, no consideration for her feelings. No one cared about her, just as no one had cared about Cassie.

With that realization – unwelcome as it was – came one small consolation. At least now, with Cassie's disappearance, there no longer was any bar to her boarding the giant aircraft carrier. At long last, she could leave Manhattan. Her home, since her birth on the Upper West Side 43 years earlier, had, in the past six days, become a frightening prison. Despite her finery, she had been reduced to existence as a homeless person. For days now, she had made her bed on the street, dependent on charity for sustenance, grubby, unwashed, and but for Cassie, entirely alone. The sense of relief at the prospect of an end to that indignity left her almost giddy.

Elizabeth picked herself up off the surface of the pier and, click-clacked her way toward the end of the still-seemingly-endless line of waiting refugees. To her gratified astonishment, less than a block away from Pier 88 a hulking man in a gray sweat suit and sneakers stopped her in mid-stride. Chivalrously, he gestured for her to slip into the queue in front of him.

A fat, balding man, in a rumpled, stained, black pinstripe suit, who stood in line directly behind him objected. The giant – blue-black, unshaven jaw outthrust – turned to scowl at him.

Elizabeth's benefactor balled a fist the size of a small ham, and warned, "Ey! Watch yer tongue, pal! Dat's my mother yer talkin' about!"

Satisfied with the objector's silence, the big man turned his back on the fat businessman. He favored Elizabeth with a conspiratorial wink.

That simple act of kindness cheered her immensely. Likewise, after nearly a full day without food of any kind, the bologna sandwich and foam cup of strong coffee a sailor handed her, at the entrance to the pier satisfied her in a way that no Beluga caviar ever had. As if observing the reactions of a stranger, Elizabeth marveled at the gratitude these small benisons evoked in her.

Near dark, she finally reached the foot of the gangplank.

A bored sailor with two red chevrons on the sleeve of his camouflage duty uniform asked her for identification. She rummaged in her Hermes Birkin. Eventually, she produced her State of New York identification and Social Security cards. The petty officer neatly printed her name and ID numbers on a thick sheaf of clipboard-bound forms, then tore the topmost one off, and handed it to her.

"Welcome aboard, ma'am," he said. "Please give this form to the rating, as you board the ship."

Elizabeth thanked him. Carefully, she ascended the gangway to the Kennedy, teetering on the incline in her Tabitha Simmons stilettos.

At the top, she was met by another man with chevrons on his sleeve. He politely asked to see the form with which she had been entrusted. While he examined it, a sailor with two diagonal silver stripes on his sleeve scanned her from head to toe with a wand-like device attached to a gray metal box. It emitted a series of ominous squeals.

"Clothes, and shoes, both," the sailor observed.

"Ma'am," the man with the chevrons told her, "I'm afraid your shoes and clothing have been contaminated with radioactive material."

At her expression of shocked alarm, he said soothingly, "Don't worry, ma'am ..."

The petty officer looked at the radiac operator. The sailor held up two fingers, and nodded.

"... it's not life-threatening," he continued. "But we are going to have to ask you to change clothes, before we can let you board a helo."

He pointed to a large tent-like structure on the Kennedy's deck.

"If you'd be so kind as to follow Seaman Albermarle to decon," he told her, "we'll get you fixed right up."

Truly frightened, Elizabeth meekly followed a very young sailor to the tent. There, a young woman in blue surgical scrubs told her to strip to the skin. She was instructed to place her clothing and shoes in a hamper marked with a black trefoil on a yellow background, and the stenciled words "Radiation Hazard". The woman gave her a bar of green soap and a tube of yellowish shampoo. She was then directed to a shower stall, with instructions to thoroughly wash her hair and skin.

Elizabeth followed the young woman's instructions religiously. With a shudder of revulsion, she discarded her Burberry coat, her Mandalay evening gown, her Tabitha Simmons stilettos, and, for good measure, her Hermes purse. Then she stood under the cold shower, furiously scrubbing every inch of her skin with the soap; washing and rewashing her hair with the chemical-scented shampoo. When she was finished, a woman in duty uniform again scanned her body with a radiac wand.

"You're clean, ma'am," the woman told her.

"Oh, thank God!" was Elizabeth's heartfelt response.

"You'll find clothing and slippers through there," the woman said, gesturing to a curtained opening in an interior partition of the tent. "And you'll want to hold on to these," she added, handing Elizabeth her identification, credit, and Social Security cards.

Elizabeth padded barefoot across the tent.

On the other side of the opening, she discovered a half-dozen long tables. They were heaped with obviously-used clothing, unopened packages of bargain-store underpants, and brassieres, and hospital-style slippers with rubberized soles. Selecting a pair of relatively-new-looking, store-brand jeans and a pink Ne-on Glowbaby sweatshirt, she dressed quickly, glad to be able to cover her nakedness.

When she was again clothed, another female sailor in duty uniform ushered her out of the decontamination tent. She pointed to a large canvas structure, across from the tall, narrow command island toward the rear of the carrier's deck.

"Please follow the yellow line to the waiting area over there, ma'am," the woman instructed her. "You'll board a helo to Fort Monmouth from there."

20 minutes later, she was on her way. The trip was short, which was welcome, because the incredible racket of the Sea Stallion's engines triggered a fierce attack of tinnitus. So it was with her ears literally ringing that Elizabeth exited the helicopter, and entered Fort Monmouth Temporary Housing Facility.

Her first experience of life at Fort Monmouth was joining a line of fellow refugees.

When she reached its head, she was escorted to a long table where she was again asked for identification. From there, she was directed to a tent where she was weighed, asked to provide her detailed medical history, and had her pulse and blood pressure recorded. Her next stop was still another table, where she was issued a laminated identification badge on a lanyard. The bored National Guardsman who handed it to her cautioned her to keep it on her person at all times. She was also given a thin sheaf of papers, including a map of the facility, a bus schedule, a list of Frequently Asked Questions, and their answers, and a cover sheet that displayed her name and billet assignment. Lastly, she was pointed to a shuttle bus stop that would take her to her new temporary residence.

It was all quite disorienting.

When Elizabeth arrived at the giant tent that would be her home at Monmouth, she was informed that she had missed dinner. Luckily, the staff – who were accustomed to new residents arriving around the clock – supplied her with another bologna sandwich and one of the ubiquitous foam cups of diluted orange drink.

Gratefully, she accepted her sandwich and cup, and retreated to a bench at one of the dozen picnic tables at the rear of the huge tent, to study the FAQ she had been given. One of its revelations was that there existed a computerized master list of all those who had been rescued from Manhattan. To access it, all she needed to do was take a shuttle to a building in another part of the facility. There, she could sign up for a turn at a PC.

Too wound up even to consider sleeping, Elizabeth immediately set out for the building that housed the public computers. It took her nearly an hour to reach it, and she spent another hour waiting for a PC to become available. Then, because she had never bothered to learn how to use a computer, she had to ask for help. Fortunately, a man who was just finishing his own turn at the station next to hers was kind enough to show her how to use the touch screen and keyboard to search the database.

She did not waste time looking for her husband's name. The firm at which Fox Shergold had been a partner specialized in securities law. It had been located across the street from Zucotti Park, well within the May Day weapon's blast zone. Instead, she first searched for her daughter's name. To her dismay, Cissy was not listed in the database.

Elizabeth was nearly overcome by fear for her daughter, and by an overwhelming sense of loss. For days now, she had been convinced that her young daughter, at least, must be safe. From the moment she had found the Dwight School unoccupied, she assumed its staff had ushered the children in their care to the Kennedy and rescue. Why that seemingly had not happened was a mystery – one that did not bode at all well for Cissy.

- *Please, God.* -

Tears streamed down her cheeks.

- *I beg you, let my daughter be safe. Please, God, I beg you.* -

Nearly blinded by tears, she searched again. The results screen displayed her son Greg's name – and his location: Monmouth Medical Center.

- *Thank you, God! Thank you for my son's life, at least.* -

It was far too late for her to go to him now. One of the first items in listed the Monmouth FAQ was the existence of a country-wide, strictly-enforced, 10:00 pm curfew.

"Violators are subject to imprisonment or execution," it warned, in bold-face type.

- *All right. If I have to wait until tomorrow, I'll try to be patient – but tomorrow morning, I am going to see my son.* -

Wearily, she pushed herself away from the computer.

She stood, and stretched. It might take another hour before the shuttle bus would return her to her assigned cot, but now she knew Greg, at least, was alive. She would try to take comfort in that thought.

Exhausted as she was, Elizabeth could only hope she would be able to sleep.

May 7, 2020, 1:23 am EDT

Highway 92, East Lake Orient Park, FL

Steve Newman was rapidly getting pissed off.

This was the third ATM he'd been to in the 20 minutes or so since his shift as an air switcher at MOR-TV ended. All three of them had given him bullshit, in place of the C-note he needed to get himself laid. Goddamnit, it was *his* fuckin' money. Just thinking about sliding his dong into some whore was making him harder than a three-point free throw.

Yeah, being a second-shift, air switcher at an indie station wasn't exactly the royal road to riches. But he made enough at it to get by, and enough extra to afford a little treat, from time to time. Tonight was supposed to be one of those times.

Angry and horny wasn't a good combination for him. Somehow the girls could always tell. Their prices went up accordingly – which never did a whole lot to improve his temper.

No, as much as he hated to pay foreign ATM charges, it looked like he was gonna have to get his money from somebody other than Wells Fargo tonight. That is, if he wanted to get laid, he was.

Muttering under his breath at the injustice, Newman got back in his six-year-old Kia, and drove a block down 92, to a SunTrust branch bank.

Pulling into the ATM drive through, he rolled down his window, then inserted his Wells Fargo card, and entered his PIN. When the device displayed its menu, he jabbed the button next to "withdraw $100 in cash".

Sure enough, the next thing he saw was a screen that read, "This transaction will incur a $4.00 fee."

"Confirm, you bloodsucking robot!" Newman snarled. He jammed his thumb hard on the button.

The ATM took a long time thinking it over – longer than normal, it seemed to Newman.

Finally, the display changed from "Please wait", to "The transaction you have requested is not available at this time." His card popped out of the slot. The screen reminded him, "Please remove your card from this machine."

"Fuck!" Newman yelled, pounding his fist on the Kia's steering wheel. "Fuck! Fuck! Fuck! *Fuck!*"

Shaking with resentment, he ripped his card out of the treacherous ATM. The little car's accelerator pedal was all the way down, when he peeled out onto the highway.

Newman had no idea that by dawn, every ATM in the country would be displaying the same, unwelcome message he had just received. All he knew for certain was that he was going to be dating his fist tonight.

That *really* pissed him off.

May 7, 2020, 2:17 am EDT

Joint Base Andrews Naval Air Facility, Prince George's County, MD

Samantha Denise Harbison was bone-weary.

Her eyes felt like they were surfaced with medium-grit sandpaper. Her hair was lank, her skin greasy. She didn't even want to contemplate how she smelled.

Harbison's day had begun more than 29 hours earlier.

Her alarm awakened her at 7:00 am, in the modest house on the outskirts of Islamabad that she shared with three other employees of the American Embassy. Her morning had been routine. However, once she returned to the Embassy from lunch at a Chinese restaurant, Marlon Wilkins, her supervisor, had summoned her to a private meeting. It turned out to be anything but routine.

"Samantha," Wilkins told her, "your trip today is going to be a little out of the ordinary."

In retrospect, Harbison Wilkins' pronouncement as, without doubt, the single most sweeping understatement she had ever heard anyone utter.

"Instead of carrying the pouch to London," Wilkins continued, "you'll be taking it all the way to DC. And this time, I'm afraid you won't exactly be traveling in comfort."

Harbison laughed – laughed aloud. Notoriously stingy when it came to travel expenses for its junior staff members, the State Department would occasionally spring for business class seats for couriers. Since Pakistan's Airblue offered only single-class seating on its Wednesday flights to Abu Dhabi, she was accustomed to flying economy whenever she made the mid-week run. By no stretch of her imagination could she consider those runs "traveling in comfort."

"It's no laughing matter, Samantha," Wilkins warned.

Then he explained what he meant. Harbison was left staring at him in disbelief.

At 1:30 that afternoon, with a diplomatic pouch handcuffed to her right wrist, Harbison folded herself into one of the Embassy's fleet of cars. She was driven to Gandhara International Airport, 25 miles south of Islamabad. On Wilkins' advice, she left her overnight bag in her cubicle at the Embassy.

As frequently happened, despite Gandhara's newness and modernity, the 3:00 pm flight to Abu Dhabi was late pulling away from the International Departures pier of the terminal's Y-shaped dock. Eventually, though, the Airbus A-320 made it off the ground. The crowded jet headed for the Persian Gulf.

The three-hour flight was largely uneventful – which is to say, it was filled with the screaming of infants and a blue haze of tobacco smoke. Harbison spent most of the time playing Sudoku on her smartphone, and listening to folk-hop MP3s. Her earbuds were cranked up nearly to the threshold of pain, to block out the cabin noise.

After passing through Customs at Abu Dhabi – where she merely had to show her diplomatic passport to be waved through – Harbison was met by a taciturn, brown-haired man. He was dressed in a Lacoste polo shirt, tan Dockers, and a pair of impenetrably-dark Ray Bans. They wended their way through the geometric, green-and-white-glass fairyland of the terminal to the open-air lot. There, they got into a black Cadillac Escalade.

For 40 minutes, they sped down the shimmering, heat-glazed E-11 highway. By the time they exited to a roundabout and the long approach road to Al Dhafra Air Force Base, they had the highway to themselves. The Escalade's driver dropped her at the airfield, and immediately sped away.

At the base's ready center, she was fitted for a G-suit. Once the inflatable harness passed its pressure test, a WAF conducted Harbison to the mission briefing room. There, Captain Marvin Starling – a short, muscular man with close-cropped, sandy hair and a lopsided grin – introduced himself.

"I'll be your taxi driver," he told her.

They walked from the briefing room out to a golf cart. Its driver took them to where the Captain's F-15SE Silent Eagle fighter stood on the tarmac. It was surrounded by ground crewmen, sweating in the ferocious desert heat. With three external fuel tanks dangling from its wings and belly, Harbison thought the dull black, needle-nosed jet looked cumbersome and menacing, at the same time.

The ground crew helped her clamber into the Silent Eagle's rear seat. A friendly staff sergeant fastened the unfamiliar flight harness around her G-suited torso. He showed her how her suit and helmet plugged into the aircraft's oxygen, electrical, and communications systems.

"Can you hear me, Samantha?" Starling's voice sounded over the earphones built into her helmet.

It seemed close and intimate, and not at all artificial, as if he was speaking directly into her ear.

Harbison nodded, then caught herself.

- Of course he can't see me – I'm sitting behind him! -

"Yes," she said, too loudly, she realized. "I can hear you fine, Captain Starling," she continued at a more normal conversational level

"It's 'Marvin'," Starling replied. "And you might want to get used to saying, 'Roger that.' Otherwise, all the fighter jocks will point at you and laugh."

"Roger that," Harbison promptly replied.

"Much better," Starling responded. "Now, just in case you didn't hear it the first 20 times I told you, you're sitting in Ninja Tweety's Weapons Systems Officer's seat. So don't touch *anything* back there. You got me?"

Harbison looked at the incomprehensible profusion of dials, lights, buttons, switches, levers, and readouts that surrounded her. She shuddered at the thought of the terrible havoc she might wreak by randomly poking buttons and flipping switches.

"Roger that," she said.

"Attagirl," Starling told her.

He gave the ground crew a thumbs-up, and lowered the clear bubble of the canopy, sealing them into the fighter. Suddenly, the loudest sound Harbison could hear was her own breathing. That changed almost immediately, as Starling fired up the jet's twin engines. Their roar was nearly deafening.

After an unfathomable exchange of jargon and numbers between Starling and the unseen control tower, they taxied to the end of the runway.

"Lima, November, one, four, seven, zero, zero, niner," she heard the tower say, "you are clear for takeoff."

"Roger that, Tower," Starling responded.

"You ready, Samantha?" he asked.

"Roger that," Harbison replied.

"Good girl," Starling said, approvingly. "Here we go."

Harbison was thoroughly accustomed to the sensation of commercial passenger jet takeoffs and landings. This was a whole other order of experience.

When Starling hit the throttle, the Silent Eagle's twin Pratt & Whitney F100-229 turbofan engines screamed like angry dragons. A giant's hand pressed her back in her seat. The F-15SE shot down the runway as if fired from a cannon. It bucked and rumbled like a jalopy racing over a washboard gravel road. Well before it reached the end of the 12,000-foot, concrete runway, it was airborne.

The shaking and rattling abruptly ceased.

Seconds later, there was a near-simultaneous triple thump, as the fighter's landing gear retracted, and folded into its hull. What happened next literally took Harbison's breath away.

Starling pulled back on the stick. The Silent Eagle stood on her tail. The giant that had been pushing on Harbison's chest decided to sit on it, instead. The F-15SE rocketed into the sky, climbing at a rate of nearly a mile every six seconds. Less than a minute later, Starling leveled the fighter out at its cruising altitude of 40,000 feet, producing a negative G force so violent his passenger nearly passed out.

"You okay back there, Samantha?" Starling asked. His tone was casual.

"Roger that," Harbison replied. Then she added, "you jerk."

Starling chuckled.

"Sorry," he said. "That was what we call a 'max performance takeoff'. You'll probably never get to experience another one, so I thought I'd give you something to tell your grandchildren about."

"Roger that," Harbison told him. "But once was enough, okay?"

"That's a 'Roge'," responded Starling. "Want a look at the Syrian desert?"

"What happens if I say, 'Roger that'?" Harbison asked, cautiously.

"This does," replied Starling

He put the fighter into a slow barrel roll.

The horizon steadily rose toward the zenith on their left, until the F-15SE was flying entirely upside-down. The desolate landscape was now straight overhead, as Starling and Harbison hung from their harness webbing. The line between earth and the heavens continued on around, until the roll was complete and their view was once again composed entirely of cloudless blue sky.

"*Please*, don't do that again," Harbison pled, as calmly as she could.

Silently, she considered the many ways in which she might enjoy committing extreme violence on the person of Captain Smarty-pants Starling.

"Roger that, Samantha" Starling acknowledged. "Just two more experiences of a lifetime, I promise."

"Two?" Harbison demanded.

"Roger that," Starling confirmed.

The jet began to vibrate, gently at first, but building rapidly in intensity. Within seconds, it was shuddering with alarming ferocity. Then, with one final, loud bang, the shaking unexpectedly stopped.

"What was *that*?" Harbison demanded.

"'That' was us breaking the sound barrier," Starling told her.

Cruising at 1430 miles per hour, they were over the Mediterranean in an hour. Ten minutes later, the Silent Eagle was making its approach to Incirlik Air Base.

Starling again engaged in a mystifying exchange of pilot-speak with an air traffic controller. Suddenly, they were descending with terrifying speed toward Incirlik's main runway. Harbison's heart pole-vaulted into her mouth. She sunk her teeth into her lip to keep from screaming in terror. Then they were down on the deck, being slammed against their harnesses as Starling reversed thrust on the jet's twin turbofan engines.

It was hot in southeastern Turkey – not oppressively scorching, as it had been in Abu Dhabi, but hot nonetheless. Taxiing to the fuel island and refueling Starling's fighter took just over half an hour.

"You ready, Samantha?" Starling asked, poking his head into the pilots' lounge, where Harbison was gratefully enjoying the air conditioning.

"Roger that," Harbison replied.

"Okay," Starling said.

His lopsided grin turned all the way up.

"I hope you realize you don't have to say that *every* time," he informed her.

"Roger that," she acknowledged, returning his grin with one of her own.

Their takeoff from Incirlik was every bit as rough as the one from Al Dhafra, but the climb to cruising altitude, although swift, was a good deal more sedate.

"We'll be home in less than two hours," Starling told her.

"How is that possible?" Harbison asked. "We have to cross the whole Atlantic, don't we?"

"To get to Andrews?" Starling replied. "Absolutely. But home base for me and Ninja Tweety is Lakenheath RAF – a rainy little garden spot, in Surrey."

"Oh," Harbison said. "That sounds nice."

The turbofan-powered jet crossed from Asia Minor into the Balkans. It passed over the Alps of central Austria, eating up distance at more than double the speed of sound. Somewhere over Germany, Starling spoke up again.

"You remember those 'experiences of a lifetime' I mentioned, Samantha?" he asked.

Harbison looked up from her smartphone, where she was fast closing in on the solution to a particularly fiendish Sudoku matrix.

"Let me guess," she replied. "I'm about to have another one?"

"Roger that," Starling confirmed.

"Am I going to enjoy this one as much as I did that 'max performance' thing?" Harbison asked, preparing to save her game and stow her phone.

"Let's just say it should be a lot less ... physical ... than that," Starling told her.

"Oh, goody," Harbison replied, sardonically. "I can hardly wait."

The Silent Eagle slowed, juddering violently, as it dropped below the speed of sound. It began descending to 30,000 feet. Soon, they were loafing along barely fast enough to keep the F-15SE airborne. Moments later, they began to catch up with a much larger, four-engine jet.

"That's a KC-135R Stratotanker up ahead of us," Starling announced.

"And ...?" Harbison responded, warily.

"Just watch," Starling told her.

The distance between the two aircraft closed rapidly, until the bigger jet was flying only 30 feet above and just ahead of the fighter. A winged boom began to extend from the rear of the Stratotanker toward the point where the Silent Eagle's left wing joined its fuselage. More than a little in awe of the prowess both pilots displayed, Harbison craned her neck to watch, as the questing boom's end mated with the F-15SE's air refueling receptacle.

The thirsty gurgle of jet fuel under pressure flowing from the KC-135R into the Silent Eagle's fuel tanks fascinated her. The way two pilots maintained their delicate, aerial dance throughout their coupling she found mesmerizing. Harbison marveled at the seemingly-effortless way they never permitted the distance between the two aircraft to vary by more than a few inches, from the time the boom docked with the fighter until the planes broke their embrace.

Refueling completed, Starling's jet peeled off, to the right.

Once they were clear of the Stratotanker, Starling closed the aerial refueling receptacle bay door, increased speed, and began gaining altitude. Just before they broke the sound barrier, he rocked the Silent Eagle from side to side.

Waggling his jet's wings, he radioed, "Romeo, Sierra, six, three, three, six, niner, one – thanks for the drink, you guys."

"Roger, Lima, November, one, four, seven, zero, zero, niner," came the response. "Y'all come back, now, hear?"

Half an hour later they were descending over the English Channel, beginning their approach to Lakenheath RAF.

While the F-15SE was being refueled, they took time out for a hot meal. Starling confessed that he hadn't eaten in nearly ten hours. Even with that delay, they were back in the air before sunset.

An hour later, over the Atlantic, they again rendezvoused with a KC-135R Stratotanker, to take on additional fuel.

"I guess that makes it a 'twice-in-a-lifetime' experience," Starling admitted.

When they touched down at Gander International Airport, almost exactly two hours after departing Lakenheath, it was full daylight once more. They had outraced the Sun, in their transonic flight across the Atlantic Ocean.

"Do I have time to go to the bathroom, Marvin?" Harbison asked.

"Take all the time you need, Samantha," Starling replied. "It looks like we might be here a while."

"Why?" she asked. "What's wrong?"

"I didn't want to worry you by mentioning it while we were in the air," Starling told her, "but the engines have been making funny noises for a while. I want a ground crew to go over them, before we take off again."

"How long is 'a while'?" Harbison demanded.

"Oh," Starling said, "about 1,000 miles, give or take."

Harbison gulped.

"Listen," Starling continued, "I can get you another ride, if you don't think you should wait."

Harbison thought it over for no more than a few seconds. By now, she trusted completely in Starling's competence, and in his commitment to his mission and his passenger.

"Thanks for the offer," she said, "but I think I'll stick with the guy what brung me."

The Gander ground crew eventually determined a clogged fuel filter was the cause of Starling's misgivings. Nearly eight full hours passed, before they were once again able to take to the sky.

The new filter worked perfectly. They flew, without incident for almost an hour and a half, before they began descending for the approach to Andrews. Starling's conversation with the control tower was incomprehensible to Harbison – but she was now used to that.

As they touched down, Harbison thought to herself, "*Just one more leg of the marathon to go.*"

She found herself torn between being happy that her journey was nearly done, and a little sad that her adventure was almost over.

Starling shut down the F-15SE's engines outside the pair of giant hangars that housed the Presidential Airlift Group. A VH-60N White Hawk helicopter was waiting on the tarmac to ferry Harbison to her destination. Her eyes went wide, when she spotted the seal beside the helo's door.

- I'm hitching a ride on Marine One? -

She dropped her gaze to the diplomatic pouch cradled in her lap.

- This must really be important! -

The waiting ground crew helped Harbison and Starling out of his fighter. With their feet on the ground, there was an awkward moment of silence between them. Starling broke it.

"Thanks for flying Air Marvin, Samantha," he said.

His lopsided grin flickered on and off.

"It's been a real pleasure," he told her, with feeling.

Doffing her helmet, Harbison clasped his offered hand.

"Roger that," she said, with a lopsided grin of her own.

May 7, 2020, 3:41 am EDT

Canoe Brook Reservoir Number 1, Short Hills, NJ

- Jesus Christ! What the fuck *are we going to* do? -

The other members of Arun "Big Sugar" Washington's gang stood, solemn-faced, in a huddle around him, as Donell Jackson fought his mounting panic. Tears streamed down "Big Willy" Dixon's face. He seemed neither to notice, nor to care about his display of weakness in front of his fellow mobsters – and none of them bothered to chide him for it.

Jackson felt like crying, too.

They had all depended on Washington's vision to guide them, and on his leadership to bolster their confidence. Now that burden had been suddenly, shockingly transferred to Donell. The gang looked to him to somehow fill the vast hole left by Big Sugar's absence. He was anything but certain he had what it took.

But he had to try. The entire gang had witnessed Washington hand the mantle of leadership to him. Now, no matter how unprepared he felt to shoulder the responsibility, Big Sugar's crew was counting on him literally to lead them out of the wilderness.

Washington's prophecy that the authorities would actively search for them among the refugee camp's residents turned out to be – as his predictions usually did – right on the money.

Big Sugar had roused his followers before dawn. He commanded them to scatter to the four corners of the East Orange Golf Course. Washington ordered his gangsters to mingle with the crowd only after the other inhabitants emerged from the huge dormitory tent structures. While his subordinates were eating breakfast, their giant commander made himself scarce, on the theory that his height and mass were simply too distinctive for him to risk being seen in public.

The mobsters each smuggled something – a roll, a napkin-full of sausage, an individual serving-sized plastic bottle of orange juice – out of the mess tent for their boss.

They spent the day assembling materials to help them breach the razor wire that now surrounded the camp. Dante Woodruff demonstrated why he was known as "Smoove", by boosting a pair of bolt-cutters from the Canadian troops' makeshift motor pool. Others pilfered planks and tarpaulins. They stashed their haul in the copse of trees, on the other side of the fairway from the point on the perimeter Washington had chosen for their breakout.

Despite the presence of a National Guard search party, they managed to avoid being spotted. Avoiding their assigned billets during daylight hours, they continued to lay low after nightfall. By 3:00 am, the entire mob was once more assembled around their leader, waiting for Big Sugar to give the word to move out.

"I have timed the sentries' passages," Washington told them.

His voice was loud enough to be heard only at close range.

"Our guardians have been patrolling the perimeter fence opposite us, since dusk," he continued. "I have determined that one of them passes by every ten minutes, with quite dependable regularity."

"That doesn't leave us a lot of time," Jackson whispered.

"You are correct, brother Donell," Big Sugar concurred, "it does not. Therefore, I have determined that our passage must be essayed in stages. Brother Dante will venture forth initially, to create a suitable gap in the wire. Once he has accomplished that task, we will bide our time until the sentry again passes our position. Only then will we attempt our actual escape."

"Works for me," Woodruff murmured.

Two minutes after the guard next appeared, Smoove was dispatched to cut the wire.

It was then that the flaw in Washington's plan became apparent. The moment Woodruff's purloined bolt cutter bit through the wire, the severed coils reacted to the sudden release of tension by springing apart. They left a sizeable – and glaringly obvious – gap in the barrier.

Instantly, Big Sugar sprang to his feet.

"Follow me!" he commanded, his voice low and urgent.

He charged with surprising speed across the fairway, to the shelter of the trees beyond the wire.

Once he was across the fairway, Washington stopped to wave the other members of his gang past him. He turned to follow them only after Chuckie D, the last man to cross the open space, entered the woods.

"Hey! Halt, there!" came a shouted command from the agitated Canadian sentry.

When his order was ignored, the guard dropped to one knee. He fired once.

Jackson was close enough to hear Big Sugar's grunt of pain. He immediately turned back, and ran to Washington's side. Panting, the mob boss laid his massive arm across Donell's shoulder. Leaning heavily on him for support, the capo attempted to continue his escape.

They made it only as far as the edge of the reservoir, before Washington collapsed to his knees. Jackson went down with him.

"I can run no further, Donell," Big Sugar gasped. "You must abandon me here, or, most assuredly, you will all lose your freedom."

Jackson heard an ominous whistle, as Washington labored to breathe.

"No, Boss!" Donell protested, feeling his eyes grow moist. "We can't leave you!"

"You must," Big Sugar said, fixing him with a sober gaze. "I have a sucking chest wound, and am incapable of running any further. It is up to you, now, Donell. You must lead our brothers to safety."

"What?" Donell asked, almost pleading. "How am I ...?"

"There is a bar called 'Manny Jack's', on Main Street, in Asbury Park," Washington told him, struggling for breath. "Brother Kendall knows it. The owners are friends. Should I survive my wound, I will get word to you there."

"Why me?" Jackson demanded.

"Because you are the only one who has the intelligence and education necessary to lead," Big Sugar told him. "I am confident that you are equal to the challenge, Donell. Now you must *go* – or else, we all will be lost."

Washington, had propped himself on his elbows for their exchange. Now, he fell back on the ground, panting shallowly.

His eyes wet, Jackson turned to face the other members of the gang – *his* gang, now, he realized. They stood clustered together, faces reflecting their shock and grief.

"Well?" he said, squaring his shoulders. "You heard the man – what are you waiting for? Let's get the fuck out of here!"

May 7, 2020, 4:34 am EDT

One Observatory Circle, Washington, DC

Diana Hunter woke to a room ringing with silence. Listening as hard as she could, she could not hear her husband Benjamin breathing.

Hunter rose from the Victorian-era arm chair in which she had spent the past three nights dozing fitfully. She stepped to her spouse's bedside, already certain of what she would find.

She turned on the floor lamp, beside her husband's hospital bed. Laying her fingers on his carotid artery, she checked his pulse. Hestia Argus, the night-duty hospice nurse who sat watch in the hallway had showed her how to use her index and middle fingers to test his radial and carotid pulse points. She could detect none.

Benjamin Hunter was dead. His lips had already turned blue. His face was slack, his chest still.

The Vice President sincerely believed she had steeled herself to face this moment with dignity. With sadness, too, of course – that was inevitable. But, still, she had convinced herself she was prepared for Benjamin's passing; that it could not, and would not take her by surprise. She had been certain she could maintain her composure, knowing that, at last, at least, her husband's suffering was over, his ordeal ended.

Now that the moment was upon her, she realized that her belief in her own preparedness had been mere self-delusion. Knowing her beloved Benjamin would die, that his death would come soon, and that there was no avoiding it turned out to be a far different thing than coming face-to-face with the reality. Now, she discovered to her dismay that resignation was no defense against the agony of her loss, of his passing, of her own vulnerability in the face of death.

Helplessly, hopelessly, against her will, despite her best efforts to suppress it, Diana Hunter's grief manifested itself in an anguished, utterly heartbroken wail. Devastated, she flung herself on the still, still body of her spouse. She found herself overwhelmed by the tears she had wrongly believed she could suppress.

In the hallway outside, waking at the sound of the Vice President's heart-rending keen, Hestia Argus, RN instinctively stood. The hospice nurse automatically started to open the door to the room where her patient's corpse lay. Then she stopped herself, and removed her hand from the doorknob.

There were things to do, she knew. At a minimum, a doctor must be notified to fill out the death certificate. A funeral home should be contacted, as well, to retrieve and embalm the body. And yet, both of those things could wait, at least for a little while.

At the moment, the Vice President needed time to herself, without medical and legal matters intruding on the first, terrible moments of her grief. She deserved the dignity of a period of privacy, in which to compose herself, to wipe away her tears, and to gather her strength. Hestia Argus was determined to give her that breathing space.

- *The poor thing. The poor, poor thing.* -

May 7, 2020, 5:54 am EDT

Seneca Temporary Housing Facility, Romulus, NY

Sean Halloran, Sr. sleepily awoke. He was unsure, at first, what had roused him.

"Are ya awake, Sean?" his wife Fiona whispered in his ear.

"I am now," Halloran confirmed grumpily.

It seemed unjust that his spouse should wake him an hour early. The fact that, for the first time in almost a week, he had finally been able to sleep through the night made it doubly unfair.

"Good," Fiona murmured in his ear. "I wanted to say 'thanks' for what ya did last night."

Her hand snaked under the blanket that covered her husband. She pulled down his briefs, and grasped his manhood. Immediately, it sprang, throbbing, to life.

The sound of their tent mates' snores reminded him of how little privacy they had. Just hours earlier, he had taken Adam Manson to task about the noise he and his wife Ruby made during their marathon copulation sessions. The thought that they, in turn, might overhear him and Fiona …

"Fiona!" Halloran gasped. "What do ya think you're doin'?"

"Sayin' 'thanks', ya zoof!" Fiona giggled, as she took him in her mouth.

May 7, 2020, 3:16 am PDT (6:16 am EDT)

Foothill Boulevard, Hayward, CA

Madeline Czerwinski, Special Agent in Charge of the FBI's San Francisco field office pushed the talk button clipped to the lapel of her windbreaker. She spoke into the headset of the APX 7000, two-way radio she carried in a belt holster.

"SWAT is 'go' for entry," she said.

It had, Czerwinski thought, been the 21st Century equivalent of good, old-fashioned police work that brought her team to this apartment building, in one of the sketchier neighborhoods of Hayward. If the Veterans Administration, and California DMV records were correct, this was the current residence of the prime suspect in the kidnapping of the President's daughter.

Within seconds of the incident, calls had begun flooding in to 911.

The Berkeley Police Department had willingly turned over its records of those calls – including the numbers from which they had originated – to Czerwinski's office. With help from the Secret Service, her agents painstakingly tracked down, and conducted detailed interviews with each caller. Some had taken cell phone videos of the abduction. The agents obtained copies of those videos, given either voluntarily or under subpoena. In the meantime, Berkeley PD had located, copied, and shared with the FBI, the footage from every Closed Circuit TV camera along the route Artemis Steele and her Secret Service detail had followed, from the U.C. Berkeley campus to the intersection of University Avenue and Grant Street, where the kidnapping of the President's daughter and the murders of the agents assigned to protect her had occurred.

The Bureau's Silicon Valley Regional Computer Forensics Laboratory in Menlo Park had spent the previous day and a half processing CCTV and cell phone videos. Two of the witnesses' videos turned out to include usable images of the face of the bicyclist who had followed Artemis Steele and her detail. He was the only member of the abduction team who had not been wearing a ski mask. The FBI's Next Generation Identification system churned through every video, isolating, and comparing each image of the hoodie-wearing kidnapper. Using an array of algorithms, it built up a biometric model of his face that was accurate enough for the Lab to compare against its own and the Defense Department's databases.

After eliminating easily-ruled-out matches, the list of suspects had been reduced to three. Of those, two had valid alibis. Both men had multiple witnesses to verify their location at the time of Steele's abduction.

That left only Herbert Richard Baumeister, a Marine who had been dishonorably discharged. His record included a pattern of deliberate racial slurs towards African-American and Hispanic fellow Marines, multiple instances of public disrespect towards non-white superiors, and repeated assaults on non-white ratings and non-commissioned officers. Cross-referencing with the California Department of Motor Vehicles and Veterans Administration databases had led the Bureau to this, Baumeister's last known address.

At Czerwinski's command, the black-clad Special Weapons and Tactics team arrayed around apartment 14's door sprang into action. The beefy agent stationed directly in front of the entryway swung his portable battering ram, smashing it into the door just above the knob. The doorframe splintered, and the door burst open. The agent stepped back, allowing the other members of his team to swarm into the apartment.

"FBI!" shouted the first agent over the threshold. "We have a warrant!"

The one-bedroom apartment – in reality, more of a studio with delusions of grandeur – swiftly filled with SWAT team members. Alien-looking, in their helmet-mounted ATN PVS7 night vision goggles, they repeatedly shouted, "Clear!" as they swept the premises for signs of the suspect.

"The apartment is vacant, Ma'am," Gary Severn, the SWAT team supervisor, radioed seconds later. "Looks like our bird has flown the coop."

Czerwinski sighed.

"Roger that," she replied. "Severn, pull your team out. Forensics – you're up."

The Bureau's team of evidence specialists would comb Herbert Baumeister's apartment for clues to his whereabouts. Baumeister's fingerprints and those of his visitors would be lifted. Discarded trash that might contain names or addresses of interest and DNA samples that might turn up hits in the NGI would be collected.

Meanwhile, her field agents and those of the Secret Service would begin interviewing Baumeister's neighbors and the building's supervisory and maintenance staff, seeking information on his habits and known associates. Many of those interviewed would have criminal records of their own, no doubt. Even so, they'd be unlikely to expend much effort protecting an avowed racist, who lived in an apartment building whose other residents were mostly African-American or Hispanic – and who was the prime suspect in the kidnapping of the President's daughter.

- We'll get you, Baumeister. You can run. You can hide. But, in the end, the Bureau always gets our man. -

She had to wonder, though.

- Why did you rabbit? No one but the Bureau and the Secret Service even knew you were a suspect. Did someone tip you off? -

May 7, 2020, 7:05 am EDT

Volta Place, NW, Georgetown, Washington, DC

The sound of cash register drawers opening and closing, and slot machines dropping coins from the intro to Pink Floyd's song *Money* was loud in the early-morning dimness of the fashionable townhouse, as the screen of Secretary Treasury Anderson Connaught III's smartphone lit up with a transatlantic call. Awakened from the depths of slumber by the familiar ringtone, the Secretary sat up, and reached for the phone.

"Huh ... hello?" Connaught said, his voice husky with sleep.

"Hullo, Andy?" inquired Bernard Lord Silkington, Chancellor of the British Exchequer.

"Uh, huh," Connaught responded, unsuccessfully trying to stifle a yawn. "Who's this?"

"It's Bernard," the Chancellor replied. "Bernard Silkington?"

"Oh," Connaught said.

He squinted at the time display on his smartphone, but couldn't quite make it out.

"What can I do for you, Chancellor?" Connaught asked, fumbling for the reading glasses he kept on the nightstand beside his bed.

"Sorry to call at such a beastly hour," Silkington responded, "but I thought it best to give you a heads-up on the banking situation here."

"Why?" the Treasury Secretary inquired.

He sat up, and inched his feet into his bedroom slippers.

"What's wrong?" Connaught demanded.

"I'm afraid we're experiencing a bit of a panic over here, Andy," Silkington told him.

"How so?" Connaught queried.

He slipped out of bed, so as not to disturb his still-sleeping husband.

"Well," Silkington explained, "the thing is, our banks have yet to open their doors today. It looks as though they've shut down their cash machine networks, as well."

"That's …" Connaught said, closing the bedroom door behind him, "… a little troubling."

"Quite," Silkington agreed.

"Have they explained what's going on?" Connaught asked.

He flipped on the light, in the hallway.

"The bankers?" Silkington replied. "Not as of yet, I'm afraid. In fact, the cheeky bastards haven't even the decency to answer, when we try to ring them up."

"How about the Bank of England?" Connaught asked.

He headed for the kitchen to make coffee.

"Naturally, Threadneedle Street is in constant communication with the Treasury," Silkington assured him. "The problem is, the private banks seem to have deliberately chosen not to follow its lead."

"That's not good," Connaught replied.

He turned on the kitchen light.

"No, it most certainly is not," Silkington agreed. "Nor is that the worst of it."

"Oh?" Connaught responded.

He pushed the button to start the coffeemaker brewing.

"What is?" he asked.

"Mr. Secretary," Silkington told him, "I'm afraid this financial panic is not confined to the UK. In point of fact, it seems to have infected the whole of the Common Market."

May 7, 2020, 8:17 am EDT

The White House Situation Room, Washington, DC

Grim-faced, William Orwell Steele stared at the wall-sized screen at the other end of the Situation Room.

General Rashid Omar Sheikh's confession to his authorship, planning, and execution of the nuclear bombing of New York City was just concluding. Watching the General sign the written transcript of his declaration of guilt, the President could not help but reflect on how drawn, and haggard, and eloquent of the certainty of his own impending death Sheikh's face was.

"Director Murdock?" Steele asked, turning to face the Director of the CIA.

His voice was low, and dangerous.

"Are you telling me that, after he signed this document," the President brandished his copy of Sheikh's confession, "your people murdered, beheaded, and sexually mutilated that man?"

"Yes, sir," Christopher Murdock replied. "That's affirmative."

"Jesus H. Christ, Chris," Steele grated.

He struggled for control.

"How can you sit there so calmly, and confess to such ... such ...?" he struggled to find a term that would adequately express his outrage.

"'Expediencies'?" Murdock offered. "Mr. President?"

"Don't bandy euphemisms with me, Murdock," Steele responded. "Murdering and mutilating a high-ranking foreign official goes against everything this nation – and I, personally – stand for, regardless of the excuse."

"Nonetheless, Mr. President," Murdock said, calmly, "you personally authorized those actions."

"Is that so?" Steele retorted, coldly. "Perhaps you can explain to me exactly how that fantastic event came about."

"Certainly, sir," Murdock replied. "You will recall that I conferred with you via our secure line, on Tuesday afternoon? And that, in that call, I told you our Deputy Chief of Station in Islamabad had reported that the ISI's search for General Sheikh was becoming intense enough to pose an imminent danger of exposing his entire network?"

The President nodded, skeptically.

"And that he was requesting permission to dispose of the General," Murdock continued, "and to try to pin responsibility for his kidnapping on the Taliban?"

"Yes," Steele affirmed, "I recall all those points. And I also recall that I authorized you to tell him to go ahead."

"Yes, sir," Murdock said.

There was a long moment, during which neither man spoke. The President's gaze was fierce. The DCIA returned it, poker-faced.

"So," Steele finally asked, "what makes you think that authorization extended to murder, and mutilation?'

"With all due respect, Mr. President," Murdock replied, "what did you think I meant by, 'dispose of him, and pin it on the Taliban'?"

"I thought," Steele responded, "you meant, 'smuggle him out of the country, and spread disinformation about who was responsible,' using that 'network of local assets' your people are so determined to protect."

Murdock shook his head.

"Again, with all due respect, sir," he said, "that simply would not have been possible."

"Why not?" Steele demanded.

"Firstly," Murdock answered, holding up his index finger, "because the level of official scrutiny was far too intense to permit the General to be safely smuggled out of Pakistan. Its border with India – the only neighboring country that's even arguably friendly – is one of the most highly militarized and heavily guarded in the world. Iran, of course, would be out of the question. Afghanistan has belonged to the Taliban, ever since we withdrew our forces from it, at the end of 2014. Had our people been caught with the General in their possession – which they very nearly were – the Paks would immediately have arrested, jailed, and tortured all our operatives. And please believe me when I tell you that they know exactly who those operatives are, just as we know who the ISI's people in Washington are. Sir."

"So," Steele responded, "that somehow meant you had to murder him?"

""Execute him,' you mean?" Murdock corrected. "Yes, sir. Mr. President, the General was, by his own admission, directly responsible for the murders of … what? A million American civilians? In the Agency's book, that's a war crime of the highest magnitude, and it deserves the harshest possible sanction."

"So your man in Islamabad took it upon himself to mutilate him in an utterly barbaric fashion?" Steele shot back. "Is that what you're telling me, Mr. Director?"

"No, sir," Murdock replied levelly. "He quite correctly asked for permission to proceed – or for alternative instructions, if permission was denied. I relayed his request up the chain of command to you, and you gave him the go-ahead."

"I still don't accept that," the President said.

"Well, sir," Murdock responded, "that takes us to," he held up another finger, "secondly, the Taliban has a recognizable 'signature' to the execution of people they kidnap. They cut off the victim's head. If the victim is male, they emasculate him, and stuff his genitals in his mouth. Once you authorized our DCS to pin the General's kidnapping on the Taliban, he did exactly what *they* would have done. It's the same thing that Khalid Sheikh Mohammed, the guy who planned the 9/11 attacks for Al Qaeda did to Daniel Pearl, the Wall Street Journal reporter, back in 2002."

"Jesus," Steele commented, slumping back in his chair.

"Mr. President," Murdock continued, "you may also recall that, back when we first discussed this operation – here in this very room – I warned you that you didn't want to know the details. You insisted on going hands-on, despite my advice."

"And this is what I get for that?" Steele replied, his voice hollow.

"Yes, sir," Murdock told him, "it is. Welcome to my world."

May 7, 2020, 9:54 am EDT

U.S. District Court, 3rd Street NW, Washington, DC

Esau Piltch stood under the portico of the William B. Bryant U.S. District Court Annex, feeling very small and forlorn in his new, midnight-blue suit. He was surrounded by a ring of private security guards. The imposing bulk of Jameson Matthew Peek, Esq., his Party-appointed lawyer largely blocked him from view of the mob of reporters, video cameramen, *paparazzi*, and curious private citizens that spilled out across 3rd Street NW.

Peek held up his hands, like Moses parting the Red Sea. The barrage of shouted questions died away, in anticipation.

"Ladies, and gentlemen," Peek proclaimed.

His voice easily carried to the back of the crowd.

"In just a moment," the lawyer announced, "my client will make a brief statement. He will not take any questions, at this time."

The assembled onlookers immediately voiced their disappointment with this revelation. Several of the more self-important media personalities shouted questions at Peek. He ignored them, and continued, voice booming.

"Let me point out that the terms of the Congressman's plea bargain forbid him from making any statement, other than the one he is about to read," Peek explained. "My client is eager to cooperate with every condition of the Court's orders. Naturally, we expect that you will respect his determination to avoid displaying even the slightest hint of contempt for Judge Lovett's instructions."

A glum silence settled over the crowd.

"Now that you understand the ground rules," Peek concluded, "Ladies and gentlemen, I give you Representative Esau Piltch."

Peek stepped aside. Piltch was left exposed to the hungry stares of the multitude. As if rehearsed, the crowd leaned forward in unison, eager to witness his abasement.

"Ladies, and gentlemen," Piltch began, reading from a typescript.

His shaky voice was so muted, even those in the front ranks of the swarm had to strain to hear him.

"A few minutes ago," the Congressman read, "I pled *nolo contendere* to the charge of involuntary manslaughter, in the case of Atticus Martial Freed, former Sergeant-at-Arms of the United States House of Representatives."

"Louder!" shouted a local television correspondent.

Piltch started at the interruption. He looked up from the page. The glittering eyes and expressions of wolfish delight on the faces of the media, whose members dominated the front ranks of the crowd appalled him. He felt sick with mingled resentment and outrage. Lower lip trembling with indignation and shame, he swiftly returned his gaze to the safety of his script.

"In pleading no contest," Piltch continued, "I stipulated to the following facts: that I physically assaulted Atticus Martial Freed, while in the performance of his official duties; that my assault on his person resulted in his death; and that there were no extenuating circumstances for my assault on Sergeant-at-Arms Freed."

"*Louder!*" insisted the same TV reporter.

He was immediately shushed by those around him, all still straining to hear Piltch's *mea culpa*.

"The Honorable Joshua R. Lovett, Judge of the DC Federal District Court, sentenced me to two years in Federal prison for my crime," Piltch read.

He stopped then, blinking back tears, fighting for self-control. The crowd watched, as the page he clutched shook like a dying leaf in the wind. Finally, Piltch forced himself to continue.

"Judge Lovett agreed to suspend my sentence," Piltch told them, half-sobbing, "in exchange for my agreement to resign both from my position as a Member of the House of Representatives and from the Idaho State Bar; to perform 500 hours of community service; and to serve two years of probation, during which I will be prohibited from leaving the city of Coeur d'Alene without written permission from my probation officer."

Overcome by emotion, Piltch crumpled the page in his white-knuckled hands.

The crowd stood silent. Waiting.

Looking up, completing his speech from memory, Piltch announced, "In accordance with that agreement, I shall tender my resignation from the House – an institution which I love, and which I deeply regret that my actions have dishonored – as of noon today. Immediately upon my return to Idaho, I shall resign from its Bar. I shall then return to private life."

Having reached the end of his prepared statement, Piltch was at a loss for what to do next. It was clear to him that the mob expected – no, demanded – something more from him; that it would not allow him to leave until its hunger was assuaged.

"May God bless the United States of America," Esau Piltch concluded.

Then his bodyguards closed ranks around him, and whisked him away.

May 7, 2020, 10:34 am EDT,

The Cabinet Room, Washington, DC

"Mr. Chairman," William Orwell Steele demanded, "the only thing I want to know is: what does the Federal Reserve intend to do about this banking shutdown?"

The President sat in his usual place, at the center of the room's long, oval conference table. His chair was flanked by American and presidential flags on flag stands, against the wall behind him. The Vice President and Secretary of the Treasury were seated to his right and left, respectively. Opposite the Chief Executive was Caldecott Nice, Chairman of the Federal Reserve's Board of Governors.

Arrayed along the table to Steele's left, and right were the members of his Council of Economic Advisers and its senior economists. Behind them, key CEA and Treasury staffers occupied chairs along the wall of windows that looked out on the Rose Garden and the Residence. White House Counsel Kenneth Watanabe stood by the door to the office of Ardin Wildehoof, Steele's private secretary. To either side of Nice were the six other members of the Federal Reserve's Board and four of the five Presidents of Regional Federal Reserve Banks who were currently voting members of the Federal Open Market Committee. Their own staffers filled the chairs against the wall, behind them.

"Mr. President," Nice replied, "I'm not sure what you want me to say."

"I want you to tell me what your plan is for getting the goddamn banks open, Mr. Chairman," Steele said.

His tone betrayed his impatience.

Nice lifted his empty hands in an elaborate shrug.

"Mr. President," he responded, "the Board has many tools it can employ to nudge our member banks towards stricter or more liberal loan standards. It has the power to fine or close banks that transgress our regulations, as well. Unfortunately, however, Congress has not seen fit to give us the power to force those member banks to keep their doors open. We have still less power over state-chartered banks that have not opted to become members of the Federal Reserve system. Quite frankly, our hands are tied in this matter."

"Then why have you chosen to waste my time by requesting this meeting?" Steele inquired, brusquely.

"Why," Nice told him, "to offer you the benefit of our counsel, and to assure you of our earnest desire to help determine a path forward for the nation's financial system, Mr. President. Of course."

"In other words," Steele grated, "to cover your own asses, and create the appearance that you're doing something useful about this mess, when all you really want to do is stick your heads in the sand, and hope it will just blow over."

"Mr. President," Nice replied, icily, "I see no benefit in my sitting here, and allowing you to insult me personally, and impugn the motives of the Board in general. I bid you good day, sir."

He stood up, and gathered the papers spread out on the table before him,

"Sit the fuck down, Nice," Steele ordered.

The Chairman blanched. His files dropped from his nerveless fingers, to cascade over the surface of the conference table and onto the carpet at his feet.

"Mr. President ..." he responded, clearly groping for words.

"Or would you rather I have you arrested for treason?" Steele offered.

"You don't have the power to do that," Nice stated.

His tone betrayed his doubt.

"Counselor?" Steele queried.

His cold gaze was fixed unwaveringly on the nation's chief banker.

"Mr. Chairman," Kenneth Watanabe responded, without moving from his post by the door, "under the current state of martial law, the President not only has the power to arrest you for, and charge you with treason, he also has the power to order your summary execution on those charges. Were I in your position, I personally would opt to sit the fuck down."

"Thank you, Ken," Steele said.

"My pleasure, Mr. President," Watanabe replied.

"Mr. Chairman?" Steele challenged.

Nice slumped into his chair.

"Now that we've settled the question of whether you and your Board have any useful alternative to offer," the President continued, "let me tell you what *we* intend to do about your fucking, asshole bankers …"

May 7, 2020, 11:19 am EDT

Monmouth Medical Center, West Long Branch, NJ

Elizabeth Shergold was devastated.

In the past six days, every vestige of her former life had been stripped away from her. She had lost her luxurious home, her privileged social position, her wealthy husband, her only daughter, and her beloved dog. Even her very clothing and shoes had been taken from her. Somehow, even reduced to the status of a homeless refugee, she had managed to persevere. But to lose her last, remaining, tiny spark of hope for the only remaining member of her family was the fatal blow to her resilience.

- My sole, surviving child! My precious, darling, only *son! -*

Her anguished, self-pitying tears blinded her. The hospital corridor and the face of the doctor before her blurred.

- He didn't recognize me! My own son, the boy I carried inside me for nine, long months – he doesn't even know who I am! -

She slumped slowly to the floor, her back against the wall, supporting her descent. Dressed in a donated Ne-on Glowbaby sweatshirt, bargain-store jeans, and already-fraying, hospital slippers, the gray roots of her brunette-dyed hair now clearly showing, after a week without a touch-up, she made a pathetic figure.

Doctor Theodore Volberding, surgeon and specialist in brain trauma at Monmouth Medical Center's Neuroscience Institute, crouched in front of her.

"Mrs. Shergold," Volberding said.

He gently reached out to cup her chin, turning her face up to meet his gaze.

"You have to pull yourself together," he told her. "I realize Gregory's condition has been a shock to you, but your son needs you now more than ever."

The doctor's features swam into focus as Elizabeth blinked away her tears.

- *So young. He looks so young.* -

"Greg," Elizabeth gulped.

Her lips quivered.

"Excuse me?" Volberding responded.

"My son prefers to be called 'Greg'," Elizabeth told him.

To her surprise, her self-control was beginning to reassert itself.

The neurologist nodded.

"Well, Mrs. Shergold," he replied, "right now, Greg really needs you to make some decisions about his treatment. Can you do that for him?"

Wiping her tears away, on the sleeve of her incongruous sweatshirt, Elizabeth nodded.

"I'll do anything for him, Doctor," she said. "He's all I've got."

Her face twisted again with pain and loss. After a moment, she rallied. Elizabeth pushed her emotions away, and forced herself to concetrate on her son's needs, rather than her own frailty.

"Good," Volberding responded, approvingly.

He took her by the elbow, and helped her to her feet.

"Mrs. Shergold ..." he began.

"Elizabeth," she corrected.

Unconsciously, she straightened her shoulders, and, once again, assumed the persona of a gracious socialite.

"Please call me 'Elizabeth'," she requested.

"Certainly," Volberding agreed. "Elizabeth, your son Greg is suffering from what's called a 'subdural hematoma.' Are you familiar with that term?"

"I've heard it before," Elizabeth replied. "But I can't say I know what it means."

"Essentially," Volberding explained, "a subdural hematoma is a blood clot on the surface of the brain, beneath the protective membrane called the 'dura mater'."

Recalling her high school Latin, Elizabeth mused, "That means 'tough mother' in Latin, doesn't it?"

Volberding nodded.

"That's correct," he said, impressed despite himself.

- That's what I need to be. A tough mother. -

"Go on," she urged.

"Greg's hematoma is just behind his left temple," the neurologist continued, pointing to the corresponding spot on his own head. "It's pressing on the part of his brain we call the 'temporal lobe'."

"Is that what's causing his amnesia?" Elizabeth asked.

Suddenly, she was afraid.

Volberding again nodded.

"Yes," he said. "At least, that's what we believe,"

"What can you ..." Elizabeth began. "Is there anything you can do about it?"

"Well," Volberding told her, "we could simply opt to do nothing – to wait, and see whether his condition improves without treatment, other than for pain. However, I don't recommend that. He's been having seizures, and that's not a good sign."

"Oh my God!" Elizabeth exclaimed.

"They're just *petit mal* episodes, so far," Volberding reassured her, "but I think we should consider more aggressive treatment, before Greg's condition deteriorates any further."

"What do you recommend, Doctor?" Elizabeth demanded.

Impatience sharpened her tone.

"We think the best course would be to remove Greg's hematoma, and attempt to relieve the intracranial pressure it's creating," the neurologist replied.

"You want to operate on his brain," Elizabeth said.

Her voice was devoid of emotion.

"Yes, Mrs. Shergold," Volberding confirmed. "And I think it's important that we do so as soon as possible. Otherwise, Greg's condition could deteriorate still further."

Elizabeth Shergold steeled herself against the lance of pure terror that transfixed her heart. She forced a calm into her voice that she did not truly feel.

"What do you need me to do?" she responded.

May 7, 2020, 12:05 pm EDT

The Senate Chamber of the Capitol Building, Washington, DC

"Madam President," requested Senate Majority Leader Vittorio Donofrio, his Brooklyn accent unmistakable, "I ask unanimous consent to dispense with the morning business."

"Hearing no objection ... ?" Diana Hunter responded, from the desk reserved for the President of the Senate.

After only the briefest of pauses, she continued, "It is so ordered."

Lightly, she rapped the hourglass-shaped, ivory gavel on the desktop.

"Madam President," Donofrio announced, "as the petition to limit debate on SB 1141, otherwise known as the May Day Relief Act, has now ripened, I ask unanimous consent to proceed immediately to a vote, under Rule Twenty-two."

"Hearing no objection ...?" Hunter again queried.

When no Senator voiced opposition to Donofrio's appeal, the Vice President brought the gavel down once more.

"It is so ordered," she finished.

The Vice President looked down, toward Marjorie Kern, the Senate's Legislative Clerk. Kern was seated on the lower tier of the dais, directly in front of her.

"The Clerk will call the roll to determine the ayes and nays on the invocation of cloture," Hunter ordered.

His head tilted slightly downward, as if perusing a document on the Majority leadership desk, Donofrio gazed at Hunter through the thick tangle of his untrimmed eyebrows.

- "*She looks like Hell.* -

The roll call vote began.

It was common knowledge throughout Washington that the Vice President's husband Benjamin – to whom she had been famously devoted – had passed away during the night. To one who did not know her well, it might have been surprising that she had bothered to assume her ceremonial duty as the President of the Senate so shortly after her spouse's death. But Donofrio had recently had occasion to become better acquainted with Hunter than most.

He understood now, as he might not have mere days ago, that the Vice President regarded her duty to the nation as a sacred obligation. Unlike a Senate President *Pro Tempore*, the Vice President alone had the Constitutional power to cast a deciding vote, in the event of a tie. Improbable as such a deadlock might be, Diana Hunter was present, despite her personal loss, to provide that crucial vote, just in case it was needed.

- The lady's got class. You've gotta give her that. -

With all the Senators present, the vote went more quickly than usual. Ten minutes after it began, the Clerk announced the tally.

"Madam President," Kern said, "on the vote to approve the petition, the ayes are 65, the nays are 35."

"Thank you, Madam Clerk," Hunter responded. "The ayes have it. Therefore, in accordance with the rules adopted by this body at the commencement of the 115th Congress, debate on SB 1141 will be limited to a maximum of 30 hours. Mr. Majority Leader?"

"Thank you, Madam President," Donofrio replied. "I ask unanimous consent to proceed to consider the matter of amendments in the foist degree to SB 1141."

"Hearing no objection ...?" the Vice President offered.

When none was raised, she continued, "it is so ordered."

She rapped the gavel.

"Madam President," Donofrio announced, "as no amendment in the foist degree has been offered by members of the Majority, we need only consider such amendments as have been submitted by the Minority. The only such amendment has been proposed by Senator Bass Ransom, of Texas. In order to waste as little of our precious debate time as possible, perhaps the Senator would care to explain the substance, an' purpose of the amendment he has put forth?"

"Senator Ransom?" Hunter responded. "The floor is yours, if you wish."

"Thank you, Madam President," Ransom replied.

He got to his feet, and clomped down the aisle from his assigned desk to the podium in the chamber's well.

"Fellow Senators," the Texan proclaimed, "the amendment I have offered to SB 1141 is a simple one. It proposes to replace the text of the original bill – including provision of free medical care and low-interest loans to refugees, block grants to affected states, and decontamination and reclamation of the Fallout Zone – with language identical in every respect, except that it deletes all provisions for funding the May Day Relief Act via the mechanism of a ten percent surtax on what the original bill defines as high-net-worth individuals, and on businesses whose net income exceeds $500,000.

"It is my personal opinion that, especially in light of the current crises in the insurance and banking industries, it would be the height of folly for this body to levy any additional tax burden on the citizens and businesses of this great nation, in this time of fiscal uncertainty. As I speak, it is yet unclear when, or, for that matter if any private citizen or company will ever regain access to its own money, let alone find outside financing for such major expenses as purchasing a car, or a house, or to expand a business. Therefore, I strongly urge you to consider adopting by unanimous consent the amendment I have offered to SB 1141. Let us leave for another, more fortuitous time the question of how to finance this bill's desperately-needed relief measures."

Ransom turned to look directly at the Vice President.

"Madam President," he stated, trying, and failing to keep a note of smug triumph from infecting his tone of voice, "I do not believe I need answer questions from my fellow Senators on the substance and details of my amendment. Therefore, I yield back the remainder of my alloted time."

Ransom turned, and strode back to his desk. The heels of his cowboy boots thudded on the chamber's blue-and-white patterned carpet.

"Would any other Member care to speak to Senator Ransom's proposed amendment?" Hunter queried, resignedly.

No one responded to her invitation.

Donofrio's heart sank. He instantly recognized that no amount of coercion on his part could stem the tide of his fellow Senators' will.

"Do I hear a motion on Senator Ransom's suggestion, that his proposed amendment to SB 1141 be adopted by unanimous consent?" Diana Hunter asked.

"So move," Ransom, now back at his desk, called out.

"I second," boomed Hale Davies of Mississippi, head of the Republican caucus, from his seat at the Minority leadership table.

No voice was raised in objection to Ransom's amendment. Even Donofrio maintained his silence.

The outcome of the vote on the freshly-amended Act itself was never in doubt. Nevertheless, for the benefit of the Congressional Record – and the campaign literature that would cite them – self-congratulatory speeches had to be made, before the time allotted for debate expired. Senators from both sides of the aisle lined up to make them.

After all, there was an election coming.

May 7, 2020, 1:15 pm EDT

The White House Rose Garden, Washington, DC

"Ladies and gentlemen," announced Yvonne Clevinger, "the President of the United States."

On cue, William Orwell Steele appeared at the top of the marble steps leading down from the West Wing's colonnade. He stepped briskly to the podium. The members of the White House press corps sat in folding chairs set up on the lawn of the Rose Garden, waiting expectantly. Treasury Secretary Anderson Connaught IV and Chairman of the Federal Reserve Caldecott Nice followed Steele. They halted just behind and to either side of the Chief Executive.

"Good afternoon, ladies and gentlemen," the President said, without preamble. "As I'm sure you must know by now, the United States of America has fallen prey to a bank panic that, in just over 12 hours, has spread from Europe around the world. Let me assure you that, while this Administration is not indifferent to the source of the problem, our focus instead is, and has been, primarily on solving it. We believe that restarting the flow of money from our nation's banks to the families and businesses to whom it rightfully belongs is our most urgent and important task."

Steele paused to look out at the many, familiar faces in his audience. He had seen most of them again and again at press conferences, photo ops, and assorted White House events. He could not, in all honesty, call any of them friends – although he was friendly enough with some of the stalwarts – but he was acutely aware that many of them had come to know him well enough to accurately judge his mood from the subtle clues of body language and tone of voice.

At the moment, the President was angry. Angry at the bankers and insurance industry executives who had added so greatly, not just to his own burden, but to the weight of anxiety that all Americans had felt since the May Day bombing. He knew, though, that allowing his anger to become visible now would be a mistake. The press – and through them the public – needed to see him as calm and in control, rather than raging.

"Make no mistake," he continued, "the money invested in America's banks, savings and loans, and credit unions does not belong to the bankers, however much they might think otherwise. It belongs to the ordinary people and the businesses both small and large who have entrusted their financial resources to those institutions, and who are now wondering whether that trust has been badly misplaced.

"I am here to tell you that it has not."

A murmur swept through the crowd. A barrage of camera flashes erupted.

"After consulting with advisors, both inside and outside the White House, I have decided to enact the following policies. Beginning as of midnight tonight, Eastern Daylight Time, any ATM network that remains shut down will be considered to have gone into involuntary bankruptcy under Chapter 7 of Title 11, USC, and it will be taken over by the Federal government. Likewise, beginning tomorrow, any bank, savings and loan, or credit union that fails to open its doors for business as usual, at its usual time – and by that, I mean the time advertised on its front doors, as of yesterday's close of business – will also be considered to have voluntarily entered Chapter 7 bankruptcy, and it will be seized. In addition, any bank that closes its doors earlier than normal will be considered to have announced Chapter 7 bankruptcy, and it will be nationalized.

"One more thing. The senior executives and members of the board of directors of any banking institution this Administration is forced to take control of will be arrested, and tried before a military commission, for fraud and malfeasance."

A buzz swept through the audience. The correspondents glanced at one another, and murmured their incredulity at the announcement of such harsh sanctions.

"To my fellow Americans," the President continued, "I say this: the money in your savings and checking accounts is protected by the FDIC and other government financial insurance programs. It is safe. You will not lose a dime. This, I promise you. In addition, beginning tomorrow, you will once again have full access to your personal and business deposit accounts, regardless of what may happen with the banking industry elsewhere around the globe.

"In exchange for this guarantee, I ask only that you continue to display the courage and dignity that has been a hallmark of the American character, since we first declared our independence in 1776. I am counting on you to help me show the world what true leadership looks like – and, my fellow Americans, I believe in my heart that it looks like *you*. All we need is faith: in each other, in our country, in our economic system. So, I am confident that you will do the right thing, tomorrow. That you will use your ATM cards, or write checks to buy only the things you truly need. That you will trust in your government to keep your money safe. And that you will show the rest of the world by your example the true greatness that is the heart of the American character.

"I thank you for your attention, and for your faith and patience. May God bless America."

The press corps began shouting questions.

Ignoring them, William Orwell Steele turned, climbed the three steps to the colonnade, and headed back to the Oval Office.

May 7, 2020, 2:17 pm

Manny Jack's Bar and Grill, Main Street, Asbury Park, NJ

"You sure about this?" Kendall "Wide Load" Broadus demanded. "Big Sugar told us to stay here, an' wait for him to send word."

"Yeah," Donell Jackson replied, "that's true. And he put me in charge of the mob, too, didn't he?"

"Well," Broadus conceded, "true, that."

"And I got us all here safe, didn't I?" Jackson challenged.

"Yeah," Broadus admitted, thrusting his hands in his pockets, "you did."

"Okay," Donell told him. "Well, now I'm telling you I got some personal business to take care of. My woman's in the hospital, and I need to see how she's doing. You just chill here with Manny and Jackie, and I'll be back in a couple, three hours."

Jackson was desperately tired, and on edge. But he understood there was nothing to be gained by antagonizing Wide Load. Like Donell, Broadus clearly was concerned about the fate of their leader, Big Sugar Washington. Wide Load just wanted Jackson, as Big Sugar's designated replacement, to remain close at hand.

After Washington had fallen to a sentry's bullet, the gang fled along the edge of Canoe Brook Reservoir Number 1, until they reached the PS&G right-of-way. Leaving the shoreline, they skirted the swampy ground around a high-voltage transmission tower to reach the access road that connected it with Passaic Avenue. In the quiet neighborhood along Dickinson Lane, they stole an unlocked Dodge Durango, then made their way, cautiously, circuitously to Asbury Park. They stuck to secondary roads, rather than taking the New Jersey Turnpike. Sometimes they had gone miles out of their way to avoid National Guard checkpoints.

Once they reached their destination, they wiped the Durango clean of fingerprints, and ditched it in the seaside parking lot shared by the Paramount Theatre and the Asbury Park Convention Hall. They then hiked almost a mile from the seaside to Manny Jack's Bar and Grill.

Manuel "Manny" Ramirez and his tall, black, Cajun wife Jacqueline greeted Wide Load like a long-lost family member, welcoming him and his cohorts into their cool, dim, neon-lit establishment.

Jackie promptly ordered her short, muscular husband, "Rustle up some launch, you."

Then, turning to Broadus, she asked, "You tursty, Wide Load? How 'bout you udder fellas?"

The ravenous mobsters eagerly devoured plates mounded with spicy chicken and ribs, cole slaw, and corn bread. They washed it all down with mugs of cold, draft beer, while Jackie clucked over them like a brood hen. Manny beamed with pride, and kept the frosty mugs coming. Predictably enough, the combination of food, alcohol, and exhaustion soon caught up with them. It wasn't long before most of the gang was stretched out in the tavern's storeroom or in Manny's office, blissfully unconscious, leaving only Jackson and Broadus awake.

"Look," Donell told Wide Load, "everyone else is conked out. Why don't you catch some zees yourself? I'll be back before you know it."

Broadus stared at him. His expression reminded Jackson of a hurt puppy.

"You better," he said. "I ain't gonna try an' stop you, Boss. But, you better come back."

"I will, brother Kendall," Donell assured him.

Broadus's verbal acknowledgement of his authority filled him with pride.

"You can depend on it," Jackson promised.

May 7, 2020, 3:17 pm EDT

National Military Command Center, the Pentagon, Arlington Co., VA

"Mr. President," Secretary of Internal Security Arleigh Solomon rumbled, "my own opinion is that, in view of General Sheikh's confession, no formal declaration of hostilities is required. It seems clear the Paks consider themselves to be at war with us. I see no advantage to be gained in letting them know what we've found out."

"I have to agree, sir," said General Winston Chung, Chairman of the Joint Chiefs of Staff. "Besides which, we're currently not prepared for a conventional war with Pakistan. Our only immediate military option would be a nuclear strike using ICBMs. Frankly, I think that would be a terrible mistake."

"Much as I want to hurt those bastards," the President replied, "I have to agree. When we hit them, we have to be absolutely certain we neutralize their nuclear weapons. All their nuclear weapons. We need to punish them for Manhattan, too, but only as a secondary goal. Disarming them as a strategic threat has to be our top priority."

An audible sigh of relief ran around the long conference table that formed the upright of a tee shape with the command desk in the Emergency Conference Room.

The heads of the five Armed Services sat behind the desk, while the Chairman and Vice-Chairman occupied the chairs on either side of the table, nearest the desk. The remainder of the chairs that surrounded the table held the members of the National Security Council, with William Orwell Steele at its head. Some distance away to the President's left were various advisors and special assistants to the NSC, behind a long, curved desk.

"So," Steele continued, "my questions are: do we have a plan to pull Pakistan's fangs, and how long will it take us to position the necessary resources?"

"Respectively, sir," General Chung responded, "the answers to those questions are: 'yes … but,' and 'at least, what …? Two to three months?'"

There was a general murmur of agreement among the members of the JCS.

"Explain 'yes … but,' General," the President demanded.

"Well, sir," Chung told him, "as a matter of policy, we – which is to say 'the DoD' –regularly generate action plans to deal with a very large range of scenarios. One of those scenarios is a clandestine raid to disable Pakistan's nuclear capability. I have personally reviewed that plan, today. While it strikes me as a basically sound framework for action, I have no doubt that it can and should be more thoroughly reviewed. It needs to be considerably refined and updated, before I'd be willing to recommend we move on it. In any case, it will be at least a couple of months before we have in place the necessary resources. We should have plenty of time to make sure our plan of action is nailed down as tightly as possible, before we ask for your go-ahead."

Steele nodded.

"That sounds good, to me," he said. "Can I assume you'll coordinate with Director Murdock on the intelligence aspects?"

"Yes, sir," Chung affirmed. "And with the NSA, too."

"Getting back to the earlier point, Mr. President," Arleigh Solomon interrupted, "the fact is, the Bush-era Authorization for the Use of Military Action has never been rescinded. I think we can make a case for our response to May Day falling under its authority."

Steele frowned.

"How so, Arleigh?" he asked.

"Well, sir," Solomon replied, reading from a printout, "section a of the Authorization states: 'the President is authorized to use all necessary and appropriate force against those nations, organizations, or persons he determines planned, authorized, committed, or aided the terrorist attacks that occurred on September 11, 2001, or harbored such organizations or persons, in order to prevent any future acts of international terrorism against the United States by such nations, organizations or persons.'

"As you know, our intelligence community has long since established that the Paks both harbored and aided the Afghani Taliban, during our war against them and afterward. The Taliban, in turn, aided and harbored bin Laden and *Al Qaeda*. As you'll recall, that's why President Bush ordered the invasion of Afghanistan, to begin with. So, given that they're firmly established as accessories to the 9/11 attacks, in my view, the Authorization to Use Military Force gives us authority to act against the Paks without needing to ask Congress's permission."

"I don't see Congressional authorization as a problem, Arleigh," Steele countered. "I'm confident they'll fall all over themselves to approve the use of any level of military force we think is appropriate against Pakistan. All we'd have to do is show them General Sheikh's confession."

"I don't doubt that's true, sir," Solomon rumbled, "but, the moment we do that, the cat will be all the way out of the bag."

"He's right, Mr. President," the Vice-President agreed. "There's no way we can rely on the Hill to keep something this big a secret. We both know that."

"Well," Steele concurred reluctantly, "I can't honestly disagree with you on that."

"While we're on the subject of secrecy," CIA Director Christopher Murdock put in, "I think we need to begin a campaign of disinformation and misdirection, in respect to our reasons for building up our forces in the region, sir."

"I agree, Mr. President," Chung said.

"Do you have something specific in mind, Mr. Director?" Steele inquired.

"Yes, sir," Murdock affirmed. "I think we should make it look like we're preparing to take action against Iran."

"Really?" the President asked. "Why Iran?"

"For a couple of reasons, sir," Murdock replied. "One, because it would be trivially easy for us to get them stirred up enough to at least *sound* like they're a credible threat. Their touchiness would work to our advantage, in that regard. And, two, because it would give us an excuse to move significant military assets into the area, without alerting the Paks to the fact that they're our real target."

The President frowned.

"The biggest problem I see with that," he responded, "is that everyone knows the Israelis knocked out their uranium enrichment facilities, back in 2014 – and I haven't seen any reports that they've rebuilt those facilities since then."

"They haven't," Murdock stated, confidently. "But there's no reason why we can't make it appear as though we think they have, sir."

"You're talking about manufacturing intelligence to provide an excuse for war," Steele said, his voice flat.

"Yes, Mr. President," Murdock agreed. "That's exactly what I'm talking about."

May 7, 2020, 4:38 pm

Flag Bridge Conference Room, USS John F. Kennedy

"The defendant will stand," ordered Captain William Plein, acting in his capacity as Presiding Officer of the Military Commission charged with trying Winslow Benton "Buck" Hatfield.

Hatfield scowled. With arms defiantly crossed, he remained seated.

Ignoring Hatfield's display of contempt, Plein continued, "Mr. Hatfield, the Members of this Commission each and severally have found you guilty of the charges of: murder in the first degree, conspiracy to commit murder in the first degree, arson in the first degree, conspiracy to commit arson in the first degree, conspiracy to foment civil unrest, in a time of national emergency, and three counts of aggravated assault upon a Federal officer, in the performance of his duty."

Hatfield snorted dismissively.

"This Commission's verdict is based upon circumstantial and forensic evidence supporting the charges of murder and arson," Plein stated, "as well as the testimony of investigators and technical experts regarding the physical evidence of your culpability in the charged acts of murder and arson; the detailed confessions of your co-conspirators, and their testimony regarding your planning, direction, and execution of the acts of murder and arson of which you have been convicted, and your avowed intent to foment civil unrest by these acts. We have also been presented with video recordings of, and the testimony of Federal agents in regard to, your assaults upon those agents. The weight of this evidence has established that you are guilty of each of these charges to a certainty well beyond the shadow of any possible doubt. Therefore, I now ask whether you have anything to say in defense or mitigation of your actions, before you are sentenced for your crimes?"

"Mr. President," interjected Hatfield's attorney, Lieutenant Commander Benedict Rosenberg of the Navy Judge Advocate General Corps' Defense Service Office, "once again, I am compelled to object most strenuously to this Commission's assertion of jurisdiction in this case. I cite as precedent *Duncan v. Kahanamoku*, where the Supreme Court held that, even in a war zone, trial before a military commission was unconstitutional where civilian courts continued to hear other criminal cases. I beg you to withhold sentencing, pending appeal."

"Your objection is out of order, Commander," Plein responded. "As you very well know, this Commission's jurisdiction derives from a direct order of the President of the United States, in his capacity as Commander in Chief. Let me quote from the bill approved by both houses of Congress, last Monday night."

Plein put on a pair of half-glasses to read from the text before him.

"'The President is hereby authorized to employ any means he deems necessary," he quoted, "including the suspension of civil liberties and the suspension of Constitutional guarantees, to preserve civil order, and protect the people and soil of the United States of America.'"

He set his glasses back on the table top, before he continued.

"That is a rather sweeping mandate, Counselor," he observed. "It seems to me to give this Commission exactly the jurisdiction to which you object."

"With all due respect, Mr. President," Rosenberg replied, "at the very least, *ex parte Milligan* makes the unsought change of venue in this case challengeable. The defense moves that this Commission stay sentencing, until we have had an opportunity to file an emergency appeal on that basis."

"Denied," Plein responded.

"But, sir," Rosenberg insisted, "the civilian court system was fully operational in the venue where the defendant's alleged crimes were committed! Presidential orders notwithstanding, transferring him here in order to try him before this Commission, rather than in a civilian court of law, purposefully flouts *Milligan*, and constitutes an outrageous miscarriage of justice!"

"Counselor," Plein told him, "we have ruled in this matter. Your protest is noted, but that ruling stands. Kindly refrain from further interruptions."

"Only under protest, Mr. President," Rosenberg replied.

"Noted," Plein agreed.

He returned his attention to Rosenberg's client.

"Have you anything to say before you are sentenced, Mr. Hatfield?" he asked.

"Yeah," Hatfield responded, uncrossing his arms. "I do."

He stood to face the Commission.

"First of all," Hatfield said, "I don't recognize this here court's authority over me. I am a sovereign citizen of the State of Ohio, and the Federal Government – including Mr. High-and-Mighty William Orwell Steele – got no legal right to try me, or sentence me for anything I did or didn't do within the borders of the State of Ohio."

The Commissioners responded to his claim with impassive silence.

Hatfield continued, "Look, everyone knows it was the rag heads what bombed New York. I say it's the duty of every right-thinking Christian in this country to wipe those murderin' motherfuckers off the face of God's Earth. Kill 'em all, before they do it to us, is the only smart thing to do. Me? I'm proud of what I done. Hell, come right down to it, you fellers ought to be givin' me a medal for doin' what Steele don't have the balls to do, 'stead of puttin' me on trial in this jacked-up, kangaroo court you got goin' on here. But, like I said, you got no right to try me in the first place. So you'd best jus' take me back to Ohio, an' let me be about my business."

He lifted his head, stuck out his chin, and squared his shoulders, striking as heroic a pose as a man in chains could manage.

"Have you anything else to add to your statement, Mr. Hatfield?" Plein inquired.

"Hell, no," Hatfield replied. "I've said what I had to say."

"Let the record show that the defendant declines the opportunity to present claims of extenuating or mitigating circumstances," Plein noted.

He replaced the half-glasses on his nose.

"For each of the three counts of aggravated assault upon Federal officers in the performance of their duty," Plein read, "you are hereby sentenced to five years at hard labor in a Federal penitentiary."

Hatfield looked thunderstruck. His mouth gaped open in shock.

"For the crime of arson in the first degree," Plein continued, "you are hereby sentenced to 20 years at hard labor in a Federal penitentiary. For the crime of conspiracy to commit arson in the first degree, you are hereby sentenced to an additional 20 years at hard labor."

"You ... you ..." Hatfield stammered, his heroic posture deflating.

"For the crime of conspiring to foment civil unrest, during a time of national emergency," Plein told him, "you are hereby sentenced to 20 years at hard labor in a Federal penitentiary."

Hatfield's mouth worked. Only silence emerged.

"For the crime of conspiracy to commit murder in the first degree," Plein decreed, "you are hereby sentenced to 40 years at hard labor in a Federal penitentiary."

He looked over his half-glasses at Hatfield, and added, "These sentences shall be served consecutively."

"*Fuck you!*" Hatfield screamed.

"For the crime of murder in the first degree," Plein continued, ignoring the red-faced defendant's foul-mouthed stream of invective, "you are hereby sentenced to be hanged by the neck until you are dead."

A pair of beefy bailiffs in dress black struggled to hold Hatfield back from lunging at the Commission table.

Plein concluded, "At dawn tomorrow, you are to be taken from here to the place appointed for your execution, where your sentence will be carried out."

He removed his reading glasses, raised his head, and looked Hatfield directly in the eye.

"And may God have mercy on your soul," he added.

May 7, 2020, 5:31 pm EDT

Seneca Temporary Housing Facility, Romulus, NY

"What's goin' on?" Sean Halloran, Sr. asked, as Ruby Manson carried an armload of her sons' toys past him.

"We're buggin' out, bro," replied her hulking, shaven-headed husband Adam. "That's what. Gettin' out, while gettin's still possible."

Halloran looked around the tent his little family shared with the Mansons. The blanket that divided it lengthwise into halves was shoved back like a shower curtain, to make it easier for his tent mates to evacuate their possessions. Their side of the enclosure was already stripped nearly bare. Only a few clothes and small items were left scattered on the floor.

"Why now, Adam?" Sean, Sr. demanded. "I mean, is there a particular reason why you're leavin' now, instead of tomorrow?"

"Haven't you heard the news?" Manson responded. "The government's seizin' the banks. By tomorrow, they'll have this place locked down tighter than a tick on a dog's ball sack – for our own protection, of course. It's *on*, bro! They're takin' over, big as shit."

He glanced around his family's side of their shared cabin tent.

"Hell, the only reason we're still here is I wanted to give you the chance to come with us," he said.

At Manson's words, a bolt of pure terror shot through Halloran. Not more than an hour earlier, his FBI handlers had finished briefing him on what to do in the event Manson attempted to recruit him to join the Aryan Revolutionary Front – the avowedly racist clandestine organization of which they suspected him of being a key member.

"Tell him you need to think about it," Klinger advised. "Ask him for more time to make a decision."

"An' what if he says 'no'?" Halloran demanded. "What if he says, 'It's now or never?' What do I say then?"

Agents Klinger and O'Reilly exchanged glances. Some unspoken communication passed between them. It seemed to Sean, Sr. that they had been anticipating his question. He was suddenly certain that their unvoiced conversation came down to deciding which of them would respond.

"Well," Klinger replied, at last, "it's up to you, of course. But probably the safest thing to say would be 'yes'."

"You're sayin' ya think he'll kill me, if I say 'no'." Halloran responded.

He was beginning to feel cornered.

"No," Klinger disagreed. "I'm saying we don't know what he'll do, if you say 'no' – but we're pretty sure he'll react positively, if you say 'yes'."

"Goddamnit!" Sean, Sr. raged. "I knew this would happen! I shoulda never let ya talk me into this, to begin with!"

"Now, Sean," O'Reilly interjected, soothingly, "we promised to protect you and your family from Manson, and we'll by-God keep that promise. You have nothing to worry about, I assure you."

"I'll tell you what, Sean," Klinger put in, "if Manson offers to recruit you, and you say 'yes,' we'll increase your weekly stipend to ... what? Would $5,000 a week make you feel better?"

"$5,000?" Halloran repeated.

"That's more than $250,000 a year," O'Reilly pointed out, helpfully.

Sean, Sr. wavered.

He could not shake the frightening conviction that continuing to act as an informant for the FBI not only would place him in mortal danger, but would imperil his wife and infant son, as well. Klinger and O'Reilly's assurances were little comfort, when it was Fiona and Sean, Jr.'s lives that were on the line. But the prospect of $250,000, plus the agents' promise to put the Hallorans in the Federal witness protection program once his employment ended was an almighty temptation to an independent contractor whose family currently lived in a tent.

"What if we make that $5,000 a week, tax-free?" Klinger offered.

"Oh, sweet Jesus!" Sean, Sr. groaned.

"Remember," Klinger reminded him, "there's a GPS unit in the boombox we gave you. If Manson insists you leave here with him, we'll be tracking you by helicopter, every inch of the way. Worst case scenario: we'll be just five minutes away."

"With a full FBI SWAT team," O'Reilly added.

"Alright, already!" Halloran snapped. "I'll do your dirty work for ya. But, so help me God, if anythin' happens to Fiona or Sean, Jr. …"

"Don't worry, Sean," Klinger told him. "We have your back. Nothing bad will happen to your family. You have my word on it."

Klinger stuck out his hand.

"Deal?" he asked.

"Yeah, deal," Halloran agreed gloomily.

He had shaken the Senior Field Agent's hand, sealing their bargain. Now the moment was upon him, and Sean, Sr. was hard pressed to conceal his terror from Manson.

"I can't leave my pickup behind," Halloran temporized. "It's got all my tools in it – that's my life savin's, Adam."

Manson shrugged.

"Not a problem, bro," he replied. "You and Fiona can just follow us in your truck. It'll be more comfortable for everyone that way."

"But I'm outta gas," Sean, Sr. protested.

He knew he was only making excuses, but he was suddenly desperate to weasel out of his deal with the FBI.

"The needle's restin' on empty," Halloran complained.

"Still not a problem," Manson told him. "I got a siphon – and a full tank of gas in the Suburban. I filled it up, right after we left the Interstate. You can just buy me a tank, when we get back to the freeway, and we'll call it square."

Sean, Sr. blinked at him, on the verge of tears, and at a loss for what else to say.

"Well?" Manson challenged. "You comin'?"

May 7, 2020, 3:01 pm PDT (6:01 pm EDT)

Alvarado Street, San Leandro, CA

Artemis Steele felt a subtle change in her environment.

For a moment, she could not grasp exactly what it was. Then she realized that the mildest of zephyrs now caressed her naked skin. Somewhere deep inside her, tremulous hope held its figurative breath.

Fingers began touching her arms and legs. The restraints that limited her movement fell away. Now she was free to reposition her limbs. But she no longer possessed the capacity for independent action.

The relentless, irresistible, constant repetition of the Voice's mantra, "Trust me – I will rescue you. Love me – I will save you. Surrender to me – I will help you," had, over the course of days, entirely robbed her of her will; made her a completely passive, helpless creature. She was capable, now, only of waiting for the Voice that owned her to keep the promise for which she longed with all her being.

Gentle hands took hold of her: cradling her head, lifting her by her armpits, supporting her lower back, raising her thighs. They hoisted her out of the warm, wet, womb-like environment that, for such a timeless time, had been the whole of her world. She felt herself lifted through the air.

Her feet touched a soft, dry, fuzzy surface. Suddenly, she was standing. Despite the helpful hands still lending their assistance, she wavered, legs unsteady after days of inactivity. Almost, she toppled over.

As her footing firmed, the hands that braced her knees, hips, and pelvis withdrew, two by two. Eventually, she was gripped only by her upper arms. At those hands' gentle urging, she turned, shuffling bit by bit. When the guiding hands returned to the task of merely supporting her, she stopped, swaying slightly. Without volition of her own, she simply waited.

The headphones that covered her ears were removed.

For the first time in nearly three days, the Voice that had become her entire universe, the mantra it had endlessly repeated, stopped. In its place, now, was a tintinnabulation of small, unfamiliar sounds: the breathing of a half-dozen or more people, the slight rustle of their clothing, as they shifted position, the hum of electronic devices, the susurrus of computer fans, the slightest of sloshing noises, behind her. Welcome as they were, not even the totality of them made up for the removal of the Voice.

Its absence was devastating. She had lost the only constant in her world, the only stimulus she had been allowed for so very long. Silent tears tried to leak from beneath her closed eyelids.

Fingers fumbled at the back of her head.

She felt the weight and pressure of the blacked-out goggles she had worn so long that she had forgotten their very existence lifted from her still-closed eyes. Gentle hands sponged away the accumulated rheum from her crusted lids. She blinked, as they withdrew.

Standing before her, his evenly-tanned, nude form bathed in the carefully-shielded light of three nine-watt bulbs, was a compact, muscular man. He had ice-blue eyes, shoulder-length, blond hair, and the most perfect, square-jawed face she had ever seen. Deprived of sight for so long, even the reflected radiance of those dim lights made him seem, in her eyes, to glow like Apollo, the Greek god of the Sun.

Then, head slightly tilted to the left, he spoke. Once again, she heard the Voice – her one, true essential; her greatest desire; her only, imperative passion.

"Hello, Artemis," said Adolph Ryan Wolf.

His tone and body language radiated self-confidence and dominance. He held out his hand to her.

"Come to me," he commanded.

Legs unsteady, heart filled with adoration, gratitude, and the overwhelming need to obey, Artemis Steele eagerly ran to her captor.

May 7, 2020, 7:12 pm EDT

Ocean Avenue, Deal, NJ

A plan began to form in Donell Jackson's mind as he passed the Deal Esplanade, on his way toward Asbury Park. He was riding the gaudy, rumbling, Harley chopper he had borrowed from Manuel Rodriguez, proprietor of Manny Jack's Bar and Grill. The wind of his passage whipped his shirt like a flag.

Donell had arrived at Monmouth Medical Center a little before 3:00 that afternoon. Circumnavigating the massive complex twice, he finally parked the Harley in an alley off Pavilion Avenue. It had dawned on him that his chances of being ticketed for illegal parking were close to zero.

- Only good thing I can think of about Manhattan getting nuked. -

He made his way around to the 3rd Avenue Hospital entrance, and headed straight to the information desk in the lobby.

"Excuse me, Miss," Jackson said, to the middle-aged, white woman at the desk.

"Can I help you?" the woman replied, with a flattered smile.

Her name badge identified her as Mabel.

"I'm looking for my girlfriend," Donell told her. "I was told she was brought here on Monday afternoon."

After an awkward, expectant pause, Mabel inquired, sweetly, "Does your girlfriend have a name?"

Jackson gave her his most disarming grin. He shook his head, ruefully.

"That would help, wouldn't it?" he allowed.

"It would narrow it down, a little," Mabel agreed.

She favored him with a sympathetic smile of her own.

"Sorry," Donell confessed, "I'm a little off my game, today."

"I understand," Mabel replied. "I think we all are – what with everything that's going on."

She spread her hands, as if to encompass the world of events that had transpired since the bombing.

"Anyhow," Jackson told her, "her name is Latonya Gramble. She's 20, about this tall."

He held his hand at the level of his chin.

"Got a Jheri curl," he continued. "Brown eyes. Nice figure."

Mabel had been searching the hospital's patient database, while Jackson rambled on. She frowned, and looked up at him.

"G-r-a-m-b-l-e?" she asked.

Donell nodded. "That's right," he confirmed. "Latonya: L-a-t ..."

"I'm afraid I don't see anyone named Gramble in our list of current patients, Mr. ..." Mabel interrupted.

"Donell ..." Jackson began.

Then he caught himself.

"... Donellson," he said. "Jack Donellson. Are you sure, Miss? Could you check again?"

Mabel did not bother to redo her search.

"I'm very sorry, Mr. Donellson," she informed him. "She's not listed. Are you sure she was admitted to this hospital?"

"Pretty sure," Donell responded. "Leastwise, that's what they told me."

"'They'?" Mabel asked.

"The soldiers," Jackson explained. "When the soldiers stopped us, they told me she was gonna be brought here."

"And why did the soldiers stop you, Mr. Donellson?" Mabel wanted to know.

"It was a roadblock," Donell replied. "See, I went to Hackensack to get Latonya and her daughter, Nakeesha. Nakeesha passed before I got there, and Latonya was real sick. From radiation poisoning, you know?"

"I see," Mabel told him, her expression suddenly grave. "Mr. Donellson, my database only includes patients who are currently registered at Monmouth. It's possible that your girlfriend Latonya has been transferred to another facility, or ..."

She stopped herself. The corners of her mouth turned down.

Jackson's heart sank.

"I'll tell you what," Mabel offered. "Why don't I send you to Patient Records? If she was admitted to Monmouth, they should be able to help you find out ... where she is now."

"I ... I'd appreciate that, Ma'am," Donell responded.

Mabel gave him directions to Patient Records. After getting completely turned around twice, he found his way to the service window.

The clerk was a painfully-thin, flamboyantly homosexual, white man in his thirties, whose nameplate read 'Rance'. He checked his database for Latonya's name. Immediately, his delicate features twisted in sympathy.

"Oh, Honey, I'm sorry," he told Jackson. "She passed away on Tuesday."

"She's dead?" Donell replied. "Latonya's dead?"

Rance nodded.

"I'm afraid so, sweetie," he said. "Her body's downstairs in the morgue, if you'd like to see her. Or make arrangements ... you know, for her funeral?"

Half-blinded by grief, Jackson somehow made his way to the basement level. He found the morgue tucked away in a corner.

The attendant, a moon-faced, 30-ish man named David, led him into the refrigerated room. Latonya's cadaver reposed on a steel table in one corner, covered with a white sheet. A triangular, yellow, plastic sign with a black radiation trefoil emblazoned on both sides balanced on top of her shroud.

David donned a lead apron before he approached Latonya's body. He neatly folded the top of the sheet down to reveal her face. He turned to Donell.

"Is this your girlfriend, Mr. Donellson?" he asked.

His face was carefully expressionless.

Donell Jackson stood for a long moment, gazing at the corpse of the woman he loved. Her sunken eyes, the ugly blisters along the side of her face, and her painfully hollow cheeks; none of those could mask her beauty. He thought of her as she had been the day before his arrest: her wide, wicked smile, her flashing brown eyes, the endearing little dimple in her left cheek, Jheri curls bouncing, as she strolled beside him. Nakeesha skipping along, holding his hand, they had ambled along the waterfront pathway at Foschini Park, like a real family.

His eyes filled with tears at the memory.

"Yes," he said – or tried to say – at last. It came out as a half-strangled sob.

"I'm sorry," David told him. After a moment, he added, "Do you want to claim the body? I ask, because there's a lot of paperwork involved, on account of the radiation."

Jackson shook his head.

"No," he managed to reply. "Not now."

"I understand," David said.

"Thanks," Jackson responded.

He turned to go

"She'll be here for another couple of days, in case you change your mind," David called after him.

For what must have been hours afterward, Donell wandered the maze-like corridors of Monmouth Medical Center. He paid no attention to where he was, or where he was going. He kept moving only because he was certain he would break down completely, should he allow himself to come to rest. Grief and loss encumbered him, until his shoulders slumped under their burden. It seemed as though his limbs must weigh 1,000 pounds apiece.

Eventually, his aimless, agonized wandering brought him to the Critical Care Unit. At its entrance, he was stopped by a soldier in Army Combat Uniform. The guard had a holstered sidearm and an M-16A4 carbine slung over his shoulder.

"You can't go in there, sir," the soldier said.

He stepped in front of Jackson, and put his hand on the butt of his pistol.

"Huh?" Donell replied, startled out of his reverie.

He looked up at the soldier, and shook his head.

"Where am I?" Jackson asked.

"This is the Critical Care Unit, sir," the soldier told him. "And I repeat: you can't go in there."

Donell took a step back. He held up his hands, reassuringly.

"Okay," he said. "I don't want no trouble, General. I'm just kinda lost, is all."

"Corporal," the soldier replied.

He was mollified enough to take his hand off his gun butt.

"If you tell me where you're trying to go, maybe I can point you in the right direction," he offered.

Jackson eyed him, speculatively.

"I was just wanderin', to tell the truth," he confessed. "I found out my girlfriend died, and I was …"

He trailed off, at a loss for how to explain any further.

"I'm sorry to hear that, sir," the soldier said. "My condolences on your loss."

"Thank you ... Corporal," Donell replied. "Like I said, I didn't mean to cause no trouble. I'm just ... y'know ... tryin' to get used to the idea that she's gone."

"I'm very sorry, sir," the soldier told him. "I lost family in the bombing, myself."

Jackson nodded soberly.

"A lotta people did, I guess," he said. "A lotta people."

"Yes, sir," the corporal replied.

"Anyhow, you got a job to do," Donell said, "so I guess I'll just be on my way, and leave you to it."

"I appreciate that, sir," the soldier said. "Thank you for your cooperation."

"No trouble at all," Jackson responded, with a dismissive wave. "You have a nice day, Corporal."

"You, too, sir," the soldier replied.

Donell turned to walk away. Then, on sheer impulse, he turned back.

"Out of curiosity, Corporal," he inquired, casually, "how come you're guarding the ... what'd you call it?"

"Critical Care Unit," the soldier reminded him.

"Yeah," Jackson agreed, "that."

"There's a dangerous prisoner inside, sir," the corporal explained.

"Really?" Donell responded. "Must be damned dangerous, if he needs you to guard him."

"Yes, sir," the soldier told him. "He's an escaped murderer. Some kind of big gangster, or so they say. 'Big Sugar' something-or-other."

"Do tell," Jackson responded, thunderstruck.

A long moment passed.

It finally occurred to Donell that the soldier might construe his hesitation as suspicious.

"Well," he continued, as he turned to leave, "like I said, you have a nice day, Corporal."

"You, too, sir," the corporal replied.

From that moment on, Donell locked his grief away in a dark corner of his soul. Instead, he concentrated on tracing every corridor that led to the Critical Care Unit, locating every stairway, and elevator, and identifying every doorway, along the way. Only once he had the floor plan and all possible routes of escape thoroughly memorized, did he leave the complex, and reclaim Manny Ramirez's chopper.

Now, passing the seaside mansions of Deal, New Jersey, all the details came together in his mind. Suddenly Jackson understood exactly how he and the other members of his gang were going to break Big Sugar Washington out of Monmouth Medical Center's closely-guarded Critical Care Unit.

Grinning savagely, he downshifted, and twisted the throttle. The Harley's throaty rumble rose to a triumphant roar.

May 7, 2020, 8:08 pm EDT

The White House Family Dining Room, Washington, DC

"Mr. Mayor," William Orwell Steele said, "thank you for joining us."

"It's my pleasure, Mr. President," replied the Honorable Zachary Copley.

He was the Mayor of Boston and the scion of a family that traced its lineage back to colonial times.

Copley turned to Diana Hunter, who sat at his left.

"It's a great pleasure to meet you, too, Madam Vice President," he added. "I've been an admirer of yours for a long time, now."

"Why, thank you, Mr. Mayor," Hunter responded.

As the White House sommelier began filling their wineglasses, the Mayor returned his attention to the President.

"So, Your Honor," Steele inquired, "what exactly can we do for you?"

"You can give me my city back, Mr. President," Copley replied. "At the moment, I'm the mayor of 48 square miles of abandoned buildings and deserted streets. Boston's people are scattered from Hell to breakfast, over God-only-knows how many different states by now. A good half of them, or more, are living in your FEMA refugee camps."

"Temporary housing facilities," Diana Hunter corrected.

"Forgive my bluntness, but I don't give a damn what you call them, Madam Vice President," the Mayor shot back. "It doesn't change the fact that my constituents – the people who elected me to govern them, and represent their best interests – are living in tents, instead of in their own homes. Which is where they ought to be, want to be, and by-God *deserve* to be. I'm here to find out when you're going to allow them to return to those homes."

He thrust out his jaw, pugnaciously.

"I'm sorry, Your Honor," Steele replied, "but I'm afraid the answer to your question is: 'Not in the near future.'"

"That's unacceptable," Copley insisted.

The President shook his head, wearily.

"Again, Mr. Mayor, I'm sorry," he explained, "but, much as I wish it were otherwise, it's not in my power to change the laws of nature."

"I understand that you're concerned about the radioactivity," Copley said. "I get that, Mr. President. I really do. But some very smart people have told me they think the worst of it should die down inside of the next few weeks – or months, at the outside. According to them, it should be safe enough for most people to return home by, say, the beginning of the school year."

"I wish that were true, Mr. Mayor," Steele told him, shaking his head gently. "Unfortunately, some very smart people who happen to have considerable expertise in the field of high-level radioactive fallout tell me it could be generations before it's truly safe for your people to return to their homes."

Copley gaped at him.

"*Generations*?" he demanded, incredulously.

Steele nodded. "I'm afraid so," he replied. "As I understand it, the problem is the May Day bomb was set off *inside* 1 World Trade Center. Because of that, the amount of fallout it created was thousands of times what an airburst would have produced. Worse still, it's a lot more radioactive than the fallout from, say, Hiroshima or Nagasaki was. In fact, in terms of contamination, I'm told it's best to think of it as more akin to Chernobyl, rather than Hiroshima. The reports on it are classified, of course, but you're welcome to read them for yourself, if you'd like."

"But," Copley protested, "*generations*, Mr. President?"

"I'm afraid so," Steele told him. "As I'm sure you know, the Ukrainian government still won't allow people to return to Pripyat – and it's been, what? Thirty-some-odd years since the Chernobyl disaster?"

"Thirty-four," the Vice President put in, quietly.

"But ... that's terrible!" the Mayor objected.

"Yes, Your Honor," the President agreed. "'Terrible' is exactly what it is."

May 7, 2020, 7:00 pm MDT (9:00 pm EDT)

Patriot Radio Studio 1, Athol, ID

The red "on air" light glowed, as Merlin Friend's earphones filled with the sound of distant trumpets. The thunder of charging cavalry galloped from right to left, and off into the distance. Friend leaned forward, his lips close to his trusty Neumann microphone.

With his distinctive baritone voice pitched at a conversational level, he announced, "Good evening, Patriots. This is your friend Merlin, coming to you, for what may be the last time ever, live, from Patriot Radio Studio 1, in Coeur d'Alene."

Friend paused, to sip from his ever-present Tanqueray-and-tonic, before continuing.

"Patriots," he proclaimed, "the day about which I've been warning you for the past four years is now at hand! The Tyrant has taken direct, personal control of that bastion of evil, the Federal Reserve. At the behest of his New World Order masters, the Rothschilds, the Bilderbergers, and the other members of the Illuminati, he is on the very brink of nationalizing our nation's banking system. Our socialist dictator's false flag attack on Manhattan has already closed our nation's stock markets, and brought our insurance industry under his personal control. Now – *right* now – our banks, and with them all our savings, are about to fall into his blood-soaked hands! Tomorrow morning, Patriots! *Tomorrow morning*!"

Friend's voice had risen to a near-shout, as he leaned away from the Neumann to keep the audio meters from pegging. Now he lowered it to a stage whisper, and bent toward the boom-mounted microphone.

"And after he has the banks?" he demanded. "Patriots, ask yourselves, 'What then?' Will his next theft be our oil and gas industry? Or, will his foul claws first close around the throats of the Internet service providers, or the telecommunications industry, instead? Because – make no mistake about it, my friends – William Orwell Steele lusts for *total* earthly dominion! Nothing less than a stranglehold on America's economy, complete control over our means of communication with each other, and the ultimate subjugation of each and every citizen of this land will satisfy him!"

Friend paused for another sip of gin.

"Patriots," he continued, his tone confiding, seductive, "there is little time left for us to stop this Tyrant, this would-be democracide. We dare not wait another hour, another minute, another second to act. Even as I speak, this vile, perverted, ambitious man is reaching for absolute power, for total control, for the utter, irrevocable enslavement of the American people! Your sons, your daughters, your friends and neighbors – everyone you care about, every single individual you treasure – and you, yourselves will be sacrificed on the altar of the Tyrant, William Orwell Steele! *This* is the moment, Patriots! *Now* is the time! If we do not act – if *you*, personally, do not act, *now* – our country will helplessly fall into the grasping claws of tyranny. It will topple forever into the abyss of Godless socialism! It will end up trampled, and broken under the hob-nailed boots of the Satanic New World Order!"

Friend practically screamed the final phrase. He had risen to his feet, fists clenched, and face gone red with passion. Still standing, he pointed an exhortatory finger at his imagined audience, and spoke in a voice throbbing with sincerity and urgency.

"Only *you* can stop this evil Tyrant, Patriots! Only *you*! Only *you* can act – *now* – to frustrate his malevolent determination to subvert, and destroy all that you hold dearest! You cannot afford to sit back, and let your neighbor act *for* you. *You* must take action! *You*, and *you alone*, can save our country from the doom that William Orwell Steele has planned for it! *You*, Patriots! *You*!"

Friend paused to moisten his mouth with Tanqueray and tonic.

"If *you* do not act," he went on, "all will be lost. Patriots, if *you* do not act *right now*, the Tyrant will take your country away from you – and *you* will *never* get it back. Only *you* can stop this spawn of Satan from stealing America from *you*! Only *you*. And *you* must act, *now* – tonight! Tomorrow will be too late. You *must* act now! Load your weapons, Patriots, kiss your wives and children goodbye – for you may never see them again – take to the streets, and *stop this Tyrant*! Stop him, *now*, before it's too late to stop him at all! Only *you* can save our country from William Orwell Steele, Patriots! *Only you!*"

Friend, head thrown back, fists aloft, had been raving at full volume. Now, still standing at his broadcast desk, he leaned close to the microphone. He cupped it in his hand, like the breast of a lover.

"Only you, Patriots," he murmured. "Only you."

Friend fell back into his overstuffed office chair, and reached for his gin-and-tonic. Letting the tension build, he drained the glass.

Then, in a businesslike voice, he announced, "We'll be right back, after this word from our friends at Goldmine."

May 7, 2020, 7:38 pm PDT (10:38 pm EDT)

Hays Street, San Leandro, CA

"No sign of the suspect, Ma'am," reported Gary Severn, Agent in Charge of the FBI SWAT Team.

His subordinates had just broken into Charles Frederick Albright's apartment.

"The place is empty," Severn said, "just like Baumeister's."

Madeline Czerwinski, Special Agent in Charge of the FBI's San Francisco Field Office, sighed in frustration.

Forensics had found traces of Albright's DNA all over Herbert Baumeister's abandoned apartment. It seemed clear to her that the two men *had* to be co-conspirators. It was equally clear that at least two to four other perps had taken part in the kidnapping of Artemis Steele, and the murders of all but one member of her Secret Service detail. If the Bureau could determine who those others were, it might be possible to locate the entire gang.

"Okay," she ordered, "SWAT Team out, Forensics in."

"Roger," Severn acknowledged.

"And good job, Gary," Czerwinski added.

"Thank you, Ma'am," Severn replied.

- *Either someone is tipping these shitheads off, or else their whole gang has gone into hiding. Either way, this doesn't feel like any other abduction I've worked.* -

The Bureau's Regional Computer Forensics Laboratory would analyze the evidence its specialists were beginning to gather just as it had done with the clues Baumeister had left behind. Perhaps that analysis would lead her to additional members of their gang. Czerwinski hoped so. Meanwhile, the only other remaining option was to wait for a possible informant to come forward.

- Or for the kidnappers to present their demands. -

That Artemis Steele was still alive was the one assumption Czerwinski had to make. It made sense to her. Otherwise, why bother to abduct the President's daughter? If Baumeister and Albright – and whoever their associates turned out to be – had wanted her dead, they could just as easily have killed her on University Avenue, three days ago.

- So she has to be alive. The question is: what are they planning to do with her? -

Her mouth twisted skeptically.

- No. The real *question is: what is whoever they're* working for *planning to do with her? -*

And that, too, seemed self-evident. It was a safe bet that neither Baumeister nor Albright were smart enough to have planned Artemis Steele's elaborate abduction. Someone else *had* to be the mastermind behind Monday's kidnapping and massacre.

Czerwinski could only wonder who he was – and what he planned to do with the President's daughter.

May 7, 2020, 11:07 pm EDT

The White House Living Room, Washington, DC

Diana Hunter purposefully hung back, as the White House living room emptied.

She fondled Duke the Great Dane's dark, floppy ears, and petted his big, boxy head, while William Orwell Steele bade goodnight to the other members of his inner circle. Eyes shining, Duke accepted her attention with an expression of utter bliss, as the President laid his hand on the shoulder of Dr. Marcus Aurelius Clement, his personal physician.

"When I clean your clock for you," he told Clement, "remember I warned you not to make that bet."

"You mean 'if', don't you?" Clement chuckled.

"Just make sure that, when we get to the nineteenth hole, you don't forget your wallet," Steele replied, smiling.

Clement and Andover Philips, the President's Chief of Staff, departed. Steele, still standing in the doorway, turned to face the Vice President.

"Diana …" he began.

"Will …" she said, simultaneously.

Steele laughed at the coincidence. Hunter's smile was brief and flickering.

"What is it, Diana?" the President asked, concerned. "Is something wrong?"

Hunter shook her head. Her trademark French twist came undone. The frosted tips of her auburn hair flew around her head like a flock of tiny birds.

"No," she said, in a small voice.

Steele closed the door that led to the hallway outside.

He went to her, and took her by the elbows. Hunter's lips trembled with emotion. She refused to meet his eyes, keeping her own cast down, as if inspecting the third button on his shirt.

Steele took her by the chin, and gently tilted her face up to his own.

"Tell me what's wrong, Diana," he insisted.

Blinking rapidly, she raised her eyes to look directly into his. This close, Steele could not help but notice the fine network of lines at their corners – lines her carefully-applied makeup could not conceal. It struck him that her husband Benjamin had passed away only hours earlier – and that, in attending to the demands of her official duties, Hunter could not yet have had enough time to properly mourn his loss.

"Oh, Will!" she said.

Tears were beginning to spill from the corners of her brimming eyes.

"I just really need a hug!" she cried.

Hunter threw her arms around him. She clutched him fiercely to her, burying her face in his neck. As he had done many times for his beloved Julia, Steele automatically placed his left hand in the small of her back, and gently pulled her to him. His right smoothed her hair. He tucked his chin atop her head, murmuring wordless, reassuring noises.

Hunter burrowed into his embrace like a tiny animal seeking refuge from a tempest. Her streaming tears soaked his shirtfront. Her shoulders rose, and fell with the small, hiccupping sounds of her weeping, as she nestled within the shelter of Steele's arms.

In time, the storm passed. Hunter pushed softly against his chest, opening enough space between them for her to lift her gaze to his. Her mascara had run in streaks down her face, but her eyes were clear now.

"Thank you, Will," she said.

On tip-toes, she carefully kissed him on the mouth.

- This is wrong. -

Steele felt her tongue slip between his lips.

- This should not be happening. I really should put a stop to it. -

He did not break their clinch. Instead, he took her head in his hands, and returned her kiss with equal ardor.

Wordlessly, without interrupting the dance of their tongues, they began to undress each other.

May 8, 2020, 12:21 am EDT

Ulster County, New York

Sean Halloran, Sr. was now convinced that becoming an FBI informant was the single worst decision of his life.

He and Fiona, with Sean, Jr. strapped into his car seat behind them, had dutifully followed Adam Manson's battered, white Suburban from the Seneca Temporary Housing Facility north to Waterton. Both men had filled their vehicles' gas tanks there. The cost of those fill-ups shocked Halloran.

- Seven dollars a gallon for regular? That's a wicked *pissah! -*

But a deal was a deal. And, in the context of the 5,000 tax-free dollars a week the FBI was paying him for his services, even seven bucks a gallon wasn't completely intolerable. So, in accordance with their bargain, Sean, Sr. paid for Manson's fill up, in addition to his own.

The two families spent two hours zooming along the largely-deserted, interstate highway system, before leaving 81 for New York State Highway 17 East. They'd stayed on 17, skirting the verdant southwestern flank of the Catskill Mountains, and skimming the border of Pennsylvania along the East Branch of the Delaware River, until they reached the little town of Liberty. There, they'd topped up their tanks, inspiring Sean, Sr. to further outrage at the naked greed of gas station owners.

Their little caravan turned off of 17 onto Highway 52, just outside of Liberty.

Almost immediately, they left the highway for a detour of several miles. Manson later explained that they had taken the roundabout route to avoid a manned National Guard roadblock. When they again reached 52, they found access to the highway was blocked by a barbed-wire barricade surrounding two signposts. Each tee-post featured large, ominous, radiation trefoils over even bigger skull-and-crossbones signs. Hung between the signposts was a long, white signboard on which was printed "Danger! Fallout Zone ahead! Do NOT enter!"

The rest of the warning was in black lettering. The words "Danger!" and "NOT" were printed in blood-red letters more than a foot tall.

Manson pulled over to the side of the road, and got out of his SUV. He walked ahead, to talk to two men in a Ford pickup parked beyond the barrier. After a short conversation, the big man shook hands with the others. He headed back to where Halloran was parked.

"Road's clear ahead, Sean," Manson reported. "We shouldn't run into any trouble."

"Adam?" Halloran asked. "Surely you're not plannin' to take us into the Fallout Zone – are ya?"

Manson shrugged.

"Well," he replied, "we won't actually *reach* the Fallout Zone for a while. The sign is just to scare people off, bro."

"I gotta tell ya, *bro*," Sean, Sr. riposted, "it's doin' a wicked good job on *me*!"

Manson banged his hand on the driver's door of Halloran's Sierra, and laughed.

"Don't be a pussy, Halloran," he grinned. "C'mon. Let's blow this fuckin' hotdog stand."

That was when Sean, Sr. had first seriously begun to doubt the wisdom of doing the FBI's dirty work – 5,000 tax-free dollars a week or no $5,000 a week.

- Your SWAT team can't save my family from radiation*, can it now, Mr. Special Agent in Charge Klinger? -*

He watched Manson ease his Suburban onto the road's shoulder, and creep around the barricade. For a long moment, Sean, Sr. sat perfectly still, considering whether he should simply turn around, and run for it.

Manson laid on his horn.

He stuck his shaved head out the window of the Suburban.

"Well?" he hollered. "You comin', bro?"

- Fuck me. I guess I am. -

They drove east for another hour. Just outside Rosendale, they turned onto 32. Less than half a mile further, they crossed the New York State Throughway. Almost immediately, Manson turned right onto a gravel road that led down to a gate chained closed with a combination lock.

Manson got out of his Suburban to unlock the gate. He drove through, parked on the side of the rutted roadway, and motioned Halloran to enter.

After Sean Sr.'s pickup was safely inside the fence, Manson carefully closed and relocked the gate. He got back into his Suburban, and pulled back onto the gravel road. Manson drove a couple of hundred feet downhill. Then he turned past a pile of old ore cars rusting in a clearing, and up a second gravel drive to a rectangular opening in the hillside.

Halloran followed. Once inside the tunnel, they drove just over 100 feet before their vehicles entered an enormous gallery. It was hewn out of the limestone hillside, and supported by massive columns of intact rock.

Fluorescent light fixtures hung in a grid pattern from eyebolts screwed into the ceiling of the cavern. Scattered around the football-field-sized volume sat other trucks and SUVs, trestle tables loaded with equipment, and canvas tarpaulins hung on pipe work frames to create spaces for sleeping quarters, work spaces, and other functions. Gym-style lockers lined the wall to Halloran's left, while massive, enameled steel cabinets extended along the one to his right.

A couple of dozen men in uniform – most of them sporting crew cuts or shaven heads – were scattered throughout the space, conversing, or working at cluttered benches. In one corner, a small group clustered around a portable blackboard, listening intently to an older man with a pure-white crew cut. A few women were also visible. Sean, Sr. noticed that the females were all dressed in civilian clothes, rather than the camouflage duty uniform worn by the men.

Manson killed his engine. He climbed out of his Suburban, and walked back to where Halloran sat, goggling at the paramilitary base that surrounded him.

"You can shut that thing off, bro," Manson told him, nodding at the purring engine under the Sierra's hood. "You're home now."

May 7, 2020, 10:15 pm PDT (May 8, 1:15 am EDT)

Alvarado Street, San Leandro, CA

Adolph Ryan Wolf stood atop the tiny stage at the foot of the suite of offices in the warehouse that served as the Bay Area headquarters for the Aryan Revolutionary Front. Wolf was dressed in a midnight-black version of the combat utility uniform worn by the corps of men who stood at parade rest before him. His head was bare, and tilted slightly to the left. His long, blond hair cascaded to his shoulders.

Wang Jing-Wei knelt by his left side, Artemis Alexandra Steele at his right. Both women were naked. Both wore chrome-steel, Cleopatra-style, slave collars, attached to leather dog leashes. Wang stared straight ahead, her eyes empty, while Steele gazed up at Wolf, her eyes shining with adoration.

"Men," Wolf announced, his voice harsh. "The moment for which we have so long waited, the moment for which we have so long trained, the moment which we have so long anticipated is finally at hand! Those of you who have been part of our cadre since its founding know that, from the very beginning, I promised we would one day rise up, and smash the power of those who coddle the takers. That we would destroy their authority and their ability to govern so utterly that generations would pass before the people of the United States would again entrust this country to their thieving ilk. That we would crush the hands of those who insist on thrusting them into our pockets to take our wealth, and give it to the lazy, shiftless moochers whose votes keep them in office. That we would trample them and the takers they support under our boot heels, grind their faces in the dust, and leave them broken in the gutter, where they belong!"

Wolf smiled a lupine smile. He placed his hand fondly on top of Artemis Steele's head. She shivered in delight at his touch.

"Now that we have captured their king's pawn," Wolf continued, "all the pieces are at last in place. That socialist swineherd William Orwell Steele already has his hands full to overflowing. You and I are about to add a hundred-fold to his burden!

"He will break, my friends. Mark my words: he will break. And *we* will break him! We will push, and push, and push, until he cannot help but push back. We will compel him to overreact to such an extreme that even the welfare queens and tree huggers upon whom his power depends will desert him! We will make him the instrument of his own downfall. And when he falls, his freeloading army of takers will fall along with him. This I promise you!"

Wolf raised his chin, and struck a pose, balled fists on his hips.

"There are 10,000 or more local militia groups in America," Wolf declared. "Once we strike, hundreds, or even thousands of them will be inspired to rise up all around the country. Steele will have no choice but to suppress that uprising with military force. When he does, *we* will lay low, and allow *them* to absorb the brunt of his anger!

"With the armed forces of this nation at war with its own people, every man's hand will turn against him! The longer and more brutal his campaign against the militias, the more of his support it will cost him. All the while, we will taunt him with the image of his daughter – his only child – as the voice of the rebellion against him! We will drive him insane, my friends! We will drive him *insane*!"

Wolf looked out over the impassive ranks of his tiny army. His heart swelled with pride at their iron discipline.

"I need not remind you," he told them, "that each of you was hand-picked to join our ranks. That you are all former members of our country's military – and patriots all. That each of you was forced to resign, because of your perfectly justified belief in the white race's responsibility for America's greatness. That all of you are victims of the political correctness William Orwell Steele was elected to represent.

"Now, at last, it is finally time to pay him back, for the injustice he has done to you and me as individuals, and to our country as a whole. We have the power now – and we will bring that traitor to his knees! We will flush him back down the toilet of socialism, multiculturalism, and multiracialism that spewed him forth! And with him will go the legions of takers who oppress us: the makers of the white race. This I promise you, my friends! This I *promise* you!"

Wolf raised his right fist to shoulder level. He shook it in passion.

"You have the equipment, and the training," Wolf shouted. "You have your assignments. You understand your duty. Now *go* – and fulfill your *destiny*!"

The warehouse reverberated with the roar of A. Ryan Wolf's cheering troops.

May 8, 2020, 2:18 am EDT

Monmouth Medical Center Critical Care Unit, West Long Branch, NJ

Donell Jackson was shocked by "Big Sugar" Washington's appearance.

- *"Sweet Jesus! He looks* terrible*! –*

Washington's closed eyes had deep, dark circles around them. His skin – normally a rich coffee color – was ashen, and his cheeks were sunken. His appearance was that of a man who, if not actually at Death's door, was surely no further away than the Grim Reaper's front yard.

- *How the* fuck *are we gonna move him, without killing him? -*

An oxygen tube was taped beneath Big Sugar's nose, and a drip line from an IV bag had been inserted into the back of his hand. The question in Donell's mind was not so much whether the gang would be able to transport their capo's oxygen tank, and his IV bag, along with the man himself. The real issue was how they were supposed to keep Washington alive once one, the other, or both ran out.

Hours earlier, Jackson had asked Manuel and Jacqueline Ramirez whether they would be willing to help with his plan to rescue the mob boss from Monmouth Medical Hospital's Critical Care Unit.

Jackie immediately replied, "Anytin' you need, just ax, you."

Her husband nodded, in enthusiastic agreement.

"Big Sugar, he's our friend, too," Manny explained. "We'd do anything for him, *jefe.*"

Donell explained the scheme he had formulated during his ride along Ocean Avenue.

"So," he concluded, "we need gats and a van, at a minimum. Can you get them for us?"

Manny and Jacqueline looked at each other. Both grinned broadly.

"Dat's easy-peasy," Jackie laughed. "You got sumptin' hard, you?"

"How about surgical scrubs?" Jackson asked.

Manny looked doubtful.

"Can it wait 'til tomorrow?" he responded.

Donell reluctantly shook his head.

"I don't think we can afford to wait," he told them. "I guarantee they'll ship Big Sugar back to Northern State the second he's off the critical list."

Jackie nodded soberly.

"You right," she agreed. "We gotta get him gone tonight."

"We'll figure something out," Jackson predicted.

He turned to Manuel.

"Let's see what you've got," he requested.

Manny disappeared into the tavern's store room, followed by Wide Load Broadus. Minutes later, they emerged bearing an assortment of firearms that included a sawed-off Remington shotgun, two AK-47 knockoffs, and three Glock 17s.

"Will these work, *jefe*?" Rodriguez asked.

"They'll do just fine, Manny," Jackson grinned.

Around 1:00 in the morning, the gang had piled into Jackie's Dodge Ram van. Ramirez insisted on driving.

"You're taking a big risk, Manny," Donell objected. "It'll be a lot safer for you and Jackie, if we go alone. That way, if we get caught, you can always claim we stole your ride."

Ramirez stubbornly shook his head.

"I tole you, *jefe*," he insisted, "Big Sugar, he's our friend, too."

Jackson shrugged.

"It's your funeral, *compadre*," he conceded.

"*Si*," Ramirez replied.

The gangsters found Monmouth Medical Hospital's main entrance locked. A discrete sign on the inside of its doors directed them to the emergency room entrance. Donell instructed Manny to circle the Medical Center complex, dropping off individual members of the gang at the ER's doors one by one.

Jackson was the first to enter the Emergency Room.

He was pleased to discover the waiting room was crowded with patients of all ages. Most of them appeared to be suffering from nothing more dangerous than colds or influenza, although there was a smattering of people with physical injuries. Luckily for the mob, shortly after they had assembled an ambulance arrived at the entrance. It disgorged an elderly white woman on a gurney who had fallen, and broken her hip. In the confusion as the emergency room staff sprang into action, Donell and his men slipped past the distracted guard into the hospital building.

After that, Jackson's plan unfolded with chronometer precision.

The gang quickly located a laundry hamper. That provided them with surgical scrubs, caps, and masks. Parked in a hallway, they found an unoccupied gurney. A sleeping patient's room yielded a wheeled IV tree and an oxygen mask. Donell snagged the patient's chart on his way out of the room.

Jackson had Wide Load climb up on the gurney, with the sawed-off Remington by his side. With a sheet thrown over him, wearing a surgical cap and oxygen mask, Broadus convincingly appeared to be a patient fresh from surgery. Putting on his own mask, Donell led the mobsters to the Critical Care Unit, stolen chart in hand.

"Let me get that for you, Doctor," offered the National Guardsman stationed at the entrance to the CCU.

He was a different sentry than the one Donell had encountered the previous afternoon. The soldier turned to push open one of the double doors.

"Thank you, Private," Jackson responded, opening the other door.

The gurney, pushed by Big Willy Dixon and Smoove Woodruff, passed through the doorway. It was trailed by Chuckie D Dickens, holding up an IV bag.

The Guardsman turned to watch them enter.

By the time he looked back, Donell had a Glock pointed at his head.

"Drop your weapons," Jackson ordered.

The sentry paled.

Carefully, he eased the strap of his M-16A4 carbine off his shoulder, and let the rifle fall clattering to the floor. He cautiously unsnapped the flap of his holster. Holding the butt of the Beretta M9 pistol delicately between his thumb and forefinger, he withdrew and dropped it, as well.

"Kick them aside," Donell commanded.

The Guardsman complied, nervously licking his lips.

Chuckie D retrieved the soldier's firearms. He tucked the Beretta into the waistband of his green scrubs.

"Inside," Donell commanded.

He gestured with the pistol.

Hands up, the PFC entered the CCU. His head was tucked between his shoulders, as if he expected a bullet in the back. A pair of terrified nurses cowered at the far end of the room.

"Let's kill this fool," Smoove snarled, gesturing to the Guardsman with his Glock.

"No," Jackson replied, firmly. "The man's just doin' his job. There's no reason for him to die. Just tie him up, and gag him."

He nodded toward the nurses.

"Them, too," he ordered.

Noting the hungry look in Woodruff's eyes, he added, "And no funny business."

When Woodruff's features hardened in resentment, Donell patiently explained.

"We don't want to give the Feds extra reasons to hunt us down," he pointed out. "Besides – there's no time for that, anyway."

Mollified by Jackson's reasoning, Smoove began ripping sheets into strips to tie up their captives.

"If you ladies cooperate," Donell told the nurses, "you'll have no reason to be afraid of us. Once we get who we came for, we'll be gone – and you can get back to tending your patients."

He could see the doubt on their faces, but Jackson declined to waste time on additional reassurances. His only concern now was Big Sugar.

Looking at Washington's sleeping form, he began to have doubts about the wisdom of his scheme. It would not do at all to rescue Big Sugar from the hands of the authorities, only to have him die for lack of proper medical care. For a moment, Donell stood still in thought, considering his options. Then he snatched the chart that was hanging on the rail at the foot of the capo's bed, and turned to the nearest of the two nurses, who was obediently waiting her turn to be bound and gagged.

"You," he said, peering at her nameplate, "Nurse Jefferson?"

He thrust Washington's chart at her.

"What's this say?" he demanded.

Glancing at the clipboard, Jefferson replied, "It says the patient suffered a penetrating gunshot wound to the right upper back and chest. The haemopneumothorax injury – that's a sucking chest wound, with significant bleeding ..."

Jackson nodded.

"Yeah," he responded, "I got that."

Jefferson's eyebrows went up.

"You 'got that', how?" she asked.

"'Haemo' – that means 'blood', right?" Donell explained.

Jefferson nodded.

"'Pneumo' means 'air'," he continued. "And 'thorax' means 'chest'. It's pretty simple, really."

Jefferson shook her head in bemusement.

"If you say so," she conceded.

"Anyhow, his injury was complicated by a collapsed right lung," Jefferson continued her voice trembling ever so slightly. "He lost a lot of blood, too. It looks like we gave him six units of A-negative. The surgeon debrided, and closed his wounds in surgery, and inserted a 32G drain. His bleeding is well-controlled, but he won't be in any condition to be moved for another 24 to 48 hours, depending on whether infection develops. He's currently getting …"

Jefferson consulted the chart again.

"Lactated Ringer's Solution," she added, "with 5 milligrams per hour of morphine via IV drip. Oh, and we also gave him 1 gram of Invanz, for prophylactic infection control."

She looked up at Donell, frowning.

"You're not planning on moving him, are you?" she asked.

"Yes," Jackson said, "we are."

Jefferson shook her head.

"I wouldn't recommend it," she advised.

"It can't be helped," Donell told her. "If we leave him here, he'll go back to Northern State. He'll die there."

"Well," Jefferson replied, "he's going to need Invanz – Ertapenem, is the generic version – for infection control, once a day for the next ten days. And you're going to want to give him morphine, too. He's going to be in a lot of pain."

"Get both things," Jackson instructed.

Jefferson shook her head.

"I can't," she told him. "Those are pharmacy items. They require a doctor's prescription. We don't keep them on hand."

Donell examined her expression carefully. Her *café-au-lait* complexion, and the light sprinkling of freckles across the bridge of her pert nose nicely framed her large, intensely-green eyes. Her expression gave no evidence that she was lying to him. Jefferson trembled slightly under the force of his gaze, but she kept her composure, in the face of his skeptical once-over.

"Any of these other patients ..." Jackson inquired, at last.

He tilted his head to indicate the other beds in the 12-unit CCU.

"... getting either of those drugs?" he demanded.

Jefferson tried, and failed to meet his eyes.

"Yes," she admitted, in a small voice.

"Get them," Donell ordered.

"Yes, sir," Jefferson agreed.

She went to collect the medications.

Jackson turned back to Big Sugar's bed. He reached down, and gently shook the capo's shoulder.

"Boss?" he queried. "Can you hear me, Boss? Wake up."

Washington groaned. His eyelids flickered open. He blinked uncertainly, and squinted as if having trouble focusing.

"Bro ... Brother Donell?" he rasped, uncertainly.

Jackson's solemn expression broke into a wide smile.

"It's me, all right," he said happily. "How are you feeling, Boss?"

Big Sugar coughed. Instantly, his features contorted in pain.

"I must confess," he husked.

His voice was weak.

"I have felt considerably better," the capo said.

"We're here to break you out," Donell told him. "Do you think you can walk?"

Washington frowned. He attempted to sit up, but immediately fell back again.

"I think not," he confessed.

His normally-resonant voice was barely a whisper.

"That's okay," Jackson said. "We have a gurney. We'll get you out."

Big Sugar nodded, mutely.

Nurse Jefferson appeared at Donell's side, carrying a handful of medication. When he reached for it, she snatched it away, and stepped back.

"Listen to me," Jefferson pleaded. "I'm trying to tell you: your friend is in no condition to be moved.

Emerald eyes flashing, she held up her free hand to forestall Jackson's reply.

"If you insist on moving him against medical advice," she insisted, "he's going to need professional care. Otherwise, there's a very good chance that he's going to die."

Donell shook his head.

"I'd like to be able to provide him with that care," he told her, "but there aren't any doctors, where we're going."

"That's what I thought," Viola Jefferson responded. "So, I'm going with you."

May 8, 2020, 12:37 am PDT (3:37 am EDT)

The East Bay Hills above Oakland, CA

"Call Davy," Joseph Paul Franklin ordered.

His smartphone dialed David Parker Ray's number. Ray answered on the first ring.

"Red Team is set," Franklin told him. "Waiting on your 'go'."

"Hang on a sec," Ray responded.

Perhaps 30 seconds passed, before he spoke again.

"Okay," he continued, "Project Headspin is 'go'. Repeat, Project Headspin is 'go'."

"Roger that," Franklin replied.

He bent over the i-kon Surface Remote Blasting Box, and armed the system.

"Fire in the hole," Franklin warned.

His teammates ducked behind the cover of nearby oaks.

Franklin pressed the firing button on the RBBS. Four loud booms echoed almost as one, on the steep East Bay hillside. Exactly three seconds later, four additional, nearly-simultaneous explosions rang out.

Franklin stood up. He peeked around the tree trunk that had sheltered him from possible shrapnel. Even though he had personally designed the custom, shaped charges of C4, years of experience in demolitions work made him keenly appreciate the wisdom of minimizing the risk to himself and others, where explosives were concerned.

He was just in time to see the two, huge, square electric pylons topple towards each other. He was pleased to note that his explosive design had worked exactly as planned. The charges he had constructed at the Aryan Revolutionary Front's San Leandro warehouse headquarters first severed the legs of the towers closest to each other, causing them to begin to lean together. The second quartet of explosions cut the outside legs of the giant, steel structures, which carried high tension wires over the ridgeline from the Pacific Gas & Electric substation in Moraga to electricity users in Oakland, freeing them to fall.

As the twin pylons crashed together in a mutual scream of tortured metal, the multiple, 115 kilovolt, high-tension lines they supported crossed in a spectacular flash and a cascade of sparks. The towers paused briefly, in a suicidal embrace. Then, electrical lines wildly flailing, they slipped past one another, and smashed to the ground.

Franklin turned to look out across San Francisco Bay.

With the fall of the pylons, it had plunged into darkness. Franklin was too late to witness the collapse of the giant telecommunications tower atop Mount Sutro, which had been brought down by the White Team demolitions squad. But he was close enough to hear the series of blasts that had ripped through the Oakland 12th Street BART station seconds earlier, courtesy of the Blue Team.

Joseph Franklin bent to retrieve the RBBS.

He called out to his three Red Team subordinates, "ATCO, boys. Time to cut a chogie."

The four men began scrambling down the steep hillside, toward the SUV they had left parked on Ridgecrest Road. The Ford sat next to the hole they had cut in the fence that had failed to keep them out of PG&E's property.

May 8, 2020, 1:23 am PDT (4:23 am EDT)

Market Street, San Francisco, CA

Donald Henry Gaskins swung the stolen gasoline tanker to the left, then cut the wheel back sharply to the right. Expertly, he turned the vehicle into the unlit, urban canyon of Spear Street. He was following a black Ford Expedition, driven by Vaughn Orrin Greenwood, the other member of Project Headspin's Gold Team.

Gaskins pulled the tanker up to the curb, next to the right lane. The big truck took up nearly a dozen spaces that would have been filled with commuters' motorcycles during the business day. Checking his rear-view mirrors, he carefully backed up the Kenworth T300, until its rear deck was exactly even with the corner of the huge, rectangular slab of concrete and glass that was 101 Market Street. Satisfied with his positioning of the truck, he put the transmission in neutral, set the brake, and turned off the engine.

Gaskins and Greenwood had waited on Eddy Street, each in his own idling vehicle, until the report from the Silver Team came over their walkie-talkies. The hand radios were a necessity, since the massive power outage caused by the Red Team's demolition of the PG&E towers had both shrouded the Bay Area in blackness, and silenced its network of cell phone towers.

"Break, break," came the voice of Paul John Knowles. "Silver is 'go' in five. Repeat: Silver is 'go' in five. Over."

"Gold One, copy," Greenwood's voice replied.

"Gold Two, copy," Gaskins confirmed. "Gold out."

The two Gold Team members waited precisely five minutes, before pulling away from the curb at the corner of Eddy and Mason Streets. Just as the Expedition rolled into the intersection, the boom of the Silver Team's bomb exploding at the Philip Burton Federal Building reached them. Seconds later, the fog-shrouded night was alive with the sirens of first responders. The blue-and-white flashing light bars of police cruisers whipped through the darkness of downtown San Francisco toward 450 Golden Gate Avenue.

Gaskins followed Greenwood in an illegal left turn from Eddy onto Market Street. Even though a cop car roared through the intersection just seconds earlier, Gaskins remained unconcerned.

- Those boys in blue have more important things to do than hand out traffic tickets, tonight. -

Now, Gaskins opened the door of the tanker, and swung out onto the corrugated steel step. Reaching back across the cab, he dragged the slumped corpse of the driver from whom he and Greenwood had hijacked the truck into a sitting position behind the wheel.

- Close enough for government work. -

He chuckled at the corniness of his own joke. Stepping down to the pavement, he slammed the truck's door.

Gaskins walked briskly towards the Ford waiting at the curb ahead. He noted, as he did so, the presence of several homeless people huddled against the outside of 101 Market.

- Nobody's gonna miss you. -

Gaskins walked around to the passenger's side of the Expedition, and got in.

"Hit it," he told Greenwood.

Greenwood put the SUV in gear. He drove up Spear to the corner of Howard Street, and stopped at the curb.

Gaskins opened the case of the Surface Remote Blasting Box. He raised its antenna, and armed the device.

"Fire in the hole," he warned.

He held the RBBS out the open window, and pressed the firing button.

At the corner of Spear and Market, five pounds of Joseph Paul Franklin's homebrew C4 that Gaskins had stashed in its belly ripped the tanker truck in two. 4,300 gallons of gasoline erupted in an awe-inspiring conflagration. Burning fuel immediately engulfed 101 Market in a literal wall of flame. That 1 Market Street was caught in the same holocaust was of little interest to Gaskins and Greenwood. What gratified them both immensely was that the San Francisco Federal Reserve Bank had become an inferno, burning so intensely that its towering flames could be seen from half the East Bay.

"Bug out, Vaughn! *Bug the fuck out!*" Gaskins screamed.

A tsunami of blazing fuel rolled up Spear Street towards them.

May 8, 2020, 2:06 am PDT (5:06 am EDT)

1100 H Street, Sacramento, CA

The Honorable George J.P. Perry, the popular, Democratic Governor of California, awoke in darkness. Eugene V. Debs, his three-legged Cavalier King Charles Spaniel was alternately barking, and growling at someone or something in the corridor outside his room at the Best Western Sutter House.

"Hush, Eugene!" Perry ordered.

He levered his rotund form up, and swung around to sit on the edge of the queen-sized bed.

Predictably, the little brown-and-white dog ignored his master's command. Eugene continued yapping and growling, challenging the unknown presence beyond the door.

Perry fumbled for the switch of the lamp on the nightstand beside the bed. He blinked against the sudden brightness. His bulbous eyes – an endlessly-lampooned symptom of his glaucoma – had been rendered exquisitely sensitive by his nightly dose of medical marijuana.

"What is it, Eugene?" he demanded.

He pushed his feet into his bedroom slippers, and rose to his feet.

"What's got you so excited, boy?" he asked.

Perry took three steps forward. He bent to collect Eugene, just as something heavy crashed against the door to his room. Alarmed, the Governor hugged his dog against his pajama-clad chest, and backed away from the entry. The backs of his knees hit the bed, and he sat down abruptly.

Again, the door shuddered, as something slammed into it with terrible force.

Perry reached for his smartphone.

He swiped his thumb across its face to wake it, and, in a shaky voice, said, "Dial 911."

The door to his modest hotel room splintered, and burst open under the impact of a final, violent blow.

May 8, 2020, 5:58 am EDT

E Street NW, Washington, DC

In the still, cool air of pre-dawn Washington, Lieutenant Commander Benedict Rosenberg could clearly hear the sound of muffled drums, drifting across the South Lawn of the White House. Jumping out of his taxi, the Judge Advocate General Corps' Defense Service officer hastily threw a couple of 20 dollar bills at the driver. In his urgency, he abandoned his briefcase in the back of the cab.

Rosenberg ran toward the sentry post, waving a page of Supreme Court stationery like a magic talisman.

"Stop the execution!" he called.

The Marines on duty leveled their M4A1 carbines at him.

"Halt!" warned a corporal.

His name tag identified him as Williams.

"Halt," he repeated, "or you will be fired on!"

Rosenberg immediately obeyed the Marine's command. He was suddenly conscious of how threatening his approach might appear from the sentry's standpoint.

"Put your hands on your head," the corporal directed.

He stared down the barrel of his weapon at the naval officer.

Rosenberg complied.

"Corporal," he explained, "I have in my hand an emergency stay of execution, signed by Associate Justice of the Supreme Court Napoleon Blackstone. Perhaps you've heard of him? It's absolutely imperative this order be given to Winslow Hatfield's executioner, before it's too late. Please, for the love of God, man, I beg you to let me through!"

At the mention of William Orwell Steele's first Supreme Court appointee, Corporal Williams lowered his carbine.

"Let me see that," Williams demanded.

To his fellow sentry, he said, "Matt, keep this bird covered, while I check his story."

"Aye, sir," the other Marine, a Private First Class named Munro, acknowledged.

Williams approached Rosenberg from the side, leaving his subordinate with a clear line of fire. He plucked the folded paper from his hand. As the corporal opened it, and began reading, the ruffle of drums suddenly stopped.

Rosenberg appeared stricken. He glanced to his left, toward the gallows that had been erected on the White House's South Lawn. Then, with a visible effort, he wrenched his attention back to Williams.

"This appears to be in order," the Marine grudgingly conceded. "According to protocol, we really should search you, before allowing you to enter the grounds, though, sir."

Frantic with anxiety, Rosenberg replied, "Corporal, a man's life is at stake! Out of simple humanity, can you please make a temporary exception? Please?"

Williams hesitated.

"Or just come with me?" the Navy officer pled. "Take me there under guard?"

Corporal Williams features, which had been clouded with doubt, immediately cleared.

"Munro," Williams commanded, "Accompany this officer to the gallows. Once he's shown his document to the executioner, bring him straight back here. Understood?"

"Aye, sir," the PFC acknowledged.

"Come on!" Rosenberg urged, as he broke into a run.

With Private Munro at his heels, Rosenberg raced toward the Visitor's Entrance at the White House's Southeast Gate. Despair dogged his footsteps, and the taste of failure was bitter in his mouth.

Dawn – the time for which Winslow Benton Hatfield's execution had been scheduled – was already breaking.

May 8, 2020, 6:30 am EDT

The President's Bedroom, Washington, DC

As it had reliably done every morning of his adult life, William Orwell Steele's mental alarm clock woke him precisely at 6:30 am.

For a single, timeless moment, as the universe of dreams reluctantly surrendered to that of objective reality, Steele found himself once again in the arms of his beloved Julia. His right leg was thrown over hers, kneecap touching her inner thigh. His right arm lay across her warm stomach, elbow bent, palm and fingers cupping her naked breast. His face was buried in the disarray of her hair; the taste of her juices still lingering in his mouth. Marinating in pure, overwhelming happiness, he stretched, like a waking animal, and rose on his left elbow to kiss her sweet cheek.

It was only then, as he came fully awake and memories of the night just past came flooding back, that he recognized who actually lay beside him.

He could not help himself. He physically recoiled from the woman who shared his bed, overcome with shame at his betrayal of Julia's memory, and guilt for his acts with his bedmate.

Diana Hunter opened one tawny eye, then the other. She smiled knowingly at him.

"Do I really look *that* bad in the morning, Will?" she asked.

Abashed, Steele protested, "Of course not, Di – you're beautiful, as always."

"That's more like it," she said, approvingly.

She put her hand up, and cupped the back of his head, to draw him toward her for a kiss. Sensing his resistance to the intimacy, as he stiffened in response, she relented. Lightly, she continued to touch his hair.

"What is it?" she inquired, concerned. "What's wrong, Will?"

"Nothing, Di," he replied, too quickly.

The tension in his neck, and his features betrayed the lie.

"Nothing at all," he insisted.

"Bullshit," she responded. "Don't lie to me, Will. Something's bothering you. Tell me what it is."

He tried, but found he could not meet her eyes. Instead, he flopped over on his back, and stared at the canopy overhead.

"I'm not sure I can explain it properly," he confessed. "Diana, I feel ... I feel as though I'm becoming somebody else: someone other than the man I thought I was. I have to say I don't much like the sensation."

"How so?" she asked.

She turned over to face him, but shifted her body back as she did so, to maintain the distance he had put between them.

"Well ..." he began.

There was pain in his voice.

"Let's see," he continued. "In the past week, I've authorized the kidnap, torture, mutilation, and murder of a high-ranking foreign official. I've ordered the Director of the Secret Service to kill my daughter's abductors – not 'capture them and bring them to justice', mind you, but kill them, without benefit of trial. I had an American citizen transferred against his will to a venue where he could only be tried before a military tribunal. Yes, I know, Hatfield was a scumbag ... but he was a citizen of this country – and I purposely deprived him of his Constitutional right to trial by a jury of his peers, simply to make a point.

"I threatened to charge the Chairman of the Federal Reserve with treason. I nationalized one industry, and threatened to do the same to another. I'm probably going to nationalize the oil industry, too, just to generate a little working capital – all without bothering to ask for Congressional authorization. And last night I ... I took shameful advantage of your grief. I seduced you, and betrayed your honor and my own in the process."

Hunter responded with a silvery laugh. It completely bewildered him.

"You really are adorable, sometimes," she opined. "Did you know that?"

"Wh ... what do you mean?" he asked, turning his head to stare at her in astonishment.

"Will, Will, Will," she replied, mockingly. "However did someone as naïve as you ever get to be President of the United States?"

Steele flushed with embarrassment.

"Explain yourself," he demanded.

Hunter sighed.

"First of all, you darling man," she told him, "*you* didn't seduce *me*. In fact, it was entirely the other way around: *I* was the one who did the seducing. Why do you think I stuck around last night, after everyone else left?"

He stared at her, in astonishment.

"Will," she explained, "I hadn't had sex in a long time. Before last night, it had literally been months ... since the night before Ben began his chemo, in fact."

She shook her head, so that her tangled hair fell over one eye, seductively.

"And, believe me," she told him, "up until then, I was used to getting it at least once a day. Occasionally three, or even four times a day. Before he got cancer, my Ben had the stamina of a porn star."

She laughed at his obvious discomfort with her frankness.

"Don't worry, Will," she said, laying a reassuring hand on his bare chest. "You were every bit as good last night as Benjamin was. Trust me, I have no complaints on *that* score! My point is that I was just as horny – and just as lonely – as you were. You didn't take advantage of me. You couldn't have taken advantage of me, even if you'd wanted to, because what happened between us last night was *my* idea, not yours."

"Diana Hunter," he replied, recovering his composure, "you have got to be the single most devious woman I have ever had the pleasure of knowing ... in the Biblical sense, that is."

She smiled, amused at his attempt at gallantry.

"Why, thank you, Will," she said.

She flipped her hair back out of her eyes, and bent to kiss him.

"Listen," she said, when she finally came up for air, "you're wrong about the other things, too. You haven't changed. You've merely been trying to do the best you can, under the most trying circumstances any President in history has ever had to deal with. Everything you've done – and I mean *everything* ... even having that racist idiot Hatfield tried aboard the Kennedy – you've done because it was the right thing to do. Even the thing with General Sheikh. Will, he was *personally* responsible for murdering a million Americans! He deserved what happened to him. And more. Believe me, in his case, justice definitely was served!"

"You could be right, I suppose," he allowed.

"You know I'm right," she declared. "After all, 'extraordinary times call for extraordinary measures' – and there have never been times more extraordinary than these."

"Perhaps so," he admitted. "I guess I'll just have to hope that history judges my actions with more mercy than I showed General Sheikh – or that fool Hatfield."

"It will," she responded. "I'm sure of it."

She gave him another quick peck on the lips.

"In the meantime," she observed, "it's past time we got up, anyway – and I really need a shower."

Hunter rolled out of bed. In the light from the fast-rising Sun that leaked through the curtained window, her toned body, still-firm breasts, and tousled hair made her appear the embodiment of feminine desirability to William Orwell Steele.

- Venus. She should have been named Venus, not Diana. -

Steele allowed himself a low wolf whistle of appreciation.

Diana Hunter smiled at the compliment, cheeks dimpling.

"Care to join me?" she invited. "there's more than one reason to share a shower, you know ..."

May 8, 2020, 7:49 am EDT

Monmouth Medical Center, Long Branch, NJ

Bleary-eyed from lack of sleep, Elizabeth Shergold sat at the foot of her son's hospital bed. She watched as a male orderly named Jason Todd carefully shaved the left side of Greg's head with a disposable razor. Greg was still just barely conscious. He had been injected with a sedative, a few minutes earlier. It was already causing his speech to slur, and his eyelids to drift further and further closed.

The dark-haired orderly had already cut off the bandages that had swathed the left side of his face, revealing the terrible damage the savage beating had done to his left zygomatic arch. Todd had asked Greg to tilt his head back, while he applied a scaffold of tape to keep his patient's eye from literally falling out of its socket. He had already employed electric clippers to shear off most of Greg's luxurious growth of black, curly hair. Now he was removing the remaining stubble, to reveal the depressed skull fracture her eldest – and perhaps only surviving – child had received when he was pistol-whipped by looters in her very own Manhattan co-op.

Elizabeth was horrified at severity of her son's injury. She unconsciously squeezed Eydis Finnursdottir's hand so hard that her son's lover squeaked in pain. Involuntarily, the Icelandic girl jerked her hand away.

"Oh, I'm so sorry, Eydis," Elizabeth apologized. "I didn't mean to hurt you."

"I understand, Elizabeth," Eydis assured her.

The girl, with her swollen, discolored features, and lovely green eyes, had also been disfigured by the same men who had injured her son

"It is difficult for me, too, to see my beautiful Greg so badly injured," she confessed.

Elizabeth turned away from the sight of the nurse technician wiping shaving cream off the skull of her now-barely-conscious son, to look appraisingly at the girl handcuffed to the wheelchair beside her.

Eydis was hardly the kind of person the socialite had expected to be her child's soul mate. But as resentful as Elizabeth had been of her presence in Greg's room when she had first arrived, she had undergone a profound change in attitude toward the Icelandic redhead. Once the kindly Naval officer who had been appointed as Eydis's legal advocate explained the circumstances of their arrival at Monmouth, Elizabeth's initial hostility quickly evaporated.

Since then, as she had been exposed to Eydis's obvious love and concern for her son's welfare – and, more importantly, the way Greg's adoring gaze followed Eydis's every move – Elizabeth Shergold had come to feel an increasing kinship and affection for the tiny Icelander with the explosion of curly red hair.

With mingled hope and dread, they gazed upon Greg's now-sleeping form. Watching Todd paint his scalp orange with poviodine-iodine solution, Elizabeth was once more overcome with a wave of gratitude towards the little foreigner.

- You saved my son's life! A little slip of a thing like you – no bigger than a minute – and you actually saved my Gregory's life! -

Once again, Elizabeth reached for Eydis's hand. This time, she took it gently in her own. The two women sat, silently keeping watch over the unconscious man each adored in her own way – one as a mother, the other as a lover.

Together, they waited for the surgical team to take him away.

May 8, 2020, 8:33 am EDT

The White House Situation Room, Washington DC

"Because it's still a few minutes until dawn on the West Coast," FBI Director John Clune noted, "and the power is still out across most of the Bay Area, we have only a limited understanding of how the attacks actually went down. I expect more details to emerge, as the day progresses. Having said that, it's absolutely clear that the entire thing was professionally planned, and executed, and staged for maximum impact, both in terms of the physical damage done and the effect on civilian morale."

"So," the President asked, "you're saying that one organization was responsible for all five attacks?"

Clune nodded.

"Yes, sir," he replied, "I am. At least, that's our working hypothesis."

"Jesus fucking Christ," William Orwell Steele blasphemed tonelessly. "What about the assassination of Governor Perry?"

"Well," Clune responded, "given the timing of the hit, it certainly seems reasonable to assume he was murdered by agents of the same group. Whoever they are."

"That's the real question, isn't it?" observed Diana Hunter.

Up and down the long, rectangular conference table, heads nodded in response to her comment.

"Just who are these people – and what are they trying to accomplish?" she clarified.

"As to that, Mr. President," Secretary of Internal Security Arleigh Solomon interrupted.

He held up his smartphone.

"It appears as though there may be a nexus between the events of last night and your daughter's abduction," Solomon announced. "My office just sent me a video that was uploaded to the Internet less than ten minutes ago."

He turned to Michelle Fargo, one of his technical advisors, who was seated behind him.

"Is there a way to hook this thing up to the big screen?" Solomon asked.

He nodded toward the video wall at the foot of the table.

"That should be no problem, sir," Fargo told him.

She took Solomon's phone, and walked briskly to the knee-high console that squatted below the wall-sized screen.

Within seconds, the 120-inch display lit with a low-resolution image of Artemis Steele. She was dressed in a midnight black version of the Marine Combat Utility Uniform, wearing a red beret. Her outfit was accented by a red ascot. Cradled in her arms was an M4 carbine, its stock collapsed.

She looked directly into the camera. Her expression was stern.

"My name is Artemis Steele," she announced. "As you probably know, I am the daughter of William Orwell Steele, President of the United States of America. I speak now for the forces of patriotic resistance to his reign as dictator of this country."

She looked off to one side, as if seeking approval. Apparently reassured, she turned back to face the lens.

"Last Friday," she continued, "my father permitted the greatest single act of terrorism in American history to occur on his watch. Even if he did not personally order the May Day attack, he surely did nothing to prevent it. For that failure alone, common decency demands that he step down from the office of President, renounce his declaration of martial law, and put an end to his disgraceful quest to impose a socialist agenda on our beloved nation.

"In the name of simple patriotism, I call upon every true American to rise up, and forcibly oppose William Orwell Steele's illegal dictatorship. If ever there was a time when we *need* to exercise our Second Amendment right to keep and bear arms, if ever there was a time when we *need* to defend our God-given freedom against the government itself, that time is *now*!

"If he will not resign voluntarily, I call upon Congress to impeach my father, and remove him from office. To insure the safety of all true Americans, I further call upon Congress to close our country's borders to the ongoing invasion by alien hordes, and to expel from our sacred soil all those who are here illegally. Finally, to make certain that those to blame for the May Day attack are brought to justice, I call upon Congress to investigate allegations that the CIA, at the behest of William Orwell Steele, placed and detonated the nuclear weapon that destroyed our greatest city, and rendered our Northeastern seaboard uninhabitable – and to punish as high treason that crime, and the criminals who were responsible for it."

The President's daughter again looked to one side, as if seeking praise. Whatever she saw there caused a smile to flicker across her lips.

She turned back to the camera to conclude sternly, "My name is Artemis Steele, and I speak for the forces of patriotic resistance."

The screen faded to black as she sat motionless, holding her carbine across her chest. Her otherwise expressionless face held the faint suggestion of satisfaction.

"Jesus *fucking* Christ!" the President exploded.

His features were a mask of terrible fury. He turned from the darkened video wall to glare first at Arleigh Solomon, then at John Clune, then back at Solomon.

"I'd say she's been brainwashed, Mr. President," Solomon rumbled.

"Of *course* she's been brainwashed, Goddamnit!" Steele roared. "Don't you get it? Artie *hates guns*! Besides – I know she blames me for her mother's death, but she would never have come up with that 'patriotic resistance' horseshit on her own. It didn't even *sound* like her! We know someone else put those words in her mouth – *your* job is to find out who!"

Solomon nodded. "Yes, sir," he assented.

"You fucking *find* whoever has done this to my daughter, do you hear me?" Steele shouted, pounding his fist on the table. "You *find* those assholes, you *kill* them, and you *get her back*! *Alive*, Goddamnit!"

"Yes sir," Solomon assented, taken aback by the President's rage.

"Yes, Mr. President," Clune agreed.

At that moment, the lights in the Situation Room flickered and went out. A second later, they blinked back on again.

"What the Hell was *that*?" demanded William Orwell Steele.

May 8, 2020, 09:03 am EDT

NYISO Primary Control Center, Rensselaer, NY

Walter Watson, first shift Chief Operator of NYISO, woke to find himself pinned, face up, beneath some heavy, but soft object that covered his head and chest. He was lying atop his right arm. It radiated a dull, throbbing pain up into his shoulder and neck. His head hurt, and his ears rang with a high, deafening whine.

Watson had trouble concentrating. At first, it was difficult for him to understand how he had come to be in the position in which he had awakened.

There had been noises – shouting and the sound of gunfire – from outside the control room where he and his staff monitored, and adjusted the flow of electricity from New York's many generating stations to cities, towns, and villages across the state. He remembered that quite clearly. Then the door that linked the power management center's wall of video displays, and rows of be-monitored control consoles to the business and executive office complex surrounding it had burst open, to admit a half-dozen heavily-armed men dressed in camouflage.

"Everybody freeze!" ordered the leader of the intruders.

He was an older man with a white crew cut. Like his subordinates, he wore a khaki bandana tied across the lower half of his face, as if they were the military version of stagecoach robbers in a cowboy movie.

"Put your hands in the air!" he commanded.

To punctuate his demands, he fired a burst into the ceiling from his machine gun. The noise was heart-stoppingly loud in the normally hushed environs of the NYISO control center. It produced instant compliance with the trespasser's instructions.

"Who's in charge here?" asked the brigands' commander.

His voice was harsh.

"I am, sir," Watson replied.

His voice quavered. He had never been so frightened in his life. The crew cut man leveled his gun, aiming it directly at his chest.

"Have your people shut off the power," he ordered.

For several seconds, Watson had simply gaped at him. His mind, frozen in terror, simply refused to process the intruder's demand.

"But ..." he finally managed to splutter. "... but that ..."

His voice trailed off. He blinked in confusion.

The leader of the interlopers fired from the hip. His bullet struck Watson in the upper chest. It spun him around, and knocked him down.

"Who's second in command," an astonished Watson heard him ask, impatiently.

"That would be me, sir," the voice of Charlie Steinmetz responded.

"Have your people shut off the power," the chief trespasser repeated.

"Operators," Steinmetz immediately instructed, "begin phased shutdown of the system, please."

"No," the head thug instantly contradicted. "No 'phased shutdown'. Just shut it off. Now."

Hesitating for no more than half a second, Steinmetz told the operations crew, "You heard the man, people. Shut it down."

"But, Charlie," the voice of Edison Duke objected, "that will ..."

A burst of firing cut Duke off in mid-sentence. Lying on the floor, swiftly going into shock from his own wound, Watson heard him emit a choking gurgle. It died away, to be followed by a soggy-sounding thump.

Then the lights went out, only to flicker back on within a second.

"The system is down, sir," Steinmetz told the leader of the intruders.

"Then why are the lights still on?" he had demanded.

"This building has its own backup power," Steinmetz told him. "I assure you, the rest of New York is blacked out."

"You wouldn't lie to me, would you, son?" the trespasser-in-chief asked.

The mildness of his tone failed to mask its underlying menace.

"No, sir," Steinmetz replied. "I know you'd kill me, if I did."

"That's right," the head thug responded, approvingly. "I would."

"All right," he continued, "wreck it, boys."

The firing had started in earnest, then. The invaders began indiscriminately shooting up control consoles and wall displays. Some of the women in the room started screaming. The raiders' commander ordered them to shut up. He shot one of them to underline his instruction.

The sounds of automatic weapons fire and breaking glass went on for what seemed like several minutes. By the time they finally stopped, Watson was phasing in and out of consciousness. He was still sufficiently awake to hear the saboteurs' leader issue his next command, however.

"Shoot them all," he ordered.

There was more screaming from both male and female voices, after that. It died away quickly, as the gunfire went on. Watson heard the bodies of his staff dropping all around him. One of them fell across his own. He reckoned that was what had saved him from a fatal wound.

At last there was silence.

"Set the charges," the voice of the crew cut man directed.

Watson was keenly aware of the sound of booted feet moving around the control center, and the crunching of broken glass under them. He lay as still as possible, concealed beneath the corpse of one of his co-workers. Minutes later, the head intruder spoke again.

"Time to withdraw," he commanded. "We'll blow them once we're out of the building."

The trespassers exited, letting the door to the control center slam shut behind them. Watson instantly began trying to extricate himself from beneath the body of his slain subordinate, but his trapped arm had refused to cooperate.

Suddenly, there was a noise as loud as the end of the world. Then darkness.

Now, once again conscious, Watson thought to himself, "*If I don't get myself out of here, I'll die.*"

That was motivation enough to give him the burst of strength he needed. He wriggled out from beneath the corpse that had shielded him from the explosives. Panting with the effort, Watson got to his knees. Then, grimacing against the pain, he rose to his feet. His right arm dangled uselessly from his shattered shoulder.

Using only his left hand, he managed to extract his smartphone from its holster on the wrong side of his belt. He swiped his thumb over its screen to wake it, and squinted at the reception indicator.

- Zero bars. Well, that figures. -

With the failure of the power grid, cell towers would be out of operation, as well.

Watson paged through the phone's menu, until he found the flashlight app. Turning it to its brightest setting, he checked the identity of the body beneath which he had sheltered. It was Charlie Steinmetz – or, rather, what was left of him.

- Thanks for covering for me, Charlie. Once again, you saved my ass. -

Turning from the mutilated remains of his lieutenant and friend, Walter Watson began slowly, unsteadily picking his way through the wreckage of his workplace.

May 8, 2020, 10:02 am EDT

The West Wing Press Briefing Room, Washington, DC

"Ladies and gentlemen, may I have your attention, please?"

Presidential Press Secretary Yvonne Clevinger paused for a moment to allow her audience to settle down. The murmur of correspondents dictating notes or conversing with their neighbors, and the tapping of fingers on computer keyboards died away quickly.

"I'd like to begin this morning's briefing by handing out copies of the Administration's insurance industry reorganization plan, as the President promised would happen in his statement on Wednesday afternoon," Clevinger told them.

She waited, while a quartet of White House interns moved down the rows of seated journalists, passing out stacks of thick, velo-bound briefing books with card-stock covers that featured the Presidential seal. Once every correspondent had received a copy, the Press Secretary continued.

"The full text of this document is also available on the White House Web site," Clevinger noted. "As you will see, for homeowners, it incorporates, and expands existing FHA-administered mortgage insurance programs. It also provides for commercially-issued business and personal insurance policies to be re-issued by the National Department of Insurance – a new Cabinet-level agency the President has proposed to replace the formerly-private insurance sector. Naturally, Congress will have to approve the creation of the new Department. The President is hoping to find time to meet with the senior leadership of both Houses this coming weekend or early next week, to initiate that process."

Clevinger paused to take a sip of water from the glass on her lectern.

"So, you're saying he's not going to wait for Congress to approve the mortgage insurance program?" demanded Reed Bullock, the White House reporter for Fox News.

"Mr. Bullock," she replied, her voice carefully controlled, "please don't interrupt me. We have a lot of topics to work through, this morning. I plan to take questions later on, but for now, I'd appreciate it if you'd just let me do my job."

"I'm just doing mine, Yvonne," Bullock retorted.

Clevinger's hazel eyes flashed with irritation.

"I'm asking nicely, *Reed*," she said, allowing her voice to reflect her frustration.

"Fine," Bullock conceded, throwing up his hands in surrender.

"And, yes," Clevinger responded, "the President believes that, because Congress has already empowered the FHA to offer mortgage insurance on FHA loans, under Section 203 – especially 203(h), the Mortgage Insurance for Disaster Victims program – he has the authority to expand the existing programs for individual homeowners."

"But, isn't that ..." Bullock objected.

"*Mister* Bullock," Clevinger said, her tone dangerous, "if you interrupt me one more time, I will have your White House press certification revoked. Is that clear?"

"You wouldn't dare," Bullock blustered.

"Try me," Clevinger invited, staring him down.

"Fine," Bullock replied, unable to meet her unwavering gaze. "Have it your way."

"I'm pleased to announce," the Press Secretary continued, "that all the major, domestic ATM banking networks returned to normal operation by the President's midnight deadline. Also, we've confirmed that, other than those affected by this morning's blackout of the Northeastern power grid, all U.S. banks that were scheduled to open before 10:00 am this morning have, in fact, opened for business. We're confident that trend will continue, as the day progresses."

Clevinger paused to raise a well-formed eyebrow. She looked pointedly at the Fox News reporter. Bullock sat silently, arms tightly crossed, refusing to rise to the bait.

Inwardly, Clevinger smiled.

- I can almost see the steam coming out of his ears. -

"As to the blackout itself," the Press Secretary continued, "our best current information is that it began as a result of some kind of unanticipated event at the New York Independent System Operator. That's the company that operates the high-voltage electrical transmission lines in the State of New York. The exact cause of that event is still under investigation, and I have no further details to share with you at the moment. However, we'll let you know as new information become available, I promise. I'm sorry to have to report that our understanding is that the Northeastern Grid will most likely remain offline until sometime tomorrow, at the earliest. Again, as additional information becomes available, we'll do our best to keep you in the loop.

"Finally," Clevinger announced, "I'd like to address last night's series of attacks in the San Francisco Bay Area, and the assassination of Governor George J.P. Perry of California."

She looked up from her bullet-point list to survey the crowd of familiar faces. Only Sheila Cubbins, the NPR correspondent, showed any trace of emotion, other than keen interest. The Press Secretary sighed, and turned her gaze back to her outline.

"The FBI has been working closely with the Sacramento, Alameda, and San Francisco County Sheriffs' offices," Clevinger told them, "and with the Sacramento, Oakland, and San Francisco Police Departments, as well. Naturally, that investigation is ongoing, and many of the details are now and will continue to be treated as confidential information, for reasons I'm sure you all understand. I *can* tell you that the FBI strongly suspects the Bay Area attacks and Governor Perry's murder were probably committed by a single organization. It appears likely that these were incidents of domestic terrorism – that is, they most likely were committed by Americans, not by foreigners. As of the moment, the FBI believes that they are *not* directly linked to the May Day bombing."

Clevinger once again regarded her audience. Her tone of voice, which had been purposefully businesslike, turned somber.

"On a related topic, I'm sure, by now, you have all seen the video of the President's daughter, purporting to speak for something called 'the patriotic resistance'. It is the FBI's belief, as well as that of the President, that Artemis Steele did not make that video of her own free will. The FBI's behavioral sciences experts think the President's daughter was the victim of psychological conditioning by her kidnappers, and that they forced her to make that video for their own propaganda purposes. And, yes, the current consensus among our law enforcement professionals is that the Bay Area attacks, the assassination of Governor Perry, and the kidnapping of Artemis Steele are all related."

She brushed a stray lock of hair away from her face.

"I also want to announce," the Press Secretary concluded, "that, at noon today, the President will address the nation, live from the Oval Office, on the subject of last night's events in California."

Clevinger squared her shoulders. She leaned forward, as if into a gale.

"I'll take your questions, now," she announced.

May 8, 2020, 11:22 am EDT

The West Wing Ground Floor, Washington, DC

Secretary of Internal Security Arleigh Solomon reached out to the speakerphone which sat on the desk of the cramped, temporary office on the ground floor of the West Wing. He had transferred himself there from the Department of Internal Security headquarters on Nebraska Street, so as to be available for immediate consultation with the President.

"Speak," commanded Solomon.

"Mr. Secretary?" the voice of FBI Director John Clune inquired.

"Yes, Mr. Director," Solomon confirmed. "What can I do for you?"

"Mr. Secretary," Clune said, "I'm calling to update you on the NYISO 'event'. There now appears to be no question that the blackout was due to a terrorist-style attack."

"Oh?" Solomon responded.

"Yes, sir," Clune replied. "We got a short-wave call from the Renesslaer County Sheriff's Office about 20 minutes ago. They had a report of shots fired at the NYISO site, and sent a cruiser to investigate. According to what they've told us, there are dead bodies all over the Operations Center building – all gunshot victims. The Control Center itself is thoroughly wrecked. Whoever did this not only shot the place up, they also apparently set off explosive charges inside the Control Center."

"I see why you're calling it a 'terrorist-style' attack," Solomon rumbled. "Were there any survivors?"

"One," Clune confirmed. "The Chief Operator – a fellow named Walter Watson. The Sheriff's people found him in the parking lot. He was pretty badly wounded and he lost a lot of blood, but they think he'll survive ... if he makes it through the next few hours, that is."

"Have they been able to get any information from him?" Solomon asked.

"That's negative, Mr. Secretary," Clune told him. "I understand he was unconscious when they found him. He should be arriving at the county hospital any minute now."

"I see," Solomon responded. "Does this sheriff have any suspects?"

"No, sir," Clune said, "not to my knowledge."

"Do you?" Solomon demanded.

"As to that," Clune replied, "our field agents at the Seneca Temporary Housing Facility have suggested it might be the work of the Aryan Revolutionary Front."

"Oh?" Solomon responded. "Explain that."

"Well, sir," Clune told him, "our people recently managed to place an informant inside the group. That's something they've been trying to accomplish for several years now, by the way. Their guy has led them to what appears to be a headquarters for ARF's New York cell near Rosendale. It's literally underground, inside an abandoned cement mine."

"And why, exactly, do these agents of yours think ARF is responsible for the attack on the NYISO center?" Solomon demanded.

"To begin with, Mr. Secretary," Clune replied, "last night, they monitored a conversation between their informant and the guy who recruited him – a fellow named Adam Manson – who's been on our watch list for a long time now. Supposedly, Manson dismissed most other right-wing militia groups as ineffective, but strongly implied that his bunch were a major exception to the rule."

"That doesn't seem like very strong evidence to me," Solomon objected.

"Well, sir, there's more," Clune responded.

"Mr. Director," Solomon told him, "get to the point. What evidence do you have that ARF is responsible for the attack on NYISO?"

"Mr. Secretary," Clune said, "I apologize for the roundabout presentation, but I needed to prepare the ground, as it were. After that conversation, my agents followed Manson and their informant to the Rosendale location, by helicopter. One of our UAVs has been surveilling it, ever since. Around 7:00 this morning, a pair of vehicles left there, heading north up US 9 West. About 20 minutes ago, those vehicles returned to Rosendale. The timing of their departure and return seems suspicious, to say the least."

"You didn't follow them to their destination, then?" Solomon responded.

"No, sir," Clune admitted, "I'm afraid not."

"Why not?" the Secretary challenged.

"Mr. Secretary," Clune replied, "the FBI is more than a little resource-constrained at the moment. Frankly, it was hard enough just to free up a drone to keep tabs on the Rosendale location. If my agents had not been convinced their informant and his family were in imminent danger …"

"All right, Mr. Director, I get the picture," Solomon interrupted. "Has this informant provided confirmation of ARF's responsibility for the attack?"

"No, sir," Clune told him. "At least, not so far. He's equipped with a clandestine radio transmitter, but, naturally, we can't pick up its signal through solid rock."

Solomon frowned.

"So, what are you asking me to do?" he inquired. "I certainly can't go to the President with evidence this circumstantial."

"No, sir," Clune agreed, "I realize you can't go to the President, yet. What I'd like you to do is request the military to assign a UAV to Rosendale for us."

"Why a military drone?" Solomon asked.

"Because our own UAVs are unarmed, sir," Clune replied. "If my people are right about this cell being responsible for NYISO, they're likely to have other, equally antisocial projects planned. We'd like to be in a position to prevent them, if possible – or to respond with force, if not."

"Hmm," Solomon responded. "I take your point about the potential risk. I'll tell you what: I'll talk to the Air Force, and see if they have an MQ-1 they can let you borrow for ... let's say 30 days ... in case your Rosendale ARF cell decides to get creative."

"Thank you, sir," Clune said. "That will help."

May 8, 2020, 12:00 pm EDT

The Oval Office, Washington, DC

William Orwell Steele stood beside the American flag, gazing out the window of the Oval Office as the red light on top of the television camera lit up. Reflected in the glass, the President could see both the floor director's signal and the red light that indicated his broadcast to the nation had started. Slowly, he turned away from the window, pausing for a moment to fix his eyes on the flag, before continuing his turn to face the camera.

"My fellow Americans," he began, "I want to speak to you today about the difference between real patriotism and the false kind. False patriotism is easy enough to distinguish from the real thing. Real patriotism is selfless, motivated only by the desire to protect and serve the country we love. False patriotism is exactly the opposite: motivated by greed and selfishness. Real patriotism is quiet: it has no need to call attention to itself, no need to shout, 'Look at how patriotic I am!' False patriotism is noisy: it waves the flag, shouting from the rooftops about its claims to be acting in the interest of so-called 'real' Americans. Real patriotism promotes the 'brotherhood from sea to shining sea' that has always been the hallmark of the American character. By contrast, false patriotism elaborately proclaims its love of country, while sowing hatred and discord between Americans.

"The sad truth is that false patriotism is, at its dark heart, divisive, rather than unifying. It is suspicious and prejudiced, rather than accepting and inclusive. It is ugly on the inside, regardless of how it may dress itself up on the outside."

The President stepped forward. The cameraman soundlessly dollied back, keeping him consistently framed in the shot. When Steele reached the edge of the Resolute desk, he perched on its corner. The camera operator stopped his dolly, and began a slow zoom in from the medium shot with which the broadcast had opened.

"As most of you undoubtedly know by now," Steele continued, "last night, a series of terrorist attacks took place in the San Francisco Bay Area. Those attacks have left millions of people without electricity, done hundreds of millions of dollars worth of damage to its public transportation and communications infrastructure, and destroyed several skyscrapers in the heart of downtown San Francisco. In Sacramento, California's capitol, masked gunmen broke down the door to Governor George J.P. Perry's modest hotel room, and shot him to death."

The camera zoom paused now. The President's head and shoulders filled the frame.

"Governor Perry was a friend of mine," Steele said.

His voice was tinged with sadness.

"We've known each other a very long time," he explained, "and I will miss him very much."

Steele paused, and looked away for a long moment.

"George J.P. Perry," the President continued, turning back to face the camera, "was a modest, unpretentious man – the kind of elected official who, when he was in Sacramento, on the people's business, stayed in a budget-priced hotel, because he felt it would be inappropriate to waste the taxpayers' money on more luxurious accommodations. He was the kind of Governor who rode his bicycle to work on days when the weather was nice. The kind of public servant who preferred and sought out the company of ordinary people. The kind of politician who despised special interest groups and their lobbyists, and refused to take their money. The kind of man who would adopt the shaggy, little dog he named Eugene – because nobody but George could find it in their heart to adopt a pet with a missing leg. I know he loved Eugene every bit as much as I love my own dog Duke. And, last night, after his cowardly assassins murdered Governor Perry in cold blood, they stomped poor little Eugene to death, too."

Steele again paused. His expression was grim.

"As I'm sure you also know," the President went on, "four days ago, in broad daylight, my daughter Artemis was kidnapped off the streets of Berkeley, California. Not content with taking her, her abductors viciously murdered almost her entire Secret Service detail – fifteen brave, dedicated, *patriotic* Americans. Since then, as those of us who love her waited hopefully for any kind of sign of her fate, her kidnappers have made no demands for ransom, and have given us no indication of whether Artie was alive or dead – until this morning."

Steele's deep blue eyes blazed with anger.

"By now," he said, "you have most likely seen the Internet video of my daughter – who never liked guns before her mother was murdered in front of her, and has deeply hated them ever since. That video shows her with an assault rifle in her hands, claiming to speak for 'the patriotic resistance', and calling for my resignation as President."

The President's lips were tight with resentment.

"The FBI's behavioral analysis experts tell me that she shows all the signs of having been psychologically conditioned to say those things," he stated. "They assure me that she was not speaking of her own free will. In other words: my daughter Artie has been brainwashed into acting as a spokesperson for the very people who kidnapped her."

Steele jabbed a finger at the camera in emphasis.

"*This* is what I mean by the difference between real patriots, and false ones. Real patriots, like Governor George J.P. Perry and the fifteen Secret Service agents who gave their lives trying to protect my daughter – and false patriots, like the people who abducted Artie, and put that gun in her hands and those hateful words in her mouth. Those murdering, terrorist criminals who have the cast-iron gall to call themselves 'the patriotic resistance'."

The President's voice crackled with intensity. His face filled the frame.

"They are not patriots," the President gritted. "They are traitors – and we will treat them as such. We will hunt them down, like the rabid animals they are, and we will punish them for their treason. This I promise you."

At extreme zoom, Steele's glittering, blue eyes filled the frame.

"At a time when we are already facing the greatest crisis in our nation's history, these false patriots have declared war on our country," the President said. "They will soon discover – just as those who attacked us on May Day will discover – exactly how horrendous a mistake that was.

"On that, you have my solemn oath."

Epilogue

May 8, 2020, 4:15 pm MDT (6:15 pm EDT)

State Capitol Building, Boise, ID

Candace Arsche, Governor of Idaho and Tea Party darling, stood at a temporary podium erected at the foot of the State Capitol Building steps. Before her stood a small crowd of reporters, cameramen, and photographers. To one side was a cluster of staffers and hangers-on. To the other stood a solitary, porcine figure, his back to the crowd, seemingly lost in contemplation of the replica Liberty Bell looming behind Arsche.

"Ladies and gentlemen of the media," the governor began.

"I thank you for coming on such short notice," Arsche announced.

She flashed her wide, wide grin at the assembled journalists.

"As you know," Arsche continued, "this morning, with the deepest regret, I accepted the resignation of Idaho's 1st district Congressman, Easau Piltch. Representative Piltch is a friend, and I wish him well in his return to private life."

Smartphones flashed, despite the sunny weather. Reporters and bloggers photographed the Governor, framed against the replica of the Liberty Bell that hung from its sturdy support structure behind her. Arsche paused to strike a pose for their benefit, before she resumed speaking.

"In these troubled times," the Governor told them, "it's especially important that the State of Idaho's interests be fully represented in Congress. I personally feel it is equally important that the person who succeeds Representative Piltch – and I say 'succeeds', because no one can truly replace Easau – be someone who epitomizes the same values and ideals that he always stood for: smaller government, lower taxes, decreased regulation, respect for unborn life, and upholding the free enterprise system as a model for the world."

Arsche paused, expecting applause. There was a thin patter from the huddle of aides and hangers-on who were gathered far enough to one side to ensure that they would not distract viewers from the Governor. Arsche reacted as if it had been an ovation, nodding affably, and smiling her wide, thin-lipped smile.

"It gives me great pleasure," she declared, "to announce that I have found just such a successor, and that he has graciously agreed to accept the challenge of serving as Idaho's Representative to Congress from the 1st District for the remainder of Easau Piltch's unexpired term. And may I add that I sincerely hope he will opt to run in November, as our party's candidate for his own first *full* term in Congress!"

The small clutch of sycophants applauded more vigorously this time, earning them a swift, malice-filled glance from the Governor, before she turned back to face the media. Her wide, wide smile was once again firmly in place.

"Ladies and gentlemen," Arsche trumpeted, "Let's have a big hand for my friend, and yours, the 1st District's own, Idaho's favorite son, and a true patriot: Congressman Merlin Friend!"

Friend stepped to the podium beside the Governor. They exchanged air kisses, and posed shaking hands for the cameras.

"We're depending on you to give that socialist bastard Hell for us, Merlin," Arsche murmured, still smiling and waving.

"Never fear, Madam Governor," Merlin Friend assured her, *sotto voce*. "You can count on me to do exactly that."

Coming in *War* – Book Two of *American Sulla*

Militia uprisings are met with drone strikes across the country.

Merlin Friend and the House of the Elect plot to impeach the President.

USS Alligator and USS John F. Kennedy arrive in the Persian Gulf.

War with Pakistan looms, while the CIA foments conflict with Iran.

Ne-on Glowbaby becomes the voice of the anti-war movement.

The global economic crisis deepens, plunging the world into depression.

Eydis Finnurdottir and Greg Shergold are again separated – by the United States Government.

Sean Halloran Sr. becomes a pawn in a deadly game of deception, his helpless family held hostage to guarantee his cooperation with the Ayran Revolutionary Front.

Donell Jackson must lead a gang to which he is no longer certain he wants to belong.

Marvin Starling and Samantha Harbison begin a tragic affair.

The search for the President's kidnapped daughter intensifies.

Americans go to the polls in a presidential election showdown.

All this and much more ... coming in *War* – Book Two of *American Sulla*!

Cast of Characters

Tariq Abdullah Aziz/ Arlington Joseph Smith – Driver of the delivery van that carries the WTC nuclear weapon.

Alicia Takahashi – Auxiliary receptionist for Global Financial Corporation's Private Banking department.

Ali bin Hamzah/ Randy Carlson – Terrorist mole within Global Financial Corporation's Private Banking department.

William Orwell Steele – President of the United States.

Special Agent Roger Waters – Special Agent in Charge of POTUS first shift Secret Service detail.

Ronald Wheaton – Deputy National Security Advisor.

Clarabelle Wong – Tourist from San Francisco.

Aragorn Northcutt Hardcastle – Goldman Sachs VP.

Robert Whiting – Video Floor Director aboard Air Force One.

Nakeesha Gramble – Five-year-old girl in Hackensack, NJ.

Donell Abraham Jackson/Jack Donnellson – Former boyfriend of Latonya Gramble.

Marqus "Marq" Collins – Current boyfriend of Latonya Gramble.

Yvonne Clevinger – Presidential Press Secretary.

Reed Bullock – Fox News White House reporter.

Preston Hollingsworth – MSNBC White House reporter.

Sheila Cubbins – NPR White House reporter.

Eydis Finnursdottir – Icelandic tourist.

Robert "Bob" Bildinsky – General contractor.

Steven Dawkins – Presidential Science Advisor.

Admiral Harlan Adams – Chief of Staff of the Navy

Sean Halloran Sr. – General contractor.

Fiona Halloran – Sean's wife.

Sean Halloran, Jr. – Sean and Fiona's year-old son.

Arleigh Solomon – Secretary of the Department of Internal Security.

Colonel Arif Fahrood Khan/Timothy James Hilliard – Operation Sword of Allah team leader.

Roshina Khan – Arif's wife.

General Winston Chung – Chairman of the Joint Chiefs of Staff.

Arun Mansour "Big Sugar" Washington – Gang boss.

Representative Walter Karman – Representative (D) from New York's 15th District.

Representative Ellen Hardin – Representative (R) from Massachusetts's 4th District.

Senator William Roland – Senior senator (D) from Connecticutt.

Senator Irwin Kurzweil – Junior senator (R) from New York.

Ramamurthi Singh – Secretary of Energy.

Merlin Friend – Radio pundit.

Alvin "Cowboy" Clemson – Northern State Prison convict.

Timothy "Tim Tim" Timmons – Correctional Officer at Northern State Prison.

David "Little Boy" Shabazz – Big Sugar Washington's chief enforcer.

Nathaniel David Lundegran – Warden of North State Prison.

Ardin Wildehoof – President Steele's private secretary.

Marlon Roosevelt – President Steele's personal aide.

Diana Hunter – Vice President of the United States.

Alvin Spreckels – Speaker of the House. Representative (R) from Florida's 16th District.

Vittorio Donofrio – Senate Majority Leader (D, New York).

Hale Davies – Senate Minority Leader (R, Mississippi).

Darcy Peligroso – House Minority Leader. Representative (D) for California's 12th District.

Kendall MacMillan – House Majority Leader (R, Pennsylvania).

Harry Walters – Official White House photographer.

Benjamin Hunter – Husband of the Vice President.

Julia (Jules) Harper Steele (*née* Grey) – Wife of William Orwell Steele.

Vincent Govan – Senior Senator from Vermont (D).

Richard Wayne Lee – Retired postal carrier.

Anderson Connaught IV – Secretary of the Treasury.

Easau Piltch – Representative (R) from the 1st Congressional District of Idaho.

Marcus Aurelius Clement – President Steele's personal physician.

Andover "Andy" Philips – President Steele's Chief of Staff.

Harold Burley – White House elevator operator.

Special Agent Nicolas Mason – Chief of the President's third-shift Secret Service detail.

Duke – William Orwell Steele's Great Dane.

Commander Anson R. McDonald – Captain of the USS Alligator.

Lieutenant Morris Abrams – Third watch Officer of the Deck of the USS Alligator.

Book One of American Sulla
PAGE 568

Chief Petty Officer Arthur Mueller – Chief of the Boat of the USS Alligator.

Lieutenant Commander Michael Valentine – Executive Officer of the USS Alligator.

Lieutenant Roger W. Young – Commander of Alpha Squad, 2nd Reconnaissance Battalion, 2nd Marine Division Radiological Survey Team.

Sergeant Louis Cukela – Member of Alpha Squad

Corporal John Pruitt – Member of Alpha Squad

Private Albert Weisbogel – Member of Alpha Squad

Private John Kelly – Member of Alpha Squad

Private David Gonzales – Member of Alpha Squad

Walter Watson – Chief Operator of NYISO day shift.

Jefferson Raymond – Director of FEMA.

Kenneth Watanabe – White House Counsel.

Marcy Collins – Secretary of Commerce

Ricardo Guitierrez – Secretary of the Navy

Gregory Alan Shergold – 23-year-old greeting card designer.

Evan Spitzberger – Attorney General of the United States.

Martin St. John – Reuters White House Correspondent.

Bernard Bonsalle – White House Correspondent for Libertyfire blog.

Susan Colson – ABC White House Correspondent.

Special Agent Richard "Dick" Wright – Chief of POTUS second shift Secret Service detail.

Latonya Gramble – Nakeesha Gramble's mother.

Curtis Suggs – Night watchman at the Hanover County Municipal Airport.

Cissy Shergold – Craig Shergold's younger sister.

Dr. Colin Ellison – Medical oncologist at Bethesda Medical Center.

Corporal Karl Smith – National Guardsman.

Ryan Patrick Cohan – Boston scavenger.

Chief Petty Officer Curtis Simmons – Crewman on USS John F. Kennedy.

"Commodore" Barnaby Collins – Navy Captain. Executive Officer of USS John F. Kennedy.

Petty Officer Second Class Darnell "Darnit" Johnson – Crewman on USS John F. Kennedy.

Seaman Samuel "Spud" Zawinsky – Crewman on USS John F. Kennedy.

Seaman Farrell "Shorty" Buehl – Crewman on USS John F. Kennedy.

Jonathan "Jake" Cordell – Captain of the tug boat Iron Maiden.

Vasily Cukor – First Mate of the Iron Maiden.

Harvey Wilkerson – Engineer of the Iron Maiden.

Silvio Fanucci – Deck hand of the Iron Maiden.

John Clune – Director of the FBI.

Charles Huffam "Chuckie D" Dickens – member of Big Sugar Washington's gang.

Luther Martin "Ugly" Congreve – Donell Jackson's original cellmate.

Adam Manson – Seneca Temporary Housing Facility resident.

Ruby Manson – Adam Manson's wife.

Jacob Manson – Adam Manson's oldest son.

Caleb Manson – Adam Manson's middle son.

Moses Manson – Adam Manson's youngest son.

Reverend William J. "Billy Joe" Barker – Chaplain of the House of Representatives.

Reverend Hiram Dunwiddie – Chaplain of the Senate.

Ne-on Glowbaby – Folk-hop superstar.

Jebediah Springer – Senior White House economist.

Emily Winston – Executive Assistant to Treasury Secretary Connaught.

Carter Hawley – Northern State Prison guard.

William "Big Willy" Dixon – Member of Big Sugar Washington's gang.

Luis Diaz – Looter.

Angel Santiago – Looter.

Diego Colón –Looter.

Kendall "Wide Load" Broadus – Member of Big Sugar Washington's gang.

Dante "Smoove" Woodruff – Member of Big Sugar Washington's gang.

Deandre James – Donell Jackson's uncle.

Jeremiah Fout – Newark, NJ homeowner.

Bernard Lord Silkington – Chancellor of the British Exchequer.

Sir Ellston St. John – Chief Executive of the London Stock Exchange Group.

Rajiv Mehta – Director of Policy Planning for the Treasury Department.

Geert de Graaf – Chairman of InterContinentalExchange (ICE).

Elizabeth Shergold – Greg Shergold's mother.

Cassie – Elizabeth Shergold's dog.

William Plein – Captain of USS John F. Kennedy.

Second Lieutenant Dolores Anunciacion de la Madonna Pena – Army National Guard commander of 2nd Platoon, 69th Infantry Regiment, 1st Battalion, 27th Infantry Brigade, 42nd Infantry Division.

Sergeant First Class Justin Charles "Kit" Carson – 2nd Platoon, 69th Infantry Regiment, 1st Battalion, 27th Infantry Brigade, 42nd Infantry Division Army National Guard platoon sergeant.

Colonel Howard Anderson Mabry – Commander of the Army National Guard 27th Infantry Brigade, 42nd Infantry Division.

Mina Tollins-Choate – Clerk of the House of Representatives for the 117th Congress.

Atticus Martial Freed – 37th Sergeant-at-Arms of the House of Representatives.

Howard Klinger – FBI Senior Field Agent.

Timothy O'Reilly – Howard Klinger's partner.

Aldon Quarleman – Housing Director for Seneca Temporary Housing Facility.

Elsa Jean Brophy – New Jersey housewife.

Christopher Murdock – Director of the CIA.

General Rashid Omar Sheikh – Director of ISI's Joint Intelligence Miscellaneous Department.

Mohammed Danish Shirani – Former Director General of the Pakistani ISI.

Bashir Qadir Durrani – Islamabad/Rawalpindi-based CIA contractor.

Hameed Rehman Davi - Islamabad/Rawalpindi-based CIA contractor.

Fahad Abbas Afridi - Islamabad/Rawalpindi-based CIA contractor.

Younis Masood Khakwani - Islamabad/Rawalpindi-based CIA contractor.

Major Hilton Morris Burke – Executive Officer of 69th Infantry Regiment, 1st Battalion, 27th Infantry Brigade, 42nd Infantry Division.

Fairuzah Sheikh – Wife of Rashid Omar Sheikh.

John James O'Brien – Deputy CIA Chief of Station for Pakistan.

Colonel Joshua T. Silverman – Senior Intelligence Officer, 325th Military Intelligence Battalion.

Clayton Reynolds – White House Deputy Press Secretary.

Susan Marie Thornton – Secretary of State.

Yves Prudhomme – Prime Minister of Canada.

Herbert Richard Baumeister – Member of Ayran Revolutionary Front.

Artemis Alexandra "Artie" Steele – Daughter of William Orwell Steele.

Charles Frederick Albright – Member of Aryan Revolutionary Front.

Katrina Ruth – White House correspondent for CBS.

Paul McConnochie – Director of the Secret Service.

Bernadette Garcia – Artemis Steele's lover.

Madeline Czerwinski – Special Agent in Charge of San Francisco FBI Field Office.

Norman LaPlace – Former CIA Director.

Special Agent Janese Meschelle Johnson – Member of Artemis Steele's Secret Service detail.

Special Agent Paul Schieffer – Member of Artemis Steele's Secret Service detail.

Special Agent Lester Conway – Member of Artemis Steele's Secret Service detail.

Special Agent Kevin Brown – Agent in Charge of Artemis Steele's second shift Secret Service detail.

Tammy Hildiger, RN – Night nurse at Monmouth Medical Center.

Hestia Argus, RN – Private-duty hospice care Registered Nurse.

Bhagat Singh – Homeowner in Beavercreek, OH.

Guneet Kaur – Bhagat Singh's wife.

Jagroop Singh – Bhagat Singh's son.

Harjinder Kaur – Bhagat Singh's daughter.

Chester K. Chester – Representative (R) from South Carolina's 5th District.

Elvin Wheelwright – Representative (R) from Georgia's 1st District.

Bass Ransom – Senator (R) from Texas.

Joad Fungo – Representative (R) from Kansas' 1st District.

Ashley Conden – Secretary of Health and Human Services.

Eric Watt Forste – Secretary of Transportation.

Joanna Muir – Secretary of the Interior.

Lieutenant Rupert Griffin Stewart – Member of Navy Judge Advocate General Corps' Defense Service Office.

Christopher "Chris" Kohler – Senior Senator (D) from Oregon. Majority whip.

Delbert Aiden Dance – Junior Senator (D) from Kentucky.

Abigail Cobelli – Junior Senator (D) from California.

Marjorie Kern – Legislative Clerk of the Senate.

Adolph Ryan Wolf – Billionaire investor.

Dr. Increase "Inky" Bright – Geneticist, biologist, friend and advisor to A. Ryan Wolf.

Tyrone Sendahl James – CIA Deputy Director for the National Clandestine Service.

Darwish Sultan – CIA asset.

Jameson Matthew Peek, Esq – Easau Piltch's attorney.

Joshua Ruth Lovett – U.S. District Court Judge for DC.

John Thomas Bailey – Uniformed Secret Service agent.

Sarah Cowell – Arlington Lady.

Mary Virginia Bailey – Widow of John Bailey.

Special Agent Kenneth Harmoody – Member of Artemis Steele's Secret Service detail.

Special Agent Bruce Kellogg – Member of Artemis Steele's Secret Service detail.

Special Agent Alice Cushing – Member of Artemis Steele's Secret Service detail.

Wang Jing-Wei – Daughter of Chenglei Wang.

Wang Chenglei – Business rival of A. Ryan Wolf.

Sandra Gale – Witness to the arson of the Sikh gurdwara in Beavercreek, OH.

John Bowditch – Governor of New York.

Fred Bowditch – Father of John Bowditch.

Commander Clifford Fisk – Commander of the Annapolis Defense Service Office North.

Sir Cyril Dunbar – CEO of Lloyd's of London.

John Philip Parks – Senior Senator (R) from Ohio.

Samuel Woodbine – West Wing Navy steward.

Guy Prince – Presumptive Republican presidential nominee.

Kelvin Conable – Former Secretary of Defense.

Anthony Taylor – Marine lieutenant.

Roberto Guzman – Special Agent of the FBI.

Barbara Collinsworth – Mortgage applicant in Bellevue, NE.

Angie Stomatopoulis – Mortgage loan officer at Wells Fargo Bank in Bellevue, NE.

Gary Stomatopoulis – Lieutenant Colonel, USAF.

Dr. Theodore "Ted" Volberding – Specialist in brain trauma at the Monmouth Medical Center Neuroscience Institute.

Xavier Wilson Harmon – Hospital Corpsman Second Class.

Marlon "Grasshopper" Keenan – NYC gangster.

Earl Harley Stoat – Suspect in the murder of Bhagat Singh, and the arson of the Beavercreek, OH *Gurdwara*.

Karl Mayther – Special Agent in Charge of the FBI's Cincinnati Field Office.

Colonel Barrett Strong – Commander of Ohio Army National Guard's 371st Sustainment Brigade.

Cassandra Cayce – Artemis Steele's mentor, thesis advisor, and supervisor at UC Berkeley.

Keith Albermarle – Seaman Recruit on USS John F. Kennedy.

Fox Shergold – Father of Gregory Shergold.

Steve Newman – Second-shift air switcher at MOR-TV.

Samantha Denise Harbison – State Department Diplomatic Service Courier.

Marlon Wilkins – Supervisor of Diplomatic Service Couriers in Islamabad, Pakistan.

"Marvelous" Marvin Starling – Captain, USAF. F-15SE Silent Eagle pilot.

Gary Severn – San Francisco FBI SWAT Operations supervisor.

Caldecott Nice – Chairman of Board of Governors of the Federal Reserve.

Manuel "Manny" Ramirez – Co-owner and cook of Manny Jack's Bar and Grill.

Jacqueline "Jackie" Ramirez – Co-owner and bartender of Manny Jack's Bar and Grill.

Winslow Benton "Buck" Hatfield – Leader of the Bhagat Singh murder and Beavercreek *Gurdwara* arson conspiracies.

Lt. Commander Benedict Rosenberg – Winslow Benton "Buck" Hatfield's legal representative.

Mabel Turlington – Volunteer at the Monmouth Medical Hospital information desk.

Rance Mohammance – Clerk at Monmouth Medical Hospital's Patient Records desk.

David Phillips – First-shift attendant at the Monmouth Medical Hospital morgue.

Zachary Copley – Mayor (D) of Boston, Massachusetts.

Viola Jefferson, R.N. – Graveyard shift nurse at Monmouth Medical Center's Critical Care Unit.

Joseph Paul Franklin – Leader of the Operation Headspin Red Team.

David Parker Ray – Operation Headspin coordinator.

Donald Henry Gaskins – Member of the San Leandro cell of the Aryan Revolutionary Front. Leader of the Operation Headspin Gold Team.

Vaughn Orrin Greenwood – Member of the Operation Headspin Gold Team.

George J.P. Perry – Governor (D) of California.

Eugene V. Debs – Governor Perry's three-legged King Charles Spaniel.

Andrew Williams – Corporal, USMC. White House sentry.

Matthew Munro – PFC, USMC. White House sentry.

Napoleon Blackstone – William Orwell Steele's first appointment to SCOTUS.

Jason Todd – Surgical orderly at Monmouth Medical Hospital.

Charles "Charlie" Steinmetz – Deputy Chief Operator of NYISO day shift.

Edison Duke – Operator of NYISO day shift.

Candace Arsche – Governor (R) of Idaho.

Sponsors

The author is deeply grateful to the following individuals who believed enough in this project to put their money where their mouths were, by pledging contributions via the Kickstarter and Indiegogo crowdfunding sites. Some of their names will be familiar to the keen-eyed reader, because the author named a character after those sponsors who vouched $50 toward each campaign.

Kickstarter:

John Bowditch, Paul McConnochie, Richard Reinholdt, Brian Ruth, Joe (no last name given), Zach Copley, John Parks, Susan and Kevin Thornton, Mary Stark, Chris Murdock, Eric Forste, Bill Plein, Mary Hogan

Indiegogo:

Eric Forste, Fred Bowditch, Zachary Copley, Abby Cobelli, Bill Plein, Manny Ponce, Evan Prodromou, (six other sponsors contributed anonymously)

About the Author

Thom Stark has been a professional writer – which he defines as "one who gets paid for it" – since 1995, when his *@internet* column began appearing in the pages of *LAN Times Magazine.* He is probably best-known as a columnist and feature writer for the late, great *Boardwatch Magazine.* He maintains an archive of his magazine columns and articles at www.starkrealities.com.

Mr. Stark currently lives in Chillicothe, Ohio, with his wife Judy and their lovable mutts Wally and Watson, where he is hard at work on *War –* Book Two of *American Sulla.*

www.ingramcontent.com/pod-product-compliance
Lightning Source LLC
Chambersburg PA
CBHW081127020726
47505CB00010B/2264